Michelle Boule

Plagues
of the
Heart

Turning Creek
Book 4

To Randi Boulé
who has the heart and hands of a healer.

ACKNOWLEDGMENTS

Books, like children, take a village and I am blessed by mine. Many thanks and hugs of gratitude go to the following:

Brenda Peregrine, my editor and friend. I would not be here without you, nor would I want to be.

The Five Fantastic Humans Book Club. We banded together exactly when we needed each other most and I thank God every day for you. Thank you for being a part of my life and for understanding my Jesus loving, feminist heart.

Stephanie Petersen, who copy edits for me, but also fan-girls with me over other authors, tells hilarious stories, and can drink me under a table every time.

My readers, who continue to go on this adventure with me. Your enthusiasm is humbling.

My husband, who has supported me and loved me through every book. You are my knight and my HEA.

God, who teaches me every day to serve and love outside of my boundaries.

CHAPTER 1

Colorado Territory, 1863

The body of Mattie Pope lay on a bed between them. Though Dora knew the woman had already left them for the life beyond, a sliver of hope remained as Lee moved the chest-piece of his stethoscope over Mattie's chest. The room was silent except for the quiet tears of three people who had moved away from the bed to give them room. Mattie's husband, Johnny, and their closest friends, L.A. and Elizabeth, held each other and waited for the news they knew was coming. Johnny and L.A. were permanent fixtures at the depot, where they played checkers and argued over the rules. The two older couples shared a small house in town.

Lee's unflinching grey eyes raised from his work and met hers. He shook his head slightly and straightened to his full height. Dora's heart plummeted further, extinguishing the small hope that remained, and she braced herself for the conversation that came next. Lee removed the earpieces of the stethoscope from his ears and handed the instrument to Dora. He stepped around the bed and crossed the room to where the mourning group stood.

Lee placed a hand on Johnny's shoulder and gave the old man a squeeze. "I'm sorry, Johnny. Her heart has been struggling for some time now. She's gone."

Johnny wiped his eyes and blinked rapidly. "Doc, could you bring her back? Call her from Tartarus and let me have more time with her?"

Dora's hand paused on the stethoscope case and she turned to watch Lee's response. Lee was the Remnant of Asclepius, a descendant of the Greek physician who had been given power over the dead by the gods. That power ran through the veins of Lee Williams, country doctor in Turning Creek, Colorado, and he used it only occasionally. Death was not something that liked to be interfered with.

Lee rolled back his shoulders. "What you ask is a hefty request. She may not want to come back. She has already lived a long life, and though she loved you, she may not come."

Dora turned her back on the conversation and tucked the hard leather case into Lee's black bag, which carried his instruments and medicines on house calls. She had heard this conversation many times, and each time it left her heart raw with grief. No matter the circumstance, almost everyone longs for another chance with someone they lost. Lee could sometimes provide that.

Lee's cultured voice broke the expectant silence. "I will try, but there are no guarantees. Some people do not want to come back. Some people should not come back. I will not interfere in death when it will cause harm. There is an order to life and death, and that order should not be disturbed. Do you understand?"

Johnny nodded, and Lee walked back around the bed. Lee ran a hand over the laugh lines and wrinkles of Mattie's face, and laid one hand on her forehead and one on her heart. He was tall, and the position meant that he was hunched over the bed. Dora's head was higher than his as she stood, and gave her the perfect perspective to watch Lee working. He raised his eyes and met hers briefly before closing them.

No matter how many times Dora watched Lee call the dead—and there had not been many—the thrill of the depth of his power called to hers. A Remnant of Asclepius dealt in death and suffering; death, and violence, were intimates of a harpy. Dora was a Remnant of Aello, one of the first four harpies, and the power of violence ran through her veins. Anticipation curled in her as she watched Lee. She opened up her senses, but was careful to keep her power tightly coiled. She did not want to interfere.

The air in the room thickened, and Dora reached out ever so slightly with her own power as Lee's hands began to glow with a dull, grey light the color of a lamp in thick fog. She felt the wall of power surrounding Lee and Mattie. It pulled at her, and Dora drank in the feel of it. Lee's power felt different than her own, less raw and violent, more deep and swift. His power was vibrant, like water and life. Hers was more like fire and ash. The harpy within her stretched and ached to fly, but Dora lashed it back down.

Dora felt the power withdrawing from the room and back into Lee. Its absence left an ache in her core, and she pushed her reactions into the small place where they belonged, far away from the surface. His hands ceased their glowing and his eyes opened. Weariness settled over him as the power left, and shadows appeared below his eyes. He made eye contact with her first then moved to the hopeful trio.

"I'm sorry. She is content where she is. I will not pull her back from that."

Will not, Dora thought, not *can't*. Manipulating death was something Lee took seriously. One of these days, Dora would ask him about the line he never crossed and how he kept it in place. She had her own lines to dance with and she knew what control it took to reign in power that deep. That control was one of the many things she admired about Lee.

Johnny sagged into himself, supported by his friends. "Thank you, Doc. You tried and that is all I asked."

Lee checked the area around for the bed for instruments he might have left. There were none. He snapped the bag closed and walked to the door. Dora paused in front of Johnny. His grief was beyond tears at the moment.

Dora laid a hand on the old man's arm, and he patted it as though to reassure her. "I'll tell Iris about Mattie. She'll want to know and will check in on you later." Iris ran the mail depot where Johnny and L.A. spent most of their days.

"Thank you, Miss Dora. Mattie always said we were blessed by the gods to be in a town protected by a harpy like you."

"The gods had nothing to do with it," she replied with a weak smile. A harpy like her had many meanings. To this grieving man, she was a protector, a shield when needed, but she knew that deep down, she was capable of ravaging the innocent along with the guilty.

Dora took a deep breath. "Please, let Iris know if you need any help. I don't know how nature nymphs are buried, so if you need a pyre built, we can do that." Mattie had been a lesser Remnant, a nymph with little power, but she was a Remnant nonetheless and she deserved whatever path to the afterlife befitted her kind.

Johnny's eyes darted to the body of his wife and his body jerked a little as if he had forgotten she was dead, lying there. "We will need a sapling tree and an appropriate place to bury her, where we can plant the tree above."

Dora nodded. "Iris and I will confer with Reed and make the arrangements."

Lee came and stood near her. "I know they are just words, but I am sorry for your loss, Johnny. She will be missed in the town. Mattie had a kind and generous soul."

They took their leave and left the three to their grief. Lee held open the door for her, and Dora left the sickroom-turned-death chamber for the bright June sun. She blinked, momentarily blinded. She blinked again. Second Street appeared busy and bustling, unconcerned that it had lost one its own moments before.

Turning Creek had grown in the last two years, enough that the aptly named Second Street had been formed to the east, running parallel to Main Street. Dora could see another house being built east of Second Street and thought Third Street would appear soon. Turning Creek was a unique place in the world, a place where Remnants, the descendants of Greek gods and monsters, lived in harmony beside mortals in the open.

The transition had not been as smooth as the tranquil days they now enjoyed. There had been plenty of bumps over the years, but this was her home, and Dora loved it with fierceness. A handful of mortal families had left when the Remnants had made their presence known, including a miller who left a half-finished mill in his wake. Others had replaced the ones they had lost and the town continued to attract Remnant and mortal families alike. Turning Creek was a safe place, and somehow the word had spread.

Lee shifted his bag to his left hand and offered her his right arm. "Would you like me to walk with you to the depot? It's on my way."

Dora hesitated before taking his arm, steeling herself for the contact. She slid her hand into the crook of his arm, and Lee led them past the Nordmans' carpentry shop, across the street, and around the south side of the saloon. Dora forced herself to concentrate on their surroundings as Lee's heat wound from her hand's contact with his arm and tangled through her body. As they turned the corner, Main Street came into view. There were more buildings on this street. A cobbler shop and a ceramics shop were farther down, wedged between the Hughes' tailor shop and Lee's office. It was midday and the street was filed with people, horses, and wagons.

Lee paused them to greet Feliks Tumanov and let him pass. Feliks had taken over the mill after Jacob Wells had abandoned the town. Anger rose up at the thought of the man who had hurt Iris's feelings. Dora pushed it down. The man deserved her wrath but not her violence, and he was long gone. They crossed the road and stopped before the door to the depot.

Dora pulled her hand from Lee's arm and he transferred his bag back to his right hand in one smooth motion. His dark, short-cropped hair gleamed in the sun. Broad shoulders filled the dark brown suit jacket he wore over a vest and a crisp white shirt. He looked like he could have stepped out of someone's drawing room. Lee did not look like a mountain town doctor.

"Would you like to come in with me?" she asked to fill the transition of leaving. "Iris always enjoys your company."

Lee inclined his head. "No, thank you. I want to go back to the office and make some notes about Mattie Pope in my log book. I will stop by and speak to the sheriff about the arrangements that need to be made for her funeral."

Dora smiled to hide her disappointment, though she had expected his answer. "All right, then. I will speak to Iris as well and we can leave that planning to them and Johnny. Depending on when the funeral is, I'll be along in a couple days at most to recheck the herbal supplies. You know where to find me if you need me."

"I do, indeed. Good day, Dora."

"Bye, Lee."

He turned and left, and she watched him walk with confident strides until he reached the Sheriff's office, where he stopped to talk to Reed, who was leaning on a post watching the street. Dora tore her gaze away from the two men and went inside the depot.

The bell over the door rang and Dora had barely closed the door when she was accosted by two toddlers. "Auntie Dee!" they screeched, in unison. Dora wondered how every child seemed to be able to instinctively find the particular decibel that pierced the ear in the most painful way possible.

Dora moved away from the door and knelt on the floor to look both children in the eye. Both girls were just over one mortal year, but were the size and had the intellect of children twice their age. Not all Remnant children aged faster than mortals. Harpies and their Messenger aged faster when they were young so they could defend themselves earlier. Aldara had Iris's blonde hair and bore the golden wing birthmark on her back that marked her as The Messenger for the new generation of harpies. Ellie was dark in all the ways Aldara was light. A riot of unruly brown curls framed Ellie's round face. She had inherited Marina's brashness along with her looks.

Though Messengers often had more than one child, only one was marked from birth as the next in line to act as guide and chronicler of the harpies. The harpies, on the other hand, had once been cursed by the gods to have only one female progeny each generation. The harpies of Turning Creek had broken many traditions, and the way they lived and raised their young ones was only a part of it, but they still would each only have one child. Nothing stopped them from adopting other children, however.

"How are my favorite young ones today?"

"Good," Aldara said.

"Hide and seek for Nina and Thomas," Ellie pointed around the room.

Iris had taken Thomas in after his mother died in the confrontation with Zeus, five years ago now. He was the Remnant of Achilles and had the gift of speed. Nina's mother, the Remnant of Demeter, had walked into a snowstorm of her own making after the rest of her family had succumbed to fever. Nina, who had inherited her mother's gifts, lived with Reed and Marina.

Dora stood and looked around the room. Iris stood behind the counter watching them. Her blonde hair was pulled away from her face with a loose braid. She swept her eyes downward, and Dora smiled. Dora put her hands on her hips and began walking around the room, looking into all its corners.

"Did you look underneath this table?" She stooped down to check underneath one of the back tables.

Aldara hopped up beside her. "They aren't there."

Dora put a finger on her lips then picked up Ellie. "Did you look upstairs?"

Aldara laughed. "Yes. Not there either."

Dora carried Ellie to the counter and Iris stepped out of the way, pretending to put letters away.

Dora hefted Ellie higher and dropped her over the backside of the counter as she said, "Did you look behind the counter?"

Ellie landed on top of Thomas, who fell into Nina. Aldara ran around to the back of the counter and jumped on top of the pile. For a moment, there were limbs and high-pitched shrieking all in a tangle. Thomas, who was sixteen, and Nina, who was seven, had a size advantage over the girls and pinned them easily to the floor.

"I have you both now. I'm going to make Messenger soup." Thomas tickled Aldara, who squealed in delight.

Ellie tried to kick Nina off her. "No, Thomas." Nina tickled her in response and the toddler collapsed into laughter.

Thomas stood up and pulled Aldara with him. "You'd make terrible soup. Too spoiled." He put her down and ruffled her hair. She beamed up at him adoringly. "I have to help your mom now. Go back upstairs with Nina."

Nina took the hands of the two girls. "Let's go read about the voyage of Jason."

Ellie pulled on Nina's hand. "Do the voices."

"Of course I will."

"Thank you, Nina. I'll finish up here and be up soon." Iris turned to Thomas and handed him a stack of letters. "These are all in town and shouldn't take you long. Can you deliver these for me?"

Thomas took a bag down from a peg by the door and stuffed the letters in while swinging the bag over his shoulders. "Sure. Can I go to the McKenzies' after?"

"Be back for supper."

Thomas ran out the door and threw a "yes, ma'am" over his shoulder.

There was some stomping upstairs as the girls settled, and the downstairs room seemed quiet in comparison to the chaos of a few moments ago. Dora put her arms around Iris and gave her a hug.

"Now I can greet you properly," Iris said. "Hello, my bird."

Dora prolonged the hug. Iris smelled of paper and sunshine, and it quieted Dora's soul to be surrounded by it. She walked around to the front side of the counter and sat on a stool.

"I have some news. Mattie Pope died this morning. Her heart gave out."

Iris laid her hands flat on the counter. "Poor Johnny. At least he has L.A. and Elizabeth to lean on."

"Johnny said that Mattie should be buried in a green space with a tree to mark her grave. Lee is talking to Reed now. If you need help finding a good tree, let me know." Dora rubbed her hand over her face. "Johnny asked Lee to bring her back."

Iris raised her eyebrows. "What did Doc say?"

Dora shrugged. "Lee gave the speech he always gives about some people not wanting to come back, that some people shouldn't come back, and that he made no promises. He tried, but she was where she was supposed to be."

Dora thought of the way his power felt and her body tightened. She took a deep breath and let that thought go.

Iris pinned her with a calculating look in her bright blue eyes. "What were you thinking about just then?"

"Nothing."

Iris made a sound in her throat, but let it go. The ceiling shook as a herd of cattle, or three girls, romped around upstairs.

Dora looked up and smiled. "I don't think they're reading."

Iris laughed. "It would seem not." Her smile faded and her forehead was marred with lines.

Dora reached out and covered one of Iris's hands with her own. "What were you thinking about that has your face looking like that? I hate to ask because that look these days usually involves you giving me a lecture on finding a mate and having my own daughter since my sisters are settled."

Iris covered their joined hands and patted Dora. "I don't want to argue today."

Iris's eyes went to Dora's hair. The blonde and red hair hid the grey well, but the light-colored strands were scattered throughout and could no longer be hidden. A harpy's hair only greyed for one reason: when her heart had been given to another. While Petra and Marina had embraced their love for their mates, Dora knew that was not an option for her. Giving in to those emotions meant losing control, and she needed to always be in control.

"If it's not me, then what are you worried over?"

Iris's shoulders dropped farther. "Aldara. What if she never gets her wings?"

"It's early yet. She may get her wings."

Iris's voice was pensive. "It's a miracle I have mine. They only manifested thanks to Zeus. Before that, all I had was a golden birthmark that was a painful burden. It hurt to not be able to fly. I think it's unlikely Aldara's will emerge. The Messengers lost their real wings only a few short generations from the first Iris. I know of no way to get them to manifest naturally or I would have done it to myself."

The first Iris, from whom all Messengers were descended, had possessed wings with feathers of the rainbow. Her Remnants were marked by a birthmark in the shape of wings, a ghost of their true power. Iris, named after the first of her line, had wings with feathers of gold. Like the harpies, she kept them hidden and only unfurled them when needed.

Dora fixed Iris with a pointed look.

"That look does not intimidate me," Iris said.

Dora raised one eye brow in response. "You who always give us hope must not give up now. She is young. They're all young. Give them time. Give her time. Besides, you ordered us around fine without wings for years."

Iris laughed then, as Dora had intended. "You're right, but I know the pain of not having them fully, of only having a ghost of what was. I don't want that for her."

"There is hope for her yet. Henry has his own power, and a Messenger has never married a Remnant of Hephaestus before you. There is power in your pairing. Perhaps that will help. There's nothing we can do but wait." Dora wanted to laugh at her advice to Iris. She handled her own dilemmas just as badly, only she responded with control where Iris tended towards worry and impatience.

Iris removed her hands from Dora's and smoothed her skirt. "What are your plans for the rest of the day?"

Dora stood. "I need to do some weeding in my garden and take care of things around my cabin. Unless Lee sends for me, it will be a couple days before I am back in town. When Johnny decides on a time for Mattie's burial, send word."

Iris walked around the counter and enveloped Dora in another hug. "See you soon, then."

Dora left the depot through the front door, thankful she no longer had to skulk through the woods to change out of the sight of mortals. Iris and Marina had released the secret of the Remnants' existence two years ago and the town had adjusted to life with monsters as easily as could be expected.

Dora breathed in and released the control she kept on her harpy. It burst over her in a flash of power, exchanging her mortal, freckled skin for brown and white feathers. Her body transformed into the sleek form of a bird of prey while her head retained the elements of its mortality, only more angular and pointed. Her strawberry blonde hair blew in the breeze over her shoulders.

Her sudden change startled Beth Kramer, who was out sweeping the boardwalk in front of the mercantile.

"Hello, Dora." Beth continued sweeping.

Dora looked past her, down Main Street. She could not see the sign that hung above Lee's door, the sign bearing a caduceus with a single snake twining about it, the sign of Asclepius. She could not see it, but she knew it was there.

"Have a good day, Beth." Dora's harpy voice was thick and ground out of her throat like glass over rocks.

Dora glanced once more down the street then launched into the air and headed home.

CHAPTER 2

A week later, restless and in need of release, Dora went hunting with Petra and Marina. Hunting with her sisters was the only time Dora allowed herself the freedom to feel the unfiltered rush of violence coursing through her veins. She let her walls drop, and her face broke into a feral grin full of pointed teeth. The power ran over her like wind in a gale and filled her with power. She was a harpy, like the Greek myths of old, and tonight they hunted.

The early summer moon ruled the sky and hung low as they flew. The eastern edge of the sky had lost the deepness of night. Dawn was not far off. Marina flew in front of Dora. Her tan chest feathers stood out in contrast to her darker brown feathers in the dark. Dora twisted her head around to check on Petra's location. Her black form was a shadow in the pale silver of the moonlight. Petra made a gesture with the claw on the end of her wing, and Dora followed the direction of the movement. Down below, four mountain sheep lay in a cluster of bushes on the side of the mountain.

The three harpies circled the sheep in a practiced formation that needed no further communication. As one, they ceased their circular movement and dove into the sleeping animals. The sheep realized their peril moments before the screeching harpies were upon them. Their prey leapt in fright and the harpies let them have the illusion of escape. The fleeing animals did nothing but raise the pressure and pleasure of the chase.

The feelings burned through Dora's blood until she was nothing but predator. Her harsh laughter spurred the sheep on in their flight. She could have caught her mark right away, but she allowed it a few feet of freedom before landing on its back.

The bleating of the sheep hit Dora's ears the same moment her talons dug deep into the flesh on the beast's back. The sheep crashed to its knees.

Dora leaned over and sunk her sharp teeth into the back of the sheep's neck. The copper tang of blood filled her mouth and her own blood roared with violence and pleasure. Dora wrapped her wings to the front of the sheep's neck and sliced its jugular with the razor sharp claws on the ends of her wings. The sheep died in a gurgle of blood and lay still.

Dora released the sheep and stood next to the carcass. She licked the blood from her lips and let the beat of the hunt echo through her soul. It pounded in her head until it was the only thing she heard. The sharp tang of the blood mixed with the smell of mountain cedar, and all was as it should be.

"Took you long enough to take that one down," Petra taunted.

Marina laughed, full and guttural. "That's because Dora wanted to play with her food first. It's more fun to let them run. Their blood tastes better when they're scared."

The taste of the sheep was still on her tongue. "It does, indeed." Dora ran her tongue carefully over her fangs.

The three harpies laughed harshly, and the sound reverberated on the rocks around them and rose in a macabre cacophony. They were many things, but in their hearts, they were predators. Few creatures, monster or mortal, would take on a harpy, let alone three. They knew their power, and tonight Dora allowed herself to revel in it.

"Let's get these home and dress them. We're closer to my house; we can go there and put them in the smokehouse." Dora hopped over to her kill and dug her talons deep into the still-warm body.

Dora put extra power into her wings as she launched off into the night sky. The weight of the mountain sheep did not keep her from cutting through the air with precision. They had found the small herd on the Western Twin, and her own home, near the top of Silvercliff, was only one peak to the south. Dora rode the ebbing feeling of power and the drumming of violence in her blood.

A night of flying and hunting should be followed by a big breakfast and a warm bed. Quiet time after a hunt gave Dora the time she needed to let her blood cool. She increased her wingbeats as she thought of home. By the time the three of them approached her cabin, the horizon was painted with orange, red, and yellow. The western peaks of the valley were bathed in crimson as the sun peered over the eastern mountains.

Dora's eyes drank it in and imprinted it on her brain. Nothing was more beautiful than a sunrise in the Rocky Mountains. She had grown up on an island in Greece filled with lush greens and sapphire seas, but that land had never claimed her. Turning Creek valley was seared into her soul. This was home.

Dora rode a warm current and covered the last of the ground to her small homestead. She scanned the area and her eyes snagged on something out of place. A horse she knew was hobbled in the grass in front of the cabin. A man she knew even better was sitting in the chair on her small porch. His head was down as he worked with something in his hands.

Something even more wild than the blood of the hunt rushed into her as she saw Lee sitting there. All her senses were wide open from the hunt and she was caught by her response before she had a chance to stop it. Before she could even give the feeling a name, Dora grabbed it back into herself, stuffing it deep. She heaped all of the violence of the morning along with it and slammed the door. The effort left her feeling raw and hollow, and the whiplash from her self-imposed emotional imprisonment caused her wingbeats to falter.

Petra was on her in a moment. "Are you all right?"

Dora pumped her wings evenly, trying to regain physical and emotional balance. "Yes," she said through gritted sharp teeth.

Marina moved to her other side into a tighter V formation so they could talk over the noise of the wind. They were still a ways off. "What's Doc doing at your house this early in the morning?"

"I don't know, but we'll find out soon enough." Dora dug her talons deeper into the meat she carried and relished the feel of it one last time.

"Hopefully, it's a social call and no one is sick or dying. We already attended one funeral this week, and that was enough." Petra kept their formation tight as she talked.

Marina gave Dora a side-eyed glance. "Maybe he's here for a reason that has nothing to do with doctoring."

Dora gritted her teeth. "There is no other reason he would come."

"Are you sure?" Petra asked.

"Absolutely." She was sure, and she *never* wanted to consider the possibility that she might be wrong. Her control was more important than whatever temptation Lee Williams posed to her.

"Well, someone has your hair turning grey. If it's not Doc, who is it?" Marina pressed.

Anger she had locked down moments ago rose to the surface. While Petra and Marina had found a balance between violence and love, Dora knew she did not possess enough control to have both without bloodshed. The violence was part of her and could not be ignored. It required all of her power to keep that one aspect of herself in check. She did not have space for the other.

"It doesn't matter," Dora said.

Marina looked like she was going to continue the conversation, but Petra widened their formation and dropped altitude. Marina followed her lead in silence.

Dora began her own descent. She pulled the pounding in her blood down into the dark place where she kept it hidden, kept it safe. She pushed aside the aftertaste of the hunt, still teasing her senses, and forced all her violence into the prison where she kept it. She slammed the door on her power again and took a deep breath. This was the one man with whom she could never afford to lose her control, never let her harpy have free reign.

Lee stood up and transferred something from his hands to his pocket. Dora did not need to be close enough to see to know that it was a piece of wood and a whittling knife. There would be shavings on her porch that would remind her of this moment until the wind blew them away. She did not need any reminders about the place Lee held in her life. Feeling petty, she called her power over the wind and directed it to scatter the wood shavings away.

Lee walked out into the yard to greet the approaching harpies. He watched them, the Remnants of three ancient monsters approaching from the sky, clutching mountain sheep in their talons, smiled, and gave a small wave of his hand. The morning sun lit his features and he squinted into the sun.

The harpies landed in front of him in the yard. Dora landed closest to him, unable to help herself from doing so. She released her talons from the sheep and hopped off the meat that would help feed her town.

Lee tilted his head up so his grey eyes could meet her own. "I'm sorry to intrude. I was down the mountain, looking after Melanie Eisler, who has chickenpox. She'll be fine, but I wanted to check in on her since Caroline is due in the next month or so. We should keep people away from their farm until Melanie has recovered."

Marina hopped over to Lee and leaned down to put her face next to his. The sound of her harpy voice, like glass being ground into stone, was striking after Lee's smooth voice. "Good morning to you, Doc. I'm sorry to hear Melanie is sick, but I'll let Iris know when I get back to town. We'll spread the word about giving the Eislers a wide berth for a bit." Marina, as the deputy of Turning Creek, and Iris, as the postmistress, had the best chance of spreading information in a timely manner.

Lee turned to Dora. "Your house was close and it was almost morning. There are some herbs I'm short of, especially after last night, and it's been a few days since I saw you. I hope you don't mind the intrusion."

Dora ruffled her feathers and struggled with the rush of emotions coursing through her. Lee was in her yard as if he belonged there, and her harpy side liked what that implied. It was harder to keep everything contained in her true form, where her passions were close to the surface. She took a deep breath, puffing out her chest feathers. With an inward sigh, she wound her harpy's power until she felt her form shifting. Instead of a towering bird of prey, her body compacted into the form of a mortal woman with hair a little too red to be blonde. The lighter strands hid the grey in her hair. Nothing hid her face, which was covered in too many freckles to be beautiful.

With the transformation, Dora succeeded in tamping down the aftereffects of the hunt, but she did not quite succeed in dismissing the pleasure at her unexpected visitor. His head was uncovered and his straight black hair shone in the early light. A dark grey frock coat was snug over his broad shoulders and showed off his lean form to perfection. His matching vest and cravat were still perfectly tied, even though Dora suspected Lee had been up much of the night.

"It's a surprise, but a nice one." Dora turned to Petra and Marina, who had not changed. "Will you two take the sheep to the smokehouse? I'll be along to help shortly."

"I vote for breakfast before we clean these up. I'm ravenous," Marina cast the comment over her shoulder as she picked up one of the dead sheep and flew it behind the house.

"It's nice to see you, Doc." Petra followed in Marina's wake. Their wingbeats kicked up swirls of dirt and grass.

Dora was left with Lee. She shifted her weight and felt her emotions level out into something manageable. She took another breath before speaking. "Marina is right, for once. We need to eat before we get to work. Would you like to stay? It's a long ride back to town."

"I will if it's not too much trouble. I've been up half the night." His eyes never left her face as he spoke.

"Come in, then. You can give me the list of things you need." Dora led the way into her cabin. She did not have to look to see if Lee followed her. She could feel his presence at her back. No matter how much time she spent with him, she never lost her sensitivity to him.

The interior of the cabin was well lit by the morning sun pouring into the eastern-facing picture window. Dora's eyes went around the room, though she knew she did not have to, and reassured herself that everything was in place. Books were carefully stacked on her shelves. A worn blue and white quilt was folded and laid in the center of the reclining couch along one wall. The wooden chairs were pushed under the table and the door to her room was open. Through the doorway she could see her bed, which she had made before leaving last night after sleeping for a few hours at dusk.

Dora waved to the kitchen table, the only one in the room. "Make yourself at home. I'll make tea. I have some bread for toast and some cured ham."

"Thank you." Lee sat with a sigh and leaned back in the chair. "I haven't seen you since the funeral."

She kept her eyes from him and concentrated on making tea. The simple movements calmed her further. Stoke the fire. Add some wood to the coals. Blow the fire to life. Fill the kettle.

"I've been patrolling the valley, and I went south to see if the huntresses had returned. Cascade Pass is finally open. I should've told you I'd be gone for a few days."

"You aren't beholden to me, but I do miss your help with patients."

Dora laughed, but it had a hard edge. The blood still rushing in her veins after the hunt could not be described as calm in any circumstance. "That's the first time anyone in the history of the world has said that about a harpy."

She pulled down four cups with a Wedgewood blue design. Instead of a pastoral English countryside, the cups featured a stylized flower and square border common on older Greek vases. She fingered a chip on the lip of one of the cups.

"You have a gift with people and the hands of a healer. And you are too hard on yourself." Lee's words were quiet but he spoke them with force, as if he believed them completely, utterly.

His words made her throat seize up. It was high praise from a man whose own hands could raise the dead. She swallowed past the lump in her throat and placed a teacup in front of him. She laid out the other cups and turned her back on him to slice bread.

She continued speaking while her hands moved. "Thank you. Now, I know you didn't come here to tell me I'm useful."

Dora looked over her shoulder and gave him a small smile. He returned it without hesitation and his eyes crinkled at the corners. Desire for an entirely different kind of hunt slammed into her and she struggled to try to get past the emotions swirling through her. She usually had better control than this. His visit was too close to their predatory adventure for her to master all her wayward feelings. She would have been better served to come up with some excuse as to why she was too busy to see him today.

Her cabin door flew open and Marina and Petra came in, arguing.

"It's not too soon to take them out hunting," Marina said as she flopped into the chair beside Lee.

Petra showed Dora a handful of eggs. "We stopped at the coop and picked up these. Marina scared your chickens with her bellowing. You might have to go soothe them later." Petra pulled a pan from the shelf and started heating it to cook the eggs.

"Who is going hunting?" Lee asked.

"No one yet," Petra said.

"Selene and Ellie," Marina said over her.

Dora headed off Petra's rebuttal by speaking over Petra's reply. "Don't ask them any more questions, Lee. It'll only encourage them. Marina wants to take Ellie and Selene on their first hunt. Petra wants to give them a little more time to grow. Hunting can be dangerous. This is a fight they've been having off and on." Turning back to her sisters, she continued, "I would like a meal with more talking than arguing." Selene was the oldest of the young ones, but Petra was protective of her only daughter.

Dora lifted the hot water off the stove and poured it over the tea in her teapot. The kitchen was filled with the sound of frying eggs. Dora poured the tea when it was done. Marina sniffed the light brown liquid in her cup and scowled at it. She pushed her chair back, retrieved a bottle of whiskey from the back of the shelf over the sink, and poured some into her tea.

"Anyone else?"

Petra pushed her cup towards Marina. Dora rolled her eyes. "It's barely past sunrise."

"Daytime, you mean?" Marina said as she and Petra clinked cups. "Good hunt and good morning."

Petra went back to the stove and resumed cracking eggs. "I hate to say this, because it makes twice you've heard it in one morning, but you're right."

Marina cupped a hand around her ear. "Sorry, can you repeat that? I thought you said I was brilliant."

"Hera preserve us." Petra flipped an egg over too hard and the yolk broke. "I said you were right, not brilliant. Even idiots have moments of intelligence. Hells. It's time for the girls to go hunting. I know, I just wish we could keep them small, contained. They grow too fast."

Understanding dawned and Lee chuckled. "That is a sentiment shared by every mother."

Marina leaned forward, her brown eyes sparkling. "They'll have the opportunity to do something we never did until we came here. They can learn to hunt and fight together. Be a cohesive unit. They'll be a powerhouse before they've even reached maturity."

Dora pulled some plates down from a cabinet. "Not to add fuel to the fire, but Marina is right. They are old enough to learn to hunt and control their harpies."

Dora loved her sister harpies' daughters like they were her own. Selene, Petra's daughter, would be two in August. Ellie, Marina's daughter, had just turned one. She thought of teaching them the joy of flying and the pleasure of blood under their talons for the first time. The idea brought joy, but it was tinged with guilt. It was past time she continued her own line.

When the first four harpies were created by Zeus, he cursed them to only have one daughter. One female progeny to continue their lines so that their power never spread. The gods frequently feared the powerful things they created and then reigned them in cruelly after the fact.

The prospect of continuing her line was fraught with complications, and the largest one was sitting in her kitchen. She could not choose the path of her sister harpies. There were some lines she would not cross again, regardless of the pool of yearning opening up inside her.

Dora kept her harpy behind a wall until she needed it again. The harpy was her true self, but it was also dangerous. Dora knew her own limits, and she preferred keeping her limits within control. As long as she had control, she would never be the monster she had once been.

Dora fixedly did not look at Lee, afraid her control would break. Lee in her kitchen after a night of hunting, his voice rubbing over her skin like silk, was making it hard to keep her emotions in check. All of them.

The walls of her cabin seemed closer than usual and the air thinner. She could feel the power of her harpy leaking from her pores. She turned to the side and tried to breathe deep, but she could feel the wildness of all those emotions threatening to overwhelm her.

Petra and Marina turned their eyes towards her as the tendrils of violence reached them. Lee swiveled his gaze towards her and remained still. Dora knew he could feel the power shifting in the room, but he would not know why. Marina raised her brows at her in a question. Her sisters would know that Dora was acting like she was being threatened. They could not know why.

Marina waved the flask at Dora. "I think you need this more than anyone else."

Dora shook her head, but it did not clear it. If anything, the movement made everything worse. "I need to go check on a few things outside." Dora left her tea and a heavy silence behind her.

Her legs moved swiftly. Dora walked into the line of trees and kept walking until she was surrounded by the cheerful twittering of birds singing to the morning. The aspen leaves rustled over her head and she took a deep breath, the first one since returning home this morning.

Dora balled her emotions up and let them go out into the world. The breeze picked up and the branches of the trees above her head trembled. Dora was descended from the Aello line of harpies. Mothers of this line passed on many things to their daughters, including the ability to harness the wind. Dora let its power roll through her and out, taking with it the memory of the hunt, the image of Lee drinking tea at her table, and the way his eyes on her warmed her soul. The trees above her bent further with the power escaping her.

A light footstep on the forest floor came from the direction of the house. The smell of rain on summer mountains reached her, and Dora knew it was Petra that had come. Dora stilled the wind, and the leaves above them quieted.

"Why did you leave?" Petra stepped up next to her and put her arm around Dora.

"I needed to get my bearings. It felt too crowded in the cabin." Dora leaned her head onto Petra's shoulder. The touch grounded her further.

"Do you want to talk about it?"

Dora gathered what was left of her control and locked everything else away. "No. I'm fine. I just wasn't ready for company after the hunt."

"Doc knows us, knows you. We don't need to be something else for him."

Petra and Marina had found a balance with their harpies, a way to be both violent and soft. Dora knew there was either the abyss for her or nothing. One or the other. She could never be both at once, and this morning she had not been given time to separate the two.

"I'm fine," Dora repeated with her teeth clenched. If she said it enough, it might be true. "Let's go have breakfast."

Petra's lips thinned into a line and her brown eyes flashed. "You're different when you are flying than you are normally. I never noticed it until this morning when I saw your reaction to Doc unfold in front of me. It was like you locked everything down at the sight of him."

Dora huffed out a breath as everything in her tensed.

"You're doing it now." Petra gave her a push on her shoulder. "Stop it. I see you backing off."

Dora rolled her shoulder away from Petra. "I'm fine."

Petra moved closer and pushed her again, harder this time. "You're not. When we hunt you are wilder, more free. What are you hiding from?"

Everything! Dora's mind screamed. Her hand curled into a fist and she ached to plant it in Petra's prying mouth. She kept it still and rigid by her side instead to prove to herself that she could. "I know what it means to lose control. I won't ever be that way." *Never again*, she promised herself.

"Because of your mother and the way she died?" Petra asked.

Dora let that assumption stand. She'd never admitted to her sisters or Iris the real reason she feared losing control. "Yes, because of my mother." The lie was necessary, but thick in her mouth.

"You aren't her."

I'm worse, Dora thought. "I know. Let's go have breakfast."

Petra's lips thinned again and she sighed, but held her peace. She followed Dora back to the cabin in silence. Dora used that time to leash her anger further until all she felt was the low hum of it in the background.

Lee eyed her with a worried look in his eye when they returned, but he said nothing. Marina pushed Dora into a chair and scooped eggs and toast onto the plate in front of her.

"I can stay and dress the sheep after breakfast," Marina said as she served out the rest of the food and sat in her own chair.

Petra chewed a bite and swallowed. "James will be waiting for me, and Selene will be beside herself when she finds out we went hunting without her. It'll be best if I'm there to help control the tantrum she is sure to throw."

Marina chuckled. "I expect Ellie, though she is much too young to be hunting full-grown sheep, will have a similar opinion. I think Reed can handle her, though."

Petra paused before shoveling eggs into her mouth. "Do you think we were this much trouble to our mothers?"

Marina laughed. "I was worse. I'm sure."

"Of that, I've no doubt." Dora sipped her tea, and its warmth helped fill the hole in her soul. She fingered the chip on the corner of the cup.

Petra hesitated. "Besides, we have cows that need milking and James would appreciate another set of hands for that."

"James has a whole slew of men now to do the milking." Marina waved her fork in the air.

"Yes, but he likes to do the work himself, and the milking goes easier when Selene is not underfoot. Plus, someone told her cows are fun to chase, and so she has been stalking them for days." Petra narrowed her eyes at Marina.

Marina shoved eggs in her mouth and mumbled around them, "I have no idea what you're talking about."

Petra snorted. "I'll bet."

The banter between her sisters filled Dora with a calmness despite the pressure of Lee's presence. Her life before coming to Turning Creek had been filled with many things, but peace had not been one of them. Flashes of the island her mother had ruled filled her. On the outside, it was beautiful, but madness ran underneath it all. Her mother had ruled that island with blood, and in the end, Dora had not been able to escape the clarion call of violence. She had fled and found her way here.

Dora shoved those memories where she kept all the things that threatened her control, far into herself. She was no longer that young harpy. She would not allow herself to be.

"Let's take the girls hunting soon. We can start with something small, like rabbits." Dora thought of the young harpies chasing rabbits, and smiled.

Lee had not spoken a word since breakfast had resumed. Dora turned to him now. "You said you're short on some herbs?"

Lee was mopping up egg yolk with his toast and looked up. "I am out of feverfew, and I gave the last of the wintergreen I had to Mrs. Eisler for tea. I use those two quite often and wanted to get more if you had it."

Dora stood up and went to the large cupboard sitting above a wooden counter. The space took up the wall perpendicular to the kitchen. The counter was free of debris, but different size mortar and pestle sets, a press for extracting oil, and equipment for making tinctures were nestled against the backsplash. The cupboard held rows of jars, clearly labeled and alphabetized. Dora pulled two jars down and shook them.

"I have both, but not much of either. I know I have some in the garden. I'll give you what I have now and start drying more this afternoon. I'll be in town in two days for Saturday dinner with Iris and Henry; I can drop it by then."

Lee smiled and the seriousness of his features softened. "I knew I could count on you to have what I needed." He stood from the table. "Let me grab my bag off my horse. I have the empty jars there."

As soon as the door closed, Marina made a rude noise in her throat.

"Do you have something to say?" Dora asked. She felt a stir of anger, but she pushed it through a door in the wall of her soul and slammed the door shut for what seemed to be the twelfth time this morning.

Marina shook her head and grabbed a peach out of the basket on the table. "I've got nothing to say. I was just clearing my throat."

"Clearly." Dora frowned and gripped her teacup to keep herself from giving Marina an elbow to the ribs.

Petra looked between two of them. "Do I need to stay and keep you two from getting into a fight?"

Dora walked over to Petra and gave her a hug. "Go. I can handle Marina. If she gets ugly, I'll hide her whiskey."

"She's already ugly." Petra winked and they all burst into laughter.

Lee came back in the cabin carrying his medicine box. He paused in the doorway when the wall of laughter hit him. "I hope I'm not the cause of so much hilarity." He smiled as he set the box down on the table.

Marina snort-chuckled. "We were just discussing how I could beat Dora to a pulp except she would never feed me or keep whiskey for me when she forces me to drink tea if I did."

"Of course," Lee said blandly, causing Dora and Marina to burst into laughter again. He handed the empty jars to Dora. She was careful not to touch him as she took the amber-colored glass.

She carried them to the counter and transferred the last of her feverfew and wintergreen into the jars. The smell of wintergreen hung in the air as she tightened the metal lids on the jars. Dora put them on the table in front of Lee and sat back down in her chair.

Petra finished her tea and carried her cup and plate to sink. "I'm off. I'll see you both Saturday. Doc, always a pleasure."

Lee stood. "It's time I went as well. It's been a long night and I still have to ride back to town before I can seek my bed."

Dora stood and went to the door to open it. "I'll cut a batch of the herbs we use the most often and bring a sack for you on Saturday."

Lee inclined his head. "Thank you, Dora. Marina and Petra, it's always interesting."

"Thanks, Doc." Marina poured more whiskey in her cup and looped her arm over the back of her chair.

Dora closed the door behind Lee and slumped into her chair. She topped off her cup with tea and moved to do the same for Marina.

Marina put her hand over hers. "I've had enough for one morning. Thanks." She lifted the bottle from the center of the table and put a finger of the amber liquid into the cup.

Dora wrapped her hands around her teacup and let the warmth of the tea soak into her hands.

Marina's words broke her thoughts apart. "You seem over-serious this morning and a bit tetchy."

Dora smiled and met Marina's brown eyes. "I was just thinking that you and Petra are the things that make my life one of contentment instead of what it could have been."

Marina smiled ruefully. "I know that's not all, but I'll let you go this time. We could've all been different things. We could've been our mothers, gods forbid."

Dora thought of her mother and the manner in which she had died, cursed and cursing in a pool of her own blood. "Yes, we could've ended up worse." She blew on her tea before taking another sip and changed the subject. "The rivers are burgeoning from the snow melt."

Marina, never one to dwell on her own mother, accepted the change of subject without question. "The snow melt isn't as bad as the year of Demeter's spring, but it was close." Three years ago, a Remnant of Demeter had dumped so much snow in Turning Creek that the rivers had run over their banks for most of the summer as the snow melted. The mud season had lasted months longer than normal.

"It's been quiet in Turning Creek these past couple years in terms of the supernatural," Dora said. There had been pockets of disputes between mortals and Remnants, but they had been solved quickly, sometimes when the less-tolerant mortals moved on from the area.

Marina scowled at her. "Don't say that out loud for the gods to hear. I'm hoping the quiet remains a bit longer."

"I thought you thrived on chaos and excitement."

"I do, but I've had my fill of major disasters. I wouldn't mind a good monster run amok in the valley, though. It's been too long since we went hunting something that was more of a challenge than mountain goats."

Dora clucked her tongue. "Careful what you wish for, sister."

Marina drained her tea cup and rose. "It's time to skin those sheep."

They made short work of the sheep, cutting the carcasses into hunks of meat and hanging most of it in the smokehouse. The smokehouse was large enough to hold enough meat to feed many families through the winter, and it often did. The harpies saw to it that no one went hungry in Turning Creek. It was early in the season, so the smokehouse was mostly empty after having been depleted through the winter. By the time fall came, the walls would be covered in cured meat to see them through the long months of winter.

After scraping and stretching the hide, they went to the creek behind the house to wash the blood from their hands and arms.

Dora stretched her back. "One more chore, then I'll release you," she said.

"Does it involve food or a drink?" Marina's curly brown hair had escaped its binding. She righted it while she looked at Dora.

"No. I need to get those herbs for Lee, and it will go more quickly with your help."

"Why don't I just move in and do all your work for you?" Marina muttered.

"That would be great. Then I can sit around pretending to be useful and drink whisky all day, like you do." Dora hit Marina with her shoulder as walked around the cabin, grabbing a small basket as she went, finally halting in front of her ever expanding garden.

Marina called after her, laughing, "I'm damn good at what I do."

Dora laughed. "No one disputes that. Come over here."

Three years ago, she had started with one small bed of mint, chamomile, and feverfew. Now she had multiple beds with various herbs, including some rare ones she had ordered from Europe or procured through Iris's mother, who lived in Tuscany. Last month, she had added a five-by-ten greenhouse so she could continue to grow things during the winter months. She enjoyed growing things that were useful to others.

She stopped in front of a section of peppermint. The leaves looked wrong. Dora dropped to her knees in the dirt, adding to the mess already on her skirt. She bent over the plants until her nose was inches from the bright green, heavily veined leaves.

"I thought you were going to pick them, not eat them off the stems." Marina's voice was laced with good humored irritation.

"Something's wrong with the peppermint," Dora said.

The surface of the leaves was marred by black dots. Dora rubbed her finger over one of the affected leaves. The blackness transferred to her fingers and Dora rubbed them together. The black substance smeared over her fingertips and was not grainy, like dirt. It was softer.

"A fungus or something," Dora said. She rubbed the fungus off them and put one of the leaves in her mouth. The acrid taste of decay bit into her tongue and she spit it out. "Hells."

Marina was still standing, but bent over to get a closer look. "It looks like dirt from up here, but I'm guessing from your reaction, it's not."

"No. Let's check the other beds."

A perusal of the other beds confirmed that some of the plants in each batch of plants were affected. With her mouth set in a grim line, Dora began pulling up the peppermint plants with black fungus, tossing them into a growing pile. Marina knelt by the feverfew and began ripping. They did not talk as they worked. The only sound was the tearing of roots from the black soil. They worked, careful to not leave any tainted plants in the beds. After the culling the bed, there were only two or three plants at most of each kind left in the ground.

"Styx," Dora muttered.

Marina wiped sweat from her brow, leaving a trail of dirt in the wake of her hand. "For Hera's sake, Dora, they'll grow back. You still have a decent bit left."

Dora surveyed the heap of ruined plants. "I've never seen fungus like this. I need to do some research. There's still enough time to do some planting, and with the greenhouse, my growing periods are extended, but what if we need something and there's not enough?"

If she was judicious with her herb usage, she could make what she had last until she could grow more plants. Most of the summer stretched before them still and there was time to plant more and then dry it before she could no longer use the outside beds.

Marina's eyebrow cocked up. "Doc managed fine before you started supplying him with herbs. He'll manage fine without this if he needs to."

Marina was right, she knew. "Let's move these."

Dora gathered up an armful of the plants and dumped them by the wood pile on the side of the house. They each made two trips before they were finished. When the plants dried, she could burn them or bury them. Worry over the fungus and her fear that it would spread to the remaining plants niggled at the base of her spine. The success of her herbs and their usefulness to others was one way Dora fought against becoming an instrument of violence alone. With her hands and herbs, she helped heal people, and she took pride and value from those actions.

Marina wiped her hands on her pants. "I've got to get back. I'll see you in a couple days."

"Thanks for staying. Tell Reed I'm sorry for keeping you so long." Dora wrapped Marina in a hug. They were tall and of the same height so their cheeks pressed together. Marina smelled like grass and dirt and Dora smiled, tightening her arms around her sister harpy.

"Fly safe." Dora released Marina.

"I will, unless something interesting happens." Marina changed and joined the clouds in the summer sky.

Dora watched her fly away until she could no longer see her go, then turned back to her cabin, which seemed even smaller now that she was alone.

CHAPTER 3

Dora placed the basket she had been carrying in her talons on the ground, careful not to topple it or spill any of the contents she had worked to gather and dry. She landed in the small yard in the back of the building that housed Lee's medical practice and his spartan apartment on the second floor. She could hear children screeching in the distance. A glance south revealed the Saturday dinner gathering, already in full swing in Iris and Henry's yard.

Dora changed fluidly, pulling her harpy into herself until she stood in Lee's yard as a mortal woman. She picked up the basket and walked across the yard to the back door. Unlike many of the other buildings on Main Street, the doctor's office did not have a back porch, but it did have a landing of flagstone with bunches of red paintbrush flowers straining towards the sun on either side of the path. Dora ran her free hand over the blooms and went into the building.

Dora closed the door behind her and paused, tilting her head. There was a hush within the walls. "Lee. Are you here?"

Dora paused for the span of two breaths, her nose filling with the smell of clean soap. The tightness in her chest eased when she confirmed Lee was not at home. It was followed by a swift disappointment.

She moved down the bare hallway and into the first door on her left. The room she entered was the size of a large closet with a wall of glass-doored cabinets on one side and a wooden counter on the other. It was Lee's dispensary. Often-used medicines and tinctures were kept in the examination room next door. This was simply storage.

Dora plopped the basket on the counter and pulled out the jars and pouches of herbs she had brought. She lined them up in alphabetical order and then put them away without pause. Her hands and eyes never hesitated. This dispensary was as familiar to her as her own house. The labeling on the jars was in her own writing. When the last jar was filled with dried yarrow, Dora found a pile of scrap papers in the corner, wrote Lee a note, then left.

The late afternoon air was heavy with the smell of green things, bursting after a long winter's rest. Dora closed her eyes and breathed deep, letting the swirl of life run over her. A shriek followed by Marina's laughter pulled her from the moment of calm. Her rambunctious, motley family of her own choosing awaited.

Selene, James and Petra's daughter, noticed her approach first. "Dee!" The harpy toddler ran on chubby legs towards Dora, her dark curls bouncing and olive skin shining with happiness. Dora knelt on the edge of the yard and scooped up the girl. She buried her nose in Selene's hair, breathing in her sweet smell, like sugar and sunshine.

Two more small bundles hurtled themselves towards her. Ellie, her copper penny eyes aglow, and Aldara, the youngest, but already as watchful as her mother. Dora tried to keep her balance but soon gave up; the four of them tumbled into a heap in the grass. The girls screeched in delight and laughter bubbled out of Dora.

"Thank you for the greetings, young ones," Dora said.

Marina scooped up the two harpy daughters, one under each arm. "Hera save us from enthusiastic children. Good of you to make it."

Dora picked up Aldara and tossed her into the air. The tiny Messenger whooped in delight before Dora caught her.

"Again," the child demanded. At one, she was younger than the two harpy girls. Dora squeezed Aldara until the little girl squealed with delight.

There was an insistent butting into her leg. "Auntie Dee." Selene had been set free and did not want to be ignored. "Dee, Mom says we are going hunting."

"Hunting!" Ellie ran around them in circles. "Hunting!"

Dora put Aldara down, and she chased after Ellie and Selene. She met Marina's wide grin over the tops of the three cavorting children. "I see you broke the news."

Aldara stopped between Marina and Dora and looked up. "I want to go too."

Selene, with all the authority a two-year-old harpy could muster, wagged a finger at Aldara. "You can't go. You don't have wings. You're still a baby."

Aldara's blue eyes filled with watery tears, and Iris left her conversation with Reed to scoop up the girl. "Momma will carry you for the hunt, small one. We can watch, but we can't interfere."

Marina grabbed Selene's arm as she raced past and knelt with one knee on the ground. "Selene, Aldara may be younger than you, but she is your Messenger, and you will treat her kindly. She is yours to defend and protect, just as she will protect you. Words have meaning. Use them well." Marina smoothed back the curls that had escaped Selene's braid. "Do you understand?"

"Yes, ma'am," the girl mumbled, the toe of her shoe shuffling against the ground.

Petra joined them. "Apologize to Aldara, daughter." The two small girls hugged and then ran off to the other side of the yard. Marina and Petra drifted away to join the lively conversation going on around the fire.

Dora linked arms with Iris, who was following her daughter with her eyes and a worried expression. "It's early yet. Remember that I counseled patience."

Iris twisted and looked up into Dora's face. "You're right." Iris rolled her shoulder against an imaginary ache.

Dora squeezed Iris's arm. "It's nice to be able to lecture you for a change."

Iris laughed. "Lucky for you, I rarely meet advice with anger and glaring." She ran a hand over Dora's hair. "Petra told me about what happened after the hunt a couple days ago."

Dora's face hardened. "I thought we'd established that I don't want to talk about that."

Iris pulled her closer. "Avoiding town for a few days won't make me keep quiet when I have something to say. Just come talk to me when you need to."

Dora relaxed and bussed Iris's cheek. "I'll take that advice under consideration. Come, let's join the others. They're having fun without us."

Marina was already in the middle of a story, regaling those gathered around the fire. "So, I grabbed him by one ankle and flew him about fifty feet in the air. He started caterwaulin', so of course I pretended to drop him." She paused to waggle her eyebrows and laugh. "That's when he started crying. He very nearly promised me everything he owned and his firstborn."

Reed said with a wry smile, "I'm fairly certain Vine didn't have trouble with cheating for two or three months at least after that."

The group laughed. Iris broke free from Dora and went to stand beside Petra. Dora continued on to join Henry, who sat on a bench at the outside table off to the side of the yard.

"Afternoon, Miss Dora." Henry's voice was low and steady. A nice change in Dora's ears from the cacophony of the group by the fire.

"How are things at the forge?" She sat across from him with her back to the yard. Henry was the Remnant of Hephaestus, blacksmith to the gods, and he made beautiful, magical things with metal.

"Things are good these days now that I have Blaine Walsh helping out. He's got a fair hand with the hammer, and I think he enjoys the independence of living away from his family." Blaine was from a large Irish family who had settled in the valley during the last two years. He lived in the cottage behind the forge that had been Henry's before he had married Iris.

Henry's curly black hair shone in the sun, and his grey eyes watched her. "How are you this fine day?"

Dora leaned forward on her elbows. "Right enough, I suppose."

Henry did not pry. It was the reason Dora had chosen to sit here rather than remain with the group. A pile of new timber was piled on the side of the depot.

"What's the wood for?"

Henry glanced over her head and smiled at someone. Dora did not have to turn around to know he was looking at Iris. "It's time we expand the depot. Iris wants to keep the extra room for you or the other harpies, and we will be outgrowing the space we have, eventually."

Dora did not miss the twinkle in his eye. She leaned closer. "Eventually, like in a few months, or eventually, like a few years?"

Henry's eyes crinkled with a smile, but he shrugged. "Time will tell. It's early yet."

"You two are wasting no time." Dora swung her legs over the bench to face the group.

"Time is best not wasted, as I've learned."

Dora knew he was referring to his own delayed courtship of Iris, but the words could have been for her. Sitting here, surrounded by her family and their burgeoning fecundity, she knew she must soon have a daughter of her own. Maintaining control ruled out a mate of the sort Marina and Petra had chosen, one chosen by the heart. That left her with the traditional choice of taking a temporary mate for the purpose of fathering a daughter. It was what all the generations before her had done.

It was not a choice she relished.

Petra, her deep, olive skin flushed with laughter, turned away from the group and came to sit by Dora. James, Reed, Marina, Iris, and the girls followed, and the peace around the table erupted with life. Dora's lap was claimed by Ellie, who yelled at Selene across the table while Aldara yelled at them both.

"Now I know why our mothers never brought us together when we were young." Marina lowered her voice, her harpy making the next words rough. "Hush, you three." The threat in the words, though only bluff, was enough to reduce the volume of the girls by half.

A blur of blonde hair zoomed by the table and stopped in front of the pot over the fire. "What's for dinner?"

"Thomas," Iris put a hand on her hip, "don't run up to the fire like that. You'll spill the stew all over everything."

"And probably burn yourself to a crisp in the process. Where's Nina?" Marina asked.

Thomas lifted the lid to the pot and sniffed the contents. "She's with Mrs. McKenzie, Stephen, and Jonas. They were walking too slow. When are we eating?"

Iris smacked his hand away from the spoon hanging by the pot. "Dinner is soon. You can wait until we all sit down to eat."

Thomas looked like he was about to protest when Henry said, "Come sit by me, son, and tell me about your day."

Thomas went as bid, but the slumping of his shoulders and his growling stomach lodged plenty of protest. The adults laughed at his expense.

Claire emerged from a path in the woods, followed by her two sons, Jonah and Stephen, and Nina. Claire was Reed's sister. She had moved to Turning Creek after the death of her husband to start over. The boys ran to join Thomas, and Nina followed Claire to the table.

Nina had grown into a willowy youth in the two years she had lived with Marina and Reed. She was a serious child who tended to create rainstorms and wind gusts when she was upset. She was the last Remnant of Demeter, a goddess with power over the seasons. Marina was not a model of control, so Nina had been working with Iris to learn how to control her powers. Iris helped her learn control, and Nina watched the younger girls when needed in exchange for the guidance.

Nina put her small hands on Dora's knees. Her brown hair had come loose from its ties and it was a tangled mess down her back. Her eyes were the color of cornflowers in the sun.

"Howdy, Aunt Dee." Though Nina was old enough to pronounce her name, she had adopted the name the younger girls used.

Dora put her hands over Nina's. "What adventures have you been up to?"

Nina leaned closer. "We've been building obstacles and mazes and timing Thomas as he runs through them. I made it rain on him and blew him off the hill once." She giggled. "He's so fast." Nina put extra emphasis on the last word.

Dora laughed. "Has Marina shown you how fast she can fly?" The girl shook her head, her eyes growing wide. "You should have her race Thomas and see who wins. It would be close." Nina laughed and went off to consult with Thomas.

The meal was served and everyone sat where they could – at the table, on logs, on the ground. The sun dipped behind the mountains, and Henry added wood to the fire. The older kids gathered the dishes and cleaned up after everyone had eaten their fill. The adults pulled the benches from the table over to the fire and placed them beside the logs already there to add more seats. Soon, the work was done and there was nothing left to do but relax and enjoy the rest of the evening.

The kids ran beyond the circle around the fire, shrieking in the growing darkness. Marina leaned an arm down behind the log and pulled up a half-full bottle of whiskey. She pulled out the cork, took a swig, and passed the bottle to Dora.

"I think your power isn't speed at all. It's being able to produce alcohol at will whenever the occasion calls for it." Dora took the bottle from her, took a drink, then passed it to James, who sat to her left.

"And on occasions that do not." James' mouth quirked into a smile before he took a drink and passed on the bottle to his wife. Petra took it with thanks and the bottle traveled around the circle.

"Hells, you appreciate me, don't act like you don't," Marina said when the bottle got back to her.

Petra snorted. "But if we tell you that, you'll start getting a big head."

"Bigger head," Dora said, grabbing the bottle away from Marina. "Can barely see around you as it is." They all laughed together and Dora's soul lightened. She was blessed by the things she had here in this circle, things generations of harpies before her had lacked.

The laughter died and Reed's easy drawl broke into the gap. "Been a while since we made the rounds. Now that I have you all together, can you three cover the valley and a little beyond in the next couple weeks? I'd like to know if everyone got help with planting that needed it and if anyone still has needed repairs from the winter."

Being the sheriff of Turning Creek was about more than upholding the law, though he did plenty of that. Reed, with Marina's help, kept tabs on all the residents of the valley, mortal and Remnant. If someone needed food, new siding on the barn, or help getting seed in the ground, Reed and Marina made sure help was available. It was just one way the harpies kept their territory running smoothly. They protected what was theirs.

"I'll check with Lee. He may want us to look in on some people in particular. He usually keeps a list of people with conditions that need periodic checking. I can get it from him and make sure I go to those houses," Dora said.

"Doc's made you a regular nurse." Reed smiled at her.

Petra's low chuckle came through the dark. "It would be the first time a harpy ever got labeled as a nurse."

Dora opened her mouth to protest, but Petra waved her hand. "I'm not insulting you. It was more of a compliment. Could you imagine what our mothers would say if they saw us like this?"

Marina snorted and took a pull from the bottle, which had gotten back to her. "She'd probably try to kill me for being soft."

Dora thought of her mother, long dead, and knew her mother would have shredded her, or at least tried to. "She wouldn't be able to get within striking distance of you without getting through me." Dora's tone was even and calm, but her words held menace.

Marina's voice was deeper than normal and ground out like gravel. "We're stronger together. I would never let anyone harm my family."

Petra's low guttural reply matched Marina's. "Or this valley."

Dora's harpy soared within her at the power coming from her sisters. She fought to keep hers down and was pleased when she said in her normal voice, "On the River Styx, may it be so."

The three harpies looked at each other, and the predators in them rose and night shine reflected from the firelight flashed in their eyes. Dora let her harpy rise just enough for a moment of triumph, but then pulled hers back down.

"Enough of that," James said in his clipped British accent, which belonged in a drawing room and not by a bonfire. "Everyone here knows you are all quite scary. Save the theatrics for the rest of the valley. I'm glad we only have you three to contend with."

Petra nudged him with her shoulder. "You should be glad. We're practically bunnies compared to our mothers."

Marina waved a cup in Dora's direction. Dora did not know where she had gotten the cup from, but it appeared to be filled with whiskey. "Except for Dora's mother. She's already dead."

The circle was silent except for the crackling of the logs on the fire. Reed gave Marina a hard elbow in the ribs and she glared at him.

"Marina." Iris's voice was filled with censure.

Dora shrugged. "She is. It was a long time ago, and it means there's one less monster in the world."

Nina broke through the adult's circle to stand before Dora. "What happened to your mother?"

Selene was right on Nina's heels. "Tell us a story."

At some point in the evenings during these gatherings, one of the adults would tell the children a story, either from the history of the Remnants or of their own adventures. It was a way for them to both teach their history and remember it themselves. Usually, Iris told the stories because she knew the most history, given her position as chronicler and her own research interests. She yielded the job when one of the others wanted to share a story they knew well.

Iris sat straighter. "I'm not sure Dora wants to tell that story."

Dora waved a hand in the air. "No, it's fine. It's been on my mind a lot lately, and it's a good cautionary tale."

The children came into the circle by the fire and arranged themselves around Dora. The adults too settled in to listen. This was a story that Dora had never told them. She rarely spoke of her mother, even though she thought of her often.

"The line of Aello ruled an archipelago of islands off of the coast of Greece. When a harpy daughter comes of age, she leaves her mother's island and finds her own to rule. The towns or villagers that resided on these islands were not usually thrilled about this, but they had no control or power that could stop a harpy.

"The island my mother chose was in the middle of a sea so blue it made the sky look dull. The village there was filled with houses that were pale white. Every window was adorned with flowers. In the spring and summer, the smell of them would rival the sea. I thought it was the most beautiful place in the world, until I came here.

"My mother did not rule her island with benevolence. She ruled with fear, blood, and violence." Dora took a sip from the bottle that was passed to her and then kept it going on its journey. "If a villager displeased her, she killed them or maimed them. My mother didn't understand that power does not have to mean violence. Some mortals left, but many could not leave, and so they stayed.

"Though she was a tyrant to others, she loved me in her way, and I adored her, especially when I was young and before I understood that fear was not a good way to rule. As she got older, she became increasingly unstable, punishing people for perceived slights or her own foul mood. When I had almost reached fifty, the age of majority for harpies, a tailor in town made a dress for my mother and she was not pleased by it. She killed the tailor and his wife and laughed while she did it."

Dora tried to shake the sound of the memory of her mother from her mind. Her mother had often *laughed* while she killed people. Dora remembered the full-throated laugh of pleasure, and the sun setting behind her mother's head in a splash of orange over purple. The incongruity of that beautiful orange fire with her mother's revelry in the carnage she had created from innocence had been seared into Dora's mind.

Dora shook her head again and addressed the children. "The tailor had a sister, a local witch, who was the Remnant of Medea. Who remembers who Medea was?"

Thomas spoke first. "She was the first wife of Jason, who betrayed her. She was a talented witch and poisoned Jason's new intended bride, killed her sons, and rode off in a chariot pulled by dragons."

Dora nodded. "Excellent summary. The sister was a Remnant of Medea and she wanted revenge for the death of her brother. She cursed my mother with an incurable sickness."

Dora paused and took a deep breath. "It was a terrible sickness, and my mother suffered greatly, but she never repented of her actions. She died in my arms."

Dora looked over the faces of the children and into the fire. "Her death taught me that violence should only be wielded with control and that vengeance can be a dangerous thing."

More than her mother's death alone had taught her those things. It was what happened after her mother died that had cemented those two lessons into Dora's soul. Those memories were not part of the story she would tell tonight, if ever. Her actions after her mother's death had shaped her, for good or ill.

"What happened to the witch?" Iris asked.

"She died." Dora smiled when she said it. The memory of it still brought her pleasure. The pleasure contained in that knowledge was one reason of many why she would not tell the full story of that night. Ever. "The end."

The children popped up and left the light of the fire to resume their games from before. Iris watched Dora for a long time while everyone else resettled. Dora avoided making eye contact with her.

One of the girls playing outside the fire laughed, Nina maybe. Dora turned and watched the young ones run in the increasing darkness. Dora could barely see Thomas as he ran in a blur after the other children. It was their version of tag, only Thomas was always "it," trying to freeze everyone before they had a chance to set their comrades free. He always won in the end.

Aldara tried valiantly to keep up, but her tiny legs could only toddle. She might be more intellectual than a mortal one year old, but her body was still awkward. Frustrated, she climbed onto a stump in the yard and yelled at the children whipping around her. The frenzy was too much for Selene, who let loose a cackle, which sounded surprisingly like Petra's, and morphed into a small black harpy with a dusting of white across her mantle.

A full-grown harpy was larger than a cow, with the body of a bird of prey and the angular face of a woman. A fledgling harpy was the size of a large dog. Selene's face had yet to develop its angular lines and still retained some of the chubbiness of childhood even when transformed. Selene let out a screech and launched into the air after Thomas.

Ellie, not to be left out, followed suit, morphing into a rust-colored harpy with black covet feathers. Thomas darted in a zig-zag formation to try to avoid the fledglings. His speed was the only thing that saved him from getting small talons in his back. Jonas, Stephen, and Nina knew when they were outmatched and dropped from the fray.

Iris stood up. "Do you think we should intervene?"

Henry pulled her back down. "Thomas will be a grown man soon enough. He can probably handle them."

Marina laughed. "He might not come out unscratched, though they'll not mean to do him harm."

"Never fear, we'll step in if need be. As long as they don't try to go after any of the others." Petra's voice shook with laughter as they watched the chase.

Aldara, still on top of her stump, yelled at the top of her baby lungs. "Wait for me. Wait. Wait." She repeated the word over and over in the persistent indignation of the young, following the trio with the angle of her body as they moved across the yard in the dark.

The air around Dora seemed to still and suck in on itself. The hairs on her neck rose, and a raw power filled the air. It reminded Dora of how it felt before Iris was overcome with a prophecy, and she looked at the Messenger. Iris stood still and pale, her eyes transfixed on her daughter. The others around the circle rose to their feet. Marina crouched down and drew a knife from her belt. Dora could feel the power within her tighten as her harpy responded to the unknown threat. She peered into darkness of the woods, searching for the source of the power making the air leaden.

Dora swept the clearing with her eyes. The other harpies were coiled tight, ready to spring. Iris's blue gaze was still centered on Aldara. Iris, her face a pale mask of hope and fear, took a step toward her daughter. Dora swiveled towards the child with a dawning realization.

The tide of power was coming from Aldara, who stood with her hands at her sides, eyes narrowed at the fledgling harpies and Thomas who had halted on the side of the clearing. Selene and Ellie were flapping in the hair above Thomas but making no move to touch him.

Everyone was silent in the heavy air except Aldara, whose fury had not abated by the cessation of the chase. "Stop chasing my Thomas."

The words were accentuated by a small popping noise and the power contracted back toward the toddler in a whoosh that made the child stumble and almost fall off the stump. Dora swayed. Her body was pulled by the surge and she dug her heels in to maintain her balance. Two golden wings appeared between Aldara's shoulder blades, the crests barely rising over the top of her head. They glowed faintly with their own golden light in the dark beyond the orange of the fire's light. They looked so much like her mother's wings that Dora had to blink to confirm what she was seeing.

Before anyone could react, Aldara snapped open her wings and leapt off the log. Her movement was punctuated by the words, "Stop. Now. Stop."

Aldara flew through the air and barreled into Selene, who had landed on the ground. The two tumbled together in a jumble of kicking legs and wings and talons. Ellie, not to be outdone, jumped on top of the fray, screeching, her talons open wide. At the sight of those petite talons opened toward Aldara, who had none, Dora's stomach dropped in fear.

Everyone moved at once. Marina got to the pile first. She grabbed her daughter by one of her taloned feet, keeping her hand free of the sharp ends, and whipped Ellie out of the way. Thomas did the same to Selene, then handed her off to Petra once she got close enough. The two small harpies flapped their wings like suspended chickens and screeched their indignation. The sight would have been funny if the situation they had been pulled out of had been less dangerous. Iris rushed between them and scooped up her still livid child. Tears flowed freely down the face of both Messengers.

"Maman, I said wait. They hurt my Thomas," Aldara hiccupped.

"Hush, darling, Thomas is fine." Iris squeezed her daughter with shaking arms.

Marina glared at the two small harpies. "Change this instant. Both of you." Selene and Ellie complied. "Sit." She pointed to the ground, and both girls dropped with eyes wide.

Iris's hands moved over Aldara, checking for injuries and running over the glowing wings that had sprouted from her back. Henry knelt beside her in the grass, his large hands cupping his daughter's face.

"Beautiful girl," Henry said.

"Is she all right?" Dora asked.

A red welt was rising on Aldara's cheek and there were three other small scratches that Dora could see. None of them were bleeding enough to be serious.

Iris laughed. "She's fine. More than fine. A few scrapes, nothing more."

Aldara squirmed and looked around her overjoyed parents. "Thomas?"

The young man ran to her side. "I'm fine. You know those two can't hurt me, but you are *very* fierce."

Aldara wiggled back in her mother's arms. "Maman, my wings look like yours." Iris squeezed her daughter tighter, mindful of the small wings flapping in her face.

Marina gave a curt nod. "Excuse us a moment. Dora, come with us."

Dora followed Petra and Marina as they hauled their now-mortal-looking daughters to the other side of the fire. They lined the two girls up, and Marina, eyes less than mortal, flashed anger at her daughter and Selene. The two girls seemed to realize in that moment the kind of trouble they were in. They both started fidgeting and trying to look anywhere but at their furious mothers.

"Never, ever raise your hand to your Messenger. You are to protect her at all costs," Marina started, her anger rolling off her in waves. Dora felt almost sorry for the two children, but this was a lesson they must learn. Even small harpies could be dangerous to others.

Petra knelt in front of them. "I know Aldara is a baby to you, but she is not that much younger than you. It's your duty to use your power to protect those around you, but *especially* her. Her duty is to serve you, to make you stronger, to make you better, and to remind you of your humanity."

Dora's voice was hard, but less angry. Ellie and Selene had not hurt Aldara. She knew the girls had lost control and could already see remorse painting their features. Remorse was enough tonight, but they could have wrought real damage and they must understand that. This was a lesson best learned young.

"You're powerful creatures. Aldara has a power of her own, but she is not a fighter. It's your job to fight for her and with her, never against her." Dora took a hand of each girl. "You are violence made flesh, and that means you have the capacity to do great harm to others. You must overcome your violence and control it or it will control you."

Selene and Ellie tried to peer around the three adults to see Aldara taking hopping flights around the circle. Petra redirected the eyes of the girls back to herself. "You can play rough with each other, but never with her. She doesn't have talons or claws, and it wouldn't be a fair fight. You could hurt her badly without meaning to. You must be careful."

"Go apologize to Aldara. She asked you to stop chasing Thomas and wait for her. In the future, heed her advice. You don't always have to follow it, but never again react to it with violence, or you will receive worse than a tongue lashing. Do you understand?" Marina demanded. Both girls nodded.

"Go then," Petra said.

The girls scrambled off the log and ran over to the huddle of people around Aldara. The girls ducked and elbowed their way into the circle where the child with the golden wings stood showing off her new acquisition. Selene cupped her hand around Aldara's ear and whispered something. Ellie bent over and leaned her head on Aldara's shoulder. The adults around them quieted to watch.

A smile bloomed on Aldara's face as the three girls erupted into giggles. The two small harpies transformed back into their harpy shapes and hopped away from Aldara who reached for them, laughing. All three girls flew into the air giggling and chasing each other. The clearing was once again filled with the sounds of children screeching and yelling in the dusk.

"Styx, what a night," Marina said.

Petra sighed, a smile tugging her lips up. "We've created monsters."

Dora ducked as Selene flew low overhead and then had to dodge Ellie and Aldara as they tried to herd in Selene from two different directions. The baby harpies had not yet acquired their deep harpy voices, and their laughter was like tinkling glass.

"The most beautiful kind of monsters." Dora linked arms with Petra and Marina.

Iris moved away from Henry to join them. Even in the fading light, joy gleamed in her eyes. "They're just children, and children can be rough."

Petra stiffened beside Dora. "They'll never be just children."

Dora leaned her head into Petra's. "They learned an important lesson. One they won't forget. All is well."

Iris ran a hand down Petra's arm and Dora felt her relax further. "They're young. No harm was done, my bird."

The four women stood with their arms linked together, watching their children cavort in silence.

"I've had many reasons to be thankful, but today is filled to the brim," Iris said.

A warm bubble of joy filled Dora and burst in the middle of her chest. She was surrounded by her sister harpies and Iris and their children and she could not imagine being more content. Adding another harpy daughter would not make this family of her choosing more joyful, but she would have to make a decision in that direction soon.

Her generation was an anomaly. Not since the first four had harpies bound their lives together to defend a land that was theirs. She did not know if the children she watched this night would grow to live in harmony like their parents, but she hoped and believed it was possible. She would spend her life teaching them that their path of violence could be a means of defense, loyalty, and peace. She knew her sisters would do the same.

Dora had seen the other path and it was paved in the blood of the innocent. At night, alone in her cabin on the mountain, the smell of blood and fear taunted her, but here, with the family of her choosing, those memories stayed away. She had left that life when she had flown away from the island her mother had ruled in blood.

Dora blinked and Petra, Marina, and Iris were all staring at her.

"Where did you go, my bird?" Iris asked.

"Nowhere I wanted to be. Not anymore." Dora tightened her arms around the three women who meant more to her than life. "Not today."

They all turned to watch the children play and the men talking. There was no one else Dora wanted to be with and nowhere else she wanted to be.

CHAPTER 4

It was late when the family gathering broke up, and Dora gave in to Iris's plea to stay the night at the depot. Though all of the harpies had houses of their own, since the beginning Iris had kept a room with three beds for them at the depot. Petra and Marina rarely used the room anymore. Marina lived down Main Street with Reed and Ellie, and Petra and James had the cows at the dairy farm to look after.

Dora woke, rested and content. She stretched, wiggling her toes and extending her arms as far as she could over her head. The amount of sun pouring into the window told her she had slept later than intended. Dora flipped over the covers and swung her legs out of the bed.

She emerged from the room and paused in the doorway. The bedrooms upstairs opened into a large living space. The kitchen on her left was empty, except for a steaming teapot sitting on the table beside an empty cup. The sitting area on the right faced a large picture window. The wall of the sitting area was lined with bookshelves. Books and parchments, many in languages Dora could not read and a handful she could, were arranged neatly. Iris, her blonde hair bound in a single braid, turned in her seat on the reclining couch at the sound of the door opening.

Dora hesitated, then went to the table to pour herself tea. A pot of honey was out, and Dora put a small spoon of it in the steaming brown liquid. She wrapped her fingers around the cup, letting its warmth seep into her skin. She walked until she stood in front of the window and leaned against the pane. The glass was cool on her arm.

Iris patted the couch beside her. "I don't bite."

Dora sipped her tea. "That remains to be seen. You have a look."

Iris blinked in innocence. "What look?"

"The look you get when you are going to give one of us the I-know-better-than-you-do conversation."

Iris sighed and patted the cushion next to her again. "You're right, but still. Sit."

Dora's stomach pinched. This was a conversation they had avoided for a long while. Iris had pestered her relentlessly when her hair had first started to turn grey, but she had given up, mostly, after a while. It seemed the cease fire was over. Dora ran a hand over her hair, smoothing it down when it did not need it. She perched on the edge of the couch.

Iris frowned at her. "I know a harpy ready to fly when I see one. Get comfortable." The last was a command.

Dora sighed loudly, but she did as Iris asked. Iris rolled her eyes at Dora's theatrics.

Iris put her tea on the small table next to the couch. It was made of rough wood with iron fixtures. Henry had made it last winter. Iris put one hand on Dora's leg and the other on Dora's arm. The gentle touch should have relaxed her, but Dora knew what Iris wanted to talk about, and Dora had worked hard to avoid this conversation.

"My bird, I have given you time. More time than I thought warranted, but it's time we talk. I know you still have years until you lose the ability to have a daughter of your own, but it's not your line I am concerned for."

Dora sipped her tea. She was seventy-one and had nine years of fertility left, plenty of time to find someone to father her daughter.

Iris ran a hand over Dora's hair. Dora leaned into the touch. "Why will you never talk about your hair?" She lifted a hand and tucked a stray strand of hair behind Dora's ear. Dora rarely looked in the mirror anymore, but she knew what Iris saw and why her eyes were sad. Her hair had been peppered with grey for two years, but she had never once wanted to talk about it.

"My bird, I wish you would be honest about this with yourself. And with him."

Dora's throat filled with a lump that she swallowed down with a reaction that had become routine. She did not look at Iris. "It doesn't matter."

Iris's voice lost its tone of comfort. "Of course it matters. Why won't you talk about what your heart has already chosen? You've already lost your immortality. You've seen how it has worked out and changed your sisters for the better. Why do you resist?"

Dora sipped her tea and stalled, considering what to tell Iris. "My love for you, Petra, Marina, and everyone else, it grounds me. It reminds me of why we are different from our mothers and why we can teach our daughters to be different." She ran a hand over her hair. "This feeling is wild. It's like a razor's edge and on either side is madness."

"Love does sometimes feel that way, like it could consume you from the inside out." Iris ran her hand down Dora's arm.

"I can't give in to that feeling. I fear the consequences would be too dire. Even if I was still interested, it's too late now. The time is long past."

Lee was always careful to treat her professionally, as his helper. He was appreciative of her presence and was fond of her as a partner or friend, but that was as far as it went. Dora knew working with him was both a knife to her heart and a necessity. On one hand, she craved being with him. On the other hand, she proved to herself every time they worked together that she was in control of her reactions and feelings. They did not control her.

Iris smoothed her hair once more and cupped Dora's cheek. Dora leaned into the caress. "You keep saying that. It's never too late."

Anger crept through her, but Dora did not pull away. "Love is losing control, and I know what losing control looks like. I won't be that. I've seen that."

"Do you think Petra and Marina are worse off for their mates?"

Dora huffed and pulled away from Iris. "They are different than me. They have better control. I can't." Dora could feel irritation pulse under her skin, itching to be free to yell at Iris, to be really angry. It throbbed with insistency, and Dora closed her eyes to keep it in.

Iris pulled her hands away from Dora, and Dora felt the loss of her touch, the grounding of it. "You don't give yourself enough credit."

"You never saw my mother. What she did." *What I did*, Dora added to herself.

Iris's voice shook. "My mother told me about your mother. She used it as a lesson for me to not forget how easily a harpy can wage war and spill blood. You aren't her."

I'm so much worse, Dora thought. "Her anger is mine, but I can hold it in, keep it in check. This is my choice. I will have a daughter in the old way. Soon. I will not follow in the path of my sisters, but I will be loyal to them and to this valley until my death. It's all I need. All I require." Anger flared in Dora but she pushed it down. "I'm not going to discuss what is already decided, even with you. Please stop asking."

Sadness filled Iris's blue eyes. "As you wish, for now, but I think you're wrong."

"It's not your mistake to make."

Iris stood and picked up her teacup. "Come, the day's wasting. I can see this has been a wasted effort. Are you headed back to Silvercliff?"

Dora rose and shook herself, leaving the conversation behind. "No, I should go see Lee. If he has rounds to do, he might want an extra set of hands. I left some herbs and tinctures in his office yesterday with a note, but I wanted to talk to him. We need to discuss planting some new herbs in my garden before the summer gets too advanced."

"Come say good-bye before you leave town." Iris took Dora's teacup.

"I will." Dora hesitated, then hugged Iris. Her head rested on top of Iris's golden hair. "Thank you for caring so much."

Iris sniffed. "It's my job. Plus, I want you to be happy."

Dora smiled. "I am happy." To her surprise, she found the words were not empty. "I have a life blessed by the gods."

***

She did not go to Lee's office right away. Instead, she walked out the back door of the depot and leapt into the air, letting her harpy free at last. All the emotions—anger, frustration, sadness, desire—rolled off her and blew away as she chased the wisps of clouds in the sky. The ceiling of the world was azure and so clear it hurt to look at it full on. Dora found a warm current and glided into it.

The valley spread out before her, green and sprawling in the summer sun. Contentment was a buzz in her blood. Dora had seen the blue of the waters lapping a Grecian beach. She had been blinded by the white of domed buildings against a sunlit sky, and smelled the air full of the perfume of sea daffodils while waves crashed against a Minoan coast. She had experienced all these things, but nothing had ever captured her heart the way this valley in the heart of this fledgling country had ensnared her.

The mountains rose into the sky as if they, not the clouds or the gods, were the highest things in creation. Their snow-capped peaks winked at her as the sun shone on them. Trees covered the lower slopes in shades of green; the smell of life, of growing things, filled her completely. This was the life she was meant to have, a life filled with this valley, these people, and her sister harpies and their families. This was her place.

Dora pumped her wings until the town was nothing but miniscule boxes in a sea of green. She circled the valley multiple times, dropping in altitude each time, relishing the fact that Remnants no longer had to hide their presence from the mortals. It was broad daylight and she could fly wherever she chose. It was a freedom she never had thought to enjoy. It also gave a warning to all those who saw her. This territory was claimed and protected. Even mortals with little understanding of myths understood a predator when they saw one. Even after centuries of civilization, instincts warned when some things were better left alone, avoided for fear of being eaten. Or worse.

Dora pushed aside those memories and angled herself in the direction of the depot. The woods behind the depot used to be unbroken. Now, the woods were interrupted with houses. Claire McKenzie and her boys lived in a small blue house on the other side of Catcher's Creek, an off-shoot of Turning Creek, after which the town was named. The frame of another house was going up near Claire's house. Reed and Marina were hoping to finish their new house before the end of the summer.

A sound of distress echoed through the air, and Dora's head whipped toward the sound. She flipped in the air and headed back in the direction of Catcher's Creek, zoning in on where the sound originated. Her heart rate

40

whipped up to match her speed as she tore through the air. She called the wind to push at her back to increase her speed a fraction.

Two brown-headed boys, Jonah and Stephen, were bent over another figure on the bank of the creek. Dora landed in front of them. Thomas, his face pale and pinched, looked up at her arrival. His hands held together a deep gash in his lower leg that was steadily seeping blood.

Dora stayed in her harpy form in case teeth and talons were needed. "What happened?" she asked in her rough voice while she scanned the area assessing threats.

All three boys started talking at once. Sweat broke out on Thomas's forehead and his face took on a sickly green color. Dora made a cutting motion with her wing. "Quiet. Jonah, what happened?"

"We dared Thomas to jump the creek. It was my idea. It's my fault." His voice trembled at the end.

Dora let out some of her power into the area, using it to check for anything that could be a danger as she leaned over Thomas's leg. The blood was coming out faster than she had thought at first, and Thomas's color had gone from green to white. She needed to move quickly or Thomas was going to lose too much blood. There was no one else but the four of them by the creek, so Dora pulled her power back into herself and transformed into her mortal form.

She ripped strips from the underside of her skirt as she gave orders. "I'm sure there's plenty of blame to go around. We'll discuss that later. Jonah, go get Dr. Williams and bring him to the depot. Stephen, run ahead to the depot and tell Iris we'll need extra linens and boiling water so she can be ready. I'll bring Thomas."

The two boys darted off. Dora wrapped the gash closed and tied the cotton strips in knots. Thomas sucked in air when she pressed her hands to the area to apply pressure.

Dora ran a hand down Thomas's cheek. "I don't think you hit anything major, but you are bleeding and will need to be stitched up. Unfortunately, no matter how I carry you, this is going to hurt like the inner circle of hell."

Dora leaned down. "Wrap your arms around my neck. I'm going to pull you up then carry you over my shoulder. I think that will be easiest on your leg and for me."

Thomas did as she asked and she pulled him up until he was standing. He swayed, and Dora steadied him. The green tint to his face deepened, and Dora held him while he emptied the contents of his stomach.

"You managed to avoid my shoes and skirt. Thank you for that. Do you feel better?"

Thomas nodded.

"Now, for the rough part." Dora put her shoulder to Thomas's middle and hoisted him up over her shoulder. Even in her mortal form, she retained enough of her harpy strength that carrying Thomas would not be taxing. She was more concerned about getting him there quickly, before he could bleed through her temporary bandage and with minimal pain to Thomas.

Thomas sucked in a breath. "Steady there," Dora said. "Iris should stop feeding you. You weigh more than a minotaur." Thomas chuckled weakly until she began to walk.

Normally, the creek was a five minute walk from the depot. Dora tried to keep her strides even and smooth. It took longer than she wanted before she walked out of the line of trees and into the open area behind the depot.

Iris paced by the back door of the depot. Her back was to them as Dora approached. Stephen hovered in the open doorway and ran towards them when he saw them emerge from the trees. Iris turned to follow his movement and then ran to them. Iris ran her hands over Thomas's back and looked at Dora with eyes full of questions and the fear of a mother.

Dora spoke before the question could leave Iris's mouth. "He cut his leg quite badly. I need to lay him somewhere where Lee and I can get him fixed up."

Iris ran her hand over Thomas's dangling head once, then led Dora into the depot. An old, but clean, blanket covered the front counter. Iris led them to it.

"I'm going to try to be as gentle as I can, but this is going to hurt. Keep breathing deep."

Dora eased Thomas off her shoulder and onto the counter until he was sitting on it with his legs dangling. She helped him ease back and then lifted his legs and swung them in one smooth motion until they both rested on the countertop. Thomas's breath hitched, then evened out. She laid Thomas down until his head was on the pillow, a swash of white on white with watering green eyes. Iris was next to him in a moment, smoothing his hairs off his forehead and murmuring to him.

Dora picked up his hand and squeezed it. "You did wonderful. Just a bit more and Lee will have you all sorted out."

Small feet clattered down the stairs and Aldara rushed to the counter and scrambled up onto a stool. "Tom?"

Dora scooped up the child. "Thomas hurt his leg, but Doc will make it better." The bell over the front door sounded. "See, he's here already."

Dora nuzzled her face into Aldara's hair, absorbing a small bit of calm before the storm. Lee, Jonah, and Henry came into the depot.

Dora held Aldara over Thomas. "He's going to be fine, but give him a kiss for luck, then go upstairs."

Thomas accepted the offering. "I'm sure I'll be right as rain now." Aldara squirmed down and ran upstairs.

Iris went around the counter and into Henry's arms. They moved to stand beside the counter. Jonah hung back, his eyes riveted on the floor. They would have to get to the bottom of the circumstances behind the injury at a later time. Dora had a feeling there was more to the story of Thomas's leg.

"Jonah, go upstairs with the others while we get Thomas patched up," Dora said.

Jonah hesitated. "It's my fault he got hurt. I dared him to jump across the creek without landing in the water."

Iris pinned him to the floor with a stern look. "While that was foolish of you, he was even more foolish to take the bait. You will both have to answer for it."

Jonah nodded and ran upstairs.

Lee put his bag down on a stool and addressed Dora. "What do we have today?"

"He has a fairly deep cut on his leg, running from below the knee to his ankle. I wrapped it at the creek and applied pressure, but I didn't clean it there. I didn't want to do an assessment without you, so I haven't unwrapped it yet."

Less nodded as she spoke and ran his hand over the bandage on Thomas's leg. "Nice work." He smiled at her briefly and then his face slipped back into a look of concentration. "We will need boiled water and strips of clean cloth. Dora, I want to cover the area in a poultice after I stitch it, so prepare that and then assist me."

Lee addressed Iris while he gently unwound the bandage Dora had applied. "The stitches will help it heal and the poultice will aid the healing process and help keep it clean. The laceration will not kill our young runner, but infection could so we always want to be careful."

Dora opened Lee's bag and handed him the scissors he needed to cut the strips she had tied on Thomas. She pulled bottles of dried yerba and marigold from the bag to make the poultice. After she had mixed the herbs into some warm water, she laid the bowl aside.

Iris held Thomas's hand and Henry stood behind her, his large hands on her shoulders. Lee had cut away all of the bindings and was washing the gash. Dora moved to stand at Thomas's feet and waited for Lee to finish. His hands were sure and his entire focus was on the task before him. Dora snatched these moments when she could watch him under the cover of work and no one would notice. It was all she allowed herself.

"Dora, please sit by Thomas's head and keep his upper body still. If you could help him stay calm while I work, this will go smoothly." Lee said this without looking up. "Henry, if you could hold Thomas's leg I will be able to stich faster. Like this." Henry moved to do as he was told.

Iris held one of Thomas's hands. Dora took a stool around to the backside of the counter and held his other hand. She gave him a reassuring squeeze. She gathered some of her power and pushed it out, willing Thomas to be calm. A harpy's words, when said with power, carried the weight of persuasion. It was one of the reasons her assistance was so valuable to Lee in situations like this.

She leaned down and said in a lowered voice, "Don't worry. Doctor Williams sews faster than Lily Hughes putting flowers on the hem of one of the twins' skirts while they are still walking. This is the worst part. Just breathe nice and slow and keep looking at my face or at Iris."

The tawny headed youth gave her a wavering smile. The skin on the sides of the gash was clean, but swollen and still seeping blood.

Lee placed a gentle hand on Thomas's ankle. The boy flinched, and the doctor's eyes softened. "All right, young Thomas. I'm going start sewing. It's going to hurt quite a lot so feel free to yell as much as you please."

Thomas's green eyes locked on to Iris and did not waver. In this moment, Dora still saw the scrawny and heartbroken child who had come to Iris after his mother's death. He was now a gangly teen, almost a man, Dora corrected herself. No matter what he was, he was theirs. Family.

Dora squeezed his hand again. "Thomas, did I ever tell you about the time Marina got tired of drinking tea at the depot and replaced all of Iris's tea leaves with coffee?"

Thomas's lips quirked up, then thinned out as Lee pierced his skin for the first stitch. She kept talking and Thomas kept his eyes on Iris and his hands holding theirs as Lee worked.

Lee was quick. Dora had stood beside him hundreds of times as he had cared for the people of Turning Creek, mortal and Remnant alike, and she was always struck that a man who was so quick and efficient could also convey such depths of compassion with his hands. Thomas whimpered occasionally, which made Dora's own leg and heart hurt for him.

Lee stitched and Dora talked

Lee tied the last stitch in place and squeezed Thomas's toes. "Next time Jonah McKenzie challenges you to jump across the creek, I would advise you tell him to stuff it. You're the Remnant of Achilles. You were made to run. Not leap."

Thomas gave the doctor a weak smile. "Thanks, Doc."

Iris ran her hands over Thomas's face and arms. "Claire is going to skin Jonah and Stephen alive." Claire McKenzie was a kind woman but she had high expectations of her two boys.

"If his uncle Reed doesn't get at him first," Henry added.

Lee straightened. Dora left Thomas's side and held out a bowl for the needle Lee had used. He dropped the needle in and she handed him the small bowl she had mixed the poultice in.

"I'm going to rub this on your stitches. It will keep the swelling down and hopefully keep infection at bay. Dora will leave you some extra herbs to mix up when you change the bandages tomorrow. After the second day, take off the bandage and let the wound have some air. I will be back to check on you, or Dora can to make sure everything is healing."

Lee handed the empty bowl to Dora and started wrapping Thomas's lower leg. "You can walk on it, but it will heal better if you stay off of it for a day and take it easy after that. I will look at it in a week and probably take the stiches out then."

Lee tied the last knot. Dora cleaned the needle while he worked and put it and the extra linen string he used away.

Lee pointed a finger at the boy. "No running for a few days. Walking only, no exceptions. You will heal faster than a normal boy, but you still need to heal."

Thomas shook his head, but responded, "Yes, sir."

Lee grabbed the toes of Thomas's good leg. "Young man, I expect you to follow all the orders you are given and do so without grumbling. There is nothing worse than a surly patient."

"Yes, sir."

Dora handed Iris a small packet of yerba and marigold. "Mix this with a little boiling water and let it sit a few minutes before applying it."

Lee picked up his bag and walked to the door. Henry met him there and shook his hand.

"Thanks, Doc."

"My pleasure."

Henry went back to stand beside Thomas and Iris. "Let's get you upstairs." Henry and Iris gently led Thomas up to his room.

Dora smoothed her hands down her blue skirt with tiny pink roses and looked at Lee standing by the door. He was lean, but strong and broad shouldered. His hair looked like black ink in this light. He was too far away for her to smell him, but she conjured the memory without the physical reminder of it.

Lee paused at the door. "Thank you for your help. You have a calming presence."

"I barely used my power at all. You always tell me that." Dora smiled.

Lee inclined his head towards her. "It is always true."

"That went well because you are a very good doctor and you do stitch people up very fast. I wasn't exaggerating for Thomas's benefit."

Lee's lips thinned. "You have a gift with people. You should take credit for it more often."

Dora puffed out a breath of air and turned her hands over. They had been created for violence. Dora could feel the pulse of it in her blood beckoning her, always. Her hands, meant to be things of violence, were instead instruments of healing and comfort. She controlled the violence in her soul by using her hands for what they had never been created to do, heal and love. Her sister harpies dealt with the power in violence in different ways. She chose healing. With each comforting touch she gave another, she felt generations of cruelty unravel. None of her efforts made the violence under her skin fade, though. That was always there.

Dora raised her eyes to meet Lee's and she took a step closer to him, nevertheless maintaining a wall of impenetrable space. "If I start taking too much credit, I may forget who I am and why I do this."

Lee did not close the gap between them. "Who are you, and why do you do this?"

Dora blinked and answered with truth. "I am a violent creature, but I heal others so that I never forget I can choose to be something else. If I do not choose to do good, I'm choosing the worse side of myself. Once that precipice is breached, I would be lost."

Lines crinkled between Lee's eyes and his mouth turned down. "Surely, you do not believe that one wrong move would turn you into something you are not forever."

"You're wrong. I am always violence. I only choose to act against my nature." The gravity of the words settled over her and she rolled her shoulders against the weight.

As if he could read her thoughts, he said, "That sounds like a heavy burden to bear, indeed." He inclined his head towards her again. "Good day." He went out into the June sunshine and did not look back.

Dora slumped against the door and wondered, not for the first time, why she insisted on keeping such close company with Lee Williams when his words alone had the power to rend her to pieces.

CHAPTER 5

The wind beat against the windows in the morning. Dora wanted to go see Petra today after she took care of a few things around the house. She made tea and tidied her already tidy cabin. She took a pair of sturdy scissors from the shelf above her herb drying counter and put them in the pocket of her dress. When the tea was done steeping, she strained it into her favorite cup and walked outside.

The wind tugged at her hair and pulled at her dress. The sun was muted by clouds, and the air smelled heavy, but the rain was still a long way off. *If I am lucky,* she thought, *the rain will hold off until the afternoon.* The cool breeze touched her face and made her tea steam. She sipped the hot liquid and felt it settle into her bones. She walked around the corner of her cabin. The wind sang gently through the aspens, causing their leaves to rattle, and Dora's spirit settled further.

She walked between the herb beds with her eyes scanning the tops of the trees and the steel-colored sky. She stopped beside the peppermint bed without looking down. When she did drop her eyes from the sky, a cry of dismay escaped her and she jostled her tea, spilling some of the hot liquid on her hand.

All of the plants in the bed were wilted and covered in the black fungus they had found a few days ago. Then, the fungus had been a light dusting. This fungus was thick. It covered the entire peppermint plant, leaving no green visible. Dora put her teacup down on the wooden border of the peppermint bed and looked at the other plots. The sickness had jumped from one bed to another. Dora examined each plant. Every single one of her plants was consumed by the fuzzy, black fungus. Cursing, she started ripping the plants from the ground. By the time she was done, her hands were black and the earth looked like it had been chewed. The smell of decay rose from the pile she had created. Not a single plant was left in the planters, which had all been teeming last week. A sourness filled Dora's stomach.

A trickle of unease went down Dora's spine and she remembered a similar feeling when she had first seen the fungus. With a twist of worry in her gut, she went into the small greenhouse in the back of her yard. Warm, moist air surround her as she stepped into the enclosed space. Underneath the smell of dirt and green plants, Dora detected a hint of rot and the sourness in her stomach rolled. Her eyes went to the small seedlings she had planted with care, and dismay bloomed. Every plant, even the citrus trees she had coaxed to life and planned to give to Iris were dead, overcome by the fungus.

Dora turned and looked at the open door. It had been closed. There should have been no way for the fungus to travel from the outside beds to inside the greenhouse. All her work, gone. Years and months of growing and she had nothing but dead plants and empty, blackened hands.

Her plants gave her peace and hope. They were proof that she could grow something, bring life to the earth with hands that fed it blood with violence. She trembled with failure amidst the destruction around her.

Dora straightened her back and ripped up the plants in the greenhouse, adding them to the pile beside the outside garden. She made a pyre of the last of her winter wood, piled the ruined plants on top, and lit the mess with a stick from her kitchen fire. The green plants did not burn easy. Dora had to coax the fire to overtake the black plants and then, when it did, the smell of rot filled the air. She swallowed down the bile and anger and watched her work burn.

Defeated and tired, Dora cleaned her hands and face, then went to seek some much-needed solace.

***

James Lloyd had expanded his dairy farm in the last few years. Dora flew over the expanded milking barn and cheese house. She had assisted in the cheese house on occasion and even milked a cow or two. While she preferred working in her garden, her heart gave a wrench at the thought of her barren beds, and she admitted that there was comfort in the routine of milking cows. Lloyd Creamery had become a regionally famous producer of some of the best cheese in the state.

Dora landed in the front yard of the main house. The inside of the house had been transformed from a male bunkhouse to a family house. A newer bunkhouse, where the men who lived and worked on the farm ate and slept, had been added to the small cluster of buildings two years ago. She changed into her mortal form just as a knee-high streak of black, curly hair burst from the door and catapulted for her.

"Auntie Dee. Auntie. Pick me up." Hands covered in biscuit crumbs waved up at her. Selene had her mother's dark skin and hair and her father's

48

wise brown eyes surrounded by long lashes. She was beautiful as a youngling. She would be breathtaking in her prime.

Dora lifted the warm child and kissed the crown of her head. "How are you today, my love?"

Selene put her hands on Dora's cheeks and spoke into her face with breath smelling of sweet biscuits. "Good. Come. Have a biscuit with me."

James Lloyd, tall and lean, walked out from the open door of the house. He wore a buttoned vest over a crisp shirt with the sleeves rolled up to his elbows. "Selene, come here, you scoundrel. You must take a nap before your mother gets home." He halted when he saw Dora and smiled. "How are you today? This is a pleasant surprise. Petra went to check on something in the northern pasture. She should be back soon. Can you stay? I have a fresh pot of tea."

"I'd love some." Dora shifted Selene's weight to her hip and followed James into the house.

James poured them tea and gave Selene another shortbread biscuit. "What brings you over today?" he asked. "You have a pinched look that suggests this is not a mere social call."

Dora sipped her tea. "I was just feeling lonely rattling around in my house and I wanted to see Selene." The toddler gave Dora a grin full of crumbs. Dora took another sip of tea. "My garden was overtaken by some fungus. I had to pull all the plants this morning, and it's put me out of sorts." Dora described the fungus to James, highlighting the clinical details and leaving her personal reaction to the rot unspoken.

"I'm not a farmer, though I have always had some crops, and I have not seen anything like that before." James made a sympathetic noise. "I know your garden has come to mean much to you. I'm sorry for all the loss of the plants. It's still early enough in the summer. You should have some time to grow some things before fall sets in."

Dora sighed and thought of the time she had poured into the plants, now ash in her yard. "I'll have to make a list and order from Simon what I can't get locally." Some of her plants she had traded for from locals, foraged herself, or ordered as seeds from botany catalogues. She loathed starting over.

The sound of boots on the porch heralded Petra's arrival. She was followed inside by Adam and Richard, brothers from Texas who had met James on his trip west and never left his side.

Robert tipped his hat. "Pleasure to see you, Dora."

Adam mimicked his brother's gesture of greeting, and Dora smiled at the brothers. "Robert, I thought you were staying over at the Nasso farm helping Pearl."

Robert poured himself some tea and joined them at the table. "We just finished a harvest on some of the plants, and so I got a break for a few days while those stalks dry. Miss Pearl told me to come over and take some days off. There's plenty to do, but I don't mind the change of scenery."

Dora turned to Adam. "And you?"

Adam shrugged. "Same as every day. Working and blessed to be alive."

"Momma." Selene waved a biscuit at Petra.

"Hello, love. I hope your father has done something else with you besides feed you biscuits while I was gone." Petra kissed her husband and ran a hand over his shoulders before scooping up her daughter. She sat in the chair next to Dora and placed Selene in her lap.

James gave his wife a pained look. "She wanted to chase the cows in the corral by the barn. I thought biscuits and milk would be a better alternative than scaring half the herd. She's a fierce harpy, you know."

Petra laughed. "Of course she is. She's mine." Petra buried her face in Selene's hair. "At least she got some of your kindness, or we'd be in real trouble."

"She's going to grow to be a wonderful harpy." Dora leaned into Selene's face. "But you mustn't chase after cows. No matter how well that worked out for your momma." Everyone laughed except the child. "It makes your father very cross." Dora dropped her voice. "He says it curdles the milk right in the udder and then when you milk them, cheese comes out."

Selene giggled in the way of small children, and all the adults paused to savor the fleeting sound.

Petra looked up from her daughter. "Something's been at our herd the past two nights." There was a note in Petra's voice that made Dora's gaze sharpen.

James put his elbows on the table. "Did you find anything?"

Adam leaned back in his chair. "I took Mrs. Petra to the kill sight I found this morning. The carcass had been moved since I found it."

Dora sat back. "Something killed one of your cows, then moved it hours later?"

Adam nodded. "It was a good fifty feet from the original site. I thought I was mistaken at first because there's no drag marks on the ground. An animal that size being dragged would've left marks. There was the puddle of blood in the original spot, then the cow fifty yards over with a few more chunks missing."

James looked to Petra for confirmation. "Adam is right. Something moved the carcass after it was killed and after Adam found it. Whatever it was killed the cow, left, then came back for a snack before leaving again."

"Maybe something killed the cow and something else tried to move it," Dora suggested.

"That was my first thought too, but I think it was the same animal. All of the marks on the carcass were the same," Petra said. Marina was the best tracker out of the three of them, but each of the harpies could follow a trail reasonably well. "At first I thought you or Marina were playing a trick on me."

"Why?" Dora's unease from this morning returned.

"Like Adam said, there were no drag marks. Whatever moved the cow tried to fly off with it. I think whatever it was decided the cow was too big and abandoned it, but it did make it about fifty yards. No small feat. The cow looked slashed with claw marks and then chewed on by something with very sharp teeth. If I didn't know better, I would say it looked like one of our kills."

A harpy could carry a kill as big as a cow or bighorn sheep for some distance, but it was not easy going. There were other things that could fly that might be able to manage it. If Selene and Ellie were a bit older and prone to pranks, they could be the culprit. They were too young to carry that much weight, though, even working together.

Dora said, "I don't know any other Remnant living in the area that would be able to kill and attempt to move something as large as a cow. Did you smell anything?"

Petra let Selene drink tea from her cup. "I couldn't get anything distinctive from the kill or the ground around it. Whatever it was, it was careful. I don't think it was a local. We'd know about another predator that big. It has to be something from out of town."

Dora felt her harpy turn within her. This was their valley. While the harpies lived in peace with the other Remnants of the region, there was no doubt who was on the top of the food chain. Predators of any variety did not take well to others encroaching on their territory. "What do you want to do about it?"

Petra looked at James before she spoke. "I want to go hunting tonight. We should canvass the valley and see if we can find any sign of something that should not be here." James nodded his agreement.

"It could have been wolves who made the kill and something else that moved the cow," Dora suggested.

Adam shook his head. "No wolf tracks. I double checked."

"Besides," Petra said, "the valley's wolf pack generally stays in the southeast corner now."

Dora stood. "I'll head to town and get Marina. We'll meet you here at dusk. Do you want Iris to come? We might want another set of eyes."

Petra shook her head. "No. This is strictly a hunt. Let her stay home with her family. What about Caroline Eisler? We could use her nose on the ground." Caroline was the Remnant of the famed hound of Zeus, Laelaps.

Dora shook her head. "Her pregnancy is pretty advanced, and remember, they have chicken pox at their house. Lee wants them quarantined until that passes. What about Pearl? She's not a hound, but I do like the idea of having someone on the ground with a good nose."

Petra looked at Robert. "Do you think she'd do it?"

Robert chuckled. "She wouldn't pass up that offer if her house was burning down." He drained his cup and slid his chair back. "I'll leave now and let her know. What time and where?"

"Let's meet here at sunset," Petra said.

Dora finished her own tea and stood. The thought of a hunt already had her blood swimming with energy. Her earlier malaise over her ruined garden and the mysterious fungus fed into the promise of violence that already thrummed under her skin.

The last thought made her pause. "I almost forgot why I came here. An odd, black fungus killed all my plants, even the ones in the greenhouse."

Petra made a sound of dismay. "Even the citrus tree for Iris?"

"Yes."

Petra put her arm around Dora. "I'm sorry for that. You can always replant."

Dora returned the embrace. "I know. Thanks. I'll go then. I should give Iris as much time as possible to start researching some possibilities of what could've done this."

Dora bid them farewell and headed down the valley to town. It was only midday when Dora reached the north side of town. She circled around and landed on the south side of Main Street. She wanted to check on Thomas.

The door to the depot was propped open to let in the sun and fresh air. Dora paused on the threshold to let her eyes adjust to the dimness of the room. She heard Marina calling her from the back.

"You're just in time to see me fleece these two because of their truly abysmal poker playing." Marina waved her to chair. Two men, their aged faces frowning, glanced up at her.

"I thought you two knew better than to play with Marina." Dora looked over Marina's shoulder at her cards.

"My luck's worse than a maiden in Zeus's bower," L.A. grumbled.

"We should've stuck with checkers," agreed Johnny.

Dora put her hand on Johnny's shoulder. "How are you doing?"

Johnny paused, then continued looking at his cards. "I miss her every day, but in the mornings I go sit by her tree and have coffee. Elizabeth keeps baking sweet rolls and I think I've added five inches to my waist. I'll survive." He looked at her then. "Thanks for asking."

Dora moved to stand behind Marina. "I want to check with Iris and see how Thomas is doing first, but don't leave. I need to talk to you."

Marina's face turned serious, and Dora saw Marina's harpy flash to the surface in her eyes. "What's wrong?"

Marina's harpy was always close to the surface, and Dora's harpy wanted to rise in response. Dora pushed it down. "Nothing. We're going hunting tonight. I'll give you details after I see Thomas."

Marina's face broke into a grin that looked more predatory than friendly. "Excellent. Iris is upstairs. She'll be right down."

On cue, Iris came down the back stairs.

"How's Thomas?" Dora followed Iris to the mail counter.

"He's restless today. He wants to run and he needs to take it easy another day or Doc will be stitching him up again. Doc is there with him now."

"Injuries are always worse after the first day or so." Dora sat on her stool in front of the counter. "How are you today?"

"Tired. I stayed up with Thomas to make sure he didn't jostle his leg in his sleep. Needless to say, I didn't get much myself." Iris rubbed her hands over her face.

"Do you want me to make you some tea?" Dora asked.

Iris smiled. "That would be lovely."

Before Dora could leave, Marina crammed next to her at the counter and leaned her elbows on the smooth surface. "So, what're we hunting tonight?"

Iris turned a questioning gaze to Dora. "Hunting?"

"Yes, something killed one of James's cattle last night and the kill was not ordinary." Dora explained about the cow being moved and the lack of wolf tracks.

Marina's eyes sparkled. "Where there any tracks at all, human or animal?"

"I didn't see the kill site. We can ask tonight. Petra wants us to meet at her place at dusk."

Iris frowned. "Why are you hunting in the dark? Don't you want to be able to see in the daylight?"

"We all have excellent night vision, but this thing is a night hunter, and we'll have a better chance of finding it when it's active."

Marina clapped her hands. "I'm going to go break the news to Reed that he has to watch Ellie on his own tonight. She'll be inconsolable when she finds out we're going hunting without her."

"Poor Reed. He has to live with both of you. At least Nina will be there to entertain Ellie." Iris filed envelopes away.

Dora stood. "I'll go make tea."

She went up the back stairs to the kitchen. Dora pulled the tin of tea from the shelf and put more water in the kettle on the stove. While the water heated, she scooped tea leaves into the pot and put cups on a tray.

The familiar movements gave Dora time to calm the excitement in her blood. Marina was much more comfortable with her violent side than the rest of them, and her casual acceptance of the bloodshed sometimes made it more difficult for Dora to keep her own harpy under wraps. The water boiled and Dora poured it over the leaves. A door opened behind her and she did not have to turn to know who it was. She added another cup to the tray. She put the teapot on the tray and gripped the handles on the try until her knuckles were white. She steeled herself before turning around. After ripping up her garden and anticipating the hunt, she was already on edge. Dora did not want to see Lee Williams today.

Dora turned and smiled at Lee. "How's Thomas doing?"

Lee stopped, keeping the table between them. "The swelling is down and there are no signs of infection or additional bruising. He should be running around the valley, delivering letters in no time. Jonah and Stephen McKenzie are there keeping him company."

"I've made some tea. Do you have time to stay?"

"Of course."

Dora led him downstairs, more aware of his presence than of the weight of the tea tray in her hands. She chose a seat at the counter so that Marina sat between her and Lee.

Lee took the cup of tea that Iris offered him. He repeated to Iris the same news he had given her upstairs about Thomas. "It's still very important that you keep him from running. He can walk and move around, but no roughhousing."

"Thank you, Doc, for taking such good care of him. Let me know what we owe you. If you want Henry to make something as payment, I'm sure he'd be happy to do it."

Lee rubbed his chin. He had shaved this morning, Dora noticed. "There is something I might need later. I'll talk to him when I get a chance." Lee leaned around Marina and caught Dora's eye. "Did you bring any herbs with you this morning? I got your note and thought you might bring me more willow bark. I'm going to see Molly Korman and I wanted to take her some more tea for her headaches."

Dora put down her cup. "I won't be able to supply you with herbs for a while. I had to pull up all my plants this morning."

Iris made a sound of dismay. "Why?"

"Some black fungus invaded the beds and killed all my plants. I first noticed it a few days ago, and got rid of the affected plants, but this morning I went out and all my plants were covered in the stuff, even the ones in the greenhouse. I'm not sure how it spread there, but I pulled all the plants and burned them to be sure." Dora could not keep the mournful tone from her voice.

"I'm sorry to hear that." Lee leaned around Marina to look at her as he spoke.

Marina gave her shoulder a pat.

"I know. It means we'll have to make do with other things until I can get the garden back up and running." Dora ran a finger over the rim of her cup.

"No," Lee said, and Dora looked up at him. "I meant, I'm sorry because I know how hard you worked on your garden and how much heart you poured into it. We can get medicine and herbs elsewhere, not as good as yours, but all will be well. Nothing can replace the labor lost, though. I am sorry."

Dora's lungs contracted painfully. She blinked slowly and looked back down at her tea, afraid of the pain in her chest and the look she knew must be in her eyes. "Thank you," she managed. "I might check with the Eislers tomorrow and see if Mr. Eisler has any suggestions for how to clean the beds of the fungus. He has a way with plants."

Marina pushed away from the counter, leaving an open space between Dora and Lee. "I've got to go finish my rounds before heading back to the office." She turned to Dora. "I'll see you at Petra's tonight."

Neither Dora nor Lee closed the space Marina left between them.

Iris frowned at them. "I can start making a list of things big enough to kill a cow and fly with it a ways."

Dora finished her tea and rose from the stool. She dug in her bag and laid the small satchel of herbs on the counter in front of Lee. "Here's what I had left that was dried. I'll come by tomorrow and make a list of things we should order. It'll take weeks for anything to get here, and by then we will only have the greenhouse as a growing space until next spring."

Lee stood and angled his body towards Dora. "I did manage without you for many years, though now I'm not sure how I did it." Lee paused to smile. "I would like to share some of the cost of replacing your plants."

Dora scowled at Iris, who had put her back to them and was sorting letters, tactfully not looking at them. She moved a step closer to Lee, though she knew it was better to keep her distance. "Thank you, but you don't have to do that."

Lee waved a hand dismissively. "It is long past the time when I should have been helping offset the cost of the herbs we use. I know you have bartered some seeds that were hard to procure, but let me pay for the ones you have to purchase."

Dora gripped the edge of the counter. "You aren't going to let me refuse, are you?"

"I am not."

His eyes wrinkled at the corners when he smiled at her, and for a moment she wondered what it would have been like if she had moved on her feelings for him before their roles had been established, before they had become too entrenched in friendship and the professional distance that even now separated them. Dora swallowed the thoughts. She would never know.

"I surrender then. I'll make a list and price out what we will need. It might take me a couple days. Do you need me for anything today?"

Lee hesitated before speaking, and Dora was unsure if he didn't know the answer or if he thought better of his first response. "Unless some emergency comes up, I think I'll be fine on my own today. Bring the list when you have it and we can discuss it."

Lee left, and Dora helped Iris flip through books for an hour, looking for a clue as to what they might be hunting once the sun sunk below the horizon.

CHAPTER 6

The sun was still perched on top of the north range when Dora landed in Petra's yard. Marina lounged at the table underneath the tree in the front. She sat with her back to the table and her long legs stretched out before her. Her hair was tamed into a braid, and two sword handles protruded above her shoulders. A young woman with brown hair and doe-like brown eyes sat opposite Marina. Pearl Nasso's back was straight and her face intent, every inch the feline that was her true form.

Dora changed as she landed, going from flying to walking in a smooth movement. She walked over to stand beside Marina.

Dora waved a hand, indicating the swords. "I thought we were flying tonight."

Marina reached back her right hand and pulled one of her short swords free with the sing of metal. The pommel of the sword was oiled brown leather and the silver blade gleamed with enchanted runes that Henry had imprinted along the deadly surface. Marina's face turned feral, and Dora felt herself responding to the violence in the look.

Marina twirled the blade in her hand and pointed it at Pearl. "I thought I might stay on the ground with Kitten here."

Instead of being insulted at the name, Pearl's face broke into a smile with a hardness around the edges. Pearl was the Remnant of The Sphinx, an ancient monster with the head of a woman and the body of a large cat. Though young, she ran her own lavender farm, which she had built from the ground up in the years since her family had been killed by the harpies. Pearl had beheaded her own mother in front of the harpies and begun a new life, free from her family. She recognized the predatory power of the harpies because she was something almost as scary.

"Hello, Pearl," Dora said. "Robert told me the lavender is coming along and that you already pulled in one harvest. I'd like some when it dries."

A pinched look came over Pearl's face.

Marina sat up and her hand tightened on her sword. "What is it?"

Pearl looked past them to the green fields of the farm. "I've got a fungus on some of my new plants."

Dora stilled. "What does it look like?"

Pearl sucked her bottom lip into her mouth and chewed it. "It's soft and black, like a sprinkling of dirt almost."

Marina put her sword away and turned towards Dora. "It sounds the same as the stuff in your garden."

The sourness was back in the pit of Dora's stomach. "I wouldn't know without looking."

"Your herb beds were affected too?" Pearl asked.

"I found some fungus on a few plants and pulled them up. Two days later, all my plants were covered in the stuff. I had to burn them all," Dora explained.

A line bisected Pearl's forehead. "Could you come over tomorrow and look at my fields to see if it's the same stuff?"

Dora shrugged. "I'm not sure what good it will do even if it is the same stuff. I don't know how to stop it."

Marina rubbed her hands on her thighs, a sign she was thinking, Dora knew. "Even if it's the same, the Nasso farm and your cabin on Silvercliff are on opposite sides of the valley. If you are both having the same issue, there has to be more people affected in between your two houses. It's unlikely your plants are isolated instances."

Petra came out of the cabin, sauntered off the porch, and walked towards them. She paused before she reached them. Dora could see the moment she felt the residual power in the air because Petra's eyes darkened.

"It seems you three are ready for the hunt." Petra lifted her lips in something that could have been a smile except for the pointed teeth she bared.

Dora forced herself to relax. "Pearl has some fungus on her plants that may be the same thing that made me lose all my beds yesterday."

Petra laid a hand on Dora's shoulder and squeezed. "All of them?"

Dora's breath escaped in frustrated puff. "Even the greenhouse."

"Hells, that can't be good." Petra sat next to Dora.

Marina rubbed her hands together. "Enough of that problem. We can't fix it today and we're running out of daylight. I want to start out in the light."

"I hate it when you get all practical." Dora crossed her arms.

Marina laughed. "I'm also right."

Dora felt her lips twitch and gave in to the smile. "Pompous bird," she added.

"Damn right."

Petra rolled her eyes. "If you two are done?"

Dora leaned into the table and pushed the mirth to the side. "Have you found anything since this morning? Other kills?"

Petra shook her head. "No. I did a quick search of the farm, but no other cattle were missing and I didn't find any wild animal carcasses. I think we should start in the field where we found the cattle and fly a circuit. James and the boys wanted to move the carcass. I told them to leave it so you could all smell it when we started."

Pearl's eyes flicked towards the milking barn. "Bet they thought that was pleasant."

Dora kept her eyes on Pearl as the young sphinx shifted in her seat. "They're used to having us around. They understand what we are."

"It was a good idea. Whatever killed that cow might come back." Marina stood. "Enough yammering. Daylight's wasting."

The three harpies took to the sky and Pearl changed into her true form, her limbs thickening and her face stretching wider and flatter. Her graceful lope ate up the ground as Dora flew over her. The late afternoon sun illuminated the lioness body of the sphinx into the color of tarnished gold. Dora had seen Pearl's true form before, but always in a stationary state, never in motion. Pearl hunted with Marina often but Dora had never joined them. Pearl was grace defined, her muscles rippling with deadly beauty.

Dora smelled the carcass before they reached the pasture, and the smell did not improve upon closer inspection. Dora leaned over the carcass of the cow and inhaled along the long gashes running down the backbone of the cow. She could detect nothing but the smell of newly rotting meat. Longer gouges in the cow's belly had spilled the entrails and offal onto the grass, increasing the bouquet of death.

Dora lifted her leg and ran her talon over the marks. "They're the same size and shape of a harpy talon. If the girls were older, I would say they had gone out for a hunt alone."

Marina tilted her head to one side, a movement more bird-like in this form. "One day they will. But these claw marks are too large to be theirs."

Petra flexed the claws on the end of her wings and pointed to some shorter gouges on the sides of the cow's neck where its jugular had been severed. "These are a close match for our claws. It looks like whatever it was landed or jumped on the cow and then opened up its neck from behind before it slashed open the belly."

In the awkward hop-walk the harpies did when they were on the ground, Marina did a circuit around the carcass. Pearl followed in her wake, sniffing the ground and the carcass with puffs of air.

"Whatever it was could've opened the throat from the front if it was fast and surprised the animal," Marina said. "It's not like a milk cow would give up much of a fight."

Dora shook her head. It was too close to home, too like something they would do when they were hunting in a pack. She waved her claws at Marina, "You're the only thing with claws I know fast enough to do that. Are you sure you weren't flying in your sleep?"

Marina shook her head. "Even asleep, I think I'd remember that James would kill me if I ever touched one of his cows. And that would be only if I was alive when Petra was done with me."

Pearl shoved her flatter, more feline looking nose into the neck of the cow and drew in a deep breath. "I have claws and I am very fast. If I was going to kill a cow from the front, I would have waited in the grass and sprung up at its feet. I would've used my teeth then, not claws." Her voice still held the same notes as her mortal voice but it was overlaid with a rasping, like the sound of a cat's tongue on bare skin.

Dora cocked her head to hear it better and thought. An anger, ancient and strong, rose from her core. "There is some kind of flying, clawed, and taloned thing in our territory. Killing where it hasn't asked leave to do so." She all but spat out the last of the words.

Dora let the justified anger take over and power rushed out from her core. It had been a day filled with strong emotions and Dora let them all go, finally. The wind around them picked up. Marina and Petra bared their teeth and looked to the sky. The hair on Pearl's back stood up and she hissed at Dora.

She was caught up in the thought of their territory being invaded and she hissed back at Pearl, putting power in the sound. The sphinx was powerful, but no match for a harpy. The response to the power was immediate though, and she arched her back and hissed at Dora.

"Stand down, young one. My anger isn't directed at you," Dora's voice ground over sharp teeth.

Pearl shook herself and her fur went down, but her eyes remained fixed on Dora.

Marina swatted the feline's nose with the back of a wing. "Settle, Kitten. If you're going to hunt with all three of us, you have to learn when our power is or isn't directed at you. Dora is just mad that something is here in a place that belongs to us."

Pearl's attention swiveled to Marina, and Dora made an effort to reign in her anger.

Marina continued. "You should respond in the sense that you get predatory and want to kill things, but not us. The prey is the target. We're not prey."

A coughing sound escaped Pearl's mouth and it took Dora a moment to realize the sphinx was laughing.

"Sorry. I suddenly was imagining chasing you like a cat does with a bird." Marina narrowed her eyes at Pearl as the feline spoke. "Which I would never, ever do. It's heady being with all of you in our true forms. I've only ever hunted with you, Marina. It wasn't like this."

Petra bared her teeth again. "This isn't just a hunt. This is more personal."

Anger still rolled off the edges of her feathers and the power coming from all of them tightened and turned more menacing.

"Let's go," Dora said.

She launched into the air and did not look to see if Petra followed. In small, tight circles with the carcass in the center, Dora flew with her eyes trained on the ground. Petra joined her and flew in circles in the opposite direction. They kept their flight slow, gliding through the heat waves more than flying, and passing each other twice in each circuit. Dora watched Pearl and Marina mimic their movements on the ground. Petra and Dora flew faster than the two on the ground, and eventually their circle widened beyond James and Petra's farm. By the time they had made a circuit of the entire valley, the sun had long sunk and the half-moon had risen, offering too little light to be of use.

In one pass, Petra changed direction and flew directly over Dora. "I didn't see anything."

"Me either. It's like whatever did it made the kill and left without eating or anything. Nothing is missing and there's no trail."

"Just a dead body, like it wanted its presence known, but didn't want to be tracked," Petra finished Dora's thought.

Dora's anger boiled over again. "Whatever it is, it isn't friendly. Plus, the damn thing can fly or else there would've been tracks."

Dora could feel Petra's anger and frustration bounce back at hers. "Hells, if there was anything on the ground, we would've already found it."

"I agree. Let's go join Marina and Pearl." Dora tucked her wings and pointed her head down, resulting in a twirling dive. The free fall cleared her head.

They found the pair near the base of The Twins, to the east of James and Petra's farm, on the border of the Mylonis family's land. Three generations of the Mylonis family, Remnants from Greece, had settled in the valley over a year ago. Pearl, still in sphinx form, sat on her haunches beside Marina, who was pacing back and forth in a clearing between cedar trees.

Dora landed and changed. "Anything?"

Marina made a swiping motion with her hand. "Nothing."

The tip of Pearl's tail twitched. "Not just nothing. There were no signs of other predators either. There should be an occasional bobcat, bear, cougar, or wolf, but there's no trace. I don't think any of those animals have been in the area recently."

Dora rocked back on her heels. "It could be unrelated. Other predators have moved out of the area in the last few years."

Marina flashed a feral grin. "Too many scary monsters in one place."

Dora sat down next to Pearl. "I don't think it's that simple. Everything about this feels wrong."

"Like we're missing a piece of the puzzle, but can't see the hole where it goes," Petra crossed her arms over her chest.

"Exactly," Dora agreed. She wanted to grab something by the throat and shake it, but there was nothing, no outlet. "We're all out here. We shouldn't waste the night."

Marina popped up to her feet. "Yes, let's go hunting for something we can find."

Dora turned to the peaks to the north. "There are always sheep on The Twins."

The three harpies took to the sky and Pearl ran on the ground beneath them. The peaks of The Twins were a dark shadow on the ink blue of the night sky. An hour passed and they had not found the herd of sheep that usually overnighted on the mountains. The thrill of the hunt had cooled to a tightness along the lines of Dora's wings.

Dora tipped her left wing down and closed the distance between herself and Marina. "The sheep have gone to ground."

"Something's spooked them." Marina kept her eyes on the ground, following Pearl's movements.

"We hunt up here often and they don't hide much from us." The tightness in her wings increased, and Dora flapped them rapidly to release the tension.

Petra flew above them both. "What's bigger and scarier than us?"

"Whatever it is, it doesn't have long to live if it keeps this up," Marina said.

The threat of the words flowed around all of them. Dora let the tension morph back into violence. Her blood raced with the drug of power that she was releasing, magnified by her sisters' power in turn. Dora let the bloodlust soak through her. The question of what was in their territory was troubling, but together, the three of them could face anything. Whatever they faced, they would not do so alone. A blur in the dark below them reminded Dora that Pearl was also with them.

Marina noticed Pearl at the same time and made a straight dive for the sphinx. Dora tried to track her movements, but Marina added a burst of powered speed to her dive and Dora lost her in the dark. Seconds later, the screeching of an angry lioness filled the night. Marina's cackling laughter could barely be heard over the noise.

"You filthy harpy," Pearl yelled from below. "For Hera's sake, you scared the life out of me."

Dora laughed. "You have nine lives. One less won't hurt you."

Petra cocked her head and circled over Pearl. "We might as well have some fun tonight."

Marina flew in line behind Petra, circling Pearl. "Let's play capture the kitty."

Pearl hissed at them and bounded away up the mountain. "Catch me if you can," she called over her shoulder.

"I'll distract her." Dora changed direction and pumped her wings hard to get to the front and right of Pearl.

The sphinx was running in a zigzag pattern, making it hard to follow her path. Soon, they left the tree line behind and Pearl had less cover for protection. Dora pushed harder until she was well ahead of Pearl. She glanced over her shoulder. Marina and Petra were in place.

Dora turned until she was flying straight for Pearl. She barreled towards the sphinx, tucking her talons up as far as possible to keep them from getting caught on the scrub bushes. Dora slowed her speed to keep Pearl's focus on her.

The dark shape of Marina dropped from the sky directly over Pearl, landing on her back. Marina wound her talons into the scruff at the base of Pearl's neck and flapped her wings. Pearl twisted in her grip, hissing and spitting. The smell of blood hit the air. Dora knew Marina had broken Pearl's skin but was not worried about the sphinx. Marina would never really hurt her. Marina pulled the hissing Pearl a couple of inches off the ground before dropping the sphynx.

"I win catch the kitten." Marina landed in front of Pearl.

Pearl crouched down and hissed at the harpy, her back arched. There were red marks in Pearl's scruff where Marina's talons had dug in. "That hurt."

Marina laughed. "I tried not to hurt you, but you wiggled too much."

With a growl, Pearl flung herself at Marina. Instead of trying to dodge the attack, Marina met her head-on and the two wrestled around the ground, hair and feathers flying.

Dora landed and watched from a safe distance. "Think we should intervene?" she asked Petra, who had landed beside her.

"That's no fun. I don't see too much blood. They'll be fine."

Marina wrapped clawed wings around the sphinx and squeezed. When Pearl refused to be still, Marina head-butted her. Both of them fell apart, rubbing their foreheads and breathing heavily. Pearl changed back into her mortal form and flopped onto the ground on her back.

"No wonder you're so stubborn. Your head is made of stone." Pearl rubbed the egg forming on her head and started laughing.

Marina loomed over the girl. "Kitten, you are more fun than hunting sheep."

Pearl tried to scowl at Marina but her mouth turned up in a smile. "I'm not prey."

Dora flapped over to them. "Maybe not, but you are good at playing catch the kitty."

"Not sure I like that game," mumbled Pearl. "I think I'd rather play harass the harpy."

Before the three of them could move, Pearl morphed back into her true form and lunged at Dora, who had been the closest. Dora jumped back, but not before the sphinx's big paw, with claws retracted, hit her in the chest.

"You're it!" Pearl screamed as she ran down the mountain in a dead run.

Dora gathered her power and leapt into the air. Marina was far ahead of her, using her speed to gain the advantage of distance. Petra was laughing like a loon directly below her. Dora called the wind and pushed it under Petra in the same moment that she dropped like a rock onto the harpy's back, squashing her between the two forces.

"Tag," she yelled as she pushed Petra from above, this time with another gust of wind, and made her own escape. Dora laughed at the scream of fury she left in her wake.

Petra righted herself and went after the closest target. Pearl was ten yards in front of her, rounding a tree and looking at Dora and Marina. Dora did a diving flip and kept Pearl's attention while Petra advanced. When Petra was close enough, she dove towards Pearl and it looked like she would be successful in grabbing the sphynx.

But the second before Petra would have made contact, Pearl flipped around and confronted Petra with extended claws and a hiss. It was too late for Petra to change her direction and she landed on Pearl. Pearl bunched her muscles and threw Petra off herself with a push of her four legs.

"Tag," Petra said in a breathless voice.

Pearl righted herself and looked around for Dora and Marina. Marina was far ahead, but Dora was close and she angled her body and started bounding towards the speckled harpy.

Dora met her halfway and called down to her, keeping her voice quiet so it would not carry. "We need to trap Marina. She's too fast to be caught on her own. Catch me and I'll chase her towards you."

Petra joined them. "Are we conspiring against Marina?"

"Seems like the only way to put her in her place," Pearl said.

Dora laughed. "You fit in just fine. Petra, you going to help?"

"It would be my pleasure."

Dora dropped altitude and made a swipe at Pearl, moving a little slower than normal and allowing Pearl to make contact.

"You're it," Pearl laughed, and Dora winked.

Pearl and Petra peeled off from their formation, each making a wide circle in Marina's direction. Dora made a beeline for Marina, not hiding her intent to keep Marina focused on her while the other two got in position.

Marina turned slightly to head west. Dora followed the movement, striving to close the distance and giving Petra and Pearl the opportunity to swing around and get in place.

"You're flying awful fast. Scared to let me get too close?" Dora asked.

Marina laughed and did a flip in the air, flying straight towards Dora until the gap between them was cut in half. Marina turned sharply to the left, away from Dora, but straight into the path of Petra. Marina could not pull up fast enough before the two collided. Petra wrapped her wings around Marina, and the two tumbled into the ground. Pearl was on them both in a second, and Dora added her weight to the fray. Petra immobilized Marina's left wing and Dora grabbed her right. Pearl leapt onto Marina's back.

"Styx, I give up. Get off." Marina's voice was muffled because her face was in the ground. Pearl shifted to get off and it was just enough to give Marina some traction.

"No, you don't." Dora bit Marina on the top of the wing, not hard enough to draw blood, but hard enough to hurt.

"You bit me. Monster." Marina thrashed around and bumped Petra off.

The four of them scuffled around, jumping on each other and being thrown off like bull riders until they all lay on the ground with chests heaving and laughing. It was a good end to an unsuccessful hunt. For all the laughter, Dora could not get rid of the twist of her stomach thinking about what was still lurking in the darkness and wondering where it would strike next.

CHAPTER 7

The next day, Dora went to the Eisler's farm to check on Caroline and
Melanie, hoping she could inform them that their quarantine from the
chicken pox could be ended. As she approached the house from above,
Dora could see Caroline kneeling beside the kitchen garden behind the
house pulling weeds. Most families had an extensive garden near the house
where they grew the vegetables the family lived on through the summer and
stored up for the winter. The yield from these plots often made the
difference between survival and starvation.

Caroline reached around her rounded belly and pulled plants up with a
yanking motion. There was an odor in the air. Something off that did not
belong. A pull of worry tugged on Dora's backbone as she landed beside
Caroline and changed into her human form. Caroline stopped and looked at
Dora. Tears ran down her face. She held up hands full of plants.

"Everything is dead," she said.

Dora's eyes moved from the distraught face in front of her to the plants
fisted in Caroline's hand. Knowing what she would find did not make it
easier. The plants heaped around Caroline were dusted with mold. The plot
behind the house was covered in the black mold that had killed Dora's
plants. In some areas, the mold had advanced, and the plants were decaying
in the ground they had thrived in days ago. Their stench wafted to her in
full force, when it had only teased her before. It smelled like death.

The worry in her spine bloomed, and she felt it in every bone in her
body. No matter the cause of this, if other families were affected, Turning
Creek was going to be in some trouble come winter if they could not get
these plants and their food replaced. Dora placed a hand on Caroline's
shaking shoulder and squeezed. She made soothing noises and thought
about what they could do if this was widespread.

Dora knew that everyone with gardens kept seeds and starter plants in reserve for future gardens. It was June. There may still be time to cultivate enough food plants to get them through the winter. They could forage for some edible plants from the mountains around them, and the harpies could hunt more. It would result in a protein-heavy diet, but they would not starve.

Dora knelt beside Caroline. "How is Melanie?"

Caroline pointed to a blanket on the side of the field. Dora walked over and looked down. A round toddler face, lost in sleep, free of the red rash of chicken pox, greeted her.

"I hate to wake her. She looks so peaceful. Is her rash gone everywhere?" Dora ran a hand along the side of the blanket and rubbed the end between her fingers, wanting to be closer, but not wanting to disturb the bubble of peace within it.

"It's gone and no one else has been sick." Caroline stood awkwardly and stretched with a hand on her back. "I will be glad when this baby comes. I'm tired of being huge."

Caroline was a beautiful woman, and pregnancy only enhanced and softened her looks. "Your time will be here soon enough. You don't have to be quarantined anymore if all has been well here. Take it easy, though. You are in your last few weeks. Do what you think you are able but don't overwork yourself."

Caroline waved a hand towards her ruined garden. "There is plenty of work to be done." She started crying again.

Dora grabbed Caroline's shoulders. "I'll stay and help pull them up. George can burn them. Where is he?"

"He went out to check on the other fields."

"Let's get these pulled up. You can replant and have something to show for all your work come fall." Dora squeezed Caroline's shoulders hard until the woman focused on her.

A determination passed over Caroline's face. "We can have new plants in the ground in a couple days."

Dora went to the front-most row and began pulling plants. It was messy work and her hands were black before she had finished the first row. The mold and dirt caked in the cracks of her skin and collected underneath her fingernails. An irrational fear that it would burrow under her skin to fill her with decay from the inside out filled her. Dora shook her hands and took a deep breath. The feeling passed, but a tight ball of anxiety remained behind.

It took them all morning to clear the field. Dora tried to do as much as quickly as she could to keep Caroline from the bulk of the load. Halfway through, Melanie woke up and toddled over to pull plants alongside her mother.

"Usually, I have to tell her which are the weeds and which are the ones to be left alone." Caroline yanked the next plant out with more force than needed.

When they were done, the beds were ripped and gaping, with piles of molding plants on the side.

"Working in the garden usually leaves me feeling satisfied with life, but this was demoralizing." Dora tried to brush some of the mold from her blackened hands. "Do you have somewhere I can wash up?"

Caroline led her to the well to the side of the house and drew a bucket up. She poured the cool, clear water into a tub on a corner of the porch. A faded rag had dried stiffly on the side of the tub. Dora swirled it in the water until it loosened up and became soft again. She scrubbed her hands and arms.

"Thank you for your help." Caroline sat on the porch with her daughter in her lap. The child curled around her mother's belly and patted the sides.

"I'm sorry we had to do it, but I'm happy I was here to help." There was mold still under her nails and it took Dora a long time to get her hands clean.

"Will you stay for lunch?" Caroline scooted Melanie off her lap and stood.

"I can't. I hadn't planned on being here long, and I have to stop by Dr. Williams's office and the depot. Send word if you find more of the mold or if you need anything at all."

"We will. Thank you again." Caroline ran a hand over her daughter's head in unconscious affection.

The flight to town did not clear Dora's head as much as she needed it to. She was burdened by what all the ruined fields might mean. The fact that the plants had decayed while they were still in the ground led Dora to believe that the fungus was not natural in origin. It felt sinister to her. She had no idea what or who could cause such devastation. Dora had planned on going to Lee's first, but she needed to talk to Iris. If there were other families affected, word of it would have already started trickling in.

Iris's back was to her as she sorted letters into slots when Dora walked into the depot. The bell over the door rang, and Iris did not turn around, but instead kept sorting letters.

"Hello, my bird. There's a plate of lunch for you on the counter." Iris turned enough to flash her a smile, then went back to work.

Dora did not ask how Iris knew she would be here or that her stomach would be trying to digest itself when she arrived. She should have stayed at Caroline's, but she could not stand to be near that ruined garden any longer, even to fulfil the needs of her loudly protesting stomach. The plate on the counter was piled with fruit, cheese, bread, and jam.

Iris stopped sorting and faced Dora, leaning her elbows on the counter. "What do you have to tell me today? I know you're not here for a social visit, though I like those too."

"Maybe I'm just here for lunch," Dora said in between bites.

"I woke up this morning knowing you would be here for lunch and bringing news that would change the way my day went, for the worse." Iris ran her hands over the smooth top of the wooden counter.

"I'm sorry to be the one to be bearing bad news. Usually, it's Marina or Petra blowing in with it." Dora wiped some crumbs from her hands. They still felt dirty even though they looked clean. "I would've been here earlier, but I stopped by the Eisler's this morning. Her kitchen garden was destroyed by the fungus that went through my herb beds and Pearl's lavender farm."

"Did anything survive?"

"Not in my garden. Not in Caroline's. Yesterday, Pearl said she still had some fields left. I'm not sure if today has changed that."

"It's not just your garden and fields," Iris said.

The knot of worry grew heavier under her skin. "How many others?"

"Everyone who has come in today is telling the same story."

"That's not possible." The food in her stomach mixed with her worry and the result was not pleasant. "Do you have any ideas?"

Iris's lips thinned into a line. "I'm thinking we need to consider something may be at work here. Something not natural."

"I agree, but what could do this? A witch?"

"I'm going to do some reading."

Dora stood, unable to sit any longer. "Reading what? Where do we even start?"

Iris walked around the counter and laid a hand on Dora's arm, cutting off the string of words forming in her mouth. "This is the same as any other time. We have very little information and a problem on our hands. What has you so tightened up?"

Everything, Dora thought. The plants. The growing need she felt to have a daughter when she did not want to continue this cycle of violence. The fear that she would repeat her mistakes and become her mother no matter what she did. Lee.

"Nothing." Dora looked over Iris's shoulder as she said it.

With a hand on her chin, Iris redirected Dora's eyes back at her. "You're not being honest with me."

The worry harboring inside her burst and her eyes filled. Dora blinked rapidly to keep them from falling. She told Iris the easiest truth. "I don't want to be my mother."

Her mother had loved Dora in her own way, but she had been unable to control her nature, and in the end so had Dora. Dora knew her mother's intentions had been good, just as hers had always been, but everything still ended in blood. It always did.

Iris ran a hand over Dora's hair and Dora leaned into it. "Poor bird.

You're not your mother. Being yourself will not always end in blood and death. You're stronger than her. More compassionate."

Dora wished that were so. One day she would tell Iris what had really happened on the island and what she'd left behind, but not today. "Did you ever meet my mother?"

"Once, when my mother took me to meet you when we were still small. Do you remember?"

Dora had never forgotten. There had been no other powerful Remnants on their small island. Generations of mortal families and Remnants whose power had been diluted by time had lived their entire lives under the rule of a monster they did not fully understand. The visit from The Messengers was one of the few golden memories of her childhood.

"My mother did not want either of you there," Dora said.

Iris's hand moved to Dora's shoulder and down her arm. "She threatened to feed my mother her own entrails if I remember correctly."

Dora gave in and moved into Iris's arms. "That sounds about right. I only remember meeting you."

Iris squeezed her and pulled back to look Dora in the face. "You sat behind her, silent, the entire time she ranted."

"I learned early not to be focal point of her wrath. I rarely was, but still I knew what she was capable of. They sent us both away while they finished their argument. I was afraid for your mother, but you took my hand and we walked in the garden. You didn't seem concerned for her."

"Maybe I should've been, but I didn't think your mother would harm her Messenger. That bond is too ingrained."

Dora snorted. "You didn't know her. She would have, given the right provocation."

Iris nodded, "I know that now, but I learned something that day about you." Dora tried to escape the clear blue of Iris's gaze and failed. "I knew you weren't like her. I knew you had compassion and goodness in you."

Dora closed her eyes. "You're right that I do have those things. I'm here in this place and we, for whatever reason, are different than the generations before us, but I am still the same. Her violence is still there, waiting inside me. It's an animal barely caged. I control it for now, but I could slip, and then I will be her. Blood and death. That is the end of all roads."

Iris shook her. "It doesn't have to be."

Dora opened her eyes and stepped away from Iris. "I can't have both. I can control one or the other. Compassion or violence. I can't do both in equal measures. It's not a balance, it's a war."

"You underestimate yourself."

"You overestimate me. You think you've seen us at our worst. You have no idea what the worst is. I won't become that." *Not again,* she added to herself. Dora turned to leave. She wanted to be angry, but she had one more stop in town and she needed to control her anger. Control herself. Iris was wrong, she could only be this middle version of herself or all was free and lost in the world.

"Don't leave angry," Iris pleaded.

Dora turned around with her hand on the doorknob. "This isn't anger. You've never really seen that. I'll be back in town tomorrow."

Dora left before Iris could ask her to stay again. Her head ached with the effort it took to hold herself back when what she wanted was to rant and yell at Iris for her naiveté. She of all people should know not to poke at this particular sore. Iris meant well, but Dora knew what lurked inside of her. She had nightmares about what happened if she let her darker emotions out of the tight-lidded box she kept them trapped in.

The door closed behind her, and Dora regretted exiting from the front of the depot. At midday, Main Street was teeming with people. There was little chance she would make it all the way to Lee's office without being stopped. Part of her was glad; she wanted some distance between the emotions she had locked down after her discussion with Iris. Another, deeper part of her, wanted to get to Lee faster.

She took a few deep breaths and put her feet in motion, walking north up the street towards Lee's office. The sounds of the busy street, the horses, the turning of wagon wheels, and people talking pressed into her skin and helped her center. The mercantile was busy. Dora could see into the large plate-glass windows as she walked past. Beth was laughing with Widow Finch and Lily Hughes. Beth saw Dora walk by and waved. Dora returned the gesture, and some of the tightness in her chest eased open. These people, this place, they grounded her.

Reed stood on the boardwalk in front of his office with his back planted firmly on the side of the building. His eyes swept the street, but they lingered on the door of the saloon longer than anywhere else. An easy smile spread over his face as she approached him.

He stood up and away from the wall. "Afternoon to you, Dora. Business with Doc?"

"That's my destination. Why are you watching Vine's so closely?" Dora turned her body to match his so she had a clear view of the saloon, which had been behind her.

"Reggie and Art both went in about an hour ago. I figure by this time they're either best friends or about to erupt into a fight to see which of them has the least amount of smarts left. You never know with those two." Reed crossed his arms over his chest.

Dora looked at the door of the saloon, which was wide open to let some of the summer breeze into the main tap room. "Why don't you send Marina over? Keeping an eye on someone at Vine's seems like just the kind of job she wouldn't mind doing."

Reed chuckled. "Why do you think I'm watching the door so hard? I sent her over twenty minutes ago. She's still there, and no one's come out, so I'm concerned I've made the problem worse."

Marina emerged from the saloon then, one hand shielding her face and the other clutching a brown bottle by the neck. She saw them and she wove between people and horses, greeting others as she went without breaking her graceful stride. Her grin was wide and her curly hair was everywhere.

"Vine filled this for me for the road. He let this stew in an old wine cask." She popped open the flip-top with a push of her thumb and thrust it at Dora. "Try it. It's wonderful."

Dora took the bottle and did as Marina asked. There was little point in resisting. The ale was sweet with the added taste of red wine as she swallowed it. Dora gave the bottle back to Marina.

"It's unique. I do like it, though I might not want a whole bottle of it," Dora said.

Marina took the bottle from her and handed it to Reed. "Who says I'm sharing the entire bottle?"

Reed took the offered bottle. "How're things inside?" He sipped the ale, then took another sip. "You're right. This is very good. You should share this with your long-suffering husband."

Marina snorted. "You don't know the meaning of suffering yet. You have a long life of being stuck to me."

He winked at Marina and she rolled her eyes, but her smile broadened. Reed took another pull from the bottle before giving it back. "So, did you check things out at the saloon or did you just go drink?"

Marina sniffed. "I can do many things at once. Art and Reggie are getting along fine. Neither one of them is grumpy, so they'll be fine today, I think. I told Vine he could come get one of us if anything changes." Her smile went down a notch. "Got some news, though." She flicked a glance at Dora. "I heard some other people talking. Other fields in the valley have had some of the fungus on their plants. It's possible this could turn into a serious problem."

"Let's start doing the rounds and check the damage. We can make note of which families may need help replanting or will be short on food come winter," Reed said.

Dora tried to remember if she had seen any damage on her way into town. "My gardens are gone, and I stopped by the Eisler's and it was there too. I'll come back into town tomorrow in case you need me to fly," Dora said.

"Where's Ellie?" Marina asked.

Reed leaned back against to wall. "Taking a nap."

Marina waved the bottle between them. "I'm going to put this away. We can have it later. And I'm going to check on her. See you tomorrow?" She directed the question to Dora.

Dora nodded. "Yes, tomorrow. I've got to get going."

She left them and made it past the Hughes' tailor shop before she was greeted by Ruben Renault, who was cleaning the windows in the front of his family's ceramics shop. He was the oldest of four children and the one Dora saw helping most often around the shop. He looked like he was about Thomas's age, though Dora knew that Thomas did not spend a lot of time with Ruben or his brother, Asher. The older Renault children helped in the shop with their father more than they played.

"Good afternoon, madam. How are you on this beautiful day?" asked the boy on the cusp of being a boy no longer. His accent lilted and exposed his French roots. The Renaults had lived in France before coming to Turning Creek.

Dora's steps slowed. "I'm fine. How are you?"

He stopping wiping the window. "My youngest sister is feeling unwell, so Maman is home with her. Only father and I came in today."

"I'm sorry to hear that. Is it something serious?" In her head, Dora was already making a list of what they may need to take along if they went to check on the child.

The boy shrugged. "I do not know, madam. Maman is worried, but then, she worries often for us. It is her job, no?"

Dora's mind eased. "It is a mother's job to worry. Tell your mother, if Aderes is not well soon, to send someone to come and get Dr. Williams or myself."

Ruben's hands returned to his task. "I will, madam. Thank you."

Dora looked through the window where Ruben had wiped it clean. Plates, pitchers, bowls, and cups stood in an appealing array of colors and sizes. At the end, in another display, were three urns, each about a foot in height and hand painted. One depicted a traditional Greek pattern of squared borders and a goddess in a garden of plenty. The middle one, painted in blues and green, was encircled with mountains. Dora leaned closer and put a hand up to the glass. She stopped herself before leaving a smudge.

The mountains were the ones circling their valley. Dora could name all of them. They were the walls that made her home. Silvercliff. The Twins. Pikus Peak. Jolly's Folly. Aspen Peak. Baldy. The others wrapped around the back and Dora could not see them. She thought about going inside to look at the urn.

Ruben's voice broke her thoughts. "Do you like that one? I painted the scenery. My father is teaching me how to do some of the more complicated painting."

"It's beautiful. I haven't seen urns like this since I lived in Greece." Dora could not keep the longing from her voice. In Greece, these urns were common. Families passed them down from generation to generation, gave them as gifts for weddings and births, and used them to hold the ashes of those who went to be with the gods.

Ruben stopped his work and came to stand near her. Dora noted that he left some space between them. He was friendly, but there was something else beneath the surface. Dora allowed a small tendril of power to reach out to him and she felt it then. The hesitation was fear—not much, but enough that he did not want to get too close. She did not blame him. Harpies were not cuddly rabbits.

"Father's family has made ceramics for generations. When my mother's people came to France, they brought this kind of urn with them and they taught us to make it."

Magda Renault, Ruben's mother, was a Remnant. His father was not. Dora wondered if whatever they were was passed only through the maternal line. It was not a question that was polite to ask. Dora reached out to Ruben again with her power. He was mortal, a fact she stored away for another day.

"Tell your parents I send my greetings," Dora said.

"I will, madam. Thank you." Ruben went back to his task.

Dora continued her journey down Main Street with the picture of the urn on her mind and thankfulness for the home she had come to from Greece.

CHAPTER 8

Dora finally reached her destination. There was no one waiting in the sitting area of Lee's front office, and Dora closed the door behind her with a sigh of relief. She leaned her back against the door and smiled. She had left the depot unsettled, but talking with Marina, Reed, and Ruben had helped her focus on things other than how she was disappointing Iris and who was affected by the fungus.

Lee came out from the back with a towel in his hands. Dora took one look at him and knew he had been cleaning. He was missing his usual vest or jacket and his crisp white shirt was rolled up past his elbows while his black pants, usually spotless, had smudges on them. His whole face smiled when he saw her. Her breath caught then evened out as if her world had not contracted for the beat of a heart.

"I didn't expect you today, though I did hope you might come."

Dora soaked in the sight of him, allowing herself that one extravagance. She blinked and let the moment go. "I need to take inventory of what herbs and tinctures we have left. Whatever we have is going to have to last us for a few months."

Lee's smile disappeared and his gaze sharpened. "Why?"

Dora explained to him about her herb beds and the other gardens in the area that she knew about. "There are some things we can order, but most of the things we will have to plant again and wait for them to mature."

Lee stepped closer to her, but did not touch her. "I'm sorry you lost all of them. Especially the lemon tree for Iris."

Dora dismissed the image of the tree, wilted and dead. "They're just plants. Others can be grown." The lie was heavy on her tongue. Those plants were part of her redemption.

Lee stood to one side. "Come in the back. I'll get some paper and a pencil and you can take inventory."

Dora walked past him, aware of how close he was and yet keeping space between them. She thought of Ruben maintaining a space during the conversation because of his fear. She created space for the same reason. She was scared of herself.

She felt Lee at her back while she walked to the examination room. Being in his presence was like having a hammer tapping away at her walls, a slow, dangerous gamble that her control would hold out long enough for her to be here. She was the dealer, though, not a player, and she was in charge of how the cards fell. Later, when she was alone once more, she would rebuild her walls again.

The exam room, always clean, now gleamed after Lee's thorough cleaning. "I think if there's any dirt left in here, it's cowering in the corner of the next room," Dora said, heading straight for the cabinet of herbs. "I'll look in here first then check the dispensary."

Lee went to the roll top desk in the corner. The dark wood had been polished and the top rolled silently up. The desktop was clear. Papers, evenly spaced, lined the slots. Dora understood and admired Lee's organization of every aspect of his office and life. From one drawer, Lee retrieved a clean sheet of paper and from another drawer, a wooden pencil. He laid them on the counter near her hand, which rested on the counter.

"Here you are. I'm going to go get the dust off my pants. I wouldn't want to examine anyone in this state if they came in." Lee left the room without waiting for a reply.

Dora opened the cabinet. All the bottles were facing label outward, soldiers waiting for orders. She began at A, aloe, and made a list, indicating if they were dried, powdered, made into a tincture, or a salve. She was on M, mullein, when Lee returned. He had changed completely. A clean, starched shirt stretched across his shoulders. He wore a black vest with grey embroidery and fresh pants. Dora noticed he was looking at her look at him and she turned away. The sound of his chuckle tickled her spine.

"What's so amusing?" she asked with more bite than intended.

"You were smiling at me."

She did not turn around, but continued with her list. N, for nettle. *N is for nincompoop*, she thought. "I smile."

"You do. Often, but not always at me. What amused you about me just then?" Dora could tell from his voice that he had remained by the door. Keeping his distance.

"I was thinking that you are probably the best-dressed person in our small town in the middle of the mountains. I knew you were cleaning when I first came in because you were missing a jacket and vest. You own more vests alone than anyone I have ever known."

He laughed then, and Dora felt it on her back, the part of her she kept towards him. A wall to keep him out, but it still reflected sound and vibrated with it.

"It's a vanity, I know, but nice clothes are one of the few things from my past that I wanted to take with me. Lily Hughes made this particular vest. She does lovely work," Lee said from his place by the door.

Dora stopped and turned towards him. "Do you miss anything else you couldn't bring when you left Philadelphia?" Lee never talked about the life he left behind. Dora knew he had some family, and it was obvious from the way he dressed and spoke that Lee Williams had come from money, the very old kind.

Pain flashed across his face, and Lee's grey eyes swept down to the floor. Dora intensely regretted her question and opened her mouth to apologize, but Lee spoke before she could say anything.

His voice was quiet. "My sister. My mother died shortly after I left or I would regret leaving her as well."

Her eyes burned with the need to cry and her feet ached with the need to close the distance between them. Dora remained still and no tears filled her eyes. "I'm sorry. You never talk about your family."

Lee visibly shook himself and redirected his gaze on her, unrelenting grey rimmed in black. "There's nothing to apologize for. I didn't leave home under easy circumstances, and my sister and I do not write often. She still lives with my father because she is not yet married and I don't want to make her life more difficult than it already is. I have other siblings, but she was the only one I was close to. The only one I miss."

"What's her name?"

"Zoe. She's a nurse. Healing runs in the family. She would like you."

Dora's feet almost moved, but the bell in the waiting room sounded and she was saved from that mistake. "I'll go see who it is."

Her skirts brushed his legs as she walked past, faded blue against pressed black. She caught his smile in the edge of her field of vision and she wondered what he thought about during that brief moment when the space was small between them. Her thoughts were a jumble and she threw the pieces into the place of chaos where they stayed. She could feel it boiling, the chaos, and it made her wary. Things that could hurt you should cause hesitation and drive you to create distance. Dora wondered how long she would continue to win this battle.

The empty waiting room was empty no longer. It was full of an assortment of the Mylonis family. They lived on the far side of the valley, past Silvercliff, at the base of the western Twin. Three generations lived on a large sprawling farm and ranch. Like many immigrant families, they had come with everything they had and everyone they could gather to start over.

Castor, the youngest adult son, came forward, leading his wife as she clutched a bloody rag to her arm. There was a spattering of blood on her skirt. Her face was pale and her lips were blue.

"Keep your arm around her, Mr. Mylonis. She's about to faint," Dora said.

Castor adjusted his grip in time to catch his wife before she hit the ground. He scooped her up and held her limp body. "She cut her arm on some of the new tools we bought from the mercantile as we were loading the wagon."

Dora addressed the rest of the room where the other members of the Mylonis family had gathered. "Everyone stay here. You can make tea on the stove in the corner if you want. Mr. Mylonis, follow me."

Dora held open the door for him. As he walked past her, he said, "Please call me Castor, Mistress Harpy. There are too many Mr. Myloniases in my family. We'll never know which of us you mean." He was friendly despite the use of her title.

"This way." Dora led him to the examination room. "You can call me Dora, then. We aren't so formal here, you know."

"Yes, mistress. Dora. It has taken some time to get adjusted. Colorado is a long way from Greece, but habits are hard to change."

Lee stood from where he had been sitting at his desk. "Place her here on this table."

The examination table was wide, covered by a worn blanket that could be washed if it got blood or other things on it, which it often did. Castor laid his wife down. Dora helped straighten her legs and smoothed out her skirts.

"Castor, what's your wife's name?" Dora wished she could remember but there were many people in the Mylonis family.

"Thera." Castor smoothed the hair back from his wife's face. It already had more color in it than it had a moment ago.

"Why is she unconscious?" Lee asked.

"She fainted," Dora said. She put a pile of clean rags on the smaller table near the head of the examination table and took the container of clean water from the counter. Lee boiled a new batch of water every day. It saved time when it was needed right away.

Lee began to unwind the blood-soaked cloth from Thera's arm while Castor explained how she had tripped while they were loading the wagon and fell against some of the tools. The gash looked bad but it was seeping, not pumping, blood. Dora handed Lee one of the cloths and he began cleaning the wound.

"I think she lost consciousness because of the sight of the blood, not the loss of it. The cut is on the top of the lower arm, away from most of the places which would have bled more and been more dangerous. She's lucky. If she would have cut the other side of this arm, we would be having a different sort of conversation." Lee continued to clean the wound.

Castor looked pale, so Dora went over to him and put her arm around his shoulders. She guided him into the chair that sat at the roll-top desk. "Sit here. You can still see. I can bring you some water or tea if you need it."

"No," Castor croaked. "I don't need anything."

Dora put a glass of water next to Castor on the desk and patted his hand. "Here's some water just in case you change your mind."

"Thank you." Castor did not look at her as he said it. His eyes were set on his wife.

Dora got the set of suture needles from the last drawer against the wall and began cleaning one of the medium-sized needles with an alcohol mixture and a clean rag. She laid the needles and string on the table, then took the bloodied rags and put them in a bin in the corner. She mixed some salve she already had prepared and laid it out.

Without looking up from his task, Lee said, "Dora, could you please hold the wound closed a fraction while I stitch? Castor, will you please stand on the other side of us in case your wife wakes up? It is good she is unconscious now, but it will hurt. I do not want her flailing if she wakes."

Castor's olive-toned skin was pale, but he swallowed and did as Lee asked. He leaned his face down to his wife's and whispered something in her ear before kissing her on the forehead. It was an intimate moment and Dora looked away from them, feeling an intruder.

Lee held the threaded needle in his hand. "Ready?"

Dora put an extra clean cloth next to Thera's arm then held the two sides of the wound closed. Lee shifted, standing next to her, and began making the first stitch. Dora glanced up at Thera but the woman's eyes remained closed and her breathing even.

Lee was focused on the tiny stitches he was making. Dora was focused on him. This close, with his intent elsewhere, she could watch without being seen. It was the only time she allowed herself to be this close. It was unavoidable when they were working.

She inhaled deeply. The air surrounding her was filled with him. She could see the inky blackness of his hair. He kept it short so it never got in his way when he was working and it never looked untidy. She wondered what he looked like when he woke up in the morning.

Dora shifted her grip on Thera's arm to one hand and used the other to wipe up blood that dripped from the wound. Thera shifted beneath her hand. Lee paused in his work and Castor put both of his hands on his wife's shoulders. She jerked awake.

Castor spoke low and with force. "You're fine, my love, but you must be very still while Dr. Williams stitches your arm."

"This is going to hurt, but we're almost done. A few more and it will be over in no time. Be as still as you can," Lee added.

Thera, dark brown eyes wide, nodded. Lee went back to work. Thera flinched as the needle pierced her skin, then her entire body went rigid in an effort to do as she was asked.

Dora's hands went before Lee's, holding the skin as he pieced it together. Her left side, the one closest to him, radiated the heat from his body back to her. Their feet were close enough to each other that her skirts covered his right leg. She allowed herself to feel the indention his leg made in her skirts and she relaxed into that feeling.

Lee tied the last stitch and straightened. Dora used the clean water and the cloth to wipe the blood from the stitches. A row of fifteen black lines marred the smoothness of Thera's arm. The lines were precise, evenly spaced and sized, but there would still be a scar. Dora handed Lee the jar of salve.

"This will help keep the wound from getting infected and keep some of the swelling down," he explained as he spread a generous amount on the row of stitches.

Lee picked up a strip of linen they used as bandages. Dora held Thera's arm while Lee wound it over the stitches.

His long fingers were gentle as he covered his work. "Keep these covered with a clean bandage for a day or two then let it breathe, but be sure to keep it clean. You need to check the stitches twice a day to make sure there isn't any swelling, redness, or pus. If you see any of those things, send someone for me or you can go to Dora's and get her. I know she is closer to your farm. As long as you keep it clean and wipe it with a damp, not wet, cloth, it should heal without complication. I will want to see you again in six days to take out the stitches and make sure everything is healing as it should."

Castor nodded. "We'll come back into town next week."

"I'm going to go get her some tea." Dora left the room and, instead of going to the front room, went up the stairs to Lee's apartment above his office. Unlike the depot, Lee's living area above his office was all one room. The stove was in the far corner from the stairs, near the front of the building. A square table made of a single slab of dark wood and two chairs stood in the middle of the kitchen area. A small pile of wood shavings littered the floor under one of the chairs. It was the only thing untidy about the room. A chair upholstered in a cream material with green floral scrollwork was positioned near the only window. The wall next to his bed was filled with bookshelves. They contained a mix of medical texts and history. The bed was large and covered by a green and grey quilt tucked into the edges and smooth on top.

The urge to flop down into the space where Lee laid his body every night was overwhelming. She stood on the precipice of that desire for a moment, allowing the anxiety and fear of what that would mean to roll over her before pulling it in and burying it where it belonged. She knew there was no way to undo a fall from the cliff she was staring down. The only thing certain about taking the plunge would be the fact that she'd be mangled by the fall.

Dora poured a cup of lukewarm tea from the pot on the stove. She added sugar, stirring with a spoon from the basket of utensils on the counter. She carried the cup downstairs and left her imaginings about beds and falling upstairs.

"Here," she said to Thera as she entered the examination room again. "Castor, help her sit so she can drink this."

Castor's eyes never left his wife as he eased her into a sitting position and held the cup while she drank.

"I'm not in danger of dying," Thera said when he removed the cup from her lips.

"I can't allow you to die. Who would take care of me and make moussaka for me?" There was humor in his eyes and he bussed her cheek with a kiss.

"Your mother makes fine moussaka. You would not starve, husband." It was a banter borne of love and daily living. Dora looked away and gathered the bloody linens from the table.

Dora continued to help Lee clean up, and soon the entire Mylonis clan left, leaving the building quiet in their wake.

Lee reached out and laid a hand on her arm. "Thank you for your help today."

His hand was a brand on her arm, fresh from the fire. He was violating the distance they kept. She looked down, thinking she might see smoke curling from her arm where the mark of his fingers would be. Her cream-colored blouse was unmarred. The rest of her was not. His fingers flexed against her arm and she felt the pressure of it everywhere. The precipice was before her and beckoned with its wildness. Lee released his hold on her arm without waiting for a reply and went back to laying the unused supplies away as if that small touch had not just stopped the world for a moment.

Dora remained in the same spot, getting herself under control. She drew a deep breath and found her voice. "It gives me purpose to help you." She flexed her fingers and thought of the claws she wielded as a harpy. "I like using my hands to heal others. My mother only taught me to wound and kill with them. It gives me great pleasure to use them for the opposite purpose."

"Like a person, your hands may be used for many things. To hurt, to heal, or to remind us of what we are." Lee gave the already-pristine counter another swipe with a damp cloth.

"That's very philosophical of you." Dora had nothing to occupy her hands at present. She crossed her arms over her chest and kept her eyes on Lee.

Lee threw the rag into the basket of dirty linens in the corner. "There was a day in my life when I had to decide what my hands were going to be for. I wanted them to heal and bring hope. My father wanted them to help our family build prestige and fear among the elite."

"You made it here, so I assume you didn't follow the mandates of your father."

There was now nothing else for either of them to do with their hands, and Lee was looking directly at her when she spoke. That was how she saw the shadow cross over his face and his shoulders sag for an instant. He righted himself quickly. The regret, though, stayed, etched on his face.

"I am here, but it took me a long time to find the courage to do what I knew to be right and stand up to my father. My delay in finding my courage came at a great price."

Dora uncrossed her arms and dropped them to her sides. She took a step closer to Lee and wanted to reach out to ease the pain of his memory. She held her hands still at her side. "What happened?"

Lee shifted his weight from one foot to the next. "Would you like to stay for tea or an early supper? I usually only have a small meal in the evening, so there's not much, but there is enough to share."

Dora looked at the small clock that ticked on the corner of the desk. "It's only four. That's early for supper."

Lee shrugged. "Perhaps, but my company is here now."

Dora knew she should leave. Nothing good could come of her spending more time with Lee today. "I can stay."

Dora followed Lee upstairs, retracing her steps from earlier, berating herself the entire way. Lee laid out the baklava the Mylonises had given him as payment for his services and added some meat pies and sliced cucumber to the spread. He made tea and gestured for Dora to sit while he finished.

She cleared her throat. "You never answered my question about what happened between you and your father. You've never talked about him before."

Lee rarely mentioned his family at all, and Dora was beginning to understand why. Her own complicated relationship with her mother had taught her that some memories were best left alone, to rot in a dark hole. The problem is that memories had a way of not staying buried as they should.

Lee joined her at the table. "Please, help yourself." He poured her tea, putting the pot of honey by her cup, and then poured his own. He made no move to put any food on his plate.

"My father was one of those people who saw every situation as an opportunity to seek advantage, for prestige, for power, for money. He even saw our gift, the healing of Asclepius, as a tool in his quest. But our birthright was meant for better things than money and power. It was meant to save lives. The first of my line died for his right to help those who needed it, even in the face of the gods who believed only they should hold sway over life and death."

Lee ran a finger around the edge of his tea cup. His eyes traced the movements and Dora's eyes followed his. "As soon as he knew how strong the power of Asclepius was in my veins, he began teaching me to use its power to its full potential for others, but he charged a high price for our services. He came to America a poor immigrant, but it wasn't long before he had clawed and swindled his way into Philadelphia's elite. They hated him and tolerated him at the same time. They needed what he could give, the chance to bring their loved ones they had lost back from the dead."

"He practiced his ability openly in a city as large as Philadelphia?" Dora paused before taking a bite from the meat pastry.

"Openly is not the correct word. It was conveyed through whispers and suggestions that he could heal anyone of any disease, any sickness. People become desperate when faced with the loss of someone they love, and they will pay dearly."

Lee placed food on his plate, the cucumbers in a line well away from the pastries. "When I came into my power, he was pleased because it meant we could make twice as many house calls. I let him use me for a long time. Much to my regret."

"What changed?" she asked.

Lee's food remained untouched. He put his elbows on the table and leaned closer to her. "He asked me to raise someone who had been dead too long and whose soul was already at peace. I refused. He threatened me, but I refused." Lee's eyes were unfocused, looking at his memory over her shoulder. "He was furious. He started to perform the task alone, though I knew it would take both of us for the deed to be done. His best effort produced something not quite human. I had to finish the job. I couldn't leave the woman like that, raving mad. I forced her soul back into her body and made her as whole as I could."

"Is she alive?"

"Last I heard, she had a husband and two children." His mouth was bracketed by lines of regret.

"So, it worked." Dora knew this story did not have a happy ending. Lee's eyes looked too haunted for that.

"It did, but she came back different. I knew the woman before we forced her back. Her laughter was like tiny bells, and her eyes lit up when she saw someone she cared about. She was one of those rare creatures of society who could get away with being herself. Everyone loved her for it. Society tends to chew up people like her, but she thrived in spite of it all." Lee smiled as he described her, and the haunted look left his face for a moment.

The smile was gone when he focused back on Dora. "After we saved her, she was never the same." He said the word saved with menace. "There was a coldness to her. People said that her illness and brush with death had stolen her youthful exuberance. I knew the truth was that we had been unable to restore her soul intact, and she was only part of the person she had been before. I allowed my father to force me to do that to her. I tried to stay for a few weeks after that, but I couldn't do it.

"I left and came here. My father loves his money and place in society too much to leave it to come to a place like this, so I know that Philadelphia will never follow me here."

Dora watched him, her food and tea forgotten. In the years they had served together, healing others and helping where it was needed, their conversations revolved around the task at hand, practical matters and practical thanks afterwards. Topics from their past had been left alone like they had power, a ghost not made corporeal except with exposure. Now, Philadelphia and all Lee had left behind sat perched on the table, digging its claws into both of them. Lee had shared the pain of his mistakes and Dora felt the curl of pain inside her own chest.

This was why she had kept a semblance of distance between them. She could feel the threads of his past pulling at her own emotions, tying her to him. She understood tragedy and the inability to completely leave mistakes that dogged you, especially mistakes committed by your own hands. Dora curled her hands around her teacup to keep them from reaching across the table.

Dora sent her words across instead. "Now I know why you never speak of your life in Philadelphia except to speak of your sister. I'm so sorry."

Lee gave her a weak smile. "There's no cause for you to be regretful. They were my mistakes. I wish I had gathered enough courage to leave my father earlier, and I live with that regret."

Dora had many regrets, but she had not come to the point of confession with Lee. Truth and confession only added to the ties binding them, and she did not want to make them stronger than they already were. "You always hesitate a long time before trying to bring someone back. Now I see why."

Dora began eating her food again, small bites at a time, and Lee joined her in silence. When they finished, Dora leaned back in her chair.

"Why tell me this now?"

Lee tapped one of his long fingers against his thigh and Dora followed the movement. "I thought it was time someone knew, and you are the person I trust the most."

Dora swallowed past the lump in her throat and stared at the empty dishes. Lee trusted her and gave her pieces of himself while she held everything back. He did not ask for anything from her in return, but she felt the burden of inequality all the same. She could not afford to let him into her past because that would mean stepping too close to feelings she could not control. That and she did not think he would look at her the same after her story was finished.

"I know the knowledge you've given me is a gift. Thank you."

Lee's lips thinned and he nodded. Dora rose from the table and put her dishes on the counter.

"I should be leaving. I'll be back in town tomorrow. You can come get me at the depot if you need me."

The silence around them was tight as he walked her downstairs. He opened the back door and held it open for her. The early twilight of night greeted her and the cold air broke over Dora's skin, easing the knot of the day's worries.

She turned back towards Lee and the house. She kept an arm's length between them and he did not close the distance. His right hand gripped the side of the door. Dora could see his knuckles turn white in the dim light. Her fingers tingled with the need to rub over those strained knuckles, the only indication that something still haunted him from their earlier conversation. Dora fisted her hand and took a step back.

"Goodnight, Lee." Dora turned away from him and released her harpy. It burst forth in a fit of anger and frustration. Her harpy was becoming displeased with how she was handling Lee. She did not allow herself a backward glance, but she heard his parting words.

"I'll see you tomorrow."

CHAPTER 9

Dora could see Petra and Selene in what was left of the house garden when she flew over the dairy farm the next morning. Petra threw the last blackened squash vine on a mound of ruined plants. The stench of rot was heavy in the air and curled around the ache of unease that seemed to be her constant companion lately. She landed beside Petra and changed into her mortal form.

Selene was on her in a moment with her hands in the air. "Pick me up, Dee."

Dora gave her an arch look.

Selene waved her hands frantically. "Please, pick me up, Auntie Dee."

Dora smiled and scooped the girl up. "You must learn to be polite, small one. While a harpy can demand, you should not unless it is necessary."

Selene nodded at the sage wisdom and pulled on the ribbon at the neck of Dora's dress. Dora leaned in and kissed Selene's forehead. The smell of warm toddler, a combination of sunshine and sweetness, overcame the other scents on the air until Dora pulled back and looked at Petra.

Lines of frustration bracketed Petra's eyes. "All of it was too far gone to be saved. James is checking on the fields of orchard grass and Adam is looking over the herd. We need the grass to help feed the cows through the winter."

Dora chuckled and Petra's gaze sharpened in anger. "Do you find this amusing?"

Dora ignored the anger coming from Petra. "No. Well, yes. Who'd have thought that a harpy, the bane of gods and Zeus alike, would be fretting and worried over hay for cows."

Petra relaxed, and the anger drained from her. She held out her arms to her daughter and Selene went from one woman to the other. "There are many things about us that would surprise the previous generations.”

“It’s a good thing they’ll never be here to see it. They’d probably kill us for becoming soft.” Dora could imagine the outrage of the older harpies well.

Petra grinned. “They would try, but they would not succeed.”

Dora returned the feral look of satisfaction on Petra’s face. “They would not succeed.”

Selene wiggled out of Petra’s arms and ran to greet James. He swung out of the saddle and kissed his daughter. He took her hand in his left one and held the reins of the horse with his right. Dora knew from the look on his face that he did not bring good news.

“All of it is gone. The entire field reeks. Usually, the grass fields are covered in birds and insects, but there was nothing living in that patch of land. The birds wouldn’t go near it.” James stopped in front of Petra and greeted her with a kiss that was more for comfort than anything else.

Petra’s hand rested on James’s chest. “Can it be replanted?”

“There may be time. I’ll have the boys help me start clearing and burning the field today and we can plant tomorrow or the next day.” James dropped the reins of the horse and covered Petra’s hand with his own.

Dora spoke up. “I replanted some of my herbs and a few of the seedlings have sprouted.”

Petra squeezed her husband’s hand. “What do you want me to do?”

James sighed. “I know you had already planned on surveying the valley to assess the damage. They will need your wings more than I need your hands. Come home tonight, though. I don’t want to sleep alone.”

Petra winked at him. “Neither do I.”

James rewarded her comment with a kiss that caused Dora to look away. “We should probably get going.” Dora motioned Selene over to her. “We have work to do, young one. Are you ready?”

“We’re going to see Iris and Aldara?”

“Yes.”

“Will Ellie be there?”

Dora squatted down next the child. “I doubt they would be left out.”

Selene nodded. “They must come. We’re a team.”

Dora cupped the girl’s face. She was so young, but harpies grew quickly and understood things earlier than their mortal counterparts. In the past, quick maturation had ensured survival. Now, it made them a force to be reckoned with on their own. *Hera help us when they’re in their middle years,* Dora thought.

“You’re a good little harpy. You’re the oldest and must help the others work together.”

Selene patted Dora’s cheek. “But Aldara is the boss of us. She’s ours.”

Dora ruffled Selene’s hair. “You are learning quickly. That’s good. You should always take her counsel when it's given and protect her."

Petra snorted. "Seems like you should listen to your own advice, sister."

Dora gave her a look that would have had most Remnants and mortals alike cowering.

Petra ignored her and spoke to her daughter. "If you come with us today, you must fly yourself. All the way, no giving up halfway there."

Selene nodded at her mother's words and immediately turned into her harpy form. She was no larger than a herding dog on some of the farms in the valley, a fraction of her adult size. Her feathers were black and shone blue in the sun like her mother's. "I'm ready." Her voice was not as low as it would be eventually, but it already rasped like sandpaper.

James dropped Petra's hand and knelt in front of his daughter and kissed her harpy face. "Be good for your mother and aunts. Be helpful. Be fierce."

Selene wrapped her wings around James. "Yes, papa." She put her mouth by his ear and whispered in a voice loud enough for them all to hear. "I love you."

Dora's heart threatened to explode. She glanced over at Petra, who had a loony grin on her face. This was Dora's family too, but at times like this, she felt like she was looking at them through a window while a storm raged around her.

***

Selene flew the entire way without complaining, and they made good time to the depot. The flight was not reassuring. All the fields they flew over were blackened tangles of death or showcased their demise with broken soil where plants had previously been ripped from the ground. They did not see one garden or field intact on their way south through the valley.

The depot was filled with people talking in huddles around the room. The tension Dora had been feeling was palpable in the room and came from everyone. Iris held court in the depot from behind the counter. Dora could see her talking to Simon when they walked in.

Marina waved to them from one of the back tables and they made their way back to her. "I was wondering when you two'd show up." She adjusted her body down to look Selene in the face. "Ellie and Aldara are upstairs plotting something. Why don't you go join them, young one."

They watched the little harpy as she rounded the corner, and they could hear her footsteps on the stairs. Petra sank into a chair and reached for the teacup in front of Marina.

Marina smacked her hand away. "Get your own cup."

"We just sat down. Let me have a sip." Petra reached for the cup again and Marina let her take it. One of Petra's eyebrows went up into her hairline after she took a sip. Instead of putting the cup back on the table, she handed it to Dora.

Dora sniffed it before taking a drink, so she was prepared for the contents of the cup. "Is there any tea at all in there?"

"Well, the first cup had some tea, but the teapot is up on the counter and getting more tea required getting up. I had the whiskey bottle here already." Marina took the cup back from Dora.

"How many cups of not tea have you had?" Dora asked.

"Just this one, but now that you two are here, I have an excuse to have another and share it with you." Marina pulled a bottle from beneath the table, refilled the cup, and handed it to Petra. They passed the whiskey around once without speaking.

Dora leaned forward after passing the cup to Marina. "There wasn't a field spared that we flew over coming in this morning."

"Philo Kalakos came into the sheriff's office this morning asking if bears attacked cattle. He said something big killed one of his cattle yesterday. Sounded like the same kind of animal we tracked." Marina gave the cup to Petra.

Philo and Katya Kalakos were a Remnant family from northern Greece who lived in the valley north of town by Aspen's Peak. Philo was good with animals, but living in the mountains of America was new and bears were not something they ever dealt with in Greece.

Marina continued, "I flew out to the site just in case, but I found about as much as we did before."

"Nothing," Petra said.

"Yep, a whole lot of nothing." Marina fingered the empty teacup that had come back to her. "I wish we could just sit around and drink all day, but I think we're going to have work to do."

Dora stood up. "Time to go talk to Iris and make a plan."

Dora led the way through the crowd. The bell over the door rang and Reed came in and met them at the counter. Dora walked around the back of the counter and greeted Iris with a hug. Dora rested her chin on the top of Iris's blonde hair. Iris gave her another squeeze before letting her go.

"I'm glad you're all here. It saved me from having to send for you. From what I can tell, every field on the valley has been ruined by the fungus. Did you two see anything different coming in?"

Dora and Petra shook their heads.

Iris reached underneath the counter and unrolled a map of the valley. "It's still June, if we act quickly, some seeds will have time to grow and there should be some harvest for the fall. I talked to Simon. He has offered to donate all the seeds he has left in stock to the people that need them. He went back to the mercantile to bag them up. We'll divide them as best we can and deliver them today. Henry said he has some extra plow heads and tools that people might need. He is making a list with Blaine of what they have and what they may need to make."

Anxiety pierced Dora's next words. "What if the fungus is based in the soil and not airborne?"

"I don't want to say this out loud, but the devastation seems too complete to be natural. Some of plants should have survived." Marina looked at each of them in turn as she spoke.

Iris ran a hand over the map. "I've been searching my books for answers, but what I am searching for is so vague. I think we are so used to everything around here being supernatural that we are starting to see monsters where there are none."

Reed ran a hand over his face. "We keep looking for monsters because it usually *is* monsters."

"None of that answers my worry about the soil," Dora said.

Petra shrugged. "We have no way of knowing except to replant and try. What would we do if it was the soil?"

No one had an answer to that.

Dora's finger traced the outline of the valley on the map. Symbols of houses and surnames marked the areas where each family had dug in roots. All of them needed help now. "Marina and Thomas can make the deliveries in town. Petra and I will take the surrounding areas. If Marina finishes early, she can help us finish."

Marina shook her head. "People might need food to eat in the meantime. I should go hunting while Thomas and Iris make deliveries."

Reed nodded. "That's a good idea, but we'll need more than meat."

"I can go foraging after I make deliveries. I know where to find some early berries and mushrooms." Dora started making a list of the things she could find and where they were likely to be in the valley.

Reed leaned against the counter. "Most people still have a bit leftover from the winter, but I want those making deliveries to ask and make sure all the families have enough for now."

The bell rang and Henry walked in and came around behind the counter. Dora made room for him beside Iris and he slid into the space she provided. He handed Iris a piece of paper.

"Here is the list. It's not much, but I can make what we need fairly quickly." His voice was almost too quiet to hear in the noise of the room.

Iris pulled paper from underneath the counter and copied the list onto three other sheets. She gave them out to the harpies, keeping the original for herself.

Dora tapped the southern end of the valley on the map. "I'll take this area: Miller, Walsh, Stewart, Eisler, and Renault. Petra, you have Neal, Mylonis, Johnson, and Kalakos. Marina, since you will be closer in town, you can go check on Pearl and the Gerlichs while you are hunting."

Reed laid his hands flat on the counter. "We all have jobs today. Tomorrow, let's reassess where we are most needed. I suspect they'll be families who need some help planting."

"Wait," Dora stopped them as they all started moving to leave. "Don't forget to ask if they've had any livestock killed by what looks like wolves or bears."

Dora could feel Iris's gaze boring into her. "What're you thinking?" Iris asked.

Dora licked her lips. If she gave all the worries floating in her mind a voice, they would manifest into something tangible. Of course, tangible things could be killed. "I think the unexplained kill at James and Petra's is related to the fungus. I think something else is going on."

"How are the two related?" Petra asked.

There was a knot at the base of her spine. It hadn't gone away since she had pulled the first plant from her garden. The anxiety had only tightened its grip. "I don't know. I just have a feeling we are missing something. It could all be natural and unrelated, but when have we ever been that lucky?"

Reed jammed his hat on his head. "Never."

Iris nodded. "I'll stay here and do some reading. Someone has to stay anyway in case people come by and need something. It might as well be me."

Dora left with the others to make her circuit of the valley. Even in her harpy form, when she was free and felt all the power she possessed running through her blood, the knot of worry remained.

CHAPTER 10

Three days of hard labor followed. The rising sun touched the people of the valley already bent over plows and the weight of bags of seedlings strapped to their backs. The sun watched them all day as they worked steadily, knowing that the only thing that stood between the people of the valley and a hungry winter were these new plants with barely enough time to grow. If one family finished their fields, they traveled to the next farm and helped their neighbors finish. Marina and Nina traveled from farm to farm, where Nina would use the power of Demeter in her veins to call to the earth and nourish the seeds there.

Saturday came and the mood in the yard behind the depot was muted. The exhaustion of the adults, however, had absolutely no effect over the children. Dora sat on a bench and watched woefully as Thomas, Jonah, Stephen, and Nina played tag with the younger kids. Lee had cleared Thomas for normal activity the day before, and he was reveling in his regained freedom. Their energy did nothing except highlight the aches and pains plaguing her.

Marina sat down next to Dora and groaned. "Styx, this farming business is much less fun than killing things. I never want to see a clod of dirt or a plow again for as long as I live."

Dora stretched her legs. "Agreed. Thank the gods that is done. I don't mind my own small garden, but I hope I've planted my last full field in my lifetime."

Reed came over carrying three mugs. He handed one to Dora and settled in next to Marina. Before he could hand Marina her drink, she leaned into him and kissed him long and hard. Reed nearly spilled the contents of the mugs as he tried to keep his hands steady. Dora laughed as some of the ale spilled despite Reed's attempts.

Marina broke the kiss, took a mug from Reed, and took a deep pull from the contents.

"Not that I'm complaining, but next time you could wait till my hands are empty so I can grab onto you proper." Reed sipped his ale and peered at his wife. "What was that for anyway?"

Marina saluted Reed with her mug. "That was a thank you for not being a farmer."

Dora reached around Marina and clinked her mug with Reed's. "That's a thank you for taking her at all."

"Well, you're both welcome. Glad to be of service."

Dora winked at Reed. "I won't kiss you like that, though."

Marina straightened and flashed her teeth. "By Styx, you will not."

Dora shoved Marina. "Simmer down. He's all yours."

"Lord, help me," Reed said.

Marina laughed, full throated, and some of the tension in Dora's shoulders rolled out of her skin. Marina jabbed her back. "Good, I'm not in the mood to fight today. I'm too damn tired."

Dora leaned back and closed her eyes. The sound of the children running around, of Reed and Marina talking, and snippets of other conversations buzzed around her. This was what she had needed all week. *All will be well now*, she thought. The plants would grow and life would go on.

None of the sounds around her changed, but something in the clearing shifted. Dora opened her eyes and looked around. Lee hovered on the edge of the yard with a large loaf of bread in his hands. Everyone else was wrapped in their own conversations and tasks. No one had noticed him yet. His body was still and he was looking at Dora with an intensity she could not name. He blinked and the look disappeared.

"Lee, I'm glad you came." Iris walked over to him and the rest of their conversation was lost in the general noise of the clearing.

The cacophony of kids ran a circuit through the yard. Ellie and Aldara were flying around and trying to catch the other kids. Dora had to duck as Ellie made a dive for Thomas. The older boy had dodged around the edge of the table where Dora was sitting, placing her in the line of fire. Iris brought the loaf of bread over to the table where Dora, Marina, and Reed were sitting. Iris smoothed her hands down her skirt and hovered in front of Dora. Lee joined Henry by the fire.

Reed stood. "I'd better offer Doc a drink if he has to keep company with our lot tonight."

At his words, Ellie swooped down from the tree above them, grabbed his hat off his head, and flew off screeching. Reed smoothed his hair down as if that was the most ordinary thing in the world, tipped an invisible hat to the three women he left behind, and went to join the men. Marina scooted over on the bench to create an opening between Dora and herself.

Iris took up the vacated space. "I hope you don't mind that I invited Doc to dinner. He's usually alone in the evenings."

Dora allowed herself to feel the fluttering of her awareness for a moment before shoving it down where it belonged. "You don't need my permission. It's nice of you to think of him. It doesn't matter to me one way or the other."

Marina snorted and took a drink. Iris elbowed Marina, and her drink sloshed close to the rim. "Watch it there. Almost made me spill my drink."

Iris fixed Marina with a glare that made the harpy squirm. "Watch the nonverbal comments, my bird. You aren't helping."

Dora took a sip of her own ale. "She is rarely helpful."

"Enough." Iris turned back to Dora. "You spend a lot of time with him. I thought it was time we included him in a Saturday dinner."

Dora tightened her grip on the tin mug in her hand. "I said it's fine. Why does it matter what I think about Lee being here?"

Marina opened her mouth to say something and then snapped her jaw closed so hard Dora heard her teeth crash together. Iris said nothing and the three sat in silence. Dora felt needled, and anger rolled around in her like a building storm.

Lee was not an option for her and this was exactly why. Every time the subject came up, her emotions were too close to the surface. She managed to keep herself in check when it was just her and Lee together working because she had the distraction of their work and she didn't have Iris and Marina henpecking her. She knew Iris was hoping she would settle soon, but she had no intention of settling in like her sisters. There was no controlling emotions that large once she gave them free reign. Having control was better than losing control. Dora didn't want to turn into the monster she knew she could be.

Dora stood up and shook out her skirts. "Excuse me. I'm going to go see if I can help Claire in the kitchen."

Dora went through the back door of the depot and leaned on the door once she closed it. Soon she would have to find a way to have a daughter. She thought of Selene and Ellie and her heart sank. She could not leave them without a third harpy. The original harpies had lost Podarge, and the wound from when they were diminished from four to three had still not healed. The thought of losing one of her sisters sent an ache through her. She simply needed to figure out how she would accomplish the task. One thing she knew for certain: it would not involve Lee Williams.

Dora helped Claire carry down plates, forks, and knives. They stacked them on the table where Iris and Marina were still sitting. Iris looked up into the sky and Dora followed her line of sight. Petra and Selene landed in the clearing. Selene took off again after the other kids. Petra's face was pinched.

"What's wrong?" Dora asked.

Petra changed into her mortal form and rubbed her hands over her arms. "Marina, I need a drink." Marina bent over and pulled a flask out of her boot and handed it to Petra, who took a long drink before answering. "That child talked my ear off the entire time."

"That's not what's wrong," Iris said.

"No, but she did distract me during the flight, which itself is a blessing. Some of our cows are dead." Petra took another sip from the flask and handed it back to Marina.

"Another animal attack?" Dora took a step closer to Petra.

Petra shook her head. "Some sickness. James said he's never seen anything like it. Three of the cows got black spots on their noses. They were dead within two days."

Dora could feel her harpy rising, wanting to fight this enemy even though teeth and claws would do nothing against this threat. Dora cleared her throat. "Any other signs of sickness?" she asked.

Petra shook her head. The men joined them. Reed handed a mug to Petra, who took it with thanks.

Henry went to stand beside Iris. "This looks like a serious conversation."

Iris leaned into him. "Some of the cows on the farm died of a sickness."

"Has it spread to other parts of the herd?" Reed ran a hand down Marina's back and she leaned into the touch.

Dora watched as the couples took comfort from each other. She stood still, on the opposite side of the circle from Lee. She met his eyes then looked back at Petra.

Petra sighed. "Yes. As soon as James saw that the three cows were sick he quarantined them, but this morning two other cows had spots on their noses. The Mylonis families keep some cattle and they are one of our nearest neighbors. I went to check and see if they had any cows affected. That's why I'm late and why James isn't here. He wanted to stay on the farm, though I told him it would do little good."

Petra took a sip of her ale and continued. "I talked to Nicolas Mylonis. He said they lost a goat yesterday and today two of their cows were sick."

"This string of luck is starting to wear on my nerves." Reed frowned and pinched the bridge of his nose.

The knot at the base of Dora's spine dug in with long-fingered claws. "I don't think it's bad luck. I think this is related to the problems we've had with our plants."

All eyes around the circle swiveled to her. Iris crossed her arms. "I don't think they're related. Something that kills plants should have no effect on animals and vice versa."

Dora nodded. "Normally, I would agree, but when does normal ever apply to Turning Creek? Plants and animals dying of a mysterious black-spotted plague? Something about all of this has been worrying me for days. I feel like we're missing something vital. I have a gut feeling they're connected."

"A sickness that affects plants does not normally affect animals. Their physiology is too different." Lee tapped a finger against his thigh as he spoke.

Dora struggled to put into words the anxiety she felt. "I don't think they are necessarily the same thing, just that they are related."

Lee nodded. "That would be more likely, though how likely, I'm not sure. I trust your instincts, though."

Iris shook her head. "I have been looking for mention of either of these things in my books and I have found nothing. If any of you has a spare moment, I could use another set of eyes."

"We should do a circuit tomorrow, see if anyone else has livestock affected," Marina said.

"I'm not sure what the point of that would be," Petra said. "Once the animal is sick, there's nothing you can do."

Reed shifted. "We still need to know who is going to need help. If families have both their crops and their livestock gone, we're going to have a lot of hungry bellies come winter."

"There'll be hungry people before winter if that happens." Henry tightened his grip on Iris.

Petra shook herself. "I'm sorry to be the bearer of more bad news and I'm sorry for ruining Saturday dinner."

Iris made a tsking noise. "Dinner is not ruined, but we should eat soon."

Children were wrangled and served so the noise level in the clearing was drastically reduced as the youngsters shoved food into their faces. Dora had offered to carve the meat as people brought their plates over, so she was the last to put meat on her plate and find a seat. The remaining place at the table was between Henry and Lee. Dora hesitated, then squared her shoulders and sat.

She concentrated on eating and listening to the conversation around her. She felt it in her core every time Lee shifted to eat or when he inclined his head to listen to a conversation. She was more aware of him like this, up close and surrounded by people, than when they were alone and she maintained her distance. Dora tried to concentrate on eating. Halfway through her mashed potatoes, Lee turned his head in her direction.

"It's quite an honor to be asked to join you tonight."

"I hope you're enjoying yourself. This has been a tame dinner so far. There haven't been any fights or heated arguments."

Lee smiled and his smoke-colored eyes warmed. "Wonderful. I have something to look forward to then."

The full force of his smile slammed into her gut, and Dora turned her attention back towards her potatoes. It was like his smile had lit something in her and now her left side, which was unavoidably flush with Lee, tingled and burned. She allowed the sensation to lick at her skin and weave through her as the minutes passed. She danced on the edge of the precipice. It was only tonight, only conversations over dinner.

"I never thought I would come west to become a farmer." Lee's voice slid over Dora. She had no protection for it. They were sitting too close, touching in too many places.

Henry leaned forward to speak around Dora. "You did a fine job with your healing hands buried the earth these past days, Doc."

Lee leaned forward as well to reply, but it also brought him closer to Dora, and she felt like the air in the space around her was becoming thinner. Every word he spoke touched her skin.

"I don't think I would like to repeat the experience. It took me a good two hours of scrubbing this evening to finally remove all the dirt from my fingernails," Lee said.

Dora cleared her throat. "With any luck, that will be the last time you ever have to play farmer. The plants should sprout and grow in the next two or three weeks. I think we may have just enough time to get a harvest in, as long as we don't get any early snows."

Reed looked down the table. "Nina, do you think you could hold off a snow storm if we got one a little early?"

Nina, all seven years of her, straightened. "I could try. I've never tried to stop a storm."

Iris frowned. "That's a lot to ask a young one."

Reed leveled his gaze at Iris. "Nina is powerful, and we've never let her have free reign. She has done beautifully these past few days, calling to the plants to grow. We might need her to try if it comes to that." Reed's face softened as he winked at Nina. The girl beamed back at him.

Lee finished the food on his plate. "That meal was lovely. Thank you for including me in your family gathering."

Petra, on the far end of the table from them, lifted her cup. "We're always dragging you into our misadventures. It's about time you got some reward for all your troubles."

"I will say one thing about living in a town ruled by harpies. Life here is never ordinary," Lee replied.

"Thank the gods," Marina said.

Dora put her right elbow at the table and pointed towards Marina. "We have to manufacture some excitement every once in a while for Marina. She gets bored."

Petra joined in. "If we don't, she spends too much time swindling everyone out of their money at cards when things are too dull. We have to keep her from becoming a permanent fixture at Vine's."

Marina shrugged. "Not my fault some people are bad at cards."

Claire spoke up. "We should invite Daniel to this dinner sometime, if we are expanding the circle occasionally."

Marina's face hardened. "He's not welcome here." Claire's face fell.

Lee stiffened. Dora felt his body tense. "You can't still be holding a grudge against him over him siding with Zeus."

Marina's fingers tightened on her fork. Dora put her hand on Lee's arm. His attention swiveled away from Marina. Surprise had replaced whatever other sentiment he had been about to speak in Marina's direction. Dora could not remember the last time she had initiated contact between them. The muscles of his arm tensed underneath her fingers and she involuntarily clenched them tighter to enjoy the movement.

"Marina likes to drag out her grudges. Besides, I think Vine is still trying to woo her good opinion with his best spirits. Marina doesn't want to give that up." Dora tightened her fingers on Lee's arm in warning, but she spoke with a lilt of laughter in her voice. Marina tolerated Daniel Vine, but she had not forgiven him for his inability to stand up to Zeus.

Marina's posture relaxed. "He does make very fine ale."

Smaller conversations filled the empty space. Lee leaned closer to Dora and dropped his voice.

"I'm sorry I hit on a point of contention. That was not my intent," he said.

Dora leaned closer to Lee and dropped her own voice. "I know. Harpies don't like to hand others forgiveness, especially when territory is involved, but Marina is really nursing this one. At this point, she's just being stubborn to be stubborn and Vine is wooing her with ale and spirits. She's not ready to let that go."

Lee's hand covered hers, and with a jolt Dora realized she had never removed her hand from his arm. His touch wove its way up her arm, past her elbow, and bloomed across her shoulders. All her intentions of keeping him at arm's length evaporated with a simple touch. This was why she kept her distance. Dora stood firmly at the maw of insanity, peering into it curiously and unable to move away.

"I've spent enough time with at least one harpy to know how stubborn they can be," Lee said.

Dora gathered the threads of her thoughts. "Sometimes I wonder why you allow me to help you so often. I don't have any formal training."

Lee's eyebrows rose into his hairline. "Healing sick people is not just training, though I would argue you have a fair amount of that at this point, it's how you put what knowledge you have into practice. You have empathy, a will to help others, and more knowledge about plants and herbs than I do. They don't teach herbalism in medical school."

"I've replanted what I could in my garden. I should be able to have some for harvest, should we need them, in a few weeks." Dora winced at her own clumsy attempt to move the subject away from herself.

She had moved closer to him as they talked and now they were inches apart. Dora's senses were overwhelmed at how close she had allowed him to come. Whether he had intended to or not, Lee had mesmerized her as easily as a snake charmer, and like the snake, she was completely fixated.

Marina laughed loudly and Dora jerked back to herself. She leaned away from Lee and pulled her arm back and laid it on her lap. It was cold where his hand had been, and Dora rubbed it. Lee's eyes followed her movements, but he didn't reach out to her or close the distance between them again.

Dora stood. "I'll help clear the table."

Petra clapped her hands together. "Grab a bucket and come with me, young ones. We're going to need some water from the creek. Doc, you come with us." Petra, Reed, and Lee led the children into the woods. Even after they were out of sight, Dora could hear the children talking.

She began stacking dishes. Her hands trembled slightly, but she did not think anyone else noticed. When all the dishes were passed to the center of the table, everyone else rose from their seats. Marina and Claire gathered what was left of the food and took it inside. Henry brought over a tub they kept outside and filled it with the kettle of water that had been sitting by the fire during the meal.

"I'll help you wash," Iris said.

Henry put the empty kettle down on the table. "Go find another task. I'll help Dora."

"Why?" Iris crossed her arms over her chest.

"Because you want to talk to her about Doc and you should leave it alone," he replied.

Heat and annoyance flushed Dora's face. Her conversation with Lee had been in the midst of everyone. Of course, Iris was going to want to talk to her about it and encourage her. That was the last thing Dora wanted.

"That's not the only thing we would've talked about," Iris huffed.

"It's not up for discussion." Dora placed her hands palm down on the table to keep from clenching them in anger, at herself.

Iris sighed then turned around and went inside.

The bucket bearers returned singing a nonsensical song about a mermaid. Dora took the water they brought and got to work. Henry took the dishes she washed, rinsed them, dried them, and stacked them on the far side of the table. Dora listened to the sounds of the conversations by the fire. Lee, Reed, and Marina were telling stories to the children. Dora's entire body was tuned to listen for Lee's voice when it rose above the rest. Even though her hands were busy and her back was turned, she knew exactly where he was sitting.

Henry's voice was low when he spoke, each word measured. "Iris worries about you."

Dora's hands paused then resumed scrubbing the plate she was holding. "I know it's her calling, but she shouldn't. I'm fine."

"I know you will be, but she has to fret until it is true," Henry said.

"You don't think I'm happy now?"

Henry finished drying the plate in his hands and laid it on the stack in front of him. He turned to face her and took a breath. "No."

"But I will be in the future?"

He gave her a half smile. "I think you'll figure out whatever it is that has you in knots before too long and then yes, you will be happy." He finished the smile then and the implicit hope in the gesture was unleashed inside Dora.

Dora handed him the last plate and started working on the forks. "You kicked Iris off this job to do some needling of your own, blacksmith." Dora nudged him with her shoulder.

Henry chuckled. "Guilty, but you've not yet been needled by me, and I thought maybe a different voice with a similar message might work better tonight."

Dora laughed. "I concede this round. You both have me outmaneuvered." She paused for a moment, and then chose to speak her truth to Henry. "I may not find happiness in the direction Iris is pushing me."

Henry put his arm around Dora's shoulder and squeezed. She leaned into the comfort he offered. "I think you're moving in that direction all on your own."

He was right. Dora turned her head to the side enough so that she could see Lee out of the corner of her eye. He was watching her and talking to Claire. She needed to keep her distance from Lee, needed to be able to contain the wildest parts of herself. Dora needed that control, but she wanted to let all of it go. She did not know if she could face the consequences. It was the consequences that had her running scared.

Dora closed her eyes and saw her mother, covered in the blood of the family she had killed, insanity shining from her eyes. Her mother had allowed every emotion free reign, regardless of the consequences. In the end, Dora had been as savage as her mother had ever been. Dora opened her eyes, expecting to see blood, but the only thing dripping from her hands was warm water. She took a deep breath. This was not Greece.

Henry's arm was still around her shoulder. He spoke quietly, his deep voice pitched only for her ears. "I don't know where you just went, but it wasn't a good place."

Dora shook herself. "I was reminding myself of the consequences of following my own whims." It was the easiest version of the truth she gave him.

Henry moved his arm from around her shoulders and nudged her back to work. "Burdens are easier to bear together."

Dora opened her mouth to reply, but she could see part of his face in the lamplight and his eyes were sad. She clamped her mouth shut and let Henry speak.

"I've seen what you do. You keep yourself apart from something that could help you bear your burdens."

Dora shook her head. "I have all of you. You help me."

"It's not the same as a partner."

"I can't control that feeling. It's too dangerous." Dora did not look at Henry.

He moved closer to her as he took utensils from her. His body was like a wall keeping their conversation from the rest of the group. "Not everything that feels wild is bad. Not everything needs to be controlled. Birds fly free and mountain laurels grow in wild places. Wild is not always dangerous. You are not always dangerous."

They finished the rest of their work in silence. Annoyance at how easily Henry touched on the very thing she struggled with daily pricked her. That feeling evaporated quickly. She remembered the look in Henry's eyes. He had spoken out of love for her and a desire to see her content, nothing more.

"Thank you. Maybe I can try less distance and see what happens."

Henry's large hand wrapped around her wrist, making her pause. "You're never alone. We are your family. Use that to ground you."

Dora nodded, unable to answer past the lump in her throat.

When the work was done, everyone gathered around the fire. Trunks from two large trees, some of the benches from the tables, and three stumps were brought over, providing plenty of seating. Normally, she would have sat on the opposite side of the fire from Lee, but tonight she was going to let a portion of her control go.

Lee sat on the ground against one of the tree trunks with his long legs crossed in front of him. There was empty space next to him and Dora claimed the open area to his right. She sat down, leaving a bare amount of space between them. She ignored the desire to see his reaction to her choice by smoothing out her skirts and tucking them around her legs, further increasing the space between them.

Marina reached behind her seat and pulled a bottle from the shadows. "I brought something for after dinner. Port."

"Where have you been hiding that?" Dora sked.

Marina pulled out the cork. "I'm not telling you my secrets."

"She kept it inside and brought it out after they put the food away," Reed said.

Marina glared at him. "Styx, you take away all my fun. You're dead to me."

Reed took the bottle from her and poured the glasses. "Your threats are meaningless to me, Sparrow." Marina tried to look offended, but she broke her scowl with a wink.

Dora came to her rescue. "Harpies are scary monsters, Reed."

Everyone laughed. It was a joke they had told a thousand times, made more amusing by the fact that harpies were the scariest of the things that lurked the night over Turning Creek. They were monsters who also loved and laughed beside a fire, sharing a bottle of port. The duality of their existence was never far from Dora's mind. She did not want to ponder it overlong tonight, though.

The bottle of port was consumed and the fire eventually burned down.

Claire rose, stretching. "It's time for me to go. I'll get the boys from inside and check on the girls."

Reed stood and held a hand down to Marina, who laughed at him and batted it away as she stood. "Grab Ellie too and we'll walk you home," he said.

Petra yawned. "Can Selene and I stay here tonight? I don't feel like carrying her all the way back home, and James is busy with the cows."

Iris put an arm around Petra's shoulders. "Of course, my bird."

They went in, leaving only Henry, Lee, and Dora still around the fire. There was a pleasant silence between the three of them, broken by the crackling fire and the leaves rattling in the aspens.

The back door of the depot opened, spilling light into the yard. Iris's head poked out of the doorway. "Henry, can you come help with the girls while Petra and I make up their beds?"

Henry's mouth tipped up in a smile. "Coming." He turned to Lee and Dora. "Looks like I've been summoned. Good night."

Dora smoothed her skirt with her hands, acutely aware that she was alone with Lee. The fire was a gentle heat on her face. Her left side, closest to him, tingled with a flame much hotter. She considered leaving. She had played with this long enough tonight when nothing safe could come of it.

Lee shifted his body slightly so that he was angled towards her. "Thank you for allowing me the pleasure of the evening."

Dora mirrored his movements so that they were almost facing each other. "It was Iris's doing."

Lee waved a hand around the circle and Dora watched as the firelight played over his long, strong hands. "I hadn't realized how much I had missed this—family gatherings. I had some cousins from my mother's side in Philadelphia, and we would come together for holidays and things. We weren't especially close, but family is family."

Dora looked around the now-empty circle and remembered where each person had sat. "I never thought I'd have such a thing."

Lee's gaze intensified on her. "You're more relaxed here, surrounded by them."

More relaxed than what? Dora thought. But she knew. Around Lee, she was always on the edge of something that felt like insanity. Even now, she could feel it clawing around, wanting to be free. It was the wildness she feared. She fought the urge to move away from him even as she resisted another urge to move closer.

Dora shrugged. "I can be myself here."

Lee looked away from her. Dora knew her words had hurt him, and she wanted to reach out and reassure him. She folded her hands in her lap and twisted them together.

"I'm sorry," she said. "That sounded like I don't care for you at all."

Lee's gaze swiveled back to her, his eyes almost black in the orange glow of the fire. "Do you care for me?"

The question was so unexpected she almost blurted out the truth. Dora felt like the fire had eaten up all the air in the space they occupied, and her lungs forgot to function. Lies, truth, and all the excuses she could give swirled through her mind in a jumble. They moved so fast she couldn't grab ahold of any of them, and Lee sat there, watching her as she untangled from the inside out.

Dora dug the crescents of her fingernails into her palms. Her human fingers were not sharp enough and she shifted the ends of her fingers into claws. They bit into her flesh and the pain jerked her back to the truth that kept her safe. It was the ghost of truth, but she grasped it and held on.

"We've known each other for a long time." The words were not the ones clamoring to be said, but they were the ones she allowed out of her mouth.

Dora watched as the words she chose disappointed him. His shoulders twitched, as if he would have slumped, but he righted himself quickly. If she had not been watching him closely, she would have thought he was just rolling his shoulders after sitting for a long time.

Lee stood and brushed off his pants with quick movements. Frustration was etched in his features. "I think it's time for me to go home."

Dora did not get up. She tilted her neck to look up at him. Her own disappointment flared along with anger at her inability to make him happy. She tried to make amends. "Do you want company on the walk home?"

He hesitated, then shook his head. "No. I need to clear my head. The walk home will do me some good. Good night, Dora."

She watched him go. His absence was palpable, and she was angry at herself for ruining what had been a wonderful evening. Her claws lengthened and bit further into her hands as she clenched them into fists. The blood dripped onto her skirt and the copper tang of it drifted up to her nose.

It did not matter if she had feelings for Lee. Those feelings held a wildness she had kept at bay since she had fled Greece. She must keep her wildness contained at all cost. She trembled with the effort, and for the first time since she was a young one still under her mother's roof, she resented what she was. Tears pooled in her eyes and spilled over her cheeks.

The back door of the depot opened and Iris walked out. Dora turned towards Iris. She could not answer the questions Iris was sure to have. Dora released her harpy, the angry wild thing inside of her, and launched into the air. Her tears disappeared during the transformation. Her harpy form had no room for tears.

Iris called to her, but Dora flew away from her and the mess of feelings that had been burning inside her by the fire. Dora let the wind hit her face and she closed her eyes, concentrating on the sensation. She flew home, thinking only of the way the air felt on her feathers and ignoring the canyon of need and despair running through her soul.

CHAPTER 11

Animals across the valley continued to die. Cows were not the only ones affected by the strange sickness. Many chickens, goats, sheep, and rabbits developed spots on their noses and faces and then died within a day. So far, only domestic animals seemed to be affected, and this raised warning bells for them all.

Dora was concerned the illness would spread to the wildlife, so she was walking a circuit around her property, looking for dead animals or other signs that any animals in the area were suffering from whatever disease was plaguing the valley. It was early morning and the sun was a gentle glow through the trees. She walked through a copse of cedar and pine, their fresh scent tickling her nose. The ground underneath the thick trees was soft beneath her feet, and her footsteps made no sound in the morning of the forest.

By the time she emerged from the trees and stood in front of her own cabin, Dora was certain no wildlife were dying of the sickness. Being alone in the woods was the most peace she had found in recent weeks. There was hope and peace to be had. She simply needed to remember to grasp some for herself.

It had been two weeks since the valley had replanted every garden and field. Two weeks in which the seeds and seedlings had flourished in the summer weather and nourishing sunshine. Dora opened the door of her cabin and grabbed one of the baskets sitting on the floor there. She wanted to check on the progress of her new herbs and pull some weeds before the sun grew too hot. She rounded the corner, a smile on her lips and the peace of the morning flowing around her.

Dora's steps faltered when she saw the garden. Seedlings that had been vibrant and green yesterday were today shriveled and black. The smell of rot rose from the dirt, and all the hope she had acquired from the morning was replaced with rage. Dora threw the basket into the ruined garden and screamed in frustration. Fury burned in her blood. She was tired of trying and failing and letting things beyond her control take over.

Dora picked up the basket and brushed off the dirt, then went to check the youngest seedlings she still had in the greenhouse. As soon as she opened the door, she knew what she would find. The smell of decay hung in the warm air of the small greenhouse. She considered pulling up all the seedlings, but they were too small. It was better to leave them where they were for now. Dora turned around, went back to the house to put away the basket, and flew into town.

Her fury rode with her on the wing and did not abate before she reached town. She landed on the doorstep of the depot, changed into her mortal form, and went inside with a burst of wind at her back. She could feel her power leaking from her as wind and anger, but she was tired of controlling it.

Iris's eyes were lined and opened wide when she saw Dora. "My bird, what's wrong?"

"My seedlings are dead. Is my garden the only one?" Dora fought to get her voice under control. They were just plants.

Iris shook her head. "No, everyone's plants are dead. I was going to send you a note this morning. All that work. Gone."

Dora sat down on a stool at the counter, and the anger deflated, leaving her empty. "It's going to be a hard winter. Perhaps we can have Simon order extra supplies."

"There's something else." Iris pulled a newspaper from the corner of the counter and pointed to the front page. It was the *Rocky Mountain News Weekly* from Denver. "There's a food shortage in the entire state."

Dora looked up from the headline—"Shelves Empty Across the West"—and asked, "Has the fungus spread outside the valley?"

Iris ran her finger to the second paragraph. "The Union and Confederate armies are fighting over the roads and blocking supplies. Routes to the south have been disrupted by some skirmishes with local tribes and everything to the east is blocked by the war. What little food is left in the cities in the central and northern parts of the state are being sent to the troops fighting the natives in the south."

"Seems like a waste of time to be messing with the tribes now when there is a war in the east." Dora felt empty where the rage had burned so hot before. She needed to be able to do something.

The bell above the door rang and Marina, Simon, Reed, and Lee walked into the depot. Dora squirmed in her seat. She had not seen much of Lee since they had lingered by the fire a week ago. She had made sure not to be alone with him. She felt his addition to the room like a physical blow, and she struggled to maintain her composure. As the days passed, it was becoming harder and harder to control her feelings and herself. Dora quaked as she thought of what she might become if she let her harpy have true reign.

She needed a few moments alone to create some space for herself. "I'll go make a pot of tea since I get the feeling this is going to be a serious conversation." She stood and smoothed out her skirts. When she got to the top of the stairs, she gripped the railing and took a deep breath.

Dora put on the water and made tea by rote while she thought. She had known Lee since he came to town years ago. She had been working with him for almost as long. Dora ran a hand over her hair and pulled her braid over her shoulder. The strawberry blonde was woven with a silvery grey. It had started turning after she had known Lee for about a year. She had known before then, but her grey hair had confirmed her suspicions. Confirmed them and convinced her she needed to keep her feelings for him buried at all costs.

What bothered her the most about her feelings was why they were erupting now. She had been struggling these past weeks to keep her harpy in check, to keep herself feeling like she was far away from the precipice she feared. Lately, it seemed like all she did was dance on the edge.

Dora considered the season and counted the months. Realization dawned and her hands rattled the teacups she was placing on the tray. This one of the rare times she was fertile and could conceive a daughter. Harpies did not mature or become fertile at the same rate as mortals, or with the same cycles. They were only able to conceive for three months of every year, and she was running out of years. Her inability to control her own feelings for Lee had more to do with hormones than her lack of restraint over her emotions.

Dora wanted to laugh at the ridiculousness of it. All she really needed to do was find someone to father her daughter and all this turmoil between her and Lee would end. She could go back to being his partner and helping people without the struggle of reigning in her own wayward emotions. The problem was that there was no one she would consider for the job in Turning Creek except Lee. She would have to look outside of her valley for a father for her daughter. If things quieted down here, she could even stay away until her daughter was born and then return to pick up her life.

Her decision made, or at least begun, Dora took the tray with the tea things downstairs. She went around to the back of the counter and placed the tray down. She smiled at Lee when she handed him a cup of tea. She could not read his shuttered expression.

Reed waved away her offer of tea. "It seems there's not one plot of land that's been spared. Everyone's lost all their crops and over half of every herd they own. Do we have any idea what is the cause?"

Iris's shoulders hunched. "I've looked in almost all my books. I haven't been able to find a thing about either the plant fungus or animals dying."

Dora tapped a finger on the counter. "Are you looking for them separately or together?"

Iris tilted her head in thought. "Both, though I couldn't think of a way they would both come from the same source."

Reed's gaze sharpened. "Could it be a witch? There were witches in ancient Greece, right?"

"Medea," Lee said. The counter was between them, but her eyes locked with his and she forgot where she was for a moment. Then she blinked and the rest of the room came back into focus. The quicker she took care of her own raging hormones, the better.

Iris nodded. "A Remnant of Medea would be powerful enough to do something like this. Prudence Gerlich is of her line. We could ask her what she knows. She might be able to point us in another direction."

Reed placed both palms down on the counter. "That solves one problem, but we've got a more immediate one. We've a valley of people that are going to be awfully hungry come winter if we don't make a plan now."

Dora turned to Simon, who had been uncharacteristically silent. "Simon, can we order extra dry goods and other supplies for the rest of the summer and winter?"

Simon took a deep breath. "Normally, I would say yes, it wouldn't be a problem, but the supply chains have been interrupted. I know the war has barely touched us here, but it's bad in the east. The wars have been going on three years now and men who are fighting aren't farming. Both armies are commandeering everything they can get their hands on, burning fields they don't take, and destroying what supply routes they can. There's nothing to order. My shelves are already bare."

Marina pointed east. "Could we go over to one of the larger towns and see if they've had better luck getting supplies?"

A pinched feeling formed between Dora's eyes. "The problem with that plan is that most of the larger towns to the east are also mining towns. Supplies there will cost more than we are willing to pay on a good day."

Iris's voice was soft. "How much is too much to pay to keep our town from starving?"

Her question hung in the air and around their necks.

Simon broke the awkward moment. "It's too bad California is separated from us by an entire mountain range and a desert. They probably have food to spare, being so far from the mess back east."

"I'll ride to Leadville and see what they have," Marina said.

Reed turned to face Marina. "You can't go alone."

"Hells, I can," Marina replied.

Reed made a chopping motion with his hand. "A woman traveling alone? That's not suspicious or asking for trouble."

Marina lifted her chin. "I don't mind a little trouble."

"That's what worries me." Reed ran a hand over his face. "I don't feel like I can go. Someone has to stay here to keep the peace. People are going to start being hungry, and hungry people don't always make the best decisions."

A plan started to form in Dora's mind. This might be the opportunity she needed. "I'll go." All eyes swiveled towards her.

Lee's fingers tapped against the counter. "Marina could travel in an official capacity as deputy and Dora could go with her. It's unconventional, two women traveling alone, but a mining town like Leadville might overlook it. They have their own rogues of a more mortal nature in their town."

Dora smiled brightly at him in thanks. He gave her a smile in return. "The two of us can travel faster alone. We can take some extra horses to switch out our rides on the way there, then act as pack horses on the way home," she said.

Reed looked like he was going to protest, but a hard glint entered Marina's eye and Dora knew they would win this battle.

"That is an excellent plan, Doc," Marina said before anyone else could speak up.

Dora nodded. "Simon, make a list of what you think we should get and what you think we should be willing to pay for it. I'll go talk to Henry about getting some horses from the stable. We might have some slim pickings after the sickness, but he should be able to scrape together something."

Marina rubbed her hands together. "Excellent. We can leave before dawn tomorrow."

Dora pushed away from the counter. "I'll come back here after talking to Henry."

Lee rose from his seat. "Can I walk with you? I'm headed to that end of the street."

Dora wanted to tell him no. She wanted to keep some distance between them, but she could not think of a way to refuse that would not sound rude. "Of course."

Lee held the door for her and Dora found herself breathing in as she walked past, allowing herself a moment to let the smell of soap and what was uniquely Lee fill her senses. She felt her harpy roll within her. *Perhaps this was a bad idea*, she thought. She should have made an excuse to maintain some distance.

This would be the time to move away from him, to put some distance from him before he could offer her his arm. Dora's harpy, however, was clamoring inside her to be closer, and she wanted to be closer to him. If everything went according to plan, she would be able to stop worrying about how she behaved around Lee and where that behavior could lead.

Dora reached out to him and wrapped a hand into the crook of his arm before he could offer it. Lee did not betray his surprise. Instead, he covered her hand with his, pulled her closer, and began walking.

He squeezed her hand. "I'm sorry I left the other night so abruptly. That was ill done of me."

Dora did not know what to say to his apology except to offer one of her own, and she was not quite ready for that.

Lee continued. "I haven't seen you much in the last week and I thought I may have offended you. I'm sorry. It was unfair of me to press you."

Dora stopped walking. They would have to cross the street soon to get to the blacksmith shop and stables. "Are we friends?"

Lee's mouth thinned into a line. "Why are you asking me?"

"You didn't answer my question."

Lee's body radiated tension. "You didn't answer my question the other night either."

Dora nodded. "Fair enough, but I am asking a similar question. Are we friends?"

Lee shook his head. "It's not the same question at all. I asked if you cared for me."

Dora pulled her hand out of Lee's and off his arm with a jerk. "They are the same question."

"They are not, Dora Aello. Not in the slightest."

Dora ground her teeth together. She could feel the slow trickle of anger build in her blood. Everything was always just beneath her skin with Lee. It was why she needed to take care of securing her line, so she could be in his company without tiptoeing on the edge of insanity.

"I'll answer my own question, then. We are friends, Lee Williams, and, as your friend, I'll allow you some bad manners occasionally. Hera knows, I put up with Marina. You're easier on my eyes and you certainly try my patience less." Dora crossed her arms over her chest because she was afraid she would use her finger to jab into his sternum to emphasize her point.

Lee leaned into her. His face close to hers. "I'm tired of being your damn friend, Dora."

Dora leaned away from him. "You never curse."

Lee closed the space she had created, little though it was. "Today, I'm making an exception."

Dora was sick of being crowded in, tired of controlling everything, and finished with this conversation. She dropped her arms and her walls. She allowed the power to wash over her and bring with it swift anger. She was not even sure why she was so very angry with Lee, but she was done.

Dora took a page from Marina and flashed pointed teeth at Lee while allowing the power of her anger to push out from herself. "I'm not tired of being your friend, but if you're sick of the sight of me, so be it. I was trying to be nice and offer you some honesty and all I got for my trouble was an argument. I like being your partner, but I see the feeling isn't mutual."

Most people would have moved back in the face of so much raw violence, but Lee gripped her upper arms with his hands and leaned closer. "That's not what I meant and you know it."

Dora hissed at him. Her voice was more harpy than human when she spoke. "Let. Go. Of me."

With what seemed like a great effort, Lee removed his hands from her arms. She shook her arms and balled her hands into fists. Her claws lengthened and she could feel the blood in her palms again. She could feel the rage roaring through her blood like a waterfall long denied passage.

Lee took a step back. "You'll think about this conversation later and regret your anger."

Dora allowed her harpy to show in her eyes, in her stance, and in the wind that whipped around her. "I doubt that."

Lee took another step back and Dora realized they had acquired an audience. Traffic on Main Street had ground to a halt. "When you do come to have doubts, my door is still open to you."

Lee turned around and walked north towards his office. Dora remained in place. Seething rage and the desire to tear apart everyone on the street battled in her veins. The urge to give in to it all and feel blood on her claws and flesh beneath her talons was overwhelming. She trembled with rage and the wind kicked up dust in the street around her.

Lily Hughes stood in her doorway not ten feet away from where Dora seethed. She slowly reached for her daughters, who had gone white and wide eyed at Dora's display, and pulled them into the door of their shop. Dora heard the latch click into place as Lily locked her door against Dora.

This was why she did not let her harpy have free reign. This was why she could not trust herself out in the open. Her friends feared her, and now she had broken something with Lee.

With great effort, Dora struggled to breathe in a slow rhythm until her heart was no longer pounding in her head. She would have left town except that she needed to talk to Henry. She took one step, then another, and then another and crossed the street to the blacksmith's shop. People gave her a wide berth as she made her way to her destination. She did not blame them.

Dora made it across the street without further incident. She walked past Blaine, working at the forge, and sat on the floor at the end of the bench by the back wall. Blaine did not greet her as he normally would. He kept his mouth sealed shut and sent her sideways glances the way one watched a poisonous snake in the grass you had to walk by.

Henry walked in from the back and paused when he saw her. He halted completely when he got a good look at her flushed face and elongated hands ending in claws. He put down his tools and went out of the shop. He returned a minute later with a glass of cool water from the well. He handed it to her and went back to his work.

"Blaine, why don't you take a break." It wasn't a question. Henry took over at the forge when the boy left, leaving the two of them alone with the roar of the fire and the heat from the flames.

Dora's teeth went back to their mortal shape and the rest of her anger drained away. Without Lee in front of her, it was easier to let it go. She took a gulp of the water and let its refreshing coolness wash away the last vestiges of her outburst.

"Thank you," she said.

Henry nodded and kept to his task.

"Marina and I need to borrow four horses that we can take to Leadville for supplies."

Henry stopped working then and wiped his hands off on a towel. "I got four you can use. Only have seven total left after that sickness, but you can take the sturdiest four. Anyone else going?"

Dora shook her head. "Just us two. We want to travel light."

"I'll have them ready to go for you tomorrow before first light." Henry moved to the other side of her and sat on the ground with her. "Want to talk about whatever it was that had you riled up?"

"No."

"Can I offer you some advice?"

"No."

"Well, I'm going to give it to you anyway. I was only asking to be polite. Have you considered that the thing you're most afraid of is not something to be afraid of at all?"

"You don't know what I could become." She raised her eyes to meet his. They were grey and shot with blue, and something in those eyes loosened the truth from her at last. "People die when I lose control."

Henry put a hand on her knee. "I know you, and Iris loves you. She knows you would never do anything to hurt anybody, and I trust her."

Dora stood. "Thanks for the advice, even though you're wrong. I have before. I could again."

"So you say."

Dora walked out of the forge. She was tired and she was done with people. She let her harpy roll over her and she shifted in the street. Before she took to the air, she thought she saw Lee looking out of his window watching her. Her anger boiled again. She was done with him.

CHAPTER 12

Dora waited until the night before they arrived in Leadville to tell Marina about her plan. There were many times during their week of travel that she could have brought it up, but she had let those opportunities slide by. Now they sat before their small campfire, in their own thoughts, listening to the popping of the pine as it burned. Marina was feeding the hungry flames small sticks, and Dora took a deep breath.

"I think it's time for me to have a daughter of my own."

Marina looked up from the fire. "Hells, it's about time."

Dora continued, "When we get to Leadville, I'm going to find the best candidate and spend the nights with him while we're there."

Marina stopped playing with the fire and really looked at her. "Let me repeat this to make sure I understand what idiocy just came out of your mouth. You're going to find a stranger in Leadville, proposition him, and hopefully conceive your daughter."

"That's the gist."

Marina dug around in her coat pocket and pulled out a flask. "I need a drink."

She unscrewed the lid, took a sip, and passed it around the fire to Dora. Dora took a drink and let the fire of the whiskey add to the already churning contents of her belly. She had thought, out of everyone, Marina, who danced with her violent side with ease, might be the most understanding. Dora often envied the nonchalant way Marina strode back and forth across that line.

"Is that why you wanted to come on this excursion?" Marina asked as Dora handed her the flask back.

"That was a factor, yes."

113

"There is a perfectly willing and able man in Turning Creek who would gladly do the honors. You don't have to do this in the way of our mothers." Marina took another drink and offered it to Dora again.

Dora waved the offer away. "He's not an option."

"Why the hells not?"

"My mother didn't love a man, but she did love me and it ate her up." Dora tried to remember the way her mother had cared for her and revealed her heart to her daughter during the years they had lived together, but it was all shadowed by the way it had ended. "She began to see everything as a threat to me. She was only calm around me. With everyone else, she became the worst part of herself. She couldn't control her love for me and she could control her violence even less. She became the nightmares harpies were supposed to be: a violent, relentless monster."

Marina's voice became hard. "Do you think that's what I am? A relentless monster? Do you think Reed makes me weak? Do you think James makes Petra a monster?"

"No, but I am. I'm like her, and I can feel the chaos inside, waiting. I can't let it loose again. I would lose everything. Lee makes me feel like I'm about to jump off a cliff and hit every jagged edge on the way down." Dora clenched her hands on her thighs and willed Marina to understand.

"You said 'again.' What happened to you before you came here?"

Dora took a shuddering breath. She needed to tell this story to her sister harpy and cleanse it from her soul. "You already know my mother was a tyrant, the violent despot of our island, but she loved me with a fierceness that scared me. The closer it got to the year of my majority, when I would have to leave, the more unhinged she became. She wanted me to stay, and I wanted desperately to go.

"She was forever finding fault with others. There was a tailor who made a dress she didn't like. It had the wrong lace on it or something trivial. I don't remember now. She went to the tailor's house and killed him and his family. A servant told me what was happening, but I couldn't get there in time.

"There was a witch in town. She was the sister of the tailor. She marched into my mother's throne room and cursed her and her household to die of a terrible disease. The witch spared me, she said, so I would remember and choose differently, but in the end, I didn't.

"When my mother died, I lost myself. All I could think about was that I was alone now and that I wanted revenge. My mother's blood was still on my hands. I went to the witch's house, dragged her into the street, and ripped her to shreds."

Marina let out a long breath. "Styx and fire. Dora, you were young."

"I killed her family too. There were two children. I killed all of them. I was in such a rage, I didn't even realize what I'd done until the next day." Dora's throat burned with tears and anger at herself.

"You were young, and that was the only thing you knew. You were alone."

"It was still me."

A wave of anger swept from Marina. Dora felt her own harpy rise in response, but Dora held it still. "You are not your mother," Marina said. "You're stronger than her. You're older now. We are stronger than our mothers. Together we are different. We don't have to be like them anymore."

Marina got up and closed the distance between them. She yanked on the braid, woven with grey, resting on Dora's shoulder. "This confessional aside, it's a little late for all this posturing. You already love him and the damage is done. You can't even say his name. It's Lee Williams. What do you think he's going to say when you come back to town carrying another man's child?"

Dora turned her head away. "It will be none of his business." Dora feared that revelation. She had not thought all the way through this plan of action, but it was still her best option for a future she could control, a future she could live with.

"Like hells it won't be. I'll give you the same advice I gave Petra all those years ago when she was torn up over James. You're a harpy, for Hera's sake. Act like it. Admit that you want Lee and go *take* him. You have us. We'd never let you be that person you were on the island again."

"I've made my decision."

"You're strong enough to handle the consequences of that decision, but doing this with a stranger is not the right way. Not anymore."

Dora let the dam free on her own fury. It blew from her like the wind, but Marina did not retreat. Dora let her anger show in every part of her face and voice. "You think I don't remember what I am every moment of every day? Do you think that with every beat of my heart I don't remember that it was created for bitterness and bile? I've seen what violence and pain a harpy can inflict. I've felt the blood of the innocent run through my talons and I've tasted their blood. The worst part is while I was doing it, I *liked* it. So don't tell me to act like a harpy. I'll never be that again. Ever. That is where chaotic love takes those of my line. If that means I have to be something less, settle for something less, then so be it."

Marina hardened her stance, then relaxed. Sorrow replaced the anger on her face. "Dora, real love doesn't make you weak. It fills all the cracks and makes you a better version of yourself. What your mother acted on was something else, and you were too young to have control of your harpy. Love isn't supposed to be like that."

Dora could not release her anger, not yet. "I can't take that chance."

Dora knew if she stayed, Marina's sorrowful gaze would hound her all night. She got up and left the glow of the fire. Marina did not try to stop her. She let her anger and misery roll through her and she shifted. The night air embraced her and she flew all night, the only escape she could stomach.

***

Leadville, Colorado was the closest city of substance to Turning Creek. It was a silver mining town with examples of the best and worst of the West. The influx of silver, people seeking their fortune, and people living off the hopeful made Leadville a bustling mass of humanity. Dora had passed through the town on her way west many years ago. The town had grown so much since then that she would not have recognized it as the same place if she had not known where she was. What she hadn't anticipated was how that much humanity in one teeming mountain town would press its weight down upon her.

There were people everywhere. Women in coats embroidered in silver and gold paraded down the same street where men begged in rags and prostitutes called from the window at passersby. The ladies in the windows seemed to have no gender preference as they waved and cat-called at anyone who looked like they could pay. One of them waved a handkerchief in their direction.

"You two ladies look like you need a warm bed for the night. I know where you can find one, and I can keep it warm." The woman had brassy red, natural-colored hair, and a wide welcoming smile.

Dora could feel a blush creeping up her neck. Marina laughed and waved back at the redhead. "Not tonight, ma'am. I'm here on business and happily married besides."

The redhead pouted. "Lucky man. What about you?" she asked Dora.

Dora opened her mouth, but Marina cut in. "You're not her type, but good luck to you." Marina reached into a pocket of her duster and tossed a coin up to the window the woman was hanging out of. The woman caught it in a smooth motion and she saluted the two harpies as they rode by.

In Turning Creek, Main Street was predominantly businesses, and the surrounding streets were where family houses stood. Here, there was a brick building next to a shack made of logs and scrap wood, next to a canvas tent from which emerged a mother and a large brood of well-groomed children. It was chaos.

Dora breathed through the feeling of being surrounded. "There are too many people here."

Marina turned around in her saddle to look at her with a gleam in her eye that Dora did not trust. "There's bound to be more than one place to get a drink in this town. We'll be here for more than one night. We can make the rounds."

Dora rolled her eyes, but Marina had already turned back around to navigate them through the foot traffic, wagons, and other riders on the road. "Do you know where you're going?"

Marina called over her shoulder. "Reed gave me some directions to a boardinghouse, and Simon gave me the name of the most reputable mercantile. We should go to the mercantile first then get a room."

"How does Reed know where we should stay?"

Marina's shoulders went up and down. "He's friends with the sheriff here. They keep in touch. I'm supposed to go by and let him know we're in town. I met him a couple years ago when Reed and I went to Denver."

After that, talking became harder as the streets became more crowded and more established. The buildings in this part of town were almost all painted clapboard or stone. The people looked less desperate and there were no ladies propositioning people as they rode by, but the press of humanity remained on the back of Dora's neck. They passed a brick building with an ornate sign that declared it was the First Bank of Leadville. Marina led them past that building to the one abutting it, a two-story white building with green trim. They tied their horses to a post underneath a sign that read, "King's Grocery and Dry Goods."

Dora secured her second horse. "Should one of us stay with the horses?"

Marina paused. "I hadn't thought of that. Who would steal from us?"

Dora smiled. "Someone who doesn't know any better."

They shared a smile. "Let's cross that river if we get to it," Marina said.

King's Grocery and Dry Goods had a brass bell over the door, similar to the one at the depot, but larger so the tone was lower. It rang when they went in, and a young man with black hair and features that revealed some native heritage in his family tree greeted them from behind a tidy counter.

"Good day to you, ladies. What can I help you with today?"

By previous agreement, Marina did the talking, leaving Dora to look around the shop. "My name is Marina Brant. I'm the deputy in Turning Creek, west of here. This is my friend, Dora Aello. Our town is having some trouble getting supplies. We were wondering if you'd be able to help us out."

"That's an awful long way to come for supplies. I'm Pierre King. Let me see what you need." The man's voice was friendly, and he was attractive with his dark hair and copper skin. Dora wondered if he would be a suitable candidate for what she had in mind.

"We have a list," Dora said.

Marina pulled the list out of the inside pocket of her duster and laid it on the counter when a tall woman with a loose bun and large brown eyes came from the back and stood beside Mr. King. They shared a look that said they were happily married. Dora walked away from counter to look at what the store had to offer.

There was a section of mining tools, dry goods like flour and beans, seeds for planting, farming tools, a plow, a wall of fabric that ranged from thick, coarse canvas to midnight blue silk, and a shelf of figurines made of porcelain and gold. It was an odd jumble. Even with the variety, there were gaps on the shelf, as if a few things stood where many used to crowd. Dora did not think they would be able to find supplies in the amount they were needing for Turning Creek here.

Mr. King's words confirmed Dora's suspicions. "This is a fairly extensive list. We've had our own problems getting supplies. The war has been wreaking havoc on deliveries. I can give you what I have of some things, and I know of some other places around town where I can gather items for you. It will take some time to get what I can organized, and it might be more than you're willing to pay."

Marina nodded. "We can afford it unless the price is unreasonable. We'll be in town for two days. Is that enough time?" The town had pooled money for this. They would have enough, but they had agreed they would not pay if the prices were too high. They needed the food though, and high at this point was relative.

Mr. King smiled and handed the list to his wife. "That sounds perfect. I will have everything ready to go the morning after next."

Marina shook the man's hand. "We appreciate your help. I have one more question before we leave."

Mr. King nodded and started making notes on the list. Marina continued, "Has there been any crop failure here or livestock dying? We've had some problems in our valley, and I was wondering if it had reached this far east."

Mr. King shook his head. "No, nothing like that here. Our main problems are keeping the scuffles over mines contained in the hills. Sometimes the arguments spill into town and cause problems."

"Thanks. I'm glad it hasn't come this way," Marina said.

Dora rounded the corner of an aisle of carpentry tools and found a skinny bookcase so filled with books that some were stacked sideways on top of the others. She ran a finger over the leather and cloth bindings and read their titles. Like the unusual variety in the store as a whole, the shelf held books on cooking, farming, and gardening, with penny novels on the bottom and classic literature on the top. One volume, in unmarked leather with black accents, caught her eye. She pulled it from the shelf. *Anatomy: Descriptive and Surgical* by Henry Gray was two inches thick and looked like it had never been opened. Dora thumbed through it, glancing at the black and white sketches of human bodies in various stages of dissection.

Dora closed the book and replaced it on the shelf. She had no reason to buy it. She did not want to give Lee any ideas. Besides, he was likely still fuming over their last encounter. Marina peered over her shoulder and saw the book before she took her hand off it.

"I know someone who might like that book," she said.

Marina had not mentioned Dora's confession, Lee, or Dora's plan since last night. Dora said nothing and walked past Marina. She was not going to engage in another argument. Her mind was set.

Their horses were waiting for them where they had left them. Dora untied her horse and faced away from the buildings before swinging up into the saddle. She arranged her skirts to cover her legs. She wished she would have thought to borrow some of Petra's split skirts to wear for the journey. This was the most time she had spent on a horse in her life.

Dora spoke. "Let's go get a room and board the horses. Then we can see about getting into the trouble I know you're craving. Which way do we go?" Dora pointed left then right, trying to decide between the two.

"I think about more than just getting into trouble."

"Somehow, I don't believe that's true." Dora rolled her eyes.

"We go right. The boarding house should be up this street a few blocks."

They continued along the street and stayed in the nicer part of town. The road was less crowded, less noisy. Not that Dora minded the more colorful parts, but there were more people there and she was surprised by how much the density of people bothered her. She had been in big cities before on her journey west, but she had never felt quite so boxed in. Perhaps she had lived in the open spaces for too long to feel comfortable around civilization any longer.

"Does being in a city with this many people bother you?" she asked Marina.

Marina stopped in front of a three-story blue building with jaunty yellow shutters and dismounted. "You mean the feeling that all these people are a lodestone around my neck dragging me toward the River Styx to drown a slow, wet death?"

Dora dismounted. "I would probably not use those exact words, but yes, that is what I mean. I'm glad I'm not the only one."

Marina leaned forward as she opened the door and said under her breath. "I don't think harpies were meant for city living. We're not exactly civilized society."

"On most days, I would say that was a good thing."

"Is today most days?"

"It's too early yet to tell." Dora smiled as innocently as she could, and Marina laughed at her.

There was a man behind a counter just inside the door. To their right was a room with tables for eating and to the left was a shabby, but clean, sitting area.

Marina nodded to the man. "We're looking for a room for two nights and a place for our horses where they can be fed and watered."

The man bobbed his head. "We have some rooms available. Some with more than one bed, if you would prefer, and a nice stable out back for the horses with a lad who cares for them."

Marina turned and raised a questioning eyebrow at Dora. Dora held up two fingers. Marina turned back towards the man. "One room, two beds it is."

"Very good. If you'll just bring your horses around the side, I'll have Ben meet you there. I'll meet you at the back door by the stables when you're done."

They handed off their horses to a round-faced boy of twelve and went inside. The room they were given was sparse, holding only two skinny beds, a washstand, and a single chair. There was not a speck of dust or dirt anywhere. Dora dropped her saddle bags in a corner and flopped down on the nearest bed. She groaned in pleasure at feeling something soft beneath her back after many nights of sleeping on the ground.

"Seventy-one is too old to be sleeping on the ground and riding all day in the saddle." Dora snuggled into the mattress.

"Don't get too comfy. The evening is young, and I want to go exploring." Marina sat on her own bed with a sigh. "Of course, this does feel nice." Marina bounced on the bed.

Dora laughed at her. "We're easily swayed by comforts."

"If only someone would bring me whiskey in bed. Now that would be a good way to spend an evening." Marina flopped the rest of the way down on her bed.

"I would pass on the whiskey, but I would love a warm cup of tea." Dora sat up. "Come. I'm hungry. Let's change out of these clothes, get cleaned up, and see if we can't find some trouble for you."

Marina lay for a minute more before getting to her feet. "Good idea. We can stop by the sheriff's office and invite him out for dinner. Kill two hellhounds with one stone."

"I don't think a hound of hell can be killed with stones."

"Probably not, but I always thought killing two birds with one stone was a poor turn of phrase. Birds are not great eating."

"I agree. Birds are too small. Not enough meat. A hellhound, though. That would be big enough, but probably too gamey for dinner. It would be a great hunt, though, don't you think?" Dora's blood beat through her just thinking about it.

"It would be adventuresome. I'd take that challenge."

They looked at each other and laughed.

Dora started unbuttoning her shirt and poured water into the basin on the washstand to wipe some of the grime of the road from her body. A dip in a stream would have been preferable, but this would have to do.

"Get dressed," Dora said, "We might find a hellhound yet."

CHAPTER 13

Dinner with Sheriff Harding and his wife was pleasant, but they did not linger when it was over.

As they walked out of the nicer part of town and back down the road where they had been propositioned by the women earlier, Dora said, "You made some very polite excuses about us being tired to Sheriff Harding about why we did not want to stay for drinks. I was surprised you didn't just tell him the truth."

"I was tempted, but Reed told me that Sheriff Harding was an old-fashioned sort, and I promised to behave out of character for me as a courtesy to my husband and his reputation." Marina's eyes never stopped moving over the people walking the street in the deepening darkness. The sun had already dipped below the peaks surrounding Leadville.

Dora stopped walking and shook her head in an exaggerated fashion.

Marina realized Dora was no longer keeping pace with her and she stopped. "What?"

Dora started walking again and caught up with Marina, a sly grin on her face. "That is very un-harpy of you. Didn't you just remind me yesterday that I needed to be more of a harpy? Here you are, being nice because your mate asked it of you."

Marina's eyes narrowed and Dora thought she might have crossed a line that would get her into a brawl in the street. Then Marina laughed and said, "I suppose that means I'm forgiven."

Marina's laughter faded. "About that other thing—"

"I don't want to talk about that again."

"It's in the past, Dora. You're different now. You have more control. Don't make a decision about your mate based on something that happened thirty years ago."

"I understand where your advice is coming from, but I need to go my own way."

"I think you're being an idiot."

"Coming from one, I don't think that's much of a problem." Dora flashed a toothy grin at Marina and they both laughed loudly, drawing looks from other pedestrians.

Marina linked her arm with Dora's and they walked down the street in silence. Though it was nearing full dark, the streets were full of people, and lamps hung on poles on the sides of the buildings giving light to the pedestrians, of which there were many. Most people who walked by them on their side of the street gave them a wide berth. Dora curled her power out around them and felt for other sources of power. She could feel Marina doing the same. Even though there were few things that could hurt them, it would be foolish to be caught unaware.

Everyone skirting them was mortal. Dora supposed Marina looked unsettling with her usual array of weapons in full view, but she knew there was a general sense of violent power that surrounded a harpy in any form. Even a mortal unaware of the existence of Remnants knew a predator when they saw one.

One person, about a block up, moved to the other side of the street. Dora's senses honed in on a squat man and the idea of what he was formed in her mind.

Marina turned her head towards Dora. "He's not dangerous, I think," she said, and Dora nodded in agreement.

"He certainly thinks we are, though," Dora replied.

Marina tipped her hat to the man who blanched and ducked into an alley. Marina's laugh was loud.

Dora tugged her along the street. "Stop pestering people. Let's find a place to get a drink and get you off the street."

Marina pointed to a new-looking two-story building with light and music spilling out of the open door and windows. "You don't have to tell me twice."

All eyes followed them as they walked into the saloon. Some of the tables made a show of not looking, but Dora felt their eyes on her as they walked to the back of the room and sat at a table along the wall.

Dora looked around the room. Most peoples' gazes slid away when she caught them looking. "People are staring at you. Did you have to bring your sword?" Dora pointed the to pommel visible over Marina's left shoulder.

Marina returned a persistent glare from a man at the end of the bar. "The sword is here to discourage anyone from getting ideas. Besides, they're staring at you."

"Me?" Dora's eyes swept over the room again. She started when she met several pairs of eyes again before they became very interested in their drinks and cards. "I look less frightening, more like regular person than you. Why would they look at me?"

"You're wearing a dress. The only other women in here besides us are paid to be here, and men have to pay extra for one-on-one conversations." Marina waggled her eyebrows and stood. "I'm going to get us some drinks and check out the card tables on my way back."

Dora rolled her eyes. "Don't stop at the tables too long. I'm thirsty."

Dora scanned the room while Marina talked up the bartender, a surly fellow with a frown covering the entire lower half of his face. The room was lit with gas lamps held in sconces on the walls and with wooden chandeliers of candles overhead. The room smelled like stale ale, wax, and wood. The building she was sitting in could not have been more than a few months old because the smell of fresh lumber still lingered over the other odors. Dora wondered if they had put it up as soon as the snow had melted this past spring.

There were two tables of men playing cards. One table was accompanied by two women whose dresses, if they could be called that, left very little to the imagination. The other table of five men looked like more serious card players. One of them chomped on an unlit cheroot and none of them spoke. There were three other tables occupied by patrons. Two already had female companions, so Dora focused her attention on the last table, which held two men. Their clothes were clean, if worn, and more importantly, they were lacking female companions of any sort.

Marina came over with two glass mugs of dark ale. "It's not as good as Vine's, but after a long day, it'll do."

Dora clinked glasses with Marina. "May Tartarus be far from you…"

"…and may the gods look favorably upon you," Marina finished.

"I think you are developing a soft spot for Daniel Vine." Dora sipped her ale. It was malty with a hint of spice. She took a larger sip and felt herself relax until she remembered her goal for the evening. She took another sip to quell the nerves blooming in her belly.

"I don't have soft spots." Marina took a sip of her own ale and closed her eyes and sighed.

"I think you do. For a drink, or a fine sword." Dora motioned towards the sword hilt nestled between Marina's shoulder blades and partially covered by her hair

"I do have some soft spots. Reed, Ellie, and Nina."

"And the rest of us?" Dora elbowed her.

"Too late to get rid of you now." Marina elbowed her back.

Dora clinked their glasses together and took a sip.

"It feels different here in Leadville. Have you noticed?" Dora asked, keeping her eyes on the table of two men alone.

Marina licked her lips. "There are not many Remnants here."

Dora nodded and she felt a twist of memory go through her. "It's been a long time since I have been in a city this large and a longer time since I have been around this many mortals in one place."

Marina turned her body towards Dora. "When was the last time you were in a city?"

Dora felt the memory of leaving the island she had shared with her mother and the pull she had felt to go west. "When I came west, I avoided most of the cities. I flew at night and slept during the day. I did stop in Denver and then Estes Park, but I stayed on the outskirts of those areas. The island I grew up on was smaller than this city. I can feel the press of all the mortals in this one place. It's disconcerting." Dora opened up all her senses and she could feel the number of people in a way she could not in Turning Creek. It felt like a boot on her neck. It felt like something she needed to escape.

Marina laid a hand on her arm, and the spiraling of thoughts stopped. "I know what you're feeling. I felt the same way when Reed and I went to Denver a couple years ago. We won't be here long."

Dora sighed into her drink. "I don't think harpies are supposed to live in cities."

Marina smiled. "Not for long, anyway. There is some fun to be had in large cities, though. You just have to know when to leave." Marina looked around the room, and her gaze landed on the men Dora had noticed sitting alone. "See anything you like?"

"Perhaps. Those two men over there might do."

"Or one of them anyway."

"One is all it takes."

Marina snorted and drained her cup. "You are still set on this, then?"

"The harpies before us took less care than that and you know it," Dora retorted. Her anger unfurled. It was close to the surface these days.

Marina slammed her empty mug on the table, drawing the eyes of the men playing cards with the women draped over their chairs. She leaned closer and hissed, "It doesn't have to be that way anymore. Are you going to kick your daughter out of your house after her childhood has passed? Will you deny her the family we have built in Turning Creek?"

Dora's anger rolled forth from her. "Of course not."

Marina leaned farther into Dora. "Then don't do this."

Dora clenched her hand around her mug to keep herself from slamming it into Marina's face and stood. "I'm going to get another drink, and then I'm going to make some new friends. I suggest you do the same for now until we both cool off."

Dora walked to the bar fuming. She pulled her anger in and locked it down where it belonged. "Another of the dark ale, please."

She took her refilled mug and turned around. Marina had already ingratiated herself into the serious card game in the corner. Dora took a deep breath and steeled herself. She had faced hydras and a power-hungry god. She could talk to a stranger and ask him to sleep with her.

Just thinking it made her stomach sour.

She shook herself and forced her feet to move towards the two men sitting alone.

They looked up as she approached their table. "Do you mind if I join you?" Up close she could see that one of them had a very crooked nose from repeated breaks and the other man had hard brown eyes.

"Not at all," Hard Eyes said as he kicked a chair out from under the table. "My name is Alex. This is my friend, Brady."

Dora sat and questioned the merits of her plan. "My name is Dora. What brings you two here tonight?"

"I could ask the same of you, a lady all alone in a mining town." There was an underlying violence in Alex's words, and Dora's harpy came to attention at the sound.

She pushed aside her reaction, thinking her nerves were making her hear things that weren't there. "I'm not alone. I'm with my friend over there." She waved a hand towards Marina, who was waving her arms and telling a story.

Alex leaned forward and rubbed his jaw. "Two women alone. If I had a woman like you, I wouldn't let her wander around the streets at night."

Brady laughed. "That's because you'd keep her locked in a room somewhere, afraid someone would see her and want to keep her."

Dora tilted her head and wondered how this encounter had gone so wrong so fast. She laughed, more at herself than them. "Do either of you think that this is the proper way to greet and woo a lady? Nothing could compel me to spend any time alone with you."

Alex reached out and placed a large hand over her wrist and squeezed until her bones ground together. "I think you're going to do just that. If you yell, I'll break your arm before any of them get over here to help you."

The anger she had so casually boxed away scorched through her and she let it show in her eyes. She could feel her hair blowing in a breeze that was not natural, a breeze that should not be there. She could feel Marina's consciousness take heed of her anger. She flashed a smile of pointed teeth at the men.

"Do you know what my other name is? The one given to every woman of my line?"

Brady looked at her from a pale face. Alex's eyes hardened further like he was deciding if he could win this fight. Neither answered her question.

"I am called Aello, Storm Swift, and you will not win this battle if you engage in it." Dora's voice had dropped an octave. It did not have the sandpaper quality it did when she was fully transformed, but there was no denying the menace in it.

Marina leaned back in her chair and called to her across the saloon, which had gone completely still. "Everything all right over there?"

The hand on Dora's wrist squeezed harder. Alex really thought he was going to get his way. She was going to enjoy hurting this man.

"Finish your card game," she told Marina, "I'll be back shortly. I need to take care of something."

She placed her hand over Alex's hand squeezing her wrist and said, "I have something to show you out back."

"Well, now, that's a bit better." Alex stood, his expression hard.

Brady's head swiveled between Dora and Alex. "I don't think you should go, Alex."

Dora smiled and she knew it looked anything but friendly because Brady paled. Alex did not notice her expression because he wasn't looking at her face. "I think Brady might be the one with the smarts in this pairing."

Alex snorted and pointed at Brady. "You shouldn't think so hard. The lady wants me to go. I'm going to go."

She gripped his wrist and dragged him towards the back of the building. Dora could see the moment Alex realized he might be in real peril. A harpy was no shrinking flower, and a fully enraged one was stronger than many men. Marina did not get up, but Brady did, trailing behind them, wringing his hands.

Alex tried to wrench out of her grip. "Let go of me, you crazy bitch."

Dora laughed and let her claws elongate enough to pierce his skin while she pulled him along. "Oh, I am something much scarier than a mangy dog."

Dora shoved the back door open with one hand and yanked the now-struggling Alex through the doorway. As soon as the door closed behind them, Brady tried to jump her from behind. He telegraphed his intention, and Dora used her free arm to elbow him in the sternum. He dropped like a sack of flour, wheezing, tears leaking from his eyes.

Dora yanked Alex to her like a lover. The irony of their positioning was not lost on her, and she laughed. He tried to use his legs to kick hers out from under her, but she elongated her claws further and dug them deeper into the hand she held.

"What are you going to do to me?" he demanded.

Her anger, righteous and hot, burned through her, and for once she let it go. She let it burn, and the rush of it was like the first bite of custard, warm and rich. "I'm going to teach you a lesson you need to learn, you sorry excuse for a man. Usually, these kinds of situations are handled by my friend in there. She's the one with a temper, but I find I'm rather short on patience lately, and I was only looking for some friendly companionship tonight. Now I know you weren't a good choice. Unfortunately for you, I can't just let you back out into the world to unleash yourself upon a woman less able to defend herself."

Dora's voice was still low, and she could feel her pointed teeth as she talked. She knew that Alex saw them, but punishing him was more important than keeping her teeth hidden. Besides, everyone would think he was just a drunk who had pushed one too many women too far.

Brady was still laying on the ground clutching his chest. Dora wondered if she had broken something. Now she knew why his nose had been broken so often. He was a bully who talked too much.

Alex tried bravado one last time. "Is your plan to talk me to death?" His voice wavered at the end. Dora heard it and drank in his fear.

Dora laughed again, full throated and low. The rush of violence had completely gone to her head, but if this was a night to be reckless, then she would comply. "No, I will not talk you to death, you foolish mortal." As she spoke she let her harpy show in her eyes. What looked out at Alex was all predator, and he understood, finally, his true peril.

"This is not my territory," she said, "but I know people who claim this land." Sheriff Harding had been a kind man, but Dora knew that in order to hold control over a mining town like Leadville, he was also ruthless when he needed to be. "I will tell them about you, and if you ever step out of line again, if you hurt a hair on anyone's head, I will know. I will come back, and you will go to meet whatever god will claim you. Tonight, I will only remind you that it is not polite to attempt to force anyone to do something they've no wish to do."

Dora dragged a claw on her left hand down his cheek. The cut opened, and blood welled up and spilled over. The iron smell of blood filled her senses. Underneath the violent anger, a twinge of fear turned and reminded her that this was a path she had long avoided. She pushed that fear down and marked his other cheek. The cuts were deep enough to need stitches.

"You'll have some ugly marks to match your personality. Take your friend and go before I decide you should lose something you treasure more than your face."

Dora let him go. For a moment, she thought he might rebel, but she pushed out her power and put suggestion in her words. "You will not accost women or anyone else any longer."

The fight went out of him and Alex picked up Brady and they walked down the alley behind the buildings. Dora looked at her hands, still clawed at the end, and she forced them to go back to their mortal shape. She went in the back door of the saloon to get Marina.

Marina was stacking up coins and putting them into the inner pocket of her duster. "Thank you, gentleman. I see that my friend here has concluded her business, so it's time to conclude mine. Thank you for your money." She pushed some of the coins back in the center of the table. "Have a couple rounds on me, and if you ever come to Turning Creek, I'll buy you a pint of the best ale you've ever had."

Once they were outside, Marina got a hold of both of Dora's arms. "Are you hurt?"

Dora laughed and she could hear the brittle quality to it. The version of her she let loose in the alley was the version of herself she tried to keep under wraps. "I'm fine. I left my new friend some souvenirs to remind him to think twice when he speaks to people like they are his playthings."

"You finding a temporary mate went worse than even I anticipated," Marina said. "As plans go, I think this is worse than most of mine."

Dora linked their arms together and started walking. "It is the only plan I have."

Marina squeezed her wrist and Dora winced. Marina pulled up Dora's sleeve to see the dark bruise forming on Dora's arm. "That bastard. I'll beat him into the inner circle of hell." Marina jerked like she was going to turn around.

Dora pulled her back to her side and kept them walking slowly away from the saloon. "It's just a bruise. It'll be gone by tomorrow, and you know it. I scared him enough. Let him go."

"I still want to punch him a couple times."

"If you see him again while we're here, go ahead, but let's try to start this evening over. Your game looked successful."

Marina laughed. "For me, it was. Are you sure you still want to go through with this cock-eyed plan?"

Dora was anything but sure. "Yes."

Marina patted her arm. "Then we had better find you another prospect. Follow me. We'll find a place more relaxed."

The streets got rowdier as they went into the part of the town that was mostly canvas tent buildings, stalls, or outside garden areas serving food and drinks. They stopped in one of the outside gardens surrounded by a canvas tent on one side and a building made of unpainted clapboard on the other. It was enclosed by a wooden fence with a gate propped open by a large rock. In the back of the enclosure was a tent open on the side facing the garden. Under the tent, a couple was pouring beer and selling meat pastries.

"This looks promising," Dora said.

"Yes, it does." Marina went through the open gate. "Find us a place to sit. I'll get drinks."

"How come I always man the table while you get drinks?" Dora grumbled as she took the only empty table in the small beer garden.

The table was a large tree stump with the top smoothed down. Three chairs had been arranged around it. A lantern sat in the middle of the stump, throwing light over the rings and marking the years the tree had grown before serving its current purpose. Dora sat down and assessed their surroundings. Most of the tables contained only men, but she did see two with women at them. The women were dressed similar to her, so she doubted they were paid companions. There was laughter and gentle conversation floating over the whole area, and Dora relaxed. This was much better than the saloon. Dora did one more scan and realized there were no tables gambling. Marina would be disappointed.

Marina brought over two small tin cups and two tin mugs. "I couldn't decide so I bought whiskey and ale."

Dora laughed. "I admit, the whiskey sounds good."

Marina nodded and toasted Dora. "To the slaying of monsters."

Dora saluted Marina and then downed the whiskey in one gulp. It burned a warm path to her stomach, and Dora felt herself relaxing more. Marina sipped hers first, made an approving noise, then downed the rest.

Dora returned her empty cup to the table. "I don't see anyone else playing cards. I'm sorry."

Marina gave her a sly look. "Don't be." She reached inside her coat and pulled out a deck of cards and some dice. "You know I always come prepared."

Dora and Marina laughed loudly. A few of the men at surrounding tables turned towards the sound, and Dora took note of them. She only had tonight and tomorrow, and she meant to go through with her plan. She picked up the mug Marina had brought and took a sip. It was lighter and had a taste she could not identify.

"Do you like it?" Marina asked.

"What's that taste? Daniel's ale never tastes like this."

Marina took a sip of her own ale and sighed with her eyes closed. "This, my lovely Dora, is made by that lovely Belgian couple over there. The spice is coriander. I haven't had ale like this since I stopped for a week in Bruges."

"I didn't know you went to Bruges." When Dora had left the island, she had followed the pull to come to the Americas and then west to Colorado Territory. She had not lingered in any one place, both because she had felt driven to Turning Creek, but also because she had been uncomfortable and full of rage and sorrow. The memory of the family she had killed had still been fresh, and it haunted her waking and sleeping hours in those early months.

"I wandered around a long time before I gave in and went to Turning Creek. I spent a few weeks in many different cities. I would stay long enough to make some money at cards and outstay my welcome." Marina took another sip. "This seems like a more promising crowd."

Dora looked around and nodded. Marina ran her finger around the rim of her cup.

Dora rolled her eyes. "You want to say something. Just get it out." She was tired of fighting and arguing, but she knew Marina would have her say regardless of how she felt. Marina was a relentless force.

Marina took another sip before answering. "I don't agree with this."

Dora's hand on her cup tightened. "You've expressed that."

"No, listen." Marina looked up. "I'll support you whatever you decide. Even if I think you're being a fool."

Dora raised her mug. "Thank you, I think."

A man came up to their table. He was wearing brown trousers and a vest over a white shirt. His hair was a thick brown and he had a trimmed beard with ginger highlights. "May I sit with you ladies?"

He hesitated on the last word and something tingled in the back of Dora's neck. On a hunch, she sent out a tendril of power towards the man and the rest of garden they sat in. He was definitely not mortal. He was something of middling power, not dangerous, but he likely knew what they were. Unlike other Remnants, harpies could not hide their nature from other Remnants because they had been created to torture souls on the way to Tartarus. There were no other Remnants in the garden.

"Of course," Marina said looking at Dora with eyebrows raised. She had felt Dora's power and knew why she had sent it out. Dora nodded.

Dora looked him over. He was nice looking enough and would have done well for her plan, except she did not want to be entangled with a Remnant.

Her voice was harder than usual when she said, "I'm Dora Aello. This is Marina Oxcypete." She gave him their full names, the ones that would leave him no doubt.

Marina gave him one of her dangerous smiles. "Do you have business here?"

He took off the cloth cap he wore and twisted it in his hands. "I'm sorry. I've never seen one of you before. I thought you'd be scarier. I grew up hearing horrific stories about raging monsters from my mother who lived on the Greek islands. Looking at you two, I can't imagine that any of those stories could be true. Maybe harpies aren't nothing to worry about after all," he blurted, then paled as he realized what he'd said.

Marina straightened up, but Dora laid a hand on her arm. Dora let her own power leak from her and Marina added her own. The other people in the garden shifted, unsure why they were so uncomfortable. The man before them paled further and broke out into a sheen of sweat.

Dora could feel her harpy at the surface, just below her skin, wanting desperately to reveal her true nature to show this simpleton what scary meant. Those stories he had been raised on were likely about her mother or herself. Her past never strayed far. Dora knew her eyes looked less-than-mortal and she leaned forward so her voice would not carry beyond their table. "Do you think we look harmless now?"

He flinched at the sound of her voice. "I didn't mean it like that," he babbled.

Marina cocked her head and placed a hand on the man's knee. "How did you mean, exactly?"

He looked like he was near tears. "I'm sorry Mistress Harpies. I didn't mean to offend you. I see so few other Remnants here, I forgot myself."

Dora took pity on him. "We aren't going to hurt you, fool. Next time you approach something bigger than you, try to keep your wits about you and try to avoid challenging them unknowingly."

"And remember that in most places Remnants should not expose themselves," Marina added.

Another man approached the table. He was clean shaven, with dark curly hair and warm brown eyes. His broad shoulders were covered by a jacket with worn elbows.

"Is this gentleman bothering you two ladies?" he asked.

Dora blinked and pushed her harpy away. "No, but he was just moving on."

The first man shoved his hat back on his head.

Marina's voice stopped him. "Wait. We got off on the wrong foot. If you're looking for a place of safety, and you find some manners, there's a town out west. Go to the depot first." Marina hesitated.

"There's a Messenger there," Dora added, so the man would know it was a safe one.

The man, still pale, nodded. He did not need the name of the town to find it. Any Remnant would be able to feel the collection of power there once they got close enough. Dora used her power to sense the second man just in case she had missed him before. He was all mortal. She relaxed and gave Marina a slight shake of her head.

"Would you care to sit down?" Dora asked him.

"Only if you want the company," he replied.

Marina gave Dora significant look. "Do you want the company?"

Dora looked him over again. He was attractive, a mortal, and, according to his first impression, a gentleman. "Yes, we would love some company."

Marina stood. "Wonderful. I'll go buy us some more drinks."

Dora remembered her manners. After threatening the previous man who approached their table, she had to pull forward the idea of being civilized. *Marina is a bad influence*, Dora thought. She blamed Marina, but if Dora were honest with herself, she had enjoyed scaring Alex in the ally tonight.

"Please sit," she said. For a moment, she had been worried the voice that came out would not be her mortal one, but it was all roundness and ease.

The man sat. "My name is Merrill Fisher." He had a deep, smooth voice and he smiled when he introduced himself. The lines around his mouth and eyes wrinkled into the expession. He spent more time smiling than not.

Dora relaxed and held out her hand. Mr. Fisher shook her hand with a firm grip. "My name is Dora Aello. My companion is Marina Brant." She gave him Marina's mortal name. They did not need to intimidate this man.

"If you don't mind my asking, even in a mining town, it's unusual to see two women alone." He rubbed his hands down his thighs.

Marina approached the table from behind him. "We can take care of ourselves." She distributed the fresh cups of ale. "Not that we don't appreciate the company of a gentleman, but—" She pulled the sword at her shoulder halfway out, then pushed it back in with a snicking sound— "it would be foolish of anyone to consider us easy prey."

Mr. Fisher smiled. "I'll take that for the veiled threat it was meant to be and behave myself."

"A wise choice, sir." Dora picked up her mug and raised it. "To new friends."

They clinked cups and drank. Marina's eyes flicked around the garden tables and landed in the back. When she stood, Dora knew where she was going. "It's been a pleasure meeting you, Mr. Fisher. I think I need to play some cards over there. Dora…" Marina hesitated and did not finish the sentence.

Dora swallowed the ale in her mouth. "I'll be all right."

Marina's jaw clenched with unsaid words, but she nodded and left.

Dora turned her attention towards her new companion. "I hope you don't mind the deprivation of company. Marina is better at fleecing men of their money at cards or dice than she is at polite conversation."

Mr. Fisher watched Marina walk away, and then he looked at Dora. "It seems then that I have been lucky to escape with my coin intact. She's a singular woman, a little rough around the edges."

Dora laughed. "You have no idea how right you are, Mr. Fisher."

He leaned forward. "Please, call me Merrill. It seems a waste to stand on ceremony with a cup of good ale under the stars in the company of a beautiful woman."

Dora felt a blush creeping up her neck and cheeks. "Thank you. Please call me Dora."

"You have an interesting name, Dora."

Dora debated how much she was going to tell him about herself, about anything. She could not tell him about Turning Creek or the truth of what she was. She could not have him looking for her afterwards.

"It's Greek. My family is from Greece, originally," she clarified.

He nodded. "My grandparents were British. They came over after the war and settled in Ohio. That was the frontier then. I wanted to see more of the world, so I went west. Ended up here working some of the larger and smaller mines, wherever I can get a job."

"You don't work a claim of your own?"

"No, having a claim of your own is dangerous. People kill for a good claim. I'm not here to make it rich. I'm here for the scenery, which improved recently, thank you. I make enough money to get by. I'll be moving on soon enough. There's some larger mining companies up north by the great lakes that are hiring. I thought I might try my luck there and get a more permanent job. Besides, I heard the north country is beautiful."

His compliment warmed her, but the knowledge that he had no intention of being a permanent resident of Colorado was what excited her. This man could be the one she needed. He seemed kind, moderately intelligent, and he was good looking. Dora smiled; this was going to work out nicely.

He sipped his ale and asked, "What're you doing in Leadville?"

Dora walked the tightrope of truth. "I'm from a town out west. We needed some supplies, so Marina and I came to get what we could here to take back."

He nodded. "The war in the east is making a lot of things scarce. Prices keep going up."

Dora took a drink. "I have an impertinent question to ask."

Merrill squared his shoulders. "Impertinent questions from pretty ladies are my favorite kinds of questions."

Dora laughed. It was nice to be flirted with. "You said your family was from Ohio. I'm surprised you aren't involved in the war."

The humor on Merrill's face clouded. "My family wanted me to come back, but I don't want to go back to war and strife. It's simpler out here, and in some ways, it feels like the war isn't a real thing out here under the watch of the mountains." He gestured towards the peaks surrounding them.

"Until there's food shortages," Dora interjected.

"Exactly."

"So many of the arguments for states' rights and slavery barely touch us out here. It's easier to turn a blind eye to the problems. Slavery is an evil thing, even though it's been practiced here and elsewhere since the beginning of time." Dora shut her mouth and took a sip. Her nerves were making her ramble.

Merrill did not seem to notice anything odd about her. "True. Just because humanity has done something one way for generations doesn't make it right. Sometimes we have to evaluate our actions against our own morality and decide for ourselves."

Merrill is more right than he knows, she thought.

He leaned closer as he talked. He smelled like campfires. Dora's heart skipped sharply as she thought about Lee and his crisp scent. She shoved that aside roughly.

"You sound like a philosopher," she said.

He gave her a sheepish grin. "Sorry. It's been some time since I talked to a woman. I think I've forgotten how."

Dora closed some of the remaining distance between them. "I think you're doing just fine."

Merrill reached across the table and took her hand. Dora held herself still to keep from flinching. "Am I now?"

His eyes were warm and open and Dora wondered if she could lie to him, lie with him, and hold all of herself back. In her mind, she had never gotten this far in her plan. She had only imagined finding a kind man, and that was it. She licked her lips and she saw Merrill follow her movement with his eyes. If she asked, he would take her somewhere else.

"I think I should buy us some more drinks. Do you like whiskey?" She squeezed his hand.

He rubbed his thumb back and forth over her hand. Despite her reservations, a thrill of excitement and power jolted through her. She smiled at him in encouragement. She could do this.

"I appreciate good whiskey almost as much as sky-colored eyes and freckles." He was a breath away from her.

Dora felt herself blushing and hoped it was too dark, even with the lamp, to see. "I'll get us some whiskey and then we can go from there."

Heat filled his eyes. "That sounds nice."

Her nerves snapped tight as she stood and walked to the bar. She was surprised she made it there without tripping over her own feet. She managed to order and carry the two tumblers back to the table. Marina caught her eye and raised an eyebrow. Dora gave an imperceptible nod. Marina's face hardened, but she nodded briskly and returned her attention to her cards. Dora noticed Marina was sitting next to the man they had run off from the table before. Dora chuckled. Marina was soft on the inside.

Dora gave one tumbler to Merrill and then sat as close to him as their chairs would allow. She raised her glass.

"May we have the blessings of the gods, new friends, and a night of possibilities." She clinked her glass with his and took a sip. It was smooth and warm and burned away some of her nerves.

If he thought her toast odd, he didn't comment as he sipped his own drink. Dora watched him, and the more she did, the more her nerves frayed along the edges. This was not going to get easier as the night went on. It would become a heavier weight to wield; she only had this one night, maybe the next, to get this right.

Dora finished the last of her whiskey and licked her lips. She spoke before she changed her mind. "Where are you staying?"

Merrill stilled beside her. "At a boarding house down the road. It's nothing fancy, but I have my own room."

Dora took a deep breath and plunged in. "Do you want company for the evening?"

Heat flamed in his eyes, but his body canted away from hers. "I've been told not to look a gift horse in the mouth, but you seem like a very nice woman. We could meet again tomorrow, maybe have dinner."

"That's not exactly what I was offering."

He hesitated, and Dora knew he would say yes. "If you don't mind my asking, why would a woman like you ask me something like that? It's not what I expected."

"My reasons are my own and don't concern you, but the offer still stands."

Merrill finished his own whiskey and stood. He held out a hand to Dora. She took it, her smooth palms gliding over the rough calluses of his hands. They were warm and firm as he pulled her to her feet.

"Come, then. It's a nice night for a walk." He tucked her hand in the crook of his arm and led her out of the drinking garden. Dora felt the bore of Marina's eyes as they left, but she did not look back.

The night air was cooler away from the warmth of the crowd, and a chill wind rambled down the street. Dora could not contain her shiver. Merrill pulled her closer, and she let him. His warmth was nice. Anticipation and something more painful lodged itself behind her breastbone. Dora took a deep breath and willed the tension running through her to dissipate.

Merrill stopped three blocks down, in front of a tidy two-story building. Dora looked up in dismay. The walk did not take very long.

Merrill rubbed her arm. "Do you still want to come up?"

Dora nodded. "Yes." Her voice sounded normal even through the pounding in her ears.

Merrill led her through the door of the building. The front room filled the front part of the house and was all open. It was a morning room and casual dining area, with tables for eating and couches along the wall for visitors. He pulled her past the empty room and up the stairs, which ran along the left side of the wall. The third stair creaked under his foot and then hers. Otherwise, they made almost no sound as they walked upstairs.

The pressure behind her breastbone increased when Merrill stopped in front of the second door on the right. He looked at her, the question in his eyes barely visible in the lamp-lit hallway. She nodded. He opened the door, letting the darkness of his room spill out into the already dim hallway. He gestured her inside.

She took three steps in and saw a bed in the corner, a bedside table, and a washstand in the darkness of the room. Merrill closed the door and moved around her by putting his hands on her waist to check her position. The pain in her chest increased at his touch. He walked to the bedside table with the careful steps of a man who can't see where he is going and then fumbled for something on the table. There was a strike of a match and then a lamp flared to life, bathing the room in a soft glow.

Merrill paused, his back to her, and it gave her the opportunity to look around the room. There was a bed, big enough for two, but barely. The sheets and blankets were neatly tucked in at the corners. The bedside table that held the lamp was bare except for the light source. A washstand stood in the corner with a bowl, urn, and small mirror. Clothes hung neatly on pegs along the wall that backed up to the hallway. The clothes were clean and well cared for. There was no hidden dirt in the corners and the floor was bare.

Dora met Merrill's eyes when he turned to face her. They were almost black in the dim light and focused completely on her. He hesitated, but when she did not move, he walked over to her and wrapped an arm around her waist. Dora placed her hands on his chest and tried to relax as he bent his head to hers. His movements were slow and measured, giving her time to back away if she wanted.

His lips were soft and tentative on hers. The piercing in her chest bloomed into full panic. Dora moved one of her hands around Merrill's waist and pulled him closer, ignoring the panic. *I chose this road*, she thought. *I will see this through if it kills me, and it just might.*

Merrill took her movements as encouragement and deepened the kiss. Dora thought he was probably very good at kissing. He seemed to be enjoying himself, if his fingers threading through her hair were any indication. She was too busy concentrating on breathing to enjoy much of anything. She had to do this. She could just control this and then all would be fine. Everything was fine. She was fine. She could feel her harpy retreating inside its fortress, hiding from what she was about to do.

He kissed his way down her jawline. "I can't believe you asked to come up here. You're the most beautiful thing I've seen in a long time." His hands started working on the buttons of her blouse while he continued to kiss her neck and tickle her ear with his breath. "Things like this don't happen to me."

Dora lifted his chin with her hands. His voice was making it harder to concentrate on not losing it. She covered his mouth with hers and his hands slipped into the open front of her shirt and under her chemise. His calloused hands ran over her sensitive nipples, and the panic she had pushed down consumed her.

Dora could not breathe. This was not what she wanted. He was not what she wanted. She did not know if she could even voice what she wanted. She tried to think the words, think the name of the man she most desired, but black spots hovered in the corners of her vision. She swayed and Merrill steadied her.

"Dora, are you all right?" He led her to the bed and sat her down.

The three breaths she took shook her entire body. "I'm sorry. I can't do this. I thought I could. I thought this was the best way, but I can't. I just can't. I'm so sorry. I'm sorry. I can't."

Merrill took both of her hands in his. "You're too nice a lady to be here with me anyway."

Dora's vision swam and she blinked it away. "You are too nice to have brought me here."

He tucked a bit of hair behind her ear. "I know that's not true."

They sat for a few minutes, holding hands in silence while her ragged breathing returned to something more like normal. With each moment, Dora could feel her harpy and her power uncurl from where she had shoved it. She was still not sure she could let herself have free reign. She could not, even now, admit what she wanted.

Dora patted Merrill's hand. "Thank you for being a gentleman."

"What would you have done if I hadn't been one?" he asked.

"I would've ripped open your gut and left you to bleed." The words came out of their own accord. They were from deep within her, from that well she had kept covered.

His hands jerked and he tried to laugh weakly, but he must have seen something in her eyes that said she was not joking. She knew he was thinking of Marina's sword. She carried no such weapon. She didn't need to. She *was* the weapon.

Dora stood and began re-buttoning her dress. She smoothed her hair as best she could. "I have to leave. I'm sorry for," Dora waved a hand weakly at the bed, "getting your hopes up."

Merrill chuckled, this time without uncertainty. "I think a little hope and disappointment are good for me. Besides, you can't keep me from thinking of you now and again."

Dora laid a hand on his cheek. "I'd be honored. Thank you."

She walked out of the room, through the dimly lit hallway, and past the third creaking stair. She pulled the night air deep into her lungs when she closed the front door behind her. Dora leaned on it and continued to breathe. Fear threatened to take hold. It teased and whispered that she had made the wrong choice. That there was nothing for her no matter where she went. She would always be doomed to repeat her mistakes, to become a creature of wanton destruction.

A shadow peeled itself off a building across the street and stalked towards her. Dora met Marina on the edge of the mostly deserted road. They wrapped each other in a fierce hug when they were close enough. Dora trembled and her throat burned.

Marina's embrace turned painful. "Styx. Did he hurt you? I'll cut off his balls."

Dora tried to laugh but it came out like a sob. "No. I couldn't go through with it. He was a gentleman about everything."

Marina squeezed her again. "Thank the gods. What're you going to do now?"

Dora slumped. "I wish I knew."

CHAPTER 14

The following day and evening they spent in town was tedious. Marina enjoyed playing cards at various drinking establishments. At the rate she was winning, they might be able to pay for the supplies with her earnings and leave the town's money untouched. Dora did not see Merrill again, and she agonized that she had made the wrong choice.

Dora's nerves were short. She itched to leave and dreaded getting back home concurrently. She was back at the beginning once again, stuck between fear of wanting something and fear of giving in to that need. Her thoughts on what she should do changed from one minute to the next. She had never felt so adrift. Dora was relieved when it was time to go back to King's.

Marina called to her over her shoulder as she led the way down the street. "Stop sighing. It's grating on my nerves. And you sound ridiculous. It's not that bad."

Dora narrowed her eyes at Marina's back. "Bold words to someone who could attack you from behind. I could rip out your neck before you knew what was happening."

"You're in a bloodthirsty mood," Marina snorted. "Try it."

Dora sighed, loudly. "You're not worth it." Both harpies laughed, and some of the weight on Dora's shoulders lifted. They tied their horses in front on King's store and went inside.

Mr. King saw them when they came in and he straightened and gripped the edges of the counter. Apprehension bloomed.

"We aren't going to get the things we needed, are we?" Dora asked.

"I tried. I did, but there were a lot of things on your list that I simply don't have and couldn't find elsewhere." He wrung his hands.

Marina stepped up to the counter and leaned over it. "Would you be able to find some of the things if the price was higher?" Mr. King's face bleached of color at the threat.

Dora put a hand on Marina. "I don't think he's trying to scheme us. Look, Marina, you've already scared him half to death."

Marina relaxed under her arm. "Were you able to get any of it?"

Color returned to Mr. King's face. "Yes, I did the best I could. I have some bags of oats and unground wheat you can take for flour. There are some potatoes and carrots. I found some sugar and vinegar and bagged those up with some dried and canned fruit. I asked around to other vendors in town. This is all there is."

Dora looked at the pile he had assembled for them. It was too small. Not nearly enough to help a town through the rest of the summer and winter.

"How often do you get supplies in?" Dora asked, her mind already working.

"Weekly or more in the summer, bi-weekly in the winter, but the shipments have been smaller lately," he said.

Marina caught her idea. "Would you be willing to set aside a certain portion of your supplies for a man named Simon Kramer starting in October? We would send someone for pick-up once a month during the winter."

Dora shared a look with Marina. Turning Creek could limp by this summer and fall but they would need more food this winter. They would have plenty of meat, but they needed to keep people healthy, not half-starved. They could not rely on Spuds and his mules alone this winter because they would need more than Spuds could deliver. It was a long journey on horseback but a harpy could fly it in a quarter of the time and carry what was needed.

Mr. King shifted his gaze between the two women, and Dora felt a flare of panic that he would refuse. "I can try, but supply lines being what they are, I can't guarantee anything."

Marina shook the man's hand. "That'll do. I'll make a list for the winter pickups."

Dora wandered off from the conversation and went to the back of the store. It was going to be a tough few months. They were going to have to hunt in earnest when they returned home, and it would mean months of eating mostly meat. She went past the farming tools and racks of mining equipment. Dora ran her hand over the bolts of gingham and flower prints. She stopped in front of the bookshelves and ran her hand over the book with the brown leather binding, black accents, and gold letters.

She pulled it off the shelf, flipped through the pages, and stopped when they fluttered open to a diagram of the human heart. Such a small thing to cause so many problems. Dora traced the lines and considered her next move. She needed to continue her line. Not doing so was foolish and unfair to her sister harpies' children. They would need their sister to help them face whatever trials life brought their way. They would raise their daughters to be a family. This was the life each of them had chosen. They were changing what it meant to be a harpy, and Dora wanted her own line to be a part of that future.

Dora snapped the book closed and carried it to the front. Marina's eyebrows shot up when she saw the book.

"Some light reading for the journey home?" Marina smirked.

Dora ignored her. "How much is this?"

Mr. King looked at her. "Three dollars."

"That's robbery."

Mr. King pointed to the book. "That book is in excellent condition and has never been used. It's also an item you'd be hard pressed to get on this side of the Mississippi, let alone in the Rocky Mountains."

Dora grumbled, but she pulled the coins from the inside pocket of her dress. She had plenty and could afford the price, even if it was high. Mr. King wrapped the book for her while Marina and Dora loaded their two pack horses.

Marina secured the last bundle. "I'll double check these bindings while you go get your book. On medicine." She winked at Dora.

Dora ignored the gibe and went inside. Mr. King handed her the book with a farewell and thanks. The weight of the book on her heart threatened to root her in place. It was a paltry offering to Lee when she had argued with him so heatedly. Dora clenched the book, now wrapped in brown paper, tighter and left the mercantile.

Dora put the book in her already-bulging saddlebag and swung up onto her horse. "Let's go home."

Marina let her stew all the way out of town and into the woods beyond. "Are you going to take up doctoring yourself, or are you going to give that book to Doc?"

Dora had thought of nothing else but how to give Lee the book. It would have to be given with an apology. "It's not for me."

Marina cackled. "Finally. Styx."

"It's just a book, Marina. I'm not offering any more than that." Dora's heart twisted and beat painfully at her lie. "Besides, we didn't part on the best terms. He said his door was open but I was harsh with him. Twice. Lee may not want to accept this for what it is."

Marina gave her an odd look. "And just what is it?"

Dora swallowed. "A peace offering."

"Is that all you want? Peace?"

"For now."

"And later?"

"We'll see how the book goes over first."

Marina never brought it up again, but it was all Dora thought about on the journey back. She went through every way the conversation could go. Every outcome scared her, and she could not answer the question Marina had asked. What did she want from Lee? She wanted to not have him angry at her, but whatever more she wanted was something she still could not completely answer.

When they finally rode through the last pass into Turning Creek Valley, they paused at the ridge and looked down over the town.

"It's the most beautiful sight I've ever seen." Marina's voice was thick with emotion.

Dora took in the sweeping floor of the valley and how it gave way to the jagged peaks that sheltered them from the outside world. The peaks were slate grey in the distance and topped with snow. The sun bounced off the snow and felt brighter this high up. Dora's horse side stepped in anticipation of a few days of rest at home. Snow crunched under her hooves. The birds sang and the air smelled sweet.

"It is good to be home," Dora agreed.

Marina started her horse down the winding trail of the pass. They still had a long day of riding ahead of them. It would be full dark before they got back to the main part of town. Dora swept her eyes over the valley one more time, wishing she could soar home instead of riding the horse. Her eyes snagged on something in the sky on the opposite end of the valley, near where Mount Baldy hunched in a row of taller peaks.

At first it looked like a harpy flying in the west, but the shape was not quite right. It was big, though, and it should not be here in their valley. All her senses immediately went on alert. It was too far away for her to get any kind of reading, but that did not stop her harpy from sending out a wave of power in frustration.

Marina reigned in her horses abruptly and turned to say something, but the words died when she got a look at Dora's face. "What is it?"

Dora pointed to the thing still flying in the west.

"What in the hells is that?" Marina spat out, and Dora felt Marina's power roll from her and collide with her own.

Dora swallowed her power. "Nothing good. Maybe that's what's been eating the cattle. Let's get home."

Marina shifted uncomfortably in her saddle. "I could fly over there and check it out."

Dora urged her horse down the path a little faster than was advisable. "Not alone you won't, and we went through too much effort to abandon these supplies. Let's get back and see what's happened while we were gone and if the others know what that is. Maybe it means no harm."

"Maybe it means to eat us in our beds," Marina muttered.

"You'd stick in its maw and give it indigestion." Dora smiled at Marina's back as they made their way down the mountain. They increased the speed of their horses.

Marina made a rude noise. "It would never get close enough to get a bite of me."

"I'd never let it, even if it tried," Dora said.

After that, they concentrated on navigating the sometimes steep descent. Every time there was a break in the trees, Dora looked for the thing they had seen flying. It never reappeared. Once they gained the floor of the valley, they pushed their horses as hard as they could. Dora checked the sky one more time, but it was empty. A feeling of dread dogged them the rest of the way.

They rode up to the depot when the last of the day had faded from the sky and the moon had taken over the horizon. Dora launched herself from the saddle and was on Marina's heels when they went into the depot. The front room of the depot was filled. Iris and Petra stood behind the counter. Henry, Reed, and James stood up from the back table when they came through the door. Screeching and high pitched welcomes came from Selene, Ellie, and Nina. Thomas hung back, striving to act more nonchalant.

Ellie and Nina launched themselves at Marina, who scooped them up, one in each arm. "Hello, my small beasties."

Selene and Aldara waved their arms at Dora, who obliged the girls and picked them up. Dora kissed the top of one girl's head, then the other. She let the warm weight of the toddlers relax her nerves. It was good to be home.

"This is a larger welcome than we expected." Dora hugged Selene, and the girl squeezed her small arms around Dora's neck. Aldara tangled her small hand into Dora's hair. Dora relaxed a fraction more.

Henry's eyes shifted to his wife. "Iris knew you would be home tonight and we all wanted to be here."

"We saw something flying in the west of the valley as we gained the pass," Dora said.

Petra's face hardened. "I saw it too, but I had Selene with me and didn't want to get into something with her. We'll have to go looking for it. Soon."

Marina put Nina and Ellie down but kept her hands on their heads. She ruffled their hair as she spoke. "Any idea what it is yet?"

Iris shook her head. "No one has gotten close enough to look at it, so I don't have any good information to go on."

Dora's spirit's fell. "I'm afraid we don't have good news either."

Marina continued, "The war in the east has caused disruption to the supply lines west. We aren't the only town having trouble getting supplies. We brought back what we could and we'll go back in a few weeks for more."

"It was precious little and we'll have to ration it." Dora put the now-wiggling toddlers down.

"Are the other towns having trouble with their crops?" Reed moved closer to Marina and stole a kiss.

"Or their livestock?" James added.

Dora shook her head. "No. That seems to be localized here in our valley."

Petra spoke up. "I spoke with Prudence and asked if the fungus could be some sort of witchcraft. She said it was possible, but she's the only Remnant in the valley powerful enough to do something like that. Prudence doesn't have a harsh bone in her body."

The adults were silent. They all knew what that meant. Something unnatural was killing their crops and livestock. Something was plaguing them. Dora did not feel any pleasure in being right.

The faces around her were all pinched. Dora asked, "How have things been here?"

Lips tightened and the tension in the room went up. Reed rubbed the back of his neck. "Things have been worse. George Eisler tried replanting again, but the seeds rotted in the ground. They didn't even sprout."

James's quiet voice added, "Most of the ranches have lost half to two-thirds of their animals. It's not just the cows, but the chickens, goats, sheep. Everything."

Dora took a deep breath. "It looks like the supplies we were able to get will come in handy then. At least we have that. It's still summer. There are animals to hunt and things to gather. We'll make do."

Iris laid her palms on the counter. "It looks like we all have a lot of things to do tomorrow. There will be research to do and supplies to distribute."

"And hunting, if we're lucky," Marina said.

The three harpies shared a look. They would not be hunting for meat. They would be hunting to protect their territory, and woe to anything that stood in their way.

CHAPTER 15

Dora's stomach rumbled the next day as she turned another page in the book she was reading. So far, she had found a few possibilities for the monster they had seen flying, but none of the pictures looked right. They were too much like a dragon. The thing they had seen was shaped more like a harpy, except the wings and body were not quite right, but she had not been close enough to see exactly how different. She sighed.

Iris looked up from her own book. "That's the third time in a handful of minutes you've made that noise. I wish you three had decided to hunt early instead of later. Go upstairs and make some tea."

Dora smiled gratefully and obeyed. She rose and stretched her arms over her head. Her muscles groaned in protest, and it felt good to walk up the stairs and work out the stiffness of her body. They had been looking through books since early morning. Dora had considered going to see Lee first thing, but she had found other things to do instead. She wasn't quite ready to grovel yet.

The muted sound of the bell over the door downstairs rang as Dora was pouring the water over the tea leaves. She paused to listen to the voices. Her stomach tightened with something more than hunger when the rumbling male voice made its way to her ears. Lee. Dora added a few more biscuits and another cup to the tray.

Their fight in the middle of the street before she left for Leadville flashed into her memory. Dora had replayed that argument, and the one before it, over and over in her mind on the ride back to Turning Creek. She was certain that she wanted more from him than friendship, but she still held herself back. She had spent years creating walls and distance. It would take time for her to get used to the idea of scaling those walls and jumping to the other side. She was less certain if her display of temper and bad behavior had ruined any tender feelings he may have harbored.

Dora was certain of very few things anymore, but she knew one thing: she did not want to lose the good opinion of Lee Williams. Even if they never became anything more, she did not want him to ever look on her with disdain or indifference.

Dora carried the tray down the stairs and ignored the rolling in her stomach. She pasted a tentative smile on her face and rounded the corner.

Lee stood in front of the counter. At the sound of her approach, he turned and his deep grey eyes swept over her. There was a question in his eyes when they met hers. Dora gave him a small but steady smile and he returned her expression.

She placed the tray on the counter and stood as close as she could without touching him directly. She breathed deep and had to force her eyes to stay open as Lee's smell rolled over her. She could feel her harpy stirring, but Dora pushed it down. She did not want a display of temper to ruin this conversation like last time. She had some apologizing to do, and harpies were not apologetic by nature. She thought of the book upstairs, but she did not want to make an excuse to go and retrieve it.

Iris glanced around the room and then down at the tray. "I think I'd like some cream with my tea this morning. I'm going to go upstairs and get it." She walked briskly around the counter and went upstairs.

Dora sent a silent thanks to Iris, but then her mind blanked. She stood staring at Lee and she could not think of anything to say. The moment stretched and her entire body tightened. Dora blinked and found her thoughts.

"I'm sorry."

"I'm sorry."

They had spoken at the same time. They both laughed.

"Ladies first. Besides, I think you are about to apologize to me. What I have to say can wait."

If she wanted to keep her head and maintain her sanity, Dora should have stepped back and given herself some space. She laid a hand on Lee's arm instead. She felt his muscles flex under her touch and then he stilled like she was a wild animal he did not want to frighten. Dora almost giggled at how close to the truth that picture was and pressed on.

"I'm sorry for the argument we had before I left. I'm sorry for threatening you in the street." Dora considered what truths to tell him and she trembled at the thought of telling him all. Some revelations she was not ready to make to herself. Others were required for this apology.

"My mother was crazy. She let all her emotions fuel anger and violence, and she had no control over either. They ruled her and saturated our island with blood. In the end, I learned I was not as different from her as I had thought. I need control." Dora paused and ran her hand down Lee's arm. "You make me feel adrift, like I'm in an ocean I can't conquer, and I fear not being in control. Control is how I stay as far away from what happened on the island as possible. I lost control the last time we argued and I'm sorry for that."

Dora took a steadying breath. "You asked me a question that I've never answered."

"What question was that?" Lee's voice was soft. He still had not moved and his stormy eyes bored into her.

"You asked me if I cared for you, and I refused to answer you. Later, you said I would remember our conversations and feel remorse for my words. And you cursed." Dora laughed a little at the memory.

Lee's mouth twitched up. "I have my own control issues, and you occasionally make me forget them."

Dora's laughter evaporated. "I'm sorry about that too. Lee, I do care for you. I'm worried about what it might mean, and I'm scared of letting any emotions have sway over me. Even good ones. I'm afraid I'll lose control completely. Turning Creek is too important to me. I won't destroy it. Even for you."

Lee wrapped his arms around her so swiftly she stopped breathing. Her arms knew what to do, though. They snaked around his waist and held on as tight as he held on to her. She had never been quite this close to him, and he surrounded her with his body. It was intoxicating. His body was hard planes and they were all pressed into her. She laid her forehead on his chest and breathed him in. Dora's harpy purred in appreciation and Dora internally rolled her eyes at her inner self.

Lee pulled back a fraction of an inch to rest his forehead on hers. "I'm sorry for the anger between us. We don't have to discuss anything beyond our apologies. We can just take one day at a time."

Lee eased his arms around her, and she moved her head to look into his face. She searched his eyes, which returned her gaze with smoldering intensity. "It's more than I deserve. Thank you."

Lee framed her face with his hands and for a moment Dora thought he might kiss her. The idea both terrified and thrilled her. "You must believe one thing, though."

"What?" She could not drag her eyes away from his.

"You are not defined by your past. Cease worrying over what was and worry instead on what you are becoming."

"What am I becoming?" Dora could feel the heat in his hands on her face. The heat traveled the length of her limbs until she wondered if his hands were the only things holding her upright.

"A good person who cares for others so deeply that you would rather lock down everything you are than harm the people you love. You are stronger than you know, and you need to believe that. My belief in you will not change."

Lee rubbed his thumbs over her cheeks and then released her. Her face was flushed and felt cool in the absence of his hands. Lee took a step back. She balled her hands at her sides to keep them from grabbing him and bringing him back to her.

He cleared his throat. "I came to the depot to look for you. Caroline is in labor. We have plenty of time to get there, but if you are willing, I would like you to accompany me."

"Do you want me to fly ahead?"

Dora saw the shift in Lee as his mind started thinking of the job ahead and what they would need. "I would. This is her second, so it's likely things will move faster than last time. Babies do have their own timetables, though. I would like to be prepared either way. I will gather my things and meet you there."

Dora nodded. "I'll see you there, then."

Lee held the door for her as they left the depot. He stopped her with a hand on her arm before she changed. "I am glad you are home."

Dora rewarded him with a wide grin. "Me too. Leadville made me realize I had more here than I knew."

Lee returned her smile and stepped back to allow her room. Dora called to her harpy and felt the change pass over her swiftly. She shook out her speckled feathers and preened for Lee, who had not taken his eyes from her as she transformed. There was appreciation in his look. She held his gaze as she called the wind to her. She created a whirlwind around Lee, who grinned wider once he realized where the wind was coming from. She launched into the air. Dora knew she was showing off, but she didn't care.

The midday sun warmed her feathers as she flew east over the valley towards Silvercliff and the Eisler's farmstead. Her conversation with Lee had left her hopeful that she could find a way to muddle through her feelings for him without losing her mind. Her flight under the warmth of the sun to help a neighbor left her hopeful about many things. Dora flexed the claws on the ends of her wings as she flew, grateful for the opportunities to use her hands to heal instead of hurt.

Dora landed in front of the door to the small house and changed before knocking and announcing her presence. She heard voices from inside.

"George, I'm having a baby, not dying. I can answer the door." The door opened to reveal a frowning Caroline. Her hair was pulled back and there were lines of worry around her eyes that belied her tone. "Dora, I'm so glad you are here. George thinks I need to be lying in bed."

Dora followed Caroline inside. She took one look at George, concern in his round face, and took pity on him. "Mr. Eisler, Caroline can walk around as long as she feels comfortable doing so. Caroline, your husband is only worried for you. Mr. Eisler, why don't you make sure we have plenty of wood for the fire and some fresh water in the pot for warming with some in reserve should we need more."

George jumped up, kissed his wife, and went outside to do as asked.

Caroline laughed, but the sound was cut off as she placed both hands on the table and breathed through a contraction. She looked up when it was over. "They are not so close or hard yet. Thank you for giving him a job. He's been flittering around me all day, and it was starting to wear me down."

Melanie scampered into the room, waving a wooden doll. "Hello."

Dora knelt in front of the child. "Hello, young one. Are you ready for a brother or sister?"

Melanie screwed up her face. "My doll. Not sharing."

Dora patted the girl on the shoulder. "That's your doll. You won't have to share it just yet, but you may want to someday." Dora stood and ran her hand over the girl's head.

Caroline went to the stove and added wood to the fire. "Would you like some tea while we wait for this one?" She stood and rubbed a hand over her belly.

"Tea sounds perfect. Let me help you."

Time passed. Lee arrived, and soon they were all waiting, drinking tea, and trying not to let the coil of anticipation make them impatient. George had the most trouble with this.

After one longer contraction, Caroline said, "George, take Melanie outside for a walk. Go pick berries or milk the goats or something."

Mr. Eisler looked out the window. "It's almost full dark."

"Well, go out and do something. You're making me nervous," Caroline snapped back before leaning against the table again.

Lee and Dora shared a look. Lee led Caroline into the bedroom and Dora ushered George and Melanie outside. "Things are moving along nicely. You should take Melanie into the barn to visit the animals. I'll fetch you before the end."

With Mr. Eisler dispatched, Dora went into the bedroom and watched Lee help Caroline onto the bed so he could examine her.

"I don't want to lay down," Caroline said.

Lee eased her back and Dora propped up some pillows behind Caroline's head. "It's just for a moment. You can get back up and walk if you want after Dr. Williams examines you."

Lee put a hand on Caroline's knee. "I need to check and make sure everything is going well."

Caroline stilled and breathed through another contraction. It would not be long now. The pains were coming close and lasting longer. Lee moved his hands around Caroline's belly. His face didn't change, but Dora knew all was well. She went to Lee's bag sitting against the wall and pulled out his stethoscope. It was one of the newer models with flexible tubing and two earpieces, and Lee was very proud of it. Dora waited until he straightened and then handed him his stethoscope. He smiled in thanks then returned to his task.

Dora sat on the edge of the bed and held Caroline's hand during the examination. Caroline gripped her hand with the strength of a woman in labor, and Dora did not flinch, though she wanted to.

"Everything is just as it should be. It will not be long now. If you want to stay in the bed, you can, if you want to move, you can do that too. You've done this before, so you're an expert." Lee winked at Caroline, who smiled before another contraction hit.

Caroline rolled onto her side and asked Dora to rub her back. Dora pressed her fingers into Caroline's back with some of her harpy strength, and Caroline relaxed into her touch. Dora continued to rub Caroline's back until her fingers were numb and her mind was in a trance.

Dora jolted when Lee placed a hand on her shoulder. Even in this setting, Dora felt the fire in his touch and could not keep herself from leaning into it. After years of avoiding his touch and resisting the urge to touch him, it was a shock to feel his hand on her multiple times in one day.

"I think you should go retrieve Mr. Eisler from the barn."

Everything went quickly after she brought Mr. Eisler and Melanie back inside. The toddler had fallen asleep, and Dora laid her on the small bed in the second room of the cabin. She took up residence next to Lee and guided Mr. Eisler to stand by his wife's head.

Lee examined Caroline again. She had been quiet for a few minutes. "All right, Mrs. Eisler. You are doing wonderful. When you feel the urge to push, you tell us, and we will help you get into whatever position feels best. Ready?" Lee asked the last question to Caroline, but they all nodded.

Everything moved in the way big events often do, in small vignettes of activity with the in-between-times getting lost in memory. Caroline was ready to push, and Dora held one leg while Mr. Eisler held the other. The baby came out with seeming ease, his protest a testament to the indignation of the situation.

Lee caught him and laid him on Caroline's belly. "You have a beautiful baby boy."

Dora grabbed a clean rag and started rubbing the vernix from his skin as his parents cooed over him. Mr. Eisler did not bother to wipe away the tears running down his rounded cheeks. He kissed his wife's sweaty brow and stroked his son's bald head.

Lee tied off the umbilical cord and offered his surgical scissors to Mr. Eisler. "Would the proud father like to cut the cord?"

George Eisler's hand shook as he squeezed the scissors closed over the blue cord that had kept his son alive for nine months. The snipping of the scissors and the sight of those shaking hands snapped something in Dora, and she had to look away.

The lock on the cage she had maintained her entire life clicked open, wrenched open by the joy of a father in his child. She had attended many births with Lee, but she had never allowed herself to feel everything a new life brought into a house. Dora turned her head and coughed to remove the restriction of her throat.

Dora helped Lee deliver the afterbirth. She wrapped it in a rag and laid it aside and then brought Lee a basin of warm water and a clean cloth. He set about cleaning and checking Caroline, and Dora went out to bury the afterbirth under the tree in the front of the cabin as Mr. Eisler had asked.

The stars were bright as she found the shovel and started digging. The work eased some of the tension of her muscles. She placed the cloth-wrapped bundle into the ground and said a prayer to the gods and a blessing for the new life. Dora filled the hole and was filled with satisfaction as she tamped down the last of the dirt with her shovel.

The smile on her face faltered when she went back inside to find Lee sitting by the crackling fire with a knife and a piece of wood in his hands. Her calm peace exploded and she felt the things she had been keeping caged claw up her throat. If she was going to allow herself to feel in his presence, she had to learn how to breathe through this sensation and trust that it was not a precursor to her going crazy.

She must have made a sound because Lee looked up from his work then, and his eyes bored into her. She imagined that he could see the monster inside of her, then he smiled. For whatever reason, he trusted her, liked her, even though he saw her for what she was. She fisted her hands in her skirt. He had confidence in her, regardless. Dora would need to tell him the whole truth of her past. Not today, though. She took one step, then another, in his direction and sat in the chair opposite him across the hearth. She took a normal breath.

"How are Caroline and the baby?" She squeaked out the question.

His eyes stayed on the work of his hands. Small curls of wood fell at his feet. "Fine. I would like us to stay until morning to make sure the child eats and all remains well. If you can, I would like you to come down off your mountain and check on her every day for a few days."

Dora nodded even though he was not looking at her. "I can do that. Would you like some tea or something to eat?"

Lee looked up then. Dora felt his gaze like a weight. "No. I'm fine. Thank you." He went back to work.

Dora pulled her chair closer to his side of the fire. "Your hands are always busy. When you are with a patient, you are always touching them, reassuring them, or working with instruments. Even when you are idle, your hands never are."

The edges of Lee's mouth quirked up. "My mother said I found trouble when I was idle. My maternal grandfather was mortal, a furniture maker, and he taught me to carve. I think mostly to keep me from under my mother's feet at first, but we enjoyed each other's company."

He turned over the piece of wood and began working on the other side. He rubbed a spot where a knot whorled in the wood. "When carving, you have to see past the surface to the heart of the thing. The surface is beautiful in its own right, but underneath, in its heart, is something more beautiful than words." His mouth curled into a full smile as he looked up at her. "It only needs patience, time, and a sharp knife to come to the surface."

"What is inside of this one?" Dora barely got the words out. They were no longer talking about the wood.

Lee laid the flat of the knife he was holding against her arm. The coolness of it throbbed even as the heat in his eyes melted her core. "I'm still working that. I'll let you know when I find out."

He removed the knife from her arm and went back to whittling as if they had been discussing the weather. Dora sat back in her chair and tried to remember how to form coherent thoughts.

Lee did not pause his hands when he broke the silence. "Now, I want to ask you a question."

Dora's stomach rolled at all the things he might ask. "Ask away," she managed with more bravado than she felt.

"I have observed that each of the harpies, including you, has some sort of extra power. Petra can harness a kind of soul-crushing darkness, Marina can move faster than anything I have ever seen, and you seem to take the wind with you when you are agitated. Earlier, you created wind in jest."

Dora felt her fair skin burn up her neck and face. "The first of my line was Aello. Her name meant Storm Swift. I can call the wind. I don't have to be upset to do it, but it sometimes happens when I don't expect it." *Because I can't control myself,* she wanted to admit. *I'm afraid I'll never be able to control myself with you.*

"That's an interesting ability."

Dora gave a short laugh. "Yes, well, it makes more sense when you live on a small island in a small sea. Many ships and sailors have felt the wrath of my line when they dared to cross us." Dora's blood pressure rose thinking of protecting her land and the people, keeping everyone safe with the power given to her by the gods.

Lee nodded as though he could not see the pleasure rippling through her at the thought of doing violence. Now that she had cracked open the cage, everything was close to the surface. For a moment, Dora felt dizzy. If she lost herself over such a small thing, how could she hope to have control when it really mattered? She pressed herself back into her chair and blinked several times, focusing on Lee's grey eyes watching her.

He went still, as though he knew how close she was to the violence roaring in her blood. It had always been there. She had simply ignored it for so long—except when she *had* to let it out—and now she had completely lost control of it. She was losing control of everything.

Lee moved his knife and the wood to one hand and placed his free right hand on her knee. The touch flared from that small focal point and she felt grounded. "Take a deep breath."

Dora obeyed and felt her blood slow to normal. "Sorry," she muttered.

Lee did not remove his hand. He leaned closer to her, threatening the calm she had found with his nearness. She could feel the heat coming off him, and her body clenched with awareness. She knew, if she held a hand mirror now, she would see no trace of her mortal eyes staring back at her.

"Why are you sorry? You are a ferocious predator who loves deeply the things that are hers. You were made to protect and defend. You should never be sorry for that."

Dora had to keep her mouth from hanging open. All her life she had been told and believed that she had been created to kill and do violence to whomever she pleased. She had viewed it as some kind of miracle that her generation of harpies had managed not to bathe everyone in blood. She had never really thought they were anything but a fluke of fate. Lee made it seem like there was purpose beyond the violence, even from the beginning. She could see he believed his words as if he could see the kernel of hope lodged deep in her soul that perhaps they could be something more, had been intended for something more from the beginning.

"I've never quite thought of it that way," she managed to say.

Lee leaned even closer to her. Her entire body screamed with his nearness, and she tightened in fear and anticipation. Instead he spoke. His words created little currents of wind over her face. "I think you are just now beginning to see what you truly are."

He leaned back and continued to work on the piece of wood in his hands. Dora stifled the disappointment that rose within her and replaced it with a realization. Lee saw her. He saw her—the her she had kept locked away her entire life—and he had leaned into it. He had not run away screaming. She watched him carve and thought maybe there was hope for her yet.

CHAPTER 16

Dora left the Eisler homestead before noon the next day. Lee had left during the early morning. She stayed long enough to make sure Caroline, baby Herne, Melanie, and Mr. Eisler were settled and well for the day. She left with a promise to return on the morrow with food and a few hours of company.

The closer she flew to her own cabin the more she felt a tug to change directions. Dora changed directions and circled over Silvercliff, wondering which way she should go. When she was pointed almost due north the tug eased, but when she circled south again it increased. It did not happen often that the harpies got a feeling they needed to follow, but when it did happen it was a pull to be together when they were apart. The last time Dora remembered it happening was when she had been drawn to this valley.

After the night she had killed the witch's family, Dora had been living like a hermit on one of the uninhabited islands of the archipelago off the coast of Greece for years when she had first felt that tug on her soul. It was a feeling of unease that she was not where she was supposed to be, not where she was needed. She had been so wrapped in her own misery those long years that it had taken some time for her to recognize the feeling for what it was, a call to action. Today, she did not hesitate. A long, mostly sleepless night meant she was exhausted, but she turned away from the comfort of her bed she longed for and flew north to see Petra.

Dora could see James's herds when she flew over the farm. They were a quarter of their previous size and her heart was full for James, who put so much of himself into his dairy farm. She caught a warm current and tilted her wings so that she was flying down in the direction of the house.

There was a pile of something in the middle of the yard. As she dropped altitude, Dora watched Petra come out with her arms full of something, throw it on the pile, then walk back into the house. Curious, Dora increased the rate of her descent. Before she reached the ground, the smell hit her. Rotten food. The pile in front of the house was rotten food.

Petra came out, annoyance sparking across her face as she dumped two loaves of bread and a slab of what looked like it may have been cured ham onto the fetid pile. She wiped her brow with the back of her hand as Dora landed.

"Nice of you to show up after I've finished all the work." Petra disappeared around the side of the house where a cistern and bucket of water were located.

Dora trailed in her wake. "What happened?"

Petra washed her hands in the bucket, then dumped out the water. "That's an excellent question. I woke up this morning to the smell of rotting food in my house. Everything had gone bad."

Dora cocked her head to one side. "What do you mean everything?"

"I mean every morsel of food that was in our house, no matter how fresh, had gone bad. Everything in the cellar for the winter. The meat pie we only ate half of last night. The berries Selene and James picked yesterday. Everything." Petra walked back to the front of the porch and sat heavily on the edge of it.

Dora looked at the mound of food. "Styx. I wonder if you're the only one."

Petra shot her a look. "What're you suggesting?"

"More and more, I believe all the unnatural things are related. They're not a coincidence."

Petra sighed. "Hells. Can't we have some good, quiet years? Why is it always dire straits and monsters?"

Dora's laughter had a thick element to it as she sat down beside Petra. "Because we live in a place filled with powerful beings and power draws power."

Petra's mouth curved into a satisfied smile. "And we are the most powerful monsters."

Dora felt the power trickling from Petra and her own rose to twine with it. "You're starting to sound like Marina. We have to find out who, or what, is causing this." Dora waved a hand towards the food pile. "All of this."

The door behind them opened and the light step of Selene approached them. Petra turned and caught her daughter in her arms. "Hello, little one. Did you finish cleaning your things like daddy asked?"

Selene nodded. "Yes." She turned and threw herself towards Dora. "Auntie Dee."

Dora moved her to her lap and squeezed her. "Hello, young one. Why did you have to clean your room?"

Serious brown eyes in a solemn brown face, so much like her mother's, looked right into Dora's face. "Daddy said I was living like a piglet and I was a girl. I told him I was a harpy, not a piglet. He said I had to prove it by cleaning up my room or else he'd make me sleep with the pigs in the mud." She scrunched up her face.

Dora tweaked Selene's nose. "Harpies do not live like pigs. He was right to make you clean it." Dora kissed Selene's forehead. "You've worked hard. Run around while your mother and I finish talking."

Selene sprang down from Dora's lap and hopped around the yard. Her power popped and she transformed into her harpy form. She flew into the air and circled about ten feet off the ground while Dora and Petra faced the problem at hand.

Petra ran a hand over her face. "I want to go to town with you after I clean up this mess. I have to talk to James too. Maybe Selene and I should stay in town overnight while we see how bad this might be. Do you want to wait on me or meet me there?"

Selene squealed and took off flying around the barn. "Auntie M is coming too." The small harpy laughed as she flew away from them.

"Marina is here?" Petra asked.

Dora followed Selene's trajectory with her eyes and saw something flying towards them. It was still far off and at first glance it did look like Marina, but something was not right about the shape. The wing beat was not right and the shape was slightly off. Thick dread slicked through Dora's veins.

They both stood.

"Gods, no," Dora pleaded as she changed into the form that would allow her to fight.

"Selene, no. Come back!" Petra's voice changed halfway through the command as her own harpy burst through her.

Whatever it was had increased its speed and was aiming straight for the young harpy. Selene turned her head around to see why her mother had yelled at her. The movement stopped her forward momentum and she looked again at the thing bearing down on her. Selene's wings faltered and she tumbled in the air before turning and flying back towards her mother. The thing was gaining on her. She could not fly fast enough to reach the safety of her mother and Dora.

The creature aimed for Selene was as large as a harpy, but it had a bat-like face and wings. Where the harpies had feathers, this monster had dark grey, leathery wings, which it flapped rapidly. Like a bat, it had claws towards the end of its wings, and its feet ended in talons.

Dora gathered every bit of speed she could and flew straight for the bat-winged creature gaining on Selene. She wished to the gods that Marina was here with her speed and swords, but she and Petra had tricks of their own. Dora pushed a gust of wind in the face of the monster, slowing it down just enough to give Selene a chance of reaching them before it reached her.

Dora felt power surge from her left where Petra pulled ahead of her. Darkness fell over them and centered on the monster, wrapping around it with tendrils that strangled. Dora had seen Petra call the darkness before, but she had never seen it reach for something the way it reached now. Despite the fact that she knew the darkness would not harm her, Dora shivered. The monster dropped a few feet in altitude as it fought the cords of despair twisting into it.

The monster jerked and screeched as it reached out of the blackness in one final attempt to reach the small, frantic harpy trying to escape. Its claw must have connected because Selene screeched in pain, and Dora saw blood fly through the air. Anger, fear, and violence were a pounding in her blood and a roaring in her ears. Dora pushed more wind into the monster, shoving it away from Selene, who was making a beeline for her with a look of determined terror on her face.

The sound of two solid bodies and walls of power collided as Petra dove straight into the monster. Black feathers and the roar of a harpy full of the fury of battle filled the air.

Selene was still flying, and she made it past Dora, who yelled at her, pushing what will she could into the command. "Get on the porch and stay there."

Dora did not look to make sure the young one listened. She dove towards the black-feathered harpy entangled with the leathery-skinned monster. Petra grappled with the beast, using her claws to rip at its face while her talons ripped at its belly. Fighting that way meant she could not fly and attack so the pair slammed into the ground, where they rolled and flapped, kicking up dirt and grass.

Up close, the monster looked even more like a bat. This close, there was also no escaping the smell. A cloud of foul air, ten times worse than the food rotting in the yard, assaulted Dora's nose and made her eyes water. Petra met Dora's eyes and she released the monster. Thinking Petra had given up, it launched itself into the air, straight into Dora's waiting talons.

The scent of blood almost covered up the stench coming from the monster. Dora could feel the warmth of its blood beneath her talons, and she tasted the copper in the air on her tongue. She wanted to roll in the sensation for days. A great need for more overwhelmed her, and she buried her pointed teeth at the base of the monsters' neck. She shook the monster like a wolf shakes its prey, all the while pumping her wings to keep them in the air. The violence was a song in her soul and she let it flow out of her and into action.

The monster managed to get one hooked claw around the back of Dora's neck. Through the euphoria of violence, Dora felt her skin open up along her neck, but she did not release the skin beneath her teeth. She only ground her teeth harder and gave the monster another toss.

Dora's onslaught gave Petra a chance to get back into the air. The moment before Petra reached them, Dora released the beast and allowed Petra to assault the creature. Petra ripped it open from sternum to tail then darted away, giving Dora an opening to repeat her assault from above. Thus, they ripped, slashed, and drove the monster down onto the ground until they both landed beside a body that resembled nothing so much as meat prepared for sausage casings.

It lay still in a pool of fetid blood. Dora and Petra stood over what was left of the body, panting. Red still rimmed the edges of Dora's vision. She wiped sweat from her brow and her claw came away bloody. Dora looked at her hand in disbelief. She did not remember getting hurt.

She looked over at Petra. There was an ugly welt down one side of her face and one of her wings hung lower to the ground than the other. There was no blood that Dora could see. She released a cry of triumph and warning that rang through the air. She crouched down, the cry and its menace still echoing in her ears. The sound of someone running intruded over the ringing in her ears and Dora spun towards the sound and hissed at the intrusion before seeing who it was that interrupted them. Petra was still focused on the kill and did not hear whatever was coming.

Dora relaxed a fraction when James and Adam rounded the corner of the barn. Adam skidded to a halt, kicking up dust as he took in the scene. James stumbled over his own feet, then ran to Petra.

James cupped Petra's harpy face as though she were the most precious thing. "Where is Selene?"

"On the porch." Dora's voice was rougher than normal. She had to struggle to form the words. She choked down the violence she was drowning in and forced herself to calm down. The monster would have killed Selene. The anger rose again and Dora shuddered under its power.

James turned and ran towards the porch. He was met halfway by a sobbing Selene. James ran a hand over and down Selene's back and made shushing noises.

With great effort, Dora turned towards Petra, who had shifted back to her mortal form. "I think she was injured."

Dora pulled her harpy back into herself. She took the swirling need for violence and packed it away, letting her mortal form come forward. The threat was past and there was work to do. Dora focused on what needed to be done. She ignored the stinging on the back of her neck and the trickle of what she knew must be blood from multiple wounds.

Dora watched Petra and James comfort their child as her own heart returned to normal. Her boiling blood cooled and the red haze in her vision faded. This was why she fought. For her family. There was nothing to be ashamed of in that. Tears mixed with the blood coming from somewhere on her head.

Petra kissed the top of Selene's head. "Let me see where you're hurt." Petra shifted the girl so Dora could get a good look at her.

"My back." Selene stretched to reveal a scratch that ran the length of the girl's back. It was long but shallow.

If the monster had not already been dead, Dora would have gladly killed it again. "We'll get you cleaned up in no time. Good thing for you, harpies heal fast. I know it hurts now, but it will be closed up by tomorrow. It's not very deep, and you don't need stitches. You'll have nothing but a bruise to show for it."

Petra squeezed the girl and placed kisses all over her small face. "You flew so fast and brave. Momma was so scared for you."

James leaned down and rested his forehead on Selene's. "I thought my heart would stop when I came around the corner and did not see you both."

Dora opened the door. "Let's get inside and clean up. I'll put some water on to boil for tea and for our wounds."

Adam stood awkwardly on the side of the porch. He was like family, close enough to be pale with worry and shock, but not close enough to intrude on the family reunion. He pointed to the bloody mess in the yard.

"What about that?"

Petra's lip curled. "It's not going anywhere. Let's take care of ourselves first. Dora and I will take care of it after that."

They all went inside. Dora put water on the stove while Petra tended to Selene, who was more frightened than hurt.

James pulled a bottle of whiskey from the shelf while they waited for the tea to brew. "I don't normally drink during the day, but I think we could all use a little fortification."

Petra raised an eyebrow at her husband. "Don't tell Marina. She'll think she's been a good influence."

James' lips held the ghost of a smile. "I am not sure she could be a good influence on anyone."

Adam brought some clean rags out from the back room and laid them on the table. Petra cleaned up Selene, and James cleaned Petra's wounds. Dora sat watching them and felt a wave of peace replace the violence from before. This is why they fought so hard to protect what was theirs.

A hand on her arm brought her focus away from the small family.

"It looks like you've some scrapes of your own. Can I help you with them?" Adam asked in his slow Texas drawl.

Dora nodded and turned so he could see her back. "I think the one on the back of my neck is the worst, though I know the one on my temple or head must be more than a little scratch. It was bleeding freely before." She no longer felt the trickle of blood on her skin everywhere, but her muscles were stiff and her skin felt stretched and cracked where the blood had dried.

Adam lifted her hair and drew in a quick breath. "Not just a scratch, I'd say. If you were human, I'd say you needed the Doc to do some stitchin'. Not sure you still don't."

He laid the warm cloth along her neck, and the gentle throb of pain that had been there bloomed into something sharper. She hissed in response and gripped the edge of the table.

Petra handed Selene over to James and walked until she stood behind Dora. "Styx and fire, Dora. Maybe you should be see Doc. I'll go to town with you."

Dora twisted around in her chair to look at Petra, but the movement wrenched her neck and she gripped the table so hard the wood groaned. "I don't need to see Lee. I'll be fine in a few hours, and then I can fly on my own."

"Oh, for Hera's sake, don't be so stubborn. Are you two still arguing?" Irritation gave way to real anger in Petra's words. Their fight was too recent for either one of them to have full control over their emotions and they both knew it.

Dora gripped the wood even harder. "No, we aren't arguing," she ground out. "I just don't need stitches."

Petra snorted and took the rag from Adam. "I'll finish with her. She's likely to get snappish before you're done, and I can handle anything she flings my way." There was a smile in her voice this time, and Dora relaxed.

James carried Selene over to Dora and placed the girl in Dora's lap. "Adam and I will drag the carcass out of the yard. We can burn it back behind the garden. It's too big to bury."

Dora looked up at him. "Wait to burn it. I want Marina and Iris to see it."

James placed a slow kiss on Petra's check and ran a hand down her back. He went to the door and opened it but did not walk through. His unexpected halt caused Adam to stumble into him.

"Bloody hell," James said.

Dora put Selene on the table and was a step behind Petra as they raced to see what James saw outside. A rush of dread and violence rose inside Dora as she moved. It was still close to the surface from the fight.

Dora looked around Petra's shoulder, and ice went through her veins. The front yard was empty. There was a puddle of bloody mud where the monster had lain but the body was gone. Petra and Dora pushed past the two men and scanned the skies.

"When I see you again, I will rip your head from your body and eat your heart!" Petra screamed at the sky.

Dora, fighting the rising violence in her own blood, felt the same conviction singing through her. She turned to address Petra. "We have to go into town to warn the others. Lee can look at my neck." Then, to herself, she muttered, "I'm fine."

Petra responded, pointing to the blood on the ground. "That thing won't be."

Dora flashed her teeth at Petra. "We will rip it into so many pieces there will be nothing left."

CHAPTER 17

Iris took one look at them and closed the depot for the day. She shoved Dora, who looked the worst, into a chair and yelled for Thomas. The boy bounded down the stairs in a heartbeat.

"Thomas, go get everyone, including Doc." The boy was out of the depot before she had finished the sentence.

"I'm fine. I lost a lot of blood and the flight wore me out." Dora leaned against the wall. "I could really use something to drink."

Iris gave her some water, and they waited for everyone to assemble. They sat in a circle at the tables in the back of the depot. The door opened and Lee's silhouette filled the doorway. The light was behind him and she could not make out his features clearly, but when she saw him, something snapped into place. Later, when she was alone, she would take time to acknowledge and assess this. Now, there was no leisure time for such revelations.

"Thomas told me to bring my bag because you were hurt." Lee came into the room and headed straight for her.

Dora was too busy watching his lithe progress to answer his unasked question. Lee stopped inches from her, and she was enveloped by the subtle scent radiating off him. Her entire body tightened at his nearness and she canted towards him.

Lee's eyes darkened to a deep, dangerous grey, but he remained still. The moment stretched impossibly long until Dora blinked. Lee's eyes swept over her, and the fingers of his right hand traced the healing gash on her temple. His hand continued down and cupped her neck. She jerked at the touch, both from the trail of heat he had been creating and from the twinge of pain as his hand wrapped around her neck.

"Are you hurt? Beyond the scratch here?" He traced her temple again and she had to steel herself not to push into his touch.

Dora shrugged, and the movement pulled the gash on the back of her neck. Lee did not miss her small wince.

"Turn around and lift up your hair."

"It's nothing. It's already half healed," she protested.

"Turn around and let me look." Lee growled out the words.

His tone tightened the coil within her. Only a harpy would get turned on when a man gets growly and bossy. Dora chuckled at herself. "Since you asked so nice."

Dora turned and pulled her hair over her right shoulder. Lee made a hissing noise.

"This is not nothing. If you were mortal, you would need stitches."

"Good thing I'm not mortal. Do I need stitches?"

Lee huffed, and she felt the warmth of it on her neck. She tried to keep the shiver to herself, but Lee placed his hand on her shoulder and rubbed a circle with his thumb.

"If I had seen this after it happened, I would have put a few stitches in for good measure, but you have shifted and waited too long. Your body heals quickly enough that these look worse than they are now. Did you clean it?"

"Yes."

"What did this?"

"That is part of why we need you here. Petra and I killed something." Dora turned back around.

Lee was still standing close enough that Dora could feel the heat of his body coming off him in waves. His eyes kept searching her face as if there was an answer there he was missing.

"Please be careful for another day or two until your back heals. It could still split back open, doing more damage. Keep it clean. If you can't reach it," Lee cleared his throat, "have someone help you."

His hesitation and his words brought images to her head she had never dared to consider before. Not trusting her voice, she nodded.

"You know how to care for wounds, but the ones with the most knowledge sometimes neglect themselves. In addition, I would be displeased with you if you got yourself killed, so nothing dramatic while it heals." He smiled at her when he said the last part.

Dora sighed dramatically. "If you insist. You're a terribly demanding doctor." It felt right to be easy in his presence after weeks of stiffness.

Lee settled into the chair next to her, still keeping distance between them. Dora was both hurt and grateful for it. "I am glad we are speaking again."

Petra leaned forward. "We're all glad you're speaking again."

Dora jolted. She had forgotten they were not alone.

A trickle of joy ran through her. Dora still had the book she had bought for Lee upstairs. She wanted to see his face when he opened it, but today seemed like a day for bad news, not gifts. She had bought it thinking it would be a peace offering after her bad behavior, but they had moved past that. The book, instead, was the start of something new.

Once everyone was assembled, and James had arrived on horseback, Petra and Dora told the story of their encounter with the monster that had disappeared. Petra still clutched Selene, afraid to let the girl go. Marina held Ellie, and Nina sat on Reed's knee. Aldara was curled up in Henry's lap. An open ache Dora had ignored for a very long time opened up in her as she sat encircled by the family of her choosing.

Iris looked ill. Her face had paled when they had told about the monster disappearing at the end of the story, and shortly after her face acquired a green tinge. Dora's eyes rested on Iris and she waited until Iris raised her own fear-filled blue eyes to hers.

"I think Iris has something to share," Dora said.

All heads swiveled.

Iris cleared her throat. "Nina, take the young ones upstairs. Thomas, you stay."

Nina started to protest, but Reed leaned over and whispered something in her ear and gave her shoulder a squeeze. The young girl clamped up her complaints and herded the three smaller girls upstairs with the promise of cookies.

While the children filed upstairs, Iris went behind the counter and retrieved a parchment. She came back to the group and angled herself so she could partially lean on Henry. He had his arm around her shoulders. With her hands free, she unrolled the parchment on the table and began to talk.

"A couple days ago, I started thinking about what Dora said about all the things going on being connected. I started looking in different places. I found a reference to a creature called a keres. I thought that might be what we were dealing with, but then I uncovered something else this morning. When we first saw the monster in the distance, it took me a while to find it in my books and papers. They looked so much like the harpies that I was distracted by that when I should have been looking at the larger picture. We're not dealing with just one monster, a keres, we're dealing with The Keres. A set of three, all harbingers of something worse to come."

Lee leaned forward. "What's the difference?"

"Keres are creatures of spite, death, and anger. Like harpies, the original Keres were created to torment souls and drive them to Tartarus. They preyed on the battlefield. When there was no war to feed them, they would stir up trouble. Plagues. Civil Wars. Famine. Descendants of the original three Keres were much less powerful, but they still fed off death and destruction, like vultures, creating death when there were no wars and creating pestilence when they were hungry."

Iris ran a hand over the parchment. "Like many other Remnant lines, The Keres disappeared a few generations after the Fall of Olympus. There were few mentions of them even before the Fall, and after that, there was nothing. When we started looking in my books, we weren't looking with the right set of facts. We were looking for something to help us identify the monster when what we should have been looking for was an event. A set of events, actually.

"The first Keres were too destructive, too violent, and a hero took matters into his own hands and trapped them for eternity in something he thought would never be opened." Her hand shook on the table, and Henry took it into his own. "The hero sealed The Keres into Pandora's Jar."

Dora hissed and sat back in her chair. "I know the myths, as I'm sure most of us do, but according to the myths, Pandora's destruction has already been unleashed upon the world. But you're acting like The Keres are not the worst thing."

Reed leaned forward and chopped a hand through the air. "Hold on. I thought Pandora had a box, not a jar."

Iris replied, "The myth of Pandora has been diluted by mortals over the ages. The vessel containing the sadness and plagues of the world was a funeral urn, called a pithos. It is a jar. As to Dora's question, the accounts of the jar are garbled. The myths say that it was only opened once, by Pandora, but according to my papers it was opened once again after The Keres were trapped there. I found an early eyewitness account of the events in a remote village in Germania. The Keres were seen as the harbinger to a wave of plagues. The village was so devastated before the end of the series of events that it had to be abandoned."

A certain dread about what was coming wrapped around Dora's shoulders. "I think we know how it started. The crops and food spoiled and the livestock died of a mysterious disease while Keres attacked the people."

Iris nodded. "But that's not all. There are three Keres, and three waves of despair that come from Pandora's Jar once it's opened. If I'm correct, then the last wave of despair from the jar has yet to hit us."

Dora felt Lee stiffen beside her. "You needed me here, but not just because I'm a Remnant. There are others who would have fit that profile who are missing. You needed me here because I'm a doctor. You keep calling the things coming from the jar plagues. The last despair is a sickness, isn't it?"

"Yes," Iris said. "The third despair is a plague on people."

"What are the symptoms? What is the survivability rate? Is there a cure?" Lee listed the questions with a calm Dora knew meant he was processing and finding solutions. His right index finger tapped nervously on his thigh.

"The records are vague. The only survivor of that village was a small boy. While he was there to see it all, he did not have a complete understanding of everything, and what he did tell later seemed unbelievable to the person who wrote down his account."

Dora pushed down the panic that threatened to tighten her throat. "Out of the entire village, there was one survivor."

"Yes," Iris whispered. "His account was simplistic because of his age and garbled because of his fear. The men that found him had no idea how long he had been alone in the village. They burned the entire village to the ground."

Lee shifted in his seat. "Did the boy say what the sickness was like?"

Iris nodded. "Yes, but the record is not complete. It starts with a fever and a rash of some kind. Then a burning of the joints, and," Iris swallowed, "the boy said they died with blood coming out of their eyes."

They looked at each other in horror. Dora had seen something like this, and she could feel the terror ripping at her. Her mother had died that way, with a fever, a rash, and then bleeding from her eyes and ears. She put a hand on the table to steady herself.

Lee cleared his throat. "This kind of illness is very contagious and known as a hemorrhagic fever. They cause the body to shut down. The patient bleeds from their orifices. They are common in other parts of the world."

Reed scowled. "That's not exactly comforting."

Petra's gaze sharpened. "Iris said there are three of the Keres, not one. That means more killing. More revenge." Her lips curled up into a deadly smile.

Marina's eyes shifted and her harpy looked out at the group. "How do we kill the Keres? If we find all of them before the last plague comes, will that stop the plague from coming?"

Dora had to control her own harpy at the sight of Marina's and Petra's so close to the surface. She felt the power coming off both of them as she spoke. "That village did not have harpies to defend it. Turning Creek will not be lost to history." Dora lost the battle with her harpy and her power leaked out to join the others.

Iris gave them a weak smile. "I think that may give us an advantage. The Keres can't simply be killed, though, as Dora and Petra learned. They have to be beheaded and burned and then a pinch of the ashes of each must be sealed back into Pandora's Jar. The pithos must be sealed with the blood of its guardian."

"Blood for the blood of others." The dance in Dora's veins was full of blood-red thoughts. Dora let the music continue without reining it in.

Lee's voice cut through Dora's dark thoughts. "Who is the guardian?"

"The guardian will be a Remnant of Pandora herself," Iris said.

Reed rubbed a hand on his chin. "I don't suppose you know who that might be?" Reed asked.

Iris shook her head. "No. It's not terribly surprising given their history that whoever it is would have kept their identity a secret. Who would want that known if it meant their possible death or the death of a loved one down the line?"

Petra looked ready to fight something that moment. "How do we find the Remnant of Pandora? Go door to door?"

Marina rubbed her hands and flashed pointed teeth. "I'll ask extra nice."

Dora made fists in her lap with her hands. The violence in the room was like blood on her tongue, and the heat from Lee's presence garbled everything. She closed her eyes and tried to center herself before speaking. She failed until Lee placed a brief hand on her knee. Everything dropped back into place. "Even if we ask Marina's way, it's likely they'll lie."

Reed cleared his throat. "There's one other matter."

"Something worse than this?" Dora asked.

Reed and Marina shared a look. "Perhaps not, perhaps so, but it complicates matters," he said. "All the food you brought back from Leadville spoiled. And not just that but all the food in the mercantile. We checked a few houses. Anything stored, canned, or baked has gone rotten."

Petra nodded. "At my house too."

Iris held up a hand. "I haven't gotten to that part yet, but that's part of the plagues from the pithos. The record, because of the source, contains very few details. According to the boy, the crops failed, food spoiled, livestock died, and there was a sickness."

Marina's eyes gleamed. "It looks like we will be hunting meat, The Keres, and a Remnant."

Dora pointed a finger at Marina. "We can't just go rushing in like a youngling. We need a plan. We have to find The Keres, find the guardian, and find the jar. I doubt they keep it on the mantel for all to see."

Henry leaned forward into the circle. "All those things take time. Hunting The Keres and the source does not solve the immediate problem of food and an impending sickness."

There were pounding feet coming down the stairs and wailing from several small people. James rose from the table with a sigh and intercepted the girls before they rounded the corner.

"There is an awful amount of tears and crying going on between all of you. What's wrong?" he asked.

Nina replied, "All the cookies are covered in mold. I went through the whole batch. When we couldn't find any to eat, the little girls started to cry."

"I made those yesterday," Iris whispered.

James dried the tears of the girls. "Now, we'll find something else for

you to eat shortly. Until then, please go back upstairs and play. Please."
Nina took all the girls back up the stairs.

Reed put his hands on the table. "Iris, you said you made those cookies yesterday?" Iris nodded. Reed turned to Henry. "Go upstairs and see if the food in your kitchen is spoiled. Bring down whatever is up there that's edible."

Henry rose and went upstairs.

Marina cocked her head to one side. "What're you thinking?"

Reed shook his head. "A notion, is all. Maybe, nothing."

Dora placed her hand on Lee's arm. It was strange to allow herself to touch him. She could feel the heat of his skin beneath her fingers and the hardness of his muscled forearm. She reveled in the simple act of contact until she realized he was watching her, waiting for something.

Dora cleared her throat but did not move her hand. "There'll be plenty to do to prepare if we have a plague coming our way. I can help you."

"I think your unique skills might be better served hunting with your sisters."

Dora removed her hand and tangled it together with her other hand in her lap. No matter how much time she spent healing people with Lee, he was right. She was best suited for hunting and killing. The weight of the day was pierced by something painful in her heart.

Lee turned and focused his attention on Dora. The rest of the table was forgotten as he spoke to her. "You misunderstand. I will need your help once the sickness arrives, but until then, I can make do without you while you attend to the matter of trying to stop this. If the gods are with us, we will be able to kill The Keres and seal the jar before the plague comes. If we fail and it does come, I'll need you with me."

Despite the danger facing them, Dora smiled at Lee. She should not have doubted him so quickly. Marina and Petra looked smug. Henry returned then, saving Dora from the heat of a full-fledged blush creeping over her neck and up her face.

Henry placed two-thirds of a round loaf of bread on the table. "This is all there is."

Reed pointed to the bread. "When was this made?"

Iris swallowed. "This morning."

Marina turned and leaned into Reed's space. "You know something. Your eyes have that shine they get when you're about to win an argument with me."

Reed leaned back in his chair, whether from frustration or to escape Marina's scrutiny, Dora could not tell. "I wish I wasn't right this once. It's like the Israelites wandering in the desert." His statement was met with blank stares by everyone except Iris, who began nodding her head.

Reed continued, "It's a good story about obedience." He cast a pointed look in Marina's direction. "I should tell you the whole thing someday." She rolled her eyes and he winked at her. "The Israelites left slavery and wandered around in the desert for forty years. They had many mouths to feed and not enough food to feed them, so God sent food to them. One of the foods he sent was called manna. It fell from the sky every day and every day they gathered it to eat. If they tried to gather enough for the next day, the manna would rot overnight. They could only gather and save enough for one day at a time. It taught them reliance on God."

The implications of Reed's theory started to sink in. Dora asked, "You think we're going to have to gather and prepare food only for what we need that day?"

Reed rubbed the back of his neck. "It's just a theory."

Petra rubbed her hands up and down her thighs. "That means gathering and hunting every day. Not everyone can do that or knows what can be gathered and eaten."

Henry said, "With the crops gone and all the stored food gone, this is going to hit people hard in the short term. Facing winter is going to be an entire other mountain to climb." That thought sobered everyone further.

"One problem at a time," Reed said.

Dora's heart sped up at the thought of all the mouths their valley now contained. Mouths she would kill to protect. "I've been doing more research on medicinal herbs. Some of the readings include lists of edible ones. If we're going to have to gather every day, we'll need to gather everything available. I can make a list of what's likely to be found in the valley."

Petra crossed her arms over her chest. "If we do that, we'll spend all our time hunting food, not finding the jar or killing The Keres."

The weight of the souls in Turning Creek settled over their shoulders. It had always been there. All of them, in some way, had willingly borne the burden for years, but now the weight threatened to crush them. Dora rolled her shoulders, trying to ease the press of what was coming.

"I do not want to offend any delicate harpy prides in the room," Lee's mouth quirked up in the ghost of a smile, "but there are others, mortals and Remnants, who can hunt game."

Dora sat up as a thought struck her. "Has anyone seen the huntresses lately?"

Atlanta and Cyrene lived in a small cabin just south of the valley during the winter and spring. In the summer, they often traveled in search of larger and more exotic hunts. They thrived on the thrill of the hunt and the company of each other. While their relationship with the harpies had not always been easy, they were their own kind of predator, and the harpies respected them.

Petra said, "They spent the first part of the summer with one of the tribes to the west. I'm not sure if they've returned yet."

"Thomas can run down and check their cabin. He can leave a message for them when they return if they're still away." Iris rose from her seat and went behind the counter of the depot. She returned with pen, ink, and paper. She started writing while they continued the conversation.

Reed stood. "We need to call a town meeting and send messages to as many in the valley as we can. We'll need to pool resources to keep everyone fed. For some, that may mean moving closer in on a temporary basis. We can meet in the morning. That'll give us time to spread the word."

Henry leaned back in his chair. "Not everyone will be willing or able to do that."

Reed shook his head. "I know, but we have to give 'em the option."

Lee made a swiping motion with his hand. "More people living closer together will mean that if we do not stop this before the plague comes, it will spread through the town quickly."

Petra sat back in her chair. "It might be a gamble we have to take."

Lee nodded. "I know, but as a physician, I don't like it."

Iris looked up from her writing. "I'll talk to Vine and see if we can meet at the saloon. The depot isn't big enough for everyone anymore."

Reed hesitated. "Are there any human families that don't know about Remnants in the valley?"

It was a valid question. There had been a time when the Remnants had been a closely guarded secret, but all that had changed a few years ago, when Marina and Iris had transformed to save a mother and child in a collapsed building. New mortal families moving in now got a visit from a select handful of Remnants, who eased them into the reality of the valley.

Dora spoke. "There haven't been any new families this season and everyone else moving in has been a Remnant, so the welcoming committee hasn't been necessary."

Lee held up his right hand. "How much information are we going to give people? All of it? If the Remnant of Pandora knows we are looking for the pithos and for them as a sacrifice, I don't think they will offer themselves easily."

Dore's heart sank further. Their choices were terrible. They could conceal information that might help them find the jar or reveal it and drive the Remnant away. A terrible thought occurred to her. "What if the Remnant already knows we'll be looking for them soon and flees?"

Marina's eyes flashed again. "The valley is too big to keep it all under our eyes and we can't round everyone up to keep them penned in. That might solve our problem, but it doesn't mean we should do it."

Dora knew Marina was right, but a part of her wished they could make the easy choice, not the morally correct one. Taking the moral high ground was more work.

Henry's voice was low and quiet. "We have to trust in the goodness of others. Perhaps they'll come forward."

Iris ran a hand down her husband's arm. "We'll trust them not to run, but I doubt they'll offer themselves up like a lamb to the slaughter."

Lee tapped his long index finger on his thigh. "I think we should leave the information about the pithos out of our meeting with the town. It could cause panic."

"I disagree," Reed said. "Searching for that from home to home will be like finding a drop of rain in a thunderstorm. Renault sells what I assume are similar jars on Main Street. We're going to need the people's help. If we at least tell Matthew Renault, perhaps he can give us guidance about what to look for."

"The truth would give the Remnant of Pandora the chance to do what's right." Henry's words were like a recrimination of the thoughts Dora was having.

Lee's finger kept tapping and Dora could see the thoughts moving across his face. "You're right, but telling the people could result in panic. People could turn on their neighbors."

Dora squeezed Lee's knee. "We can't tell them. The chance that they'll step forward is too small. It's more likely they'll go into hiding. We can look for it without telling people that is what we're doing. We'll need to visit all the houses to check on them and to get a measure of their food supply anyway."

Lee added, "If we don't find it before the sickness starts, Dora and I will be visiting people for that purpose as well. That will give us more access deeper into people's homes without raising suspicion."

"Besides, Marina, Petra, and I can usually sense a lie. We can make sure to ask some pointed questions whenever we make a home visit." Dora relaxed. Having a plan meant they would have a direction, and they had never failed yet when they stood together.

"What do the rest of you think?" Henry asked.

Marina spoke first. "I agree with Dora." She gave her husband an apologetic shrug.

"Me too," Petra said.

"Well, I won't deny I'm disappointed in you and even more disappointed that you might be right," Reed conceded. "The meeting will be tomorrow afternoon. We'll serve a community supper after and make a plan together on how to feed people."

"Right then," Marina said. "Let's stop yabbering and get to work."

Dora moved her hand from Lee's knee and grabbed some of the paper Iris had brought to the table. "I'll start making copies of lists of the plants and their descriptions. We can hand them out at the meeting."

"I'll make a list of what we'll need if a plague does reach us." Lee rose and gathered more writing supplies from behind the depot counter.

Henry ran a hand down Iris's back then stood. "Reed and I can spread the word amongst the townsfolk."

Thomas, who had remained silent, stood. "I'll take the message to the huntresses and then help deliver news of the meeting."

Marina and Petra looked at each other. Marina spoke. "I suppose that means we are flying all over the valley with the good news. Not everyone will come."

"They don't have to come, especially if they can feed their own, but there will be few who can shoulder that burden alone. Just make sure everyone gets the invitation." Reed put a hand on Marina's arm and gripped hard. "You two fly safe. Don't take on The Keres unless you have to, and if you do, make sure the bastard is dead."

Marina grinned and placed a loud kiss on Reed's lips. "I like it when you tell me to kill things."

Dora rolled her eyes and laughed. Even with a challenge as daunting as this, they all knew their strengths and worked as a unit. The next few days and weeks would not be easy, but they would do it together. She looked at Lee through the corner of her eye. His dark head was already bent over the list he was making. They were in the lee of the rock and the wind was shifting. It would not be long before the brunt of the storm was upon them. When it came, they would be together, fighting.

James stood. "I will go back the farm to ready things and return to town tomorrow."

Petra rubbed her hands over her thighs. "I'll leave Selene here, if that's all right. I can travel faster without her."

Iris patted Petra's hand. "Don't worry. We'll take care of her."

Petra and James went upstairs to take leave of their daughter. Everyone dispersed to their own duties.

With a pointed look at Lee, Iris leaned over to Dora and said in a voice meant only for her to hear, "When we have a moment alone, I think you have some things to tell me, my bird."

Dora's eyes slid to Lee again, and she could feel a blush heating her neck. She cursed her fair skin and how it always gave her away. She nodded and returned to the list she was making. There would be time later. Now, they had work to do.

Everyone dispersed to take care of their tasks, and Dora left the depot and headed to the Renault's ceramic shop. The inside of the shop was bright with the light coming in through the large glass windows at the front of the shop. There was a kiln and a workshop behind the storefront and the air smelled like clay and fire. Ruben was sweeping the floor when Dora came in.

Ruben paused in his work and smiled at Dora. "Good day, madam.

What can I do for you today?"

"I need to speak to your father or mother if they are here." Dora returned his smile.

"Father is in the back working on some new pots. I will fetch him." The boy disappeared behind a curtain that acted as a doorway behind the sales counter.

Dora wandered around the inside of the shop. The vessels for sale ranged from plain and useful to ornate and decorative. She ran her finger over the edge of a green mixing bowl. It was the color of grass in the summer.

"I made that one because Magda is always telling me a good cook can never have enough mixing bowls," a kind voice said behind her.

Dora turned to find Matthew Renault drying his hands on a towel. He had on an apron that was covered in grey clay. "I agree with your wife. This is a lovely bowl. I'm sorry to interrupt your work."

Mr. Renault's eyes crinkled when he smiled. "I don't mind the interruption. What can I do for you?"

"We have a situation in the valley and there will be a town meeting about it tomorrow." Dora explained what they knew about the plagues minus the link to Pandora. She let a bit of her power reach out to Mr. Renault to judge his reaction. He was afraid, but that was normal, considering what she revealed.

Dora continued. "I also need to ask you some questions. We are in need of your ceramics expertise."

"I will tell you anything you need to know," he said without hesitation, and Dora could feel the truth of his words.

Dora needed to ask about the jar without actually asking about the jar. "What do you know about the old Greek-style pithos jars? More specifically, if I was looking for one, what would distinguish it from other jars?"

Mr. Renault hesitated and Dora saw it before he started speaking. "The style of an early pithos would vary greatly depending on who was kept in it. A person of means would have an elaborate pithos. A peasant, if they had one at all, would have something plainer, without carvings or color. Some were made large enough to hold the entire body, others were made only to fit ashes. They are usually vase shaped and some have handles.

"Though it is not a common practice, I still occasionally get requests for them from those who follow the old ways." He cocked his head. "Are you wanting something particular?"

Dora could still feel his underlying tension. "I am looking for something that has been misplaced. Thank you. This conversation has been helpful."

"I'm glad I could be of service. If you want to commission something, I would be pleased to make something special for you."

Dora turned towards the door to leave. "Thank you, Mr. Renault. I appreciate that. I'll see you tomorrow at the meeting."

Once outside on the boardwalk, Dora sifted through the conversation. The description he had given was general, but it might be helpful in finding Pandora's jar. His fear and hesitancy could be explained away by the news she had relayed first. She liked Matthew Renault. He seemed like an honest man, and Dora did not want to doubt her instincts. In the search for the jar, she did not want to lose her trust of people in the valley.

CHAPTER 18

The next week was a relentless cycle of securing food, dispensing the food before it spoiled overnight, and waiting for the plague to appear. The burden of waiting for what was coming made every step, every wingbeat, twice as hard as it should have been. It was like swimming across rapids with no sight of the other shore. The skies were clear of The Keres, though the harpies flew all over the valley every day, scouring every nook and cranny. The harpies spent so much of their time hunting for The Keres and hunting and delivering food that they had precious few minutes to spare looking for Pandora's pithos. The relentless pressure was exhausting to the point of numbness.

"Pass that bottle over here," Petra demanded of Marina.

They sat on the front porch of Petra's house. The moon was high, and Dora rubbed her aching shoulders against the post she leaned against. She had spent most of the morning hunting food and the elusive Keres, and the afternoon delivering food. Her stomach rumbled, reminding her that she had never slowed down enough to eat more than a handful of berries today.

"Do you have any food?" Dora asked.

Petra took a long pull from the bottle Marina had reluctantly given over. "I think there is some nut flour flatbread I made this morning and some milk from today's milking. We might as well eat what we have since it will all be rotten after midnight." Petra gave the bottle to Dora and rose to go inside.

Dora swirled the contents of the half full bottle before taking a sip. The heat of the whiskey burned its way straight to her empty belly and made her head light. She tilted the neck towards Marina; when she tried to take the bottle, Dora yanked it back and took another sip. Marina gave her an evil glare. Dora winked at her.

"I suppose you're quite pleased that liquor seems to be exempt from the manna rule." Dora gave Marina the bottle. They had taken to calling the daily spoilage the manna rule after Reed had told them the story of the Israelites in the desert.

Dora leaned her head back against the pole. "Sure would be nice, though, if some god would send manna every day for us to eat. Save us the trouble of searching for it."

Petra came back out with a plate of food that she put in the middle of their small circle. "I never thought I'd say this, but I'm tired of hunting."

Marina grabbed a small flatbread. "I never thought I'd agree with that statement, but I wish I could waste a day fleecing someone of their coin and drinking. Just one whole day."

Dora laughed. "You haven't done that since Ellie was born."

Marina shrugged. "Still, I'm tired. I've never been so tired in my life, and I have a young one at home."

A screech rent the night air. All three harpies jumped to their feet and looked at each other. Only one thing made a noise that harsh.

"The Keres." A surge of relief at the appearance of the thing they had hunted slammed into her, renewing the adrenaline in Dora's veins. The whiskey she had consumed burned a hole of anger in her soul.

"It's about damned time." Marina's words went from human to harpy as she changed and shot into the air.

Dora released her own power and let her harpy take over. She launched herself into the air, aware of Marina in front of her and Petra at her side. The night became brighter with her harpy vision and her senses exploded with information. Dora zeroed in on their prey and sliced through the night sky to apprehend the beast.

There was enough of a moon that the Keres was a murky black stain on the deep blue of the night. Dora watched as Marina collided with the monster first, a tangle of wings and claws. Dora could smell the warm blood on the air the moment the first injury was made, and her own blood rioted in response.

Marina slashed and pushed off the Keres. Dora used the Keres's disorientation to slide under its neck and reach in with her talons. She found purchase with both feet and curled her talons into fists, ripping into the Keres right above its chest. The wet warmth of blood poured between her talons, and Dora screeched with pleasure. Petra answered her call and landed between the shoulder blades of the monster.

Dora felt the Keres shudder with Petra's weight. She gave one last wrench of her talons before releasing the creature to Petra's ministrations. Before she could get herself clear, the Keres swung its head down and aimed its many toothed maw at Dora's head. She reared back, but not before the teeth made contact with her cheek. Dora felt the burn as her cheek opened up and blood poured down the side of her face.

Dora whipped her clawed wing up and swiped at the monster's bat face. She dug her longest claws into its eye socket. Dora felt the pop when the eyeball came out of the socket and the Keres screamed. Dora looked down and saw the ground rising to meet them. Petra, her talons dug deep into the shoulders of the Keres, eased them down to the ground with a jarring, but not bone-crunching, impact.

Even with the help, they all tumbled to the ground in a heap of claws and talons. Dora rolled away from the Keres, and Marina dove in from above. The beast flopped wildly, and Dora moved and sat on one wing while Petra grounded the other. Marina used all her strength and speed to dive into the downed monster. She used claws and teeth and ripped half of the Keres' neck open. Blood and flesh flew in all directions. The lifeblood of the Keres gushed into the ground.

Dora stepped off of the Keres and shifted into her mortal form. The left side of her face throbbed, and she swayed on her feet. It had been too many days since she had eaten a full meal. Her lips were wet and when she licked them, they tasted of blood and victory. Dora licked them again and then brought her hand to her mouth and licked the blood off one of her fingers, careful not to nick her mortal skin on her still pointed teeth. It was only after she had cleaned a third finger that Dora and the others realized they had an audience.

Like a replay of a scene they had acted out before, James was running towards Petra. A semi-circle of ranch hands stood off to the side. Adam held a lantern. Dora could see an array of shock and disgust on their faces. Knowing what the three women were was one thing; seeing them destroy a monster with teeth and claws was quite another.

Dora ignored James running towards Petra and looked at her harpy sisters and grinned. "This is the best hunting we've had in weeks."

Petra moved away from their kill to meet James a few feet away from the blood pooling onto the ground.

James reached up and ran his hands over Petra's head and over her harpy shoulders. She stooped down to allow him better access. "I heard the fight from inside. It sounded like the very devil itself challenged you. You are all right?"

In a breath, Petra changed into her mortal form and leaned her forehead onto James'. "I'm fine. Gods, that felt good. Dora is hurt, though."

"I'm fine." Dora licked another finger and her vision went dark around the edges.

Marina was at her side in a moment. "You're not fine. When's the last time you ate?"

Dora had to think about it. "Yesterday, maybe. It's hard to eat and fly."

Marina led her back to the porch, sat her down, and shoved a cup of milk into her hands. "Drink that, if you can manage it with your cheek like that. You need stitches.”

“I’ll be fine.” Dora took a sip of the milk and ignored the searing pain running from her temple to her jaw.

Marina leaned into her face. “If you don’t want a hell of a scar, you need to go see Doc.”

Petra hollered at them. “There’s more work to do. Marina, we need your swords to finish the job you did on its neck.”

Marina kicked the dirt. “I knew I shouldn’t have left them on my saddle.”

She ran off towards the grassy field where her horse was hobbled. Dora could see the moon glinting off the blade as Marina pulled it from its custom saddle sheath. Marina ran back to the body of the Keres, where it lay on the ground. She grabbed the back of its head. With one sure movement, she sliced the blade through what was left of the Keres’s neck. Marina threw the head a few feet from the body.

Petra, her arm around James, called to the ranch hands, still standing and watching. “Adam, organize the men and build a small pyre here. We need to burn the body. I have a jar inside we can use to store the ashes.”

Adam immediately began issuing orders and Petra and James came over to where Dora was sitting. Dora pulled a small piece of flatbread off the loaf and popped it into her mouth. She chewed it with small agonizing movements. Her face throbbed with the beat of her heart.

Petra sat heavily on the porch steps. “James, will you please get a lantern from inside?”

Petra picked the whiskey bottle back up and took a long drink. “Styx, that felt great.” A full-bodied laugh escaped her mouth.

Dora felt her own bloodlust morph into something more joyful, and she joined Petra in her laughter, though it sent spiders of fresh pain over her. Marina swiped the bottle from Petra, took a drink, and started laughing. The mirth was a combination of relief at being alive and joy at their victory, achieved together. James returned to find them still cackling.

“I simply do not understand what the three of you find so divertingly hilarious about this. You just brutally slayed a monster who was trying to kill you, and Dora’s face is slashed open.”

His declaration was met with more laughter. Dora’s face throbbed and she could feel blood dripping from the wound. James mumbled something under his breath and plunked the lantern at their feet. He left the porch to go help build the pyre taking shape in the yard.

Marina wiped her eyes and raised the lantern to get a better look at Dora’s face. Dora turned her head to the side and closed her eyes against the brightness of the light. Marina grabbed her chin gently and turned Dora’s head to and fro. She did not tell Marina to stop, though the movement sent daggers of pain through her face.

Petra was looking over Marina's shoulder and hissed. "That is deep and needs to be cleaned."

"And stitched." Marina released her chin. "Can you fly to town?"

"Yes," Dora said immediately. When she opened her eyes, black dots danced before her eyes until she closed them again. "Maybe not. I think the whiskey on an empty stomach and the blood loss may be catching up to me."

Marina put a hand on Dora's knee and spoke to Petra. "Changing will help her heal, and I can fly back with her to town to make sure she gets there. Can you finish up things here?"

Petra looked out at the men working. "I've plenty of help here. Go, take her to Doc."

Dora sat up, a new thought in her head. "I don't want him to see me like this."

Marina cocked her head. "Like what? With your face ripped open or with blood on your hands?"

Dora shuddered. "The blood." Dora swallowed a sick feeling in her throat.

Petra laughed at her. "For Hera's sake, he knows what you are. If he can't be proud of that, you need to choose a better mate."

Dora frowned. "He's not my mate."

Marina snorted. Petra made a sound in the back of her throat.

Dora averted her gaze. "We haven't talked about it yet. I'm not ready."

Petra chuckled. "I think there needs to be less talking between the two of you."

Another stab of pain went right up into Dora's brain. "While I really hate both of you right now and I'd like to claw you for your ill-timed advice, can we move this along? If I'm going to get stitches, I'd like to get moving before I pass out. I might have hit my head on that last dive."

Dora and Marina changed again and flew southwest towards town. Dora knew the cut on her face was not life threatening, but the throbbing pain was starting to take over her head and spread down her shoulders, and that worried her. Her head felt like it had doubled in size and weighed fifty pounds. By the time they landed by the back of Lee's house, she could barely keep her eyes open.

Dora fumbled with the door latch. Her fingers had lost their feeling. Marina reached around her, yanked open the door, and wrapped Dora's arm around her shoulders to keep her upright.

"Doc," Marina yelled. "Doc!"

The sound was too close to her ears and pulsing head. Dora closed her eyes and felt the few bites of food she had eaten earlier rise into her throat. She leaned against the door frame and took deep breaths, willing herself not to lose the measly contents of her stomach on Lee's doorstep.

Dora kept her eyes closed and heard Lee's bare feet coming down the stairs. She felt his hands on her as he steadied her. "What happened?"

His voice centered her, and she opened her eyes. His face was inches from hers. "We killed one of The Keres. I got scratched a little."

"A little? It looks like it took half your face with it. Can you walk?"

"Yes." Her knees gave out, but Marina and Doc kept her from crashing into the ground. "Maybe not."

"No," Marina said at the same time. "I'm surprised she was able to fly all the way here. I don't think the cut is all that bad, but she hasn't eaten much since yesterday and she said she hit her head when we crashed into the ground."

Dora closed her eyes again. Now that they had made it here, she was tired. "I'm fine."

Lee shifted and placed an arm across her shoulders and behind her knees. He scooped her up into his arms before she could protest. She did not want to protest, though. "Let's take her into the examination room. I can clean her up there. Does she have any other injuries?"

Dora roused herself a bit. "I'm still awake. You don't have to talk about me like I'm not here. I hit my head and now it weighs fifty pounds. We have to stop meeting like this, Lee."

"You mean with you covered in your own blood?"

"Not all of it's mine."

Marina chuckled. "It's a good thing we have you around to patch us up, Doc."

Lee's arms tightened on Dora slightly as he carried her into the examination room. "Marina, there are matches on that table next to the lamp. Please light it for me."

Lee laid Dora on the table. His arms tightened on her again, then slid from underneath her body. Despite the pain in her head, Dora wanted to curl towards him and crawl back into his warmth. A golden light from the lamp filled the room, and she could see his face. There were lines bracketing his mouth, and his grey eyes were calculating, thinking. Dora wanted to reach up and smooth the tension away from his face, but her limbs were heavy.

Lee lifted his eyes from hers and addressed Marina. "Can you light the ones on the wall and the small stove over there now too? I need as much light as possible, even though it will probably exacerbate her headache. I'm going to get some fresh water. I'll be right back."

Lee returned with an ewer of water. He put some of the water in a pot on the stove to heat and threw a pinch of dried herbs into the water. He turned back to them and pulled one of the lamps on a stand closer to the table. Dora watched his movements. This was the first time she had seen him from this perspective. She usually stood where Marina hovered now, at his side, ready to help him. She had never been on the table beneath his warm, long fingers. For a moment, she wished she was looking up at him from a soft bed.

The throbbing in her face cut through her thoughts.

Lee turned her face so that she was looking away from him. He smoothed her hairs away from the mess of her cheek. "Can you tell me what hurts?"

Dora tried to laugh, but the movement cracked the wound, which had begun to seal. She could feel the blood start to run. "Everything. The pain from the gash wasn't so bad, but I have a roaring headache."

Lee felt the back of her head and Dora hissed in pain. "You have a nice goose egg back there. How did you do it?"

"I landed between the ground and a very angry Keres. I had just popped out its eyeball." Dora smiled at the memory and she shared a look with Marina before they both started laughing.

Lee's hands continued down her arms and over her torso, thorough and clinical movements, ignoring her colorful description and their laughter. "Nothing else?"

Dora could feel the path of his hands, clinical though they may be, spreading warm fire as they traversed over her. "No."

Marina shifted her weight beside Lee. "Is she going to be all right?"

Lee did not look up from where he was running his hands down Dora's legs. "I think she is fine except for her face and that bump to her head. The pain from that combined with the adrenaline and lack of food is what is causing her headache. A few stitches will do the trick and she will be healed up nicely in a couple days. It's possible she may have a concussion, so we will need to keep a close eye on her tonight."

"Do you need me here? If I'm more in the way than naught, I'd like to go talk to Iris. I'll check back before I head to my own bed. That should give you time to work. I will bring some soup back with me to feed her when you're done."

"I can handle one harpy on my own." He looked up and smiled at Marina before turning his grey eyes back to Dora's face.

Marina walked around the table to Dora's good side and cupped the side of her face. "Try not to be stubborn and do what Doc says." Marina leaned forward and kissed Dora's forehead. "You scared me a little."

"Nothing scares you." Dora tried to smile but it hurt too much to do so.

"Plenty scares me. I need you pretty to talk me out of being a horrible monster all the time. I only listen to pretty people." Marina squeezed Dora's shoulder.

Dora rolled her eyes instead of smiling. "Next time I'll be sure to get a nice gash in my side and keep my face injury free."

"Good." Marina nodded. "I'll be back shortly."

Dora watched the concentrated fervor of the face that Lee wore when he was deep in his work. His eyes stayed warm, but there was a calculating glint in them he only had when working. That look had never swung her way before, and she felt both pinned and comforted by it. He moved out of her field of vision briefly and came back with the steaming pot of water and a clean cloth.

"You already know the process, but I'm going to talk through it just like normal so you're not startled." He pulled the wheeled stool from beneath the table and sat. It brought his face closer to hers and she could smell him over the blood. "This water will clean and numb the area a bit but the stitches are still going to hurt."

Dora turned her head away from him to give him a better view of her cheek. It meant she could no longer see his face and she felt the pinprick of worry without that anchor. She had never been hurt enough to need a doctor's care, to need his care, in a real way.

Lee's warm hand covered hers where it lay on the table as if he knew her fleeting fears. "Don't worry. I hear I'm a decent enough doctor. You heal fast, and these stitches will only be in for a couple days. With luck, you will have no scar at all. If you do, it will be barely visible." He squeezed her hand before letting go.

The cleaning hurt bad enough, but the stitches were worse than the cut itself. She was tempted halfway through to tell him to leave it and let her have a scar. Having her face intact wasn't worth the pain and mess, but she ground her teeth, took deep breaths through her nose, and kept her protests to herself.

Marina arrived with a ceramic bowl of soup clutched in her hands as Lee tied off the last stitch. "You look prettier already."

Lee stood from his stool and waited until Dora turned her head towards him. "Are you still with me?"

She nodded and made a move to get up. He put a firm hand on her shoulder and pushed her down. "Stay lying down. I'm going to move some of this out of the way, then I'll take you to a bed."

When Lee slid his arms under her again, she did not resist the urge to snuggle into his chest. She was tired and hungry, and her head still ached. She did not want to deny herself the comfort his arms provided. Instead of taking her to the small room on the ground floor with the beds, where he usually put patients, he carried her up the stairs. Marina followed with the soup.

Lee nodded towards the table near the kitchen area. "Marina, put the soup there, and then can you pull back the quilt on the bed over there?"

Marina set the ceramic bowl down and walked over do as he asked. A wardrobe stood in the corner of the room, a shelf with books was in the other, and the large bed was flanked by side tables. Dora realized he meant to put her in his own bed. The smell of soap and something uniquely Lee enveloped her as he laid her down on the mattress.

His hands lingered over her as he adjusted her into a sitting position. He turned to Marina. "I need to clean up. Feed her what you can and I'll be back."

Lee hesitated by the bed, his eyes traveling over her body and resting on her face surrounded by his pillow and headboard. His eyes pinned her there with a look that said he was imagining her there under different circumstances. Dora returned his look even though she felt the heat of a blush tinged with desire spreading from her center to her limbs.

Marina coughed. "It's late and I need to finish this to get to my own bed. If I'm lucky, I'll have one of those looks waiting for me at home."

To Dora's delight, a bright red covered Lee's neck. She wanted to reach out to touch it. She had never seen him blush so darkly before.

Lee grabbed a shirt from the wardrobe and fled down the stairs to change.

Marina chuckled and starting feeding Dora small spoonsful of soup. "I'll hold my comments until a later date."

Dora raised an eyebrow at her. "It's unlike you to hold back at all."

"You're right. You two need to stop dancing around each other and dance in this nice big bed, instead."

Dora blushed. "We're still working out the details."

"Details are no fun. Figure it out as you go."

"I'm not used to jumping into things. I feel like I'm doing this in fits and starts instead of one smooth motion. I feel like we keep getting interrupted by bigger, more important things."

Marina smiled at her like she was a wayward child. "Jumping into this bed would be a good choice, unlike others you've made recently. You seemed to jump easily enough in Leadville."

Dora sighed. "I know. I messed up in Leadville."

"It's not like Petra and I didn't have some bumps on the way. Give yourself some grace."

Dora swallowed the soup Marina gave her. "You know I can feed myself."

Marina's eyebrows went up into her hairline. "I'm feeding you so I have an excuse to talk to you and encourage you stop letting yourself be interrupted."

Marina gave her the last of the soup and left. Dora stared up at the wooden beams in the ceiling and tried to stay awake until Lee returned. She failed.

***

Dora woke up pinned beneath the quilt. Without opening her eyes, she wiggled her body in an attempt to loosen whatever had caught her covers.

She managed to create just enough slack to roll over, and found her face inches from Lee's. He lay on top of the quilt, which was why she was having trouble moving. He lay on his side, facing her, with his hands tucked under his chin.

In sleep, his face lost the efficient control he usually exuded. The lines that had been bracketing his mouth last night were gone, and he looked younger, more at ease. His hair had gotten longer in recent weeks. She was able to get an arm free, and Dora reached out to brush a lock of hair from his forehead. His hair was smooth, and she moved it away from his face. She trailed her fingers from his temple to his jawline. His eyes, soft like grey wool, full of dreams and unfocused in the morning light, opened.

Dora felt her mouth curve up at his expression. This was something she wanted to see more often. Lee without all his layers in place. Lee's eyes flashed into focus and his body snapped to attention. Layers of cotton separated them, yet she felt the heat grow in the space between them like a fire catching dry kindling and blazing to life.

Dora stopped breathing, unable to draw air into her lungs. Her ears were filled with the sound of her blood roaring through her pounding heart and the ragged sound of Lee breathing. His eyes turned from soft wool to molten steel. The moment stretched, endless. Her entire body began to ache and she wanted to move closer to him, but she was still trapped beneath the weight of his body on the quilt. That thought made her skin burn with the need to touch him.

She made a sound full of frustration and need. In one swift motion, Lee moved into a sitting position and swung his legs over the side of the bed. His spine curled away from her and his hands balled into fists on his thighs. His fists dug into his legs and a ragged breath tore through him. Unable not to, Dora scooted closer and placed her hand flat on Lee's back. He trembled beneath her touch.

"I'll go put on some tea and start breakfast. After that, I'll look at your stitches." Lee rose and went to the kitchen area without looking back.

Dora frowned at his retreating form, her frustrated desire turning into the pinch of uncertainty. She gripped the sheets and curled her hand into a fist, flopping face first into a pillow. The side of her face protested, but it felt more like a deep bruise than the gash from yesterday. Having her face in the pillow turned out to be a mistake. It brought her nose in direct contact with the space Lee's head had occupied all night, and she was engulfed in his smell. Dora groaned.

After years of denying her feelings, it seemed admitting they existed had given them free reign to control her at will. Lee had been more warm with her lately, though he still tended to slide into professionalism. She thought again of Lee's reaction this morning: he had rolled away from her, then trembled at her touch.

Perhaps he is struggling too, she thought. She hoped.

That hope gave her a measure of comfort as she watched the object of her thoughts move around the kitchen, not looking at her. Dora sat up in bed and realized her shirt still had blood on it. She got out of bed and decided to push the matter. She unbuttoned her blouse as she walked to the wardrobe. She pulled out a shirt of Lee's. It smelled of cedar and Lee, and she tried not to think too hard about Lee watching her out of the corner of his eyes while she slid her arms into the clean shirt. It was too big, but she tucked it into her skirt. She kept her back to Lee as she buttoned the shirt. She could feel the weight of Lee's eyes on her the entire time.

When Dora joined him in the small kitchen, Lee was setting eggs and tea on the table. His eyes flashed in her direction and his hand tightened on the spatula in his hand before turning back to his task.

"Sorry, all I have is eggs. Claire leaves two or three eggs on my doorstep each morning." He sat across from her and kept his eyes down.

Dora shrugged though he couldn't see it. "Food is food, and there is a scarcity at the moment. I'm not going to complain about eggs." She took a fortifying breath and continued, "I would like to lodge a complaint about how you ran out of the bed earlier."

Lee's eyes flashed up and a dull redness rose on his neck. "I'm sorry."

"What happened?"

Lee shifted in his chair. "I needed some space."

Dora sat back in her chair. The pinch of uncertainty was back. She opened her mouth but nothing came out. Mortified that he had been escaping her presence, she put eggs in her mouth to fill it with something.

Lee pinched the bridge of his nose. "I'm bungling this. I left because I was afraid I would take advantage of having you in my bed when I currently have no right to do so. Then you changed into my shirt and I realized my thoughts may not be safe anywhere."

Relieved laughter escaped her. "Apparently, I'm no better at this than you. I was hoping you would take advantage of me."

They both smiled at each other stupidly.

Lee cleared his throat. "Well, I will keep that in mind for the future should I ever wake up to find you in my bed again. I'm inordinately pleased to see you wearing my shirt."

Dora started to say something but she was interrupted by a muted pounding on the front door and then a man's voice.

"Doc Williams. Doc!"

Lee stood and yelled as he ran, "I'm coming down."

Dora followed him, their flirty banter forgotten. Paul Hughes stood at the bottom of the stairs. His head was bare and his face pale with red cheeks. Lee took him by the arm and led him into the examination room.

"You have to come. The girls are sick."

Lee felt Mr. Hughes's forehead. "How long have *you* been sick?"

Mr. Hughes swiped Lee's hand away when he tried to take his temperature. "I'm fine, but Agnes and Amy have been sick for a day now, and this morning, Lily couldn't get out of bed."

Lee put a hand on the man's shoulder. "Mr. Hughes, look at me." Lee waited until Mr. Hughes's feverish eyes stilled on his face. "You have a fever. I'm going to give you some water, and then Dora and I will take you home and we'll take a look at your family."

Lee shared a look with Dora over Mr. Hughes's head. The plague had come to Turning Creek.

CHAPTER 19

Halfway to the tailor shop, Mr. Hughes's knees buckled, and Lee caught him before he fell face first onto the ground. Dora slid Mr. Hughes's arm around her shoulder and helped Lee carry him the rest of the way. His arm was like a hot, dry towel wound around her neck. By the time they got to the tailor shop, Mr. Hughes was barely trying to walk.

One of the benefits of tending the sick was that you were in their houses frequently, giving you knowledge of where things were, like where the family members slept and where they kept clean linens. Dora and Lee did not need to ask where the main bedroom was because they had been there before. Lee helped Mr. Hughes in bed beside his wife and Dora left Lee to finish while she examined Lily.

Lily's feverish brown eyes followed Dora's movement as she skirted around the bed. Lily, a Remnant of Medusa, usually had an undercurrent of power about her. Today, Dora felt none of the usual strength coming from the woman. Dora ran a hand over the pale, dry skin of her forehead. It was hot and her lips were chapped.

Dora saw a cup of water on the bedside table. "Here, take a sip of this. How long have you been sick?"

Lily's eyes flicked over to her husband. "Since yesterday morning, right after the girls became ill. I didn't want Paul to know, so I didn't tell him. He was so worried about the girls already, but this morning I couldn't get up."

Dora looked over at Lee, who was busy examining Mr. Hughes. "We'll check on the girls in just a moment. What can you tell me about your fever? How long have you had it?"

"I started feeling weak yesterday morning, then I got the fever about midday. By dinner my joints felt like the fever was burning them from the inside out."

Dora nodded while she talked and tried not to show the trickle of panic she felt. The symptoms Lily was describing could be attributed to many different kinds of fevers. Iris had not known what form the plague from the pithos would take, and Dora prayed to the gods now that it would not be the one she suspected.

Lee stood up from where he had been bending over Mr. Hughes, talking to him quietly. "I'm going to check on the girls. Will you join me when you're done here?"

Dora nodded.

Lily kept talking. "My head hurt so bad I went to bed early. The girls had a rash on their bellies but they said it didn't itch. I haven't been able to check myself this morning."

Dora motioned to the ties keeping Lily's nightgown closed. "May I?"

"Of course."

Dora undid the lower laces and exposed the skin underneath Lily's breasts. Her upper torso was covered in small pinpricks of red, as if each pore had been filled with blood and raised up in protest. Dora's whole body clenched at the sight of it. It looked painful, but Dora knew the rash was the least painful part of this illness.

"I need to check your legs. Can I pull the quilt down farther?"

Lily nodded. Dora held the side of the quilt and moved it over to expose Lily's legs; they were covered in mottled bruising. Slick dread coiled through her body like a snake.

Dora kept her voice steady. "I'm going to go see Dr. Williams and help him with the girls. I'll be back with something for you to eat."

Lily placed a burning hand on Dora's arm. "Thank you. Please don't let anything happen to my girls."

Something squeezed the back of Dora's throat. "I'll take care of them as if they were my own." Then Dora said words she did not know to be true. "You'll be better soon enough and fretting over what kind of new bad habit Marina has been teaching them."

That made Lily smile. "You're a blessing to your line, harpy. I can go to Tartarus knowing that if I am gone, my girls will be raised by warriors with hearts of blood and steel."

Dora swallowed past the constriction in her throat. "Stop talking like you're not going to see another sun, daughter of Medusa. Now, let me go check on Lee. I'll be right back."

Dora blinked back the tears in her eyes as she walked across the hall to the where the girls slept. People who were sick often got maudlin when confronted with the possibility of their mortality. It had never affected Dora as strongly before.

That's not quite true, she thought, remembering her mother. *If this is a similar sickness and Pandora's plague has come, I will not have enough tears to see through the end.*

Lee was talking in a low voice to Agnes as he listened to her heart. Agnes followed his movements with dull bloodshot eyes, but she did not speak. Dora went to the other side of the bed and took a rag from a basin there, squeezing out the excess liquid.

"How are you this morning Amy?"

"My bones hurt."

Dora continued to run the rag over the girl's feverish and thin limbs. Each one was a little thinner than the last. It amazed Dora how quickly a fever could sap the life from someone. "I know, sweet girl, but you'll feel better soon. Dr. Williams is going to take special care of you and Agnes and you'll be running around in no time. I'm going to look at your stomach and arms now. Your mother said you had a rash. I want to see it."

The girl nodded, and Dora lifted the girl's short nightdress to expose her torso. It was covered in the same pin prick rash. Dora looked up to make sure Lee saw it. He nodded. Dora took another look at the pinkish hue of Amy's eyes and with a shaking hand exposed the girl's legs. She breathed a sigh of relief when she saw that the skin was clear. Dora closed her eyes.

Lee's eyes went from assessing Agnes and Amy to assessing Dora. He smoothed a hand over Agnes's forehead. "Ms. Dora and I are going to go outside and talk. We'll be right back."

Dora walked out of the room like the air was molasses. She went to the first place she found, a front sitting room, with chairs covered in a floral print and walls painted a bright yellow. Sunlight bounced off the bright walls, searing her eyes. Dora groped for a chair as black spots swirled in her vision. Her stomach dipped when she dropped into the chair moments before she would have lost the ability to stand.

She put her head between her knees and tried to breathe. "It can't be the same thing. It can't. It cannot. It cannot." She kept repeating.

Dora could feel Lee's movement as he knelt in front of her, but she did not want to open her eyes. She did not want to acknowledge the reality of what was about to happen in her town. In her home. Again.

Lee's hand rested on her back. "Are you ill?"

"No," she whispered.

"Tell me what has upset you." His hand moved then, sweeping up and down her back.

Dora took a deep breath and lifted her head. She wondered briefly if her abject fear showed on her face because Lee wrapped her in his arms and anchored her in place. She breathed in his solid presence and let that fill the places the fear had started to grow. She would not be alone this time. She had her sister harpies and Iris. She had Lee. With a jolt, Dora realized that she had more to lose this time too.

She moved a little and his arms loosened enough to allow her to lean back and look into his eyes while she talked. He kept his arms on hers and she concentrated on that contact to anchor her.

"My mother died of a bleeding fever like this."

Lee's hands rested on her forearms and they tightened. "Tell me about it."

The story Dora was about to tell him had never been revealed in one sitting before. She had told parts now to Iris, Petra, and Marina. She had confessed her own transgressions in the matter to Marina. Dora wanted to, needed to, tell Lee all of it.

"I grew up on an island in the Grecian sea. The harpies of my line have lived and ruled that archipelago for almost the whole of our line. My mother loved me, but she was unhinged. She ruled her island like a despot, always terrified of being overthrown by the people who lived there. It was a groundless fear. She was too powerful, and they were too scared of her. She killed people on whims and tortured others for perceived slights.

"One day, a tailor delivered a dress that somehow displeased my mother, and she saw the flaws of the garment and the failure of the tailor as an indictment of her and her rule. She arrived at his shop to deliver her punishment. I wasn't there, but in the end, my mother had murdered two families in totality, the original family and another who sought to defend them, including their small children. One of the servants came to get me during the attack. I was barely out of childhood myself, but I could normally talk her down."

Dora's voice shook and she closed her eyes, but the vision of her mother standing over the ruined bodies of the children followed her. "I was too late. She'd killed all of them before I could get there."

Lee used his grip on her arms to shake her into opening her eyes. "What she did was not your fault. That was her choice."

"No, what she did was not my fault, but what happened at the end was."

Lee's hands gripped her arms but he remained silent.

Dora shook her head. "Gods, how I wish I would have gotten there in time. I dragged her away from the scene and took her home."

"There was a witch. Some said she was a Remnant of Medea, but she never admitted to anything. She came up to the palace that night and she cursed my mother with a disease she said had no cure. The witch said my mother and all those loyal to her would die in agony. The witch paused before she left, though, and told me I would be spared so that I could spend the rest of my life making better choices."

Dora felt her eyes burn. It had been years since she had shed a tear for her mother. She was astonished to find she still had tears for her. "It started out as a high fever and a headache. She kept complaining that her joints were on fire. She screamed in agony as the fever consumed her. She was in such pain that she nearly lost her voice by the end.

"Her eyes became bloodshot after a day, and though all she had done was lay in bed, her legs were covered in bruises. On the second day, her nose started to bleed. She died an hour later, in my arms. When a couple of the servants fell ill, the rest of them fled. I cared for those that were sick until they died. Then I went to find the witch."

Lee's grey eyes pinned her to the chair. "What happened next?"

Dora took a shaking breath and closed her eyes. "It was sunset when I arrived at her house. The sky was orange and red over the sea, and it burned almost as bright as the rage within me. I killed her the moment she opened the door. I wish I could say my swiftness was to avoid another curse, but by this time my anger was so great, I was no longer in control. I searched the house and killed everyone else in it. She was married." Dora shuddered. "She had two small children. When I left the house, the sky was as red as the blood covering my hands."

Dora opened her eyes then, expecting to see revulsion on Lee's face, but the expression instead was somber.

Dora kept her eyes on him then. "It frightened me, what I'd done. It frightened me even more that I still felt enough anger to not feel remorse. It took a while for that particular feeling to catch up to me. I am ashamed that I killed innocent children, but I have no regrets about killing the witch. I fled the island. I did not want to ever be that…thing again."

Lee leaned forward and placed a chaste kiss on her forehead. "I'm sorry." He wiped a tear from her cheek.

"My mother brought the witch's wrath on herself. I know that. It's one of the reasons why I have tried so hard to control myself. I won't be that monster again."

Lee's eyes melted into hers and Dora found herself feeling safe despite her racing anxiety. He spoke, and she believed him. "You will never be."

Dora traced the planes of his face with her eyes and thought about what was to come. There was no cure for this illness. They must find the jar and kill The Keres. The thought of Lee, who would run towards this trouble instead of away from it, being brought low by this plague and leaving her made it almost impossible to breathe. Black spots returned to her vision, and she had to suck in air like she was dying herself before they subsided.

"I thought the worst thing in the world would be watching my mother die and the madness and violence that I succumbed to after, but now I know it's not. It's not the worst thing." Dora swallowed around the vise circling her neck and spoke the truth. "I couldn't live if that happened to you. I will not hold you while you die." Her voice hardened and she pushed power into it. "Do you understand me, Lee Williams? No matter what else happens, you cannot die."

Lee moved his hands to cup her face. She had expected disappointment and distance after her confession. That is not what she saw in his face. His eyes were soft with compassion and tenderness.

She crumpled then, the fear overcoming her bravado. Dora leaned forward until her head rested on his shoulder. "I just can't do that. I'm not strong enough."

Lee smoothed a hand over her hair, then he put a hand along her jawline. He tilted her face to look at him again. "You are the strongest person I know. You will face this and everything that is to come ahead of us because you are fierce. You don't need me." Dora started to speak, but he cut her off. "That being said, I promise by the River Styx that I will do my best not to die."

Lee ran his thumbs over her cheekbones and jaw, wiping away tears she did not know had escaped. Dora followed the movement of his eyes with her own, so she saw the moment they shifted from tenderness to something else entirely. She felt the air stretch and grow heavy moments before the heat raced between them, their point of contact his hands cupping her face. If a person could melt from a look alone, she would be gone already.

Dora could not melt, though, so she was solid when Lee leaned forward and pressed his lips against hers. She had always expected him to be gentle in everything he did, but the gentle press of his warm lips on hers blazed into something wild and unexpected. Dora could feel her harpy inside her reveling in it.

Lee deepened the kiss immediately and plunged one hand into her hair, angling her mouth for better access. His other hand slid down her side to the small of her back where he used it to pull her forward. Dora opened her legs, and Lee moved into the space she created, never breaking contact, and pulling their bodies flush with one another. Dora wrapped her arms around his neck and through his hair, urging him on.

This was what she had been missing. Dora felt the wildness of their connection but did not feel out of control. It burned like the forge of Hephaestus, but she did not feel like it would consume her. Her entire body was tight and laser focused on the man running his hand from her back to her front to cup her aching breast through the shirt that was his. None of it was out of control; it was just right, like this was what she had been waiting for.

Everything clicked into place.

Her harpy wanted more of this man and Dora did too. She must have let some of her power leak into her contact with Lee because he groaned deep. Dora felt his own power push back at her. Instead of the two forces clashing together, they intertwined and molded together, settling over the two lovers like a mantle. The addition of their power flowing between them made Dora tremble with desire. She should not have waited so long to claim this man.

Lee pulled back and broke contact. The only sound in the room was their ragged breathing. Lee's eyes were molten steel on her face, and she started to pull him back to her.

"Wait," he said, his breath coming out in a rasp.

Dora paused and then remembered why they were here. She had forgotten everything in the power of that kiss. She tried to steady her own breathing. Her lips felt swollen and the core of her body screamed at her for release.

Lee leaned forward and rested his forehead on hers. They sat that way for a long time. Breathing together and trying to get back in control. Dora could not resist sending out a tendril of power while they sat so close. She felt Lee's own power, crisp where hers was heavy, meet hers. She could see it in her mind's eye and feel it in her skin when the two met and joined into something else, something that set her blood on fire like nothing else. Her hands tightened where they gripped Lee's shoulders.

She leaned back enough to see his face again, but she did not pull back her power. Lee's power stayed joined with hers when he spoke.

"You and I have some things to discuss between the two of us, but we have more pressing matters at hand." Lee's eyes were shifting from steel to soft wool again and Dora knew he was thinking of the things they needed to do to get ready for the plague that was upon them.

She was not ready to give up this moment yet. She had waited for years for this. She pushed more power into the meld between them. A smile she had never seen on Lee spread over his face. Dora was unprepared when the full brunt of Lee's power slammed into her seconds before his mouth claimed her again. She was so used to being one of the most powerful things in the room, she sometimes forgot that strong power not born of violence existed. Lee had a depth and breadth of power she had not expected. It was a heady thing to feel the weight of someone else's power tangled with her own.

He broke away too soon and his voice was firm. "We can't do this now, beloved. You know it, so stop tempting me. I've waited a long time for this, a few more days won't kill me. Or you."

Dora crossed her arms and frowned. "Might kill me."

Lee pecked her on the lips. "You will live." He ran his fingers over her face, gentle when they had been insistent before. "I am not done with you yet, Dora Aello."

Dora smiled and let her harpy show from her eyes. "By the River Styx, you will never be done with me."

As if by unspoken agreement, they both pulled the bulk of their power back into themselves. But Dora couldn't resist keeping a tendril of power coiled toward him. She purred in pleasure to find that it wrapped easily around a small tendril of his own power he had left for her to find. He gave her that smile again and she wanted to forget everything.

Despite the smile, Lee was all business. "The Hughes are going to need someone here to nurse them, and they will need food. There will be other families who need food and similar help. We're going to need some kind of hospital. I made a list of what we'll need after Iris told us this may happen. We need to get the leaders together and discuss how to address our needs."

Of course he made a list, she thought. "I'll find someone to bring food here and take care of the family while we plan, then I can come back and check on them."

Lee was still kneeling in front of her. He put a hand back on her arm. "As much as I will want you by my side for this, your skills may be needed elsewhere."

Dora had almost forgotten. "The Keres." Her resolve tightened as she held Lee's silver gaze. She would finish this, protect the valley, and take this man as her mate.

CHAPTER 20

It was eleven before they were able to gather at Vine's to discuss plans. Iris came to over to Dora as soon as she came into the saloon.

Iris ran a finger over the stitches on Dora's cheek. "Poor bird. Marina told me what happened. Are you all right?"

Dora went into Iris's arms. "I am more than fine despite how my face looks. Lee has been taking good care of me."

Dora smiled a little too wide before she caught herself and schooled her features. Although the kiss was hours behind them now, Dora's lips still felt the pressure of Lee, and her body remembered all too well the imprint of him between her legs. Iris's eyes narrowed, and Dora felt herself blushing.

"I see." Iris smoothed a hand over Dora's hair. "We can talk later, then."

They assembled and sat at the large banquet-style table in the back. Dora sat near Petra and Marina, with Lee on her right side. Claire McKenzie, Daniel Vine, Widow Finch, Reed, Henry, Simon and Beth Kramer, Philo Kalakos, who was there representing his large family, and Blaine Walsh filled out the meeting.

Reed stood from where he had been sitting on the end of the table. "There's work to be done, so we need to make this quick."

The door to the saloon opened and Atlanta and Cyrene strolled through. The huntresses were the only people Dora ever saw with more weapons on than Marina, and today they glistened with the amount of steel they carried.

Atlanta put a hand on her hip. "We heard there was hunting to be done."

Marina stood and clasped arms with both women. "You know you missed me terribly and couldn't stand to be away any longer."

Cyrene pulled up two chairs and settled into one. "Looks like we got here just in time. We found the note young Thomas left at the cabin and came straight away."

Atlanta took a seat. "What did we miss?"

Reed filled the huntresses in, then said, "Now that the plague is here, we have some additional problems. Doc has a list on how to address the sick we are likely to have on our hands so I'll let him talk about those plans."

Lee smoothed out a piece of paper in front of him on the table. Dora did not think she could get away with touching him for support, so she sent her power out to make contact instead. His mouth curled up when he felt it and he responded in kind. That small connection was enough to bring a smile to her face and a sense of peace, despite what they faced. She felt indestructible with him at her side.

Petra and Marina had both straightened, and Dora could feel their harpies rising in response to the added power in the room. Petra leaned around Marina to peer at Dora and raise an eyebrow in her direction. Dora smiled blandly at her and winked. Petra gave her a lecherous grin. Marina elbowed her in the ribs and chuckled. Iris and Henry shared a look and a smile.

Reed looked at the three harpies. "Something you three chuckleheads want to share?"

Dora felt a blush painting her cheeks. "No."

"Yes," Marina and Petra chimed together.

Dora pushed power into the next word and shot a murderous glance at her sister harpies. "No."

Reed nodded. "Moving on then."

Lee cleared his throat and spoke. "We're going to have some problems on our hands that will be exacerbated by the food scarcity. People caring for sick family members will be unable to forage for food every day. In the event that an entire family falls ill, like the Hughes family has, then there will be both no one to care for them and no one to find food for them. I think that we should set up a sort of hospital where people can come to be fed and cared for."

Reed placed a flat hand on the table. "Is this plague contagious?"

Lee's eyes were steady. "We don't know. I would surmise, because of its magical nature, that it is probable that contact is not needed for it to be contagious. We all need to be aware of the symptoms so we can escort people to the hospital we set up as soon as they appear ill. Knowing the symptoms will also make it easier for us to monitor our own health. Here is what we do know.

"As I thought from the earlier account Iris found, this is a type of hemorrhagic fever. It will start with a high fever and a severe headache. The person might also complain of their joints or bones aching or being on fire. This fever also presents a non-itching rash that resembles small pin pricks across the torso. Eventually, their eyes may become bloodshot and large bruises will appear on their legs. This happens because the fever breaks down the organs and blood vessels, shutting down the body. Toward the end of the illness, their ears, nose, and other orifices will bleed. If they develop bruises, their chance of survival is very low." Lee delivered this information in a calm manner, but it was not enough to keep everyone at the table from squirming.

"The Hughes family is currently sick, and their symptoms matched what Lee already suspected to be true about the plague from Pandora's jar. My mother and some of our servants died of a similar disease before I left Greece." Dora put her hand in Lee's, and he twined her fingers with his.

Marina wrapped an arm around her shoulders and squeezed hard. Dora felt cocooned between her sister harpy and Lee. The feeling was so comforting she wished today could be a good, ordinary day.

Lee took back over the conversation. "We need a place to set up a hospital."

"What about the boarding house?" Widow Finch asked.

"I thought of that," Lee said, "but the rooms are smaller, and it may be easier if we were able to keep people in larger rooms and only use smaller rooms as needed."

Daniel, his green eyes serious, leaned forward. He almost never spoke during these meetings. "We can use the saloon. I have this large room here and there are some living quarters and rooms upstairs as well. We would also be able to use the bier garden out back for storage or more beds as long as the weather holds."

Marina crossed her arms over her chest. "I loathe to even hear these words coming out of my mouth, but Vine is right. The saloon is the best choice for a hospital."

Daniel pointed a finger at Iris. "I want that to go into the official accounting of this generation. Marina Oxcypete agreed with something I said."

"Won't happen again," Marina muttered.

"Most of the rooms at the boardinghouse are empty because of the food problems, so we can use the extra mattresses and sheets to make beds up here. I'll need help bringing them over," Widow Finch said.

Philo Kalakos waved a hand in the air. "I can gather men to do that. Maybe Grant Korman and Matthew Renault can lend a hand."

Lee nodded. "Good. I will stay here to help organize the setup. I'll need to bring some things from my office, but I can manage that on my own. We will also need help here in the saloon once we have people here."

Henry's low voice broke through the conversation. "This isn't something we want to think about, but we need a plan on how to handle our dead."

A vise tightened around Dora's middle. "Maybe we can have people willing to dig graves be on call for when that happens." She choked on the word when instead of saying if.

They went around the table, laying out plans for who would help where and what supplies would be needed. After the planning, there was only one more thing left. Petra pulled a jar of ashes and placed them on the table.

"We have the ashes of one Keres. We still have two more that need to be killed," she said.

"Where should we start the hunt?" Atlanta asked.

Marina rubbed her hands together. "We can look at a map and decide where to start. I want Pearl Nasso to help us."

Dora leaned forward. "We should ask Caroline Eisler too. She should be recovered enough from her birth to support us."

Reed stood. "We've all got work to do. Let's get to it."

Lee stopped Dora with a hand on her arm before she could leave the table. "I want to look at those stitches before you leave. With your increased capacity for healing, they will need to come out sooner than they normally would."

"Let me go talk to Marina and Petra first, then I'll meet you at your office."

Lee ran a hand down her arm, and Dora leaned into the contact, unable to stop herself from doing so. Not for the first time today, she wished the rest of the world to an inner circle of hell. His touch, while innocent in a room of people, warmed her skin and made her yearn for something more than his hand grasping her own. He gave her hand a squeeze before leaving the saloon. Right before he went through the doors, Dora could feel his power retract. She felt its loss almost as strongly as she felt his physical absence.

Dora turned to discover Petra, Marina, and the huntresses watching her with knowing gleams in their eyes. She tried for nonchalance and walked over to where the women stood against the bar. Marina walked around behind the bar and took a bottle from the shelf.

Daniel scowled at them from across the room. "You can't just take whatever you want, Harpy."

Marina ignored him and placed five glasses on the bar. She pulled the cork out of the bottle with a pop. "Put it on my tab." Marina poured the whiskey and scooted glasses towards them all.

Dora did not pick hers up. "It's a bit early."

"It's never too early, and we have two things to drink to." Marina picked up Dora's glass and handed it to her. "The first thing I want to toast is to a good hunt. The second, and more important, thing we need to toast is you getting your head out of your backside."

Petra and Cyrene started laughing. Atlanta quirked a smile and raised her glass to Dora.

Dora decided not to bluster her way out of this. She threw back her head and shoulders and said, "I've decided it's time for me to settle down."

The others laughed as they all clinked their glasses together. "You've made the Doc wait long enough. Many happy returns," Atlanta said.

Dora almost choked on the liquid fire she'd swallowed. "Am I the only one who didn't know?"

Marina chuckled and poured another drink for herself. She waved the bottle at them. "Anyone who pays attention won't be surprised, but I'm glad there will be no more moping from you. I can't abide too much moping. One more, then we go."

Reed walked over to them as Marina poured. "Someone's been moping? Are you telling stories about how you used to pine for me, Sparrow?"

Dora laughed. For a moment she enjoyed this feeling, allowed it to push back reality.

Marina put the cork back in the bottle and put it away. "I was chasing you, not moping. Dora is going to do some chasing of her own."

They lifted their glasses again. Petra said, "May our hunt be thrilling and may we all escape Charon's boat."

The clink of glass was loud in the room, their laughter stolen with the serious ending of Petra's toast. The whiskey burned less the second time, and Dora felt the well of warmth in her stomach expand.

Dora put her glass in a pile with the others. "I'll go get Caroline and meet you at the Nasso Farm. It's on one side of the valley, so we might as well start there."

Petra pointed to her face. "You need to get those stitches out first. I'll get Caroline. Atlanta and Cyrene can go with Marina to get the map and then go to Pearl's."

Dora nodded. "We still haven't decided how to find the pithos."

"We can keep an eye out while we hunt, but I'd be happy just to get these things out of the sky. One problem at a time," Marina said, coming around to their side of the bar.

Atlanta nodded. "One hunt at a time, lest we lose focus."

Daniel joined them. "Thanks for cleaning up after yourselves and for serving yourselves. Don't do it again." His voice had an edge to it, but his eyes were glittering with amusement.

Marina patted him on the shoulder. "I think I'm starting to like you, Vine."

Daniel went around the back of the bar muttering, but he had a smile on his face.

Marina was the last of them to leave the saloon. Dora was right in front of her when Marina turned to face Daniel again. "Is there anyone else in this town who knows how to make whiskey?"

Daniel raised an eyebrow at her. "I expect so, but it wouldn't be nearly as good as mine and might leave you blind."

Marina nodded. "Thanks for turning this place into a hospital. Don't die."

"I don't intend to."

***

It had been a long time since all the hunters had gathered in a room together for the purpose of hunting, and the space vibrated with the amount of contained violence. Their power danced up and down Dora's skin. If she ever was afraid of losing control, it would be now, but amazingly, she felt the calm that comes before the storm. She was soaking up all the energy and tension to be released when they went up into the sky to hunt the last two Keres.

Dora's nerves snapped and she kicked off the discussion. "We don't know much about The Keres, but here is what we do know. They are as large as a full-grown harpy, but they look like a bat. They are more active at dusk and night. They have talons and claws like a harpy. They are monsters. There is no mortal side of them that we know. They don't appear to be that intelligent. We think there are two left."

Petra jumped in. "After we kill them, they have to be beheaded and burned, and then we have to gather a portion of ashes from each corpse."

After some deliberation, they decided to fan out in pairs and sweep the northern half of the valley today, then repeat the exercise tomorrow on the southern half. They paired those on the ground with a harpy to better cover both land and air. Dora and Caroline took the north point, Petra, Atlanta, and Cyrene took the middle, and Marina and Pearl swept the bottom, always within sight of each other.

Atlanta and Cyrene, the only ones with free hands—or rather, hands at all—carried sacks slung between their shoulder blades. As they walked, the huntresses pulled berries, mushrooms, and edible grasses into the sacks. In this way, they would have some food when they stopped for the noon meal. Though they had no plans to stop before noon, they would pause their sweep if they came upon a homestead to ask questions about the pithos. It had not taken much discussion to decide that the time for concealing the search was long past.

Dora kept her eyes on the sky and the land below. She looked for any signs that seemed out of place: flattened grass, carcasses without a predator around, or a Keres itself.

They crossed the first homestead early in the morning. The Kalakos house was a cabin with its back dug into the bottom of a hill. Philo Kalakos was in town helping set up the hospital, leaving Katya and their young son, Rasmus, at home alone. Katya and her son, a young child of five or six, came out of the cabin as Dora landed and Caroline approached the house.

Katya was tall and thin, but thinner than she should have been. Her skin looked wan and there were dark circles under her dull brown eyes. Rasmus, in contrast, watched them with bright eyes in his rounded face. Dora did not doubt where most of the food in this house was going.

The boy tried to throw himself forward to get closer, but he was stopped with a firm hand on his shoulder. "Greetings, harpies and hunters. What can I do for you?" Katya's voice was full of the music of her native Greek.

Caroline, in her laelaps form, swung her tawny hound head towards Dora and waited for her to answer. The others continued to fan out around the homestead.

"We saw Mr. Kalakos in town yesterday. He is helping set up the hospital to take care of the sick people," Dora said.

The woman softened as a smile spread across her face. "Philo is a generous man. Thank you for bringing me news of him. He said he would return when he could. He wanted to help and I assured him we would be fine without him for a few days."

Rasmus squirmed until he broke free from his mother's grip and bounded up to Caroline. "Mama, can I pet the dog?"

Caroline shook her head and sneezed in that way dogs can when they are irritated. Dora laughed and Marina's laughter echoed from behind the chicken coop on the side of the yard.

Mrs. Kalakos rushed to her son's side. "This is not a dog. She is a Remnant like you." The woman cocked her head and looked into Caroline's large hound eyes. "I believe this is a laelaps. I have never met one of your line." Mrs. Kalakos bowed her head down. "It's a pleasure to meet you, mistress."

Dora nodded. "This is Caroline Eisler. You may have met her in town sometime. She has two daughters and lives with her husband southeast of here. She is helping us search for something called a Keres. It is the size of a harpy and looks like a bat."

Mrs. Kalakos's dull eyes filled with fear. "By Athena's grace."

"Exactly. We believe that they are here because Pandora's jar has been opened," Dora said.

"That cannot be possible."

"We believe that it is why the crops have died, why the food is spoiling, why The Keres are here, and why people are falling ill. I need to ask you if you know anything about the jar or if you have seen The Keres." Dora let her power out enough to sense Mrs. Kalakos's mood to determine if she was lying.

"I did see something in the sky two days ago, but from a distance it looked like one of you, and I didn't give it much attention." Mrs. Kalakos's words rang true.

Dora could taste the tang of Mrs. Kalakos's fear on her tongue. As a predator, fear was almost as heady as violence, and Dora allowed herself to drink it down, but kept herself still. A memory flashed, of her mother getting drunk on the fear of the village, then slaughtering a herd of sheep after Dora had begged her to leave the people in the village alone.

Dora pulled herself out of that memory. She was not her mother. "Do you have any burial jars? A pithos in your house?"

Mrs. Kalakos's fear shifted to sorrow. "We only brought one with us from Greece, and it is at my parents' house on the other side of the valley. We left the three we've had for generations with my sister, who stayed back home with her husband. My mother wept for days at leaving them, but we couldn't carry everything. Will you be visiting my parents and brothers today?" Katya Kalakos was the younger daughter of Nicolas and Helia Mylonis, who had a large spread with their two sons and their families on the east side of the valley.

Dora nodded.

"Please send my love to them and tell them Rasmus and I will be traveling there tomorrow to stay until this is over."

"We will."

Caroline moved and sniffed Rasmus's face. She ran her body along his and leaned into him. The boy giggled and the serious adult conversation stopped to watch as a boy took pleasure in petting a dog larger than he was.

Atlanta and Cyrene joined them. "Everything's clear here. No sign of The Keres," Cyrene said.

Atlanta looked at Mrs. Kalakos. "Ma'am, do you have a basket or a bowl?"

Confused, Mrs. Kalakos nodded and went inside the cabin. She returned with a large basket and handed it to Atlanta, who pulled the bag off her shoulder and dumped its contents into the basket. Cyrene upended her bag into the basket as well.

"It's not much," Atlanta said, "but these grasses make a decent broth and the berries are good."

Mrs. Kalakos took the offered basket with eyes that shone with unshed tears. "Thank you."

Dora turned away from that scene and launched into the air. They had to finish this hunt for The Keres and the pithos before families like the Kalakos succumbed to hunger or the plague or both. She did not want to have to bury Rasmus or his mother. She didn't want to bury anyone.

Dora heard Atlanta say as she flew away, "If you see anything, send word if you can."

Their search continued without incident, unfortunately. By the time they were passing through the Lloyd farm, Dora was feeling antsy. This hunt needed to end with something dying. Petra peeled off from the rest of them when they saw James, some men, and Selene in one of the far pastures. She rejoined them about ten minutes later and they continued on. While the ground trackers found an occasional large kill or landing spot, there were no

Keres sightings.

They stopped at the Mylonis homestead, which was a cluster of four cabins with outbuildings spread in a circle. An older woman, Helia Mylonis, with olive skin and steel hair, emerged from the smallest cabin as they approached. When she saw who had come, she paused, and Dora could see her spine straighten. The Mylonis family were Remnants, but they had not disclosed what they were. They had been here about a year, long enough to be settled, but not long enough to trust completely.

The doors to the other three cabins opened and they were joined by an assortment of women and children. Dora sent out a small bit of power to Mrs. Mylonis. Whatever they were, it was not anything as predatory as what approached them, and Mrs. Mylonis knew it.

Mrs. Mylonis bowed her head in greeting. Her fingers twisted her skirt and her eyes darted between the members of the hunting party. "Greetings. It's a bit late for a normal welcome party, so I think you must have other business here."

Dora felt a bit sorry for all the firepower they were bringing to this household. She changed into her mortal form to ask her questions. "We're only here to ask you some questions and check in on you." The others fanned out and continued to search while Dora talked.

Mrs. Mylonis indicated the other two women, who came forward. "You know my daughters-in-law? Kepa and Thera."

"I do, nice to see you both again. We started out by Philo and Katya's house this morning. Philo is in town helping set up the hospital with Dr. Williams, and Katya sends her greetings. We left some food for her and Rasmus until Philo comes home."

Dora knew that information and family news was as important as her other questions. Being separated by miles from your nearest neighbor meant that any visitor was expected to share news and greetings before anything else. Plus, she thought if Mrs. Mylonis knew they had already seen and helped Katya, she would be more likely to help them.

Mrs. Mylonis nodded. "I never thought I would live to see a place where a harpy gave food to the needy. The blessing of the gods on you."

Dora felt her neck heat. "We're not like our mothers."

Mrs. Mylonis's eyes softened. "We know that and thank Hera for it every day."

"Does your family have enough to eat?"

Kepa stepped closer. Her belly was rounded with child, the first of this family to be born in their new home. "We're getting by, but some days are tight. The men are out hunting now, and we were going to forage for some greens to make a stew but we were late leaving because two of the children are sick."

Dora's stomach dropped. She had hoped it would take a while for the plague to come this far north into the valley. If it spread from one point of origin, then it should move from one individual and family to the next. Since it was supernatural in origin, perhaps it could just appear wherever it pleased in the valley.

"Can I see them?"

Thera led Dora into her cabin. It was a mix of wooden surfaces and old world items, rugs, a jar, cups, and a handful of books. Like the people living in the cabin, it was a blend of history and hope in a new land. The cabin had a main living area and one larger bedroom off the side. There was a large bed on one side of the room and a lower trundle bed next to it. A boy and a girl lay in the large bed.

The girl cried when she saw her mother come in. "Mama, everything hurts." The boy said nothing. The only thing that moved were his eyes, dull and bloodshot, as he watched them.

Thera went to her daughter and gave her some water.

Dora knew what she would find, but she examined the children anyway. From hours of watching Lee, she knew that part of the role of doctor is simply taking time with people. Both children had the rash on their torso and the boy already had a large bruise blooming on his right thigh. Dora tucked the sheets around him and smoothed his hair from his face.

"Mrs. Mylonis, can I speak with you in the other room?" Dora indicated the door with a movement of her head.

"Please, call me Thera." She tucked her children in and kissed them both. "I'll be right back."

Dora went into the other room, giving Risto Mylonis another glance before she left the room. She did not relish the news she had for this mother. Lee was always the one who did this with his kind words and gentle manner. She was supposed to help in the background. Dora searched for the right words.

Thera's eyes were hopeful until she saw Dora's face. "What's wrong with my children? Is it the plague we were told might come?"

Dora put a hand on the woman's arm and squeezed. "Yes. I'm sorry." Dora gave her instructions on how to make the children as comfortable as possible.

Thera grabbed Dora's hand. "They're going to get better, though, in a few days. Right?"

Dora thought of the bruises on Risto's legs, and Thera must have seen some of the truth in her face.

"No. They can't be that sick. I was yelling at them yesterday for running through the house." Thera sat heavily in one of the chairs by the kitchen table.

"I can't say for sure. They may still recover, but Risto has a bruise on his leg. Once the bruising starts, it is not likely that he will recover." Dora laid a hand on Thera's shoulder and felt the woman shudder. "You need to make him as comfortable as possible and tell him how much you love him. Asta does not have bruises yet, and her eyes are clear. She may yet recover. Keep the others away from them. We're not sure how it spreads, but keep them isolated, just to be safe. We'll try to check in on you when we can, but there will be many others who are sick."

Thera nodded.

"One more question. I know you have a pithos here. We're looking for a particular one that once belonged to Pandora. Is it here?"

Thera shook her head, her eyes growing wide. "I did not think such a thing existed. No, we do not have it."

They went back to the room where her children were fighting for their lives. Dora placed her hands on the table and leaned on them. This situation could get out of control quickly. Every hour they did not find The Keres or the pithos meant more people would get sick, more people would die.

Petra caught her eyes as Dora joined the others outside. Dora nodded her head at the unasked question.

Dora turned to Mrs. Mylonis. "Keep the others away from Thera's children and house if you can. We must go. The sooner we complete our hunt, the sooner this ends for everyone."

It was full dark by the time they all stumbled into Dora's small cabin, tired, hungry, and frustrated. A full day of searching and almost nothing to show for it but bad news. Their visit to the Neal ranch had revealed no evidence of The Keres, but Thomas Neal and his youngest son, Joseph, were both ill.

The women crowded around Dora's table, meant for four, not seven, and ate what they had, berries and a roasted rabbit, in near silence. Atlanta and Cyrene brought in bedrolls from their horses. Dora made a pallet on the floor for Pearl. Caroline went down the mountain to go home. A full day away from her baby was long enough. Petra, Marina, and Dora crowded onto her bed, which was just big enough for the three of them if they did not move too much.

It was silent in the dark cabin when Marina spoke. "We'll find what we are searching for tomorrow."

"Telling the future?" Petra asked.

"Just being optimistic," was her reply.

"We've faced worse before. Remember the night we spent in the lean-to on Atlas's Peak after Zeus's feast?" Dora had thought then that if they could get through that night and the next day, it would be the worst thing they would ever have to do. She wished she had been right.

Petra sighed. "There is nothing about that night I forget."

Dora reached out and wrapped her arm around Petra and pulled her close. "We're together. We can face this."

Marina shifted and Dora could just make out her rising up on her elbows to face them. "Do you think this is how the first four harpies got along, like we do? Do you think they stayed up late, plotting the downfall of Olympus and hoping for something better?"

"I do," Petra said. "There were nights after coming to the valley that I only stayed because of you two. And Iris."

"I've always feared becoming my mother or getting lost in my own violence, but I should've known you two would never allow that. I think it's because we have each other that we've all found our humanity." Dora thought of Lee and included him in her reasons why she felt more grounded than ever.

Marina laid back on her pillow. "We will finish this hunt tomorrow."

"This is our valley," Petra added.

"If we don't succeed, people will die. That is not acceptable." Dora reached across Petra to touch Marina's hip, then did the same to Petra before tucking her hand under her head. "We've never failed when we're together. Good night."

CHAPTER 21

The first stop the next day was the Eisler farm to get Caroline for the day's hunt. George came out to greet them. His eyes were rimmed in red and he was pale.

"Caroline can't go today. She and the baby are both sick."

The five of them froze at the news, then Dora moved. "I'll check on her. The rest of you go ahead and I'll catch up by Renault's."

Dora's shoulders slumped when she saw Caroline lying in bed with her new baby. Both were covered in the rash, but their eyes were still clear.

Caroline spoke first. "I want to go today, but everything hurts."

Dora sat on the side of the bed. "I know. I'll try to come back and check on you, but…"

"But there may be too much to do. I know." Caroline grabbed her hand. "Please keep an eye on George. He'll be lost without me."

Dora squeezed Caroline's hand. "You're going to be fine. You have to get better to teach Melanie to be as good of a hunter as her mother."

Caroline tried to smile, but a tear escaped instead. "Please promise me, Dora. George won't understand how to teach Melanie to hunt, to be a laelaps, but you can. She will need you."

Dora's eyes burned and her throat felt closed off. This was why they could not fail. "I promise, but you'll never have to hold me to it."

Caroline moved the sheets and exposed the rash on her belly. "I know the signs. I am getting worse."

They were losing too many people. Dora could see Caroline loping through the aspens yesterday, strong and healthy. She did not fight the tears. "It's been an honor being your friend. On the River Styx, I swear to watch over your family as if it was my own as long as I draw breath. May our lines always be entwined with friendship and fidelity."

Caroline sniffed and smiled. "Thank you. Turning Creek is the place I'm happy to have called home. Go now, and send in George. I have many things to tell him before I go."

Dora nodded, unable to say more. She left the room and knelt down by Melanie, who was sitting by the front window. "Today will be a hard day, but I will be back to check on you when I can. Help your father."

Dora hugged the child, gave instructions to George, and left with mourning in her heart.

The day only got worse from there.

At the Renault farm, Magda answered the door when Petra and Dora knocked. She looked haggard. Dora was coming to dread that look.

"Who is sick here?" Dora asked without preamble.

Magda said, "Matthew and two of the children are sick. How did you know?"

"There is a plague spreading in the valley. We believe it is caused by Pandora's jar. We're hunting The Keres and the pithos to try to stop it. Dora already spoke to Mr. Renault earlier, he told us what to look for in a search for an older pithos. With your family's background in ceramics, we were hoping you would be able to help us look, but you have sick to tend to." Petra made an effort to look non-threatening. Even in mortal form, they were still predators.

Dora tasted Magda's fear on the back of her tongue. "You're afraid, now that we're here. Why?"

Magda looked shaken. She grabbed the door handle to steady herself. Circling her wrist was a geometric Grecian tattoo. "Generations ago, my family fled from a region ruled by a harpy. We were always taught to be wary. Matthew wanted to settle here. He said we would have protection with the three of you so close. I'm still not sure. He's mortal and does not always understand the world I am from."

Dora sighed. They would never escape the sins of their mothers. "You must know by now that we're not like that. I ask again, can you help us find the pithos?"

Magda hesitated. "I want to trust you, but trust is a hard won commodity. I might be able to help you, but not while so many in my family are sick."

"No one will get better until we find The Keres and the pithos," Petra said.

Dora took a painful breath. "The more time we take, the more people will die. It's not an if, but a when." Dora thought of Caroline and the Hughes twins and prayed to see them again.

Magda nodded, the lines deepening around her eyes and mouth. "Let me tend to my family."

Dora pushed her power towards the woman, slowly so she did not startle her, but enough so that she would know with what she tangled. "If you can help us, you should not hesitate. The day may come when we do not ask nicely. Do you have enough food for your house?"

The question caught Magda by surprise. "Yes, we do."

Dora gave Magda instructions for caring for her sick, and they left to join the other hunters.

"She is hiding something," Petra said.

"Yes, but I don't know if it has anything to do with our current problem or something else entirely. She has some old, bad feelings about harpies and I suspect it has more to do with that than anything else."

"You don't think she can help find the pithos?"

Dora changed and pushed off into the air. "I had more hope that Matthew would have some answers. He is the ceramic expert after all."

Petra flew beside her. "But he is not a Remnant. She is."

"Either way, she'll have to tell us soon, and she did say she knew something that may help us. She just doesn't trust us yet."

Petra chuckled. "I suppose the bright side of that conversation is if Marina had been the one talking she would've tried to scare the information out of Magda and that would've backfired. It would've proven Magda's fears about us true."

"Might have been more effective, though. Intimidation does have its place."

***

By the afternoon, Dora was beginning to think the hunt was going to be a complete loss. Her stomach protested the lunch they had skipped as she flew over a brushy area again to check it. Dora tried sending out her power, trying to feel for The Keres, but with so many other predators in the area, all the feedback was tangled. She sighed, which in her harpy form came out more like a wheeze, and kept looking.

Marina circled low ahead, her eyes stuck to a brush-covered hollow. She made a motion to Pearl, who was closest to her. Pearl bounded back towards Atlanta and Cyrene. Marina flipped and flew straight back to Dora. They landed under a tree. Petra saw the movement and joined them about a thousand yards downwind from the hollow. They were soon joined by the other three.

"There's something in the hollow over there. I am almost certain it's The Keres. They smell terrible," Marina said without preamble.

Adrenaline surged in Dora's blood and her hunger for lunch was forgotten. "Both of them?"

"I'm couldn't tell for sure," Marina said.

Pearl spoke up. "There are multiple landing areas around the hollow, which means one of them has been using the hollow for some time or both of them for a shorter period of time." She still retained her face on her sleek lion's body and could speak more clearly than the harpies.

Dora was impressed and it must have showed. She'd thought Pearl's skills lay mostly in her sense of smell and feline quickness in this form.

Pearl beamed and looked at Marina.

Marina gave the young sphinx a toothy grin. "You track almost as good as I do. Maybe better with your sniffer there."

Pearl preened as only a feline can. "The smell in the hollow is rank, like death. I couldn't separate two distinct smells."

Dora could feel the hunt in her blood, her mouth fairly watered at the anticipation of the blood that would soon fill it, but she was in control. She thought of Lee, working with the sick in town, of Iris, who always guided her, and Henry, and Reed. The women in this circle and the people waiting for her in town grounded her. They were the ones who kept her from losing herself to the violence inside herself. She never had been in danger of losing herself. There were far too many people who would fight to their last breath to make sure that never happened to her.

Dora started laughing, not a pleasant sound in her harpy form.

Atlanta raised an eyebrow at her. "You harpies are the strangest lot, but anyone who laughs before a hunt is my kind of crazy."

This just made Dora laugh all the harder. She was so relieved at her revelation. She wanted nothing more than to fly back to Lee and tell him what an idiot she had been. She had wasted so many years because of her ignorance.

"The most important thing," Petra said, "is that we not allow them to fly away. We need to flush them out to give us room to maneuver, but the three of us," she gestured to herself, Marina, and Dora, "will make sure they don't get far."

Marina took up the plan. "We will keep them close to the ground or on the ground itself to give you three a chance."

Dora eyed the large rifle butt sticking out of the holster on Atlanta's back. The huntress smiled. "Don't worry, harpy. I won't shoot you unless you get in the way."

Dora stretched out her wing so that it bumped Atlanta.

Atlanta laughed. "Hunting with you three is always the most interesting. I'd never kill one of you. It would mean that many fewer hunts in my life, and hunting is the thing I like second best in the world." She winked at Cyrene.

Cyrene rolled her eyes but smiled. "Flatterer."

"Works though, doesn't it?" Atlanta said. Cyrene answered her by placing a quick kiss on Atlanta's cheek.

"If you're all done joking around, we have some monsters to kill," Petra said.

Cyrene uncoiled a rope from her hip and ran her fingers over the twine. "What's that for?" Marin asked.

"I've been practicing roping. I thought I might try roping a Keres."

"Styx, they aren't dairy cows," Marina replied.

Cyrene's eyes flashed with something Dora recognized. She had seen it often enough in her harpy sister's eyes. It was the gleam of a predator before they ripped out your throat because it amused them to do so. "I never said I was roping cattle."

Petra flapped her wings with impatience. "Enough. Marina and Dora, with me in the air. Atlanta and Cyrene, drive them from the hollow. Pearl, stay close to Marina. Atlanta and Cyrene, stay below Dora and me. Keep partnered as much as possible. That will make it less likely that we'll lose them. Marina, if you see one make a dash for it, you'll chase them down."

"May Artemis guide you." Atlanta bowed to them.

The three harpies took to the air while the other three approached the hollow at opposite directions. Pearl's feline body blended with the grasses, and Dora lost sight of her once or twice. Dora looked at her sister harpies, closing in on the hollow. There was no hiding their forms against the blue of the summer sky. Harpies were not made for stealth, they were made to intimidate, torture, and kill. Pearl was made for a different kind of hunting.

Cyrene paused about twenty yards from the hollow, unhooked the rope at her waist, and nodded to Atlanta and Pearl. Dora tightened her circle and her heart rate sped up. Atlanta shouldered her rifle and pointed it into the hollow. Pearl pushed down on her haunches, ready to spring.

Dora could not hear the verbal command, but she saw Atlanta's mouth move. "Now," she said.

The sound of the rifle rang in Dora's ear. A rumble filled the air as Pearl let out the loudest roar Dora had ever heard. She did not have time to appreciate the sound. Two black Keres burst from the hollow with the surprised squawking of ravens caught unaware.

One of the Keres had the misfortune to fly almost directly into Marina, who whooped in triumph as she dropped like a weight on top of it. Tan and brown feathers filled the air as the Keres clawed back at the harpy savaging its back.

Dora and Petra circled the other Keres, now hovering between them. It feigned to the left and was cut off with a quick dive from Petra. It corrected its trajectory away from the talons of one harpy and flew straight into Dora's. Dora used the element of surprise to get a good swipe at the Keres's eyes with her claws. She opened a deep gash across the entire length of the Keres's head, blinding it with its own blood. Blood dripped from her claws and over the Keres's face. The warm smell of gore filled the air, and Dora roared. It was not as loud as Pearl's but the Keres jerked away from her nonetheless.

Dora flapped away before the Keres could regroup and retaliate. The Keres did not get a chance to recover; Petra's body slammed into from the side while angling herself so that she could grab its wing and wrench it back until Dora heard the bone snap. Petra followed the injured Keres to the ground.

With Petra in control of their Keres, Dora chanced a glance at the other group in time to see Cyrene throw an expert loop around the head of the Keres they still fought. With a yank, she tightened the rope and began pulling it to the ground. Marina circled over the beast, laughing and dive bombing the trapped, oversized bat.

Dora dove and tried to land on top of the Keres Petra had pinned to the ground. Before she could reach the pair, the Keres flipped over and dislodged Petra from its back. It was unable to fly and mostly unable to see because of the blood fillings its eyes. One wing dragged on the ground, but it tried to hop away from the two harpies.

Pearl had been waiting, crouched and watching the fight. She chose this moment to leap into the air. The tawny sphinx pushed the Keres back onto the ground and wrapped her jaw around the neck of the monster. The strange bat gurgled as its windpipe was crushed, then severed. While the body thrashed, Pearl bit down harder.

Dora landed on the still-moving Keres and used her weight to keep it still.

Petra joined her. "This kitten has a big mouth and pointy teeth."

"The better to eat you with, my dear," Dora said, laughing.

The Keres gave one final thrash, then stilled. The air was thick with gore and the weight of violence. Dora closed her eyes and drew a deep breath. Though her blood raced like fire, peace filled her soul.

Pearl released the Keres and sat back on her haunches. She raised a paw and licked it with a bloody tongue. "Blood tastes best when you squeeze it from their throat."

Marina flapped over to them and landed next to Pearl. She swiped a wing at the sphinx, who tried to bite at it playfully. "This is why I like this woman."

Dora licked blood from one of her own claws. It was delicious. "I see you've been teaching her your bloodthirsty ways."

Pearl straightened and gave Dora a haughty look. "A Sphinx does not need training to be a killer. A true hunter knows to enjoy the blood of a good kill."

Atlanta walked over, her face broken by a wide grin. "If you monsters are done licking blood from gods-know-where and congratulating yourselves, there's work to be done." Atlanta pulled a long knife from her boot.

Marina changed into her mortal form in a snap. She reached behind her shoulders and pulled out her matched swords and twirled them. "I'll get this head, you get that one."

Dora, Petra, and Pearl changed into their mortal forms and began building the pyre they would need for the bodies. With six of them helping, the sun was just hitting the western peaks as they watched the last of The Keres burn. Dora scooped up some of the ashes in a pouch and put them in the pocket of her skirt. She was careful to gather enough to ensure she had some of each of the creatures' remains.

"I have to get home," Petra said. "I want to make sure James and Selene are all right."

They were all silent, thinking of Caroline and wondering who else had fallen sick while they had been out hunting.

Dora wrapped Petra in a hug. "I'll come check on you when I can."

Marina walked up behind them and hugged them both. "We're going to be fine. The gods aren't done with us yet." Her words were filled with bravado, but Dora saw fear of the truth in Marina's eyes.

They stood with their foreheads touching. "In this life, or the next, you two are who I would choose to fight with me against any foe."

Petra's arms tightened on them both. "I'm leaving before I cry. Be safe. If any of you die, I will hunt you down in whatever circle of hell you are in and make you regret it," she said to the entire assembly.

"I have no wish to die, but death comes for us all in time." Cyrene bowed to the harpies. "Thank you for the hunt today."

Petra left, and Dora watched her go with a twist in her heart.

Pearl changed back into her sphinx form. "I am headed home as well. I left Robert there, and I want to make sure he is fine. We will probably come into town tomorrow to help." She bounded off across the grassy hills.

Atlanta and Cyrene shared a look that held a conversation. Atlanta said, "We'll meet you in town later. We'll hunt along the way and bring some meat for a communal dinner tonight."

Dora nodded. "See you then." With a smile at Marina and a prayer sent to whoever was listening, the two harpies changed and flew back towards town.

CHAPTER 22

Marina went straight home to Reed and the girls. After some thought, Dora flew to the depot first to clean up from the fight and retrieve something she should have given to Lee weeks ago. Iris did not ask any questions when Dora handed over the pouch of ashes. Dora told her about the hunt and Iris let her talk.

"We didn't find the pithos. I do think something is going on at the Renaults, but it might not be related. I think it has more to do with the fact that Magda doesn't like harpies much." Dora fingered a patch of dirt or ash or both on her blouse.

Iris took her hand. "We will find it. You killed The Keres, all three of them, and that is a victory. Go get cleaned up."

Dora stood and swayed on her feet. Iris caught her elbow. "When was the last time you ate?"

"Breakfast? Maybe some berries along the way. We didn't take time to stop today."

"What about yesterday?" Iris pressed.

"We had rabbit for dinner."

"Let's get you upstairs. You're going to eat, clean up, then rest."

Dora shook her head as Iris led her up the stairs. "I have to go see Lee."

"You won't see anyone if you're dead. You have some time to eat and rest before going to the saloon."

Dora did not have the energy to argue. "You like bossing us around."

Iris laughed. "I do."

Dora let Iris feed her and help her get undressed. She rinsed off the worst of the dirt in a basin of warm water then tumbled into one of the beds in the extra room.

"Don't let me sleep long," she told Iris as her eyes closed.

"No promises."

***

Dora woke up and the room she was in was completely dark. She lay there for a moment, remembering where she was and thanking the gods for Iris. She rose from the bed and felt her way in the dark to the door. A red glow from the banked kitchen fire eased the darkness enough for Dora to find a candle on the table beside the bed. She took it to the fire and used a small twig from the wood box to light it.

Dora got dressed, putting on a new skirt and blouse that Iris had laid out for her while she slept. She went to the large bookshelf in the sitting room and ran her hand over the bindings. She found the volume she was looking for and removed it from the shelf. Dora blew out the candle and left it in the middle of the kitchen table.

Night still held the world in its grip as Dora crossed Main Street to Vine's. The moon was beginning its decent through the inky curve of the sky, but dawn was still a few hours away. The air smelled cool and sweet, filled with the floral scent of summer flowers and dirt. Dora clutched the book tighter in her hand and smoothed her other hand over her hair. She had left it down and now wondered if she should have pulled it back.

When she passed the threshold of the saloon, all the gentle smells of the night were wiped away by the scent of suffering and death. Dora steeled herself and looked around the room.

The tables had been pushed to one side and the floor was covered in pallets. Half of the beds were filled with the sleeping forms of the sick, who tossed and turned with their uncomfortable dreams. Widow Finch sat in a back corner, knitting. Dora approached her.

In a low voice, Widow Finch said, "Doc's out back in the garden. Take him some of these. I couldn't get him to eat earlier." She pushed a bowl of berries and a slice of cooked meat in Dora's direction. Dora nodded and picked up the bowl with her free hand.

Lee was sitting on one of the benches with his head in his hands. Dora put the bowl down on the far side of the bench and then sat beside Lee so that their shoulders touched. After a moment, she rested her head on his shoulder. She sent her power to him and wrapped him in it. Connecting with him this way, she could feel the way his power wavered with fatigue, and icy fear touched her spine.

He took a shuddering breath but did not look up. "The Gerlichs almost died today. I brought them all back from the brink. The Hughes girls pulled through just in time to watch their parents die because I didn't have enough power to save Paul and Lily. I can't save them all."

"Oh, Lee—"

"There's more. Elizabeth Smith was dead before she could make it here for care. L.A. and Johnny stumbled in soon after, burning up. They told me to let them go be with their wives. They died within an hour of each other. Shelly, Widow Finch's girl, died too. Most of the town is sick."

Dora wrapped her arm around Lee's shoulders and squeezed her eyes against the burning in them. So many empty spaces in their town. Her voice was rough when she spoke. "I left Caroline Eisler and her baby this morning. They both had rashes. They could be dead by now."

Lee straightened up and turned to face her. "Did you get The Keres?"

Dora nodded. "Both. Now we have to find the pithos."

"Before the entire town dies. I can't save everyone."

"Lee, not everyone will die." Dora was not sure she was speaking truth or just what her sore heart wanted to believe.

He gripped her arm. "I can't save them all. I want to but I can't. I don't even know how I would start to choose between who to save. Instead, I've been giving extra strength to the sick here and there as much as I'm able."

Dora smoothed her hand down his cheek. "You don't have to save everyone. We just have to do our best and save who we can."

"I can bring people back, but not everyone wants to come. But I can't bring everyone back. Even if I could, I wouldn't do it. I won't ever do that ever again."

Dora used her free hand to hold Lee's hand. He covered it instantly with both of his hands. She had trouble imagining a younger version of this man, one who could be manipulated. His strong will and purpose were something she loved about him. She knew the story of his past, but now she could feel how deep the hurt from that lesson was buried in his soul. Connected to him, she could feel the pain of his words.

His whole body shook, and he gripped her arm hard enough to leave a bruise, but Dora stayed silent. "If I bring people back that don't want to come, they don't really come back. Too many people are dying now, and I can't save them all. I'm not strong enough. I'm afraid they won't come back right. I'm afraid if I use my power now I won't be able to use it when it will matter most to *me*.

"I'm a selfish bastard."

Dora broke into his rambling. "What are you saying?"

Lee lifted his face. There were deep shadows under his eyes, but they glittered fiercely. Dora felt his power snap against her own and each word he spoke burned against her skin. "I won't watch you die. I'm telling you now so you'll come back willingly. I can't bring you back if you don't want to come, and you're the person I want most to save."

Dora shook her head. "I'm not going to die."

"That's what everyone thinks."

Dora moved her hand out of Lee's and picked up the book on her lap. "I bought something for you on my trip to Leadville. In all the chaos, I never gave it to you."

Lee took the book. He ran his fingers over the cover and Dora had a flash of desire to feel those fingers elsewhere. He opened the book and lifted it to use the light from the lamp at his side to read the inside page.

"Where on earth did you find a copy of Gray's anatomy book?"

"A soldier who'd deserted sold it to a merchant in Leadville. I knew you didn't have it, and I wanted you to know I was thinking about you, quite a lot, on that trip. Do you like it?" Dora found she was nervous. She had more important things to tell him, and this book was a gateway. If he didn't like this, the other things she might keep to herself for now.

Lee closed the book and leveled his gaze on her. His look went from appreciation of a book to something else entirely, something that made her neck hot and desire unfurl in her belly. "You thought of me on your trip?"

Dora nodded. "Yes, and I did some thinking the last two days on the hunt. I realized something."

Lee put the book behind him on the bench and gave her his full attention. "What, may I ask, did you realize?"

"My mother was not in control of her harpy and of the violence it represented. She allowed the violence to rule her, and I allowed it to overcome me. I thought that was what it meant to be a harpy, to become violence. Then I came here, and Petra, Marina, and Iris taught me differently. I was in control. I was never going to be pure violence as long as I was in control. With you, though, I didn't feel in control. It scared me. I couldn't control the way I reacted to you and I thought I would lose myself if I allowed myself to feel anything."

Warm hands gripped hers, and Dora held on. "You spent time with me even though I scared you?"

"I know. Not the smartest thing I ever did, but I couldn't stay away from you."

A smile broke the serious lines on Lee's face. "And now?"

The desire that had been filling her now filled with something she detested in herself. Fear wound its way through her. She thought he knew how she felt, but she had to be sure. She had to say the words.

"We never got to talk at the Hughes' house and then everything went sideways."

Lee's eyes darkened. "We did something better than talking."

She plunged ahead. "You are not just my friend. I love you, Lee Williams. I have for a very long time now, probably from the beginning, when we rescued you from that mob, but I never thought I could have you as mine. I didn't trust myself. I do now. I'm not certain how you feel about me. I think I know but—"

Dora never got a chance to finish her sentence. Lee's lips covered the rest of what she wanted to say. His lips were not tender this time, but demanding. His hand wrapped around the back of her head and into her loose hair. He groaned and deepened the kiss.

Dora opened to him, and he tasted of mint tea. Everywhere his hands went, Dora's skin felt like it burst into flames. She ran her hands up his chest and around the back of his head, pulling him farther into her. She wanted to consume him or to be consumed by him.

When Lee pulled back from their kiss, they were both breathing heavily. Dora closed the distance between them, already craving the heat of their contact Lee had halted. Lee pushed on her forehead with his own.

"Wait," he said between breaths. "You got to say what you needed to say. Now it's my turn." Lee ran his hands down her face and cupped his hands around her jaw. "Gods, it feels like I've waited so long to touch you again like this, but I have to tell you something first."

Dora leaned forward and kissed him quickly on the mouth. "Tell me then so you can show me all the touching you've been thinking about."

Lee groaned. "I think now you may be the death of me. Plagues be damned."

Dora felt like laughing. Her harpy was doing backflips in her head, pleased with the turn of events, finally. She tried to kiss him again, but Lee dodged her.

"Wait. I have waited a long time to tell you this." Lee took a deep breath and looked right into her soul. "I wanted you from the moment you and your sister harpies saved me from that mob, but it was spending time with you that made me love you. It was experience that showed me that you were meant to be the wife of my heart. Love is daily life lived in partnership, and you are my partner. You waited up with me at the birth of babies. You comforted the sick and gave peace to the dying. You cared for me when I was dead on my feet. With your actions, you showed me every day that I would never find anyone who was more loyal or loved me more than you have. My heart and my body have always been yours. They have been for years. I have never loved anyone, nor will I love anyone else, the way I love you."

Dora swallowed past all the emotions clogging her throat and blinked them out of her eyes. "All these years? Why didn't you tell me?"

Lee chuckled, and Dora felt the vibrations of it in her core. "I knew, but you did not. I know you now and I knew you then. I knew that if I told you the truth of how I felt, you would run, so I waited. I had faith that you'd come to your own realization about what I had known from the beginning. You are mine, and I have always been yours."

Dora laughed. "You're right. I would've flown so fast out of here."

"I admit I was starting to worry your stubbornness would win out and I would have to die a lonely old man."

"No chance of that happening now. Of course, I come with a large and obnoxious extended family."

"I think I can hold my own."

"Good, because I'd hate to have to fight them for you."

They both grinned at each other. The world was a mess, but she had this to come back to, to ground her, no matter what else was happening.

They closed the distance between them and Dora never wanted to stop feeling the pressure of his lips on hers or the feeling of his tongue as it invaded her mouth. She pushed her power fully into him and he pulled it to him, circling it around his own before slamming the combined weight back into her.

Dora's hands found the buttons on his shirt and undid them enough to get her hands on his warm skin. She ran her hands through the crinkling hair on his chest. Lee pulled her closer, then lifted her so she was sitting across his lap. The fierceness of his desire was apparent from her new perch and she shifted on his lap to let him know she felt it. His hand in her hair yanked in retaliation, and he pinched her hard nipple through her blouse.

Dora looked around the garden, assessing the corners, hoping they were dark enough for what she had in mind. She didn't think they could get from the garden to Lee's house with all their clothes on. She ran her hands over his chest again and looked down to follow her hand's progress. Everything in her froze. Spread over his skin, hidden by the hair there, were the first signs of an unmistakable rash.

"Why didn't you tell me?"

Lee's hands tightened on her, which was good because she felt like everything was spinning. "I'm fine now. I have no fever or achiness."

"You have to go lie down."

"I have a job to do." He said the words like they alone would overrule everything.

Dora's hand shook and her eyes started to fill. "You can't be sick."

Lee ran his fingers down the sides of her face. "Everything will be fine."

Dora did not believe him, though she desperately wanted to. The back door of the saloon opened, breaking into the moment. Instead of pushing her away, Lee's arms tightened around her and held her in place. Dora resisted the urge to curl into him like a puppy. She did not want to be interrupted.

Marina was silhouetted in the doorway. "I need Dora to come with me." Her voice had an even deadness to it.

The hairs on the back of Dora's neck rose and all thoughts of escape with Lee flew into the night air. "What happened?"

Marina's body gave a small shake. "The girls are sick. I need you to come look at them. Tell me how bad it is."

Dora did not know it was possible to have such joy and despair inside herself at the same time, but the universe had managed it. A band of fear wound around her.

Lee smoothed her hair and kissed her gently on the lips. "Go. We both have work to do."

"I love you," Dora whispered and marveled at the ease with which the words came out of her mouth. "I'll come by after."

"I love you too. Go."

Marina did not speak as they walked across and down Main Street. Dora wanted to say something, but there were no words of encouragement to give and she did not feel like sharing her own tangle of despair and happiness. If Dora ever felt out of control, it was right now, when there was very little she could do to stop the tide of death crashing towards them. It felt like freefalling while watching Tartarus rise up to consume them all.

Marina led her into the room Nina and Ellie shared. Reed sat with his head bowed in a chair between their beds. He looked up when they walked in. He looked years older than when Dora had seen him days ago. Deep shadows bruised his eyes.

Marina went down on her knees on the side of Ellie's bed. Both girls were asleep, but their skin was pale. Dora went to Nina's bed first. She lifted up the covers and the girl's night gown to expose her stomach; it was bare. She did the same examination of Ellie, who woke up as Dora moved the covers.

The child's eyes were clear as Dora sat next to her on the bed. "Hi, Auntie Dee."

"Hello, youngling. How are you feeling?"

"Cold and hurting."

Dora put a hand on Ellie's forehead. She definitely had a fever. "I know, but your mama and daddy are going to take very good care of you. You'll be better in no time."

Dora spoke to Reed. "Keep bathing them with cold water and a rag. It will help with the fever. I have some herbs for a tea that will also help if you can get them to drink it." Reed left the room with the basin, which was almost empty. "Marina, can I talk to you in the hallway?"

Marina kissed her daughter on the forehead. "I'll be right back, small one."

When the door was closed, Dora said, "Neither of them have the rash yet, and their eyes are clear. Even if they get the rash, they could still recover. If they develop bruises on their legs, though…"

"I know."

Marina gripped the doorframe so hard the wood creaked. "I can't lose either of them. They are my heart."

Dora gripped her shoulders. "You haven't lost them yet. We killed The Keres. We just have to find the pithos."

Marina shook and her voice was angry. "How are we going to find it? Styx, it's like looking for a needle in a haystack. It could be anywhere, in any house. How can we find it before the whole damn town dies?"

Dora shook her by the shoulders. "We will. We have to."

Marina nodded and seemed to gather herself back up.

"I'm going to help Lee at the saloon. Come get me once the sun is up. We're finding that pithos *today*."

Reed came up the stairs then, and Dora said her goodbyes. She had not thought it possible for her heart to be even heavier, but she felt like she dragged it behind her in the dust as she crossed the street to the saloon. Before going through the door, she reeled it back in and shoved it into her chest. She took a deep breath. She had a job to do and she needed a clear head for it.

Lee was kneeling between two pallets on the floor. When Dora looked over Lee's shoulder, she was able to see Simon and Beth Kramer holding hands across the small space between their pallets. Simon was flushed with fever. Beth looked pale but not feverish. Dora tried to school the despair from her face when she met Beth's eyes.

Lee did not turn around but somehow knew she was there. "Dora, will you please make Simon some tea and help Beth walk around if she feels up to it?"

Dora put a hand on Lee's shoulder. "Of course. Anything else?"

Lee stood and faced her. His movement meant there was very little space between them, and despite the room full of sick people, Dora felt her cheeks heat. "I'm going to check on each patient and then see about getting some kind of broth or something for them all to eat."

His eyes roamed over her face and he allowed a small smile to turn up his lips. Lee dropped his voice so only she could hear. "You have the most beautiful blush I have ever seen. I'll have to think of new ways to make your cheeks turn that particular color."

Dora could not untie her tongue fast enough to reply before he slipped away to the next bed. She was still smiling when she knelt down beside Beth.

"I am glad someone is happy in this room," Beth said.

Dora covered her mouth. "I didn't mean to make you think anything about this situation was cheerful."

Beth reached a hand from under her cover and took Dora's hand. "I didn't mean it that way. I mean that if it took an actual plague to bring you two together, then so be it. You have both doted on each other long enough."

Dora did not want to think about how observant the town had been of her relationship with Lee. "How are you feeling?" Dora felt Beth's forehead. "You don't have a fever."

"No, mine passed a couple hours ago. Simon's, though, is still very high."

A small bit of hope that Beth had recovered filled Dora. If Beth could get better, then others could as well. Dora turned her attention to Simon, who had been quiet. His silence caused the well of worry to overflow. His eyes were closed.

"Simon, are you awake?" Dora asked quietly.

He opened his eyes. They were still clear. Dora heaved a sigh of relief. "Do you have a rash or bruises?"

He shook his head, then winced. "But everything hurts," he rasped.

"Let me get both of you some tea and then some broth."

Beth stopped Dora before she could get up. "Is he going to be all right? Doc didn't want to say either way."

Dora dreaded answering. Lee had not wanted to answer this question because it was the one every loved one of every sick person wanted to know, and it was the one question to which there was almost never a good answer. A patient could be fine one day and dead the next or deathly ill and recovered completely in days. Fate was a harsh mistress.

Dora took another look at Simon. He watched her. "I can't say. Only time will tell. If I have my way, however, this will be finished soon."

"Thank you." Beth took her husband's hand in her own again.

Dora left them to make tea. Over the course of the next two hours, she had the same conversation with everyone that was able to speak. She was not always able to be so hopeful. Zaneta Tumanov and her son, Misha, kept vigil over her husband Feliks, who had started to develop bruising on his legs. When Dora checked on them, Misha also had a fever. Dora made him lay down next to his father. Zaneta was silently weeping when Dora left them to go to another bed.

The morning came, like it did every day, and Dora was outside in the garden getting some air when the sun peeked over the tops of the eastern summits. The birds were singing to the sunrise, and Dora could not have felt more out of sync with the beauty around her.

Marina come through the back door of the saloon. Her face was flushed. Dora put a hand on her forehead. She could feel the heat coming off her before her palm even made contact.

"You should be in bed."

Marina sat with a groan. "Good morning to you too. I feel like my bones are on fire."

"Go to bed."

"No."

"How is you driving yourself into a grave going to help anyone?"

Marina turned feverish eyes on Dora. "I can't just lay in bed and watch my family die. I can't do it. By the River Styx, I will save them or die trying, but I can't sit there any longer. Reed will take care of them. That's his job right now. This is mine. I stopped by the depot to get the ashes from Iris."

Dora nodded. "All right. Have you eaten?"

Marina shook her head. "I'm not hungry."

"You will force some food down your throat or I won't fly with you today. Wait here.”

Dora brought Marina back a boiled egg and a cup of chicken broth. “It’s not much, but it’s all we have. I’m going to tell Lee we’re leaving, then we can go.”

Dora found Iris before she found Lee. Dora asked a question she did not want the answer to. “Is everyone at the depot all right?”

“Thomas is sick.”

Dora licked her lips. “What are his symptoms?”

“He had a fever, but now he has a rash and his eyes are bloodshot. I came to see if there was anything you had found that helped.”

“Prayer. Pleading with the gods.”

Iris’s shoulders sagged, and Dora wrapped her arms around her. “We will get through this. We have to.”

Every moment, every new patient, made the world that much heavier. Dora brought Iris the herbs she needed. As she handed Iris the satchel, Iris stilled and the air around them tightened. Iris’s eyes lost focus, and she gripped Dora’s arm with a strength she did not normally have. Power surged from Iris. Her voice was flat and toneless as she spoke words; their power pounded into Dora’s breastbone.

“The lost daughter will be found, and madness will follow on her heels.”

Iris’s body shivered and her eyes focused once again. Dora steadied her with her free hand. Iris still had a vice-like grip on her other arm.

“Are you all right?”

Iris shook her head. “This is bad timing for a prophecy.”

Dora shook her head. “We’re in the middle of a plague, and we get more prophecies about doom. Next time, I want a prophecy about rainbows or a Pegasus.”

Iris released her grip on Dora’s arms. “I’ll take that into advisement.”

“What does it mean?”

Iris’s frown deepened. “I’m afraid we won’t know until it is already too late.”

Dora looked around the room, at all the sick people, some of whom would not last the day. “I only have time for one problem today.”

Iris kissed her forehead. “Be safe, my bird.” She left clutching the satchel like it was her last line of hope. Dora continued her search for Lee.

She found him in a back storage room filled with casks and bottles. He sat on a cask in the corner. He looked up when he saw her. His cheeks were flushed with fever and bile rose in her throat at the sight. With shaking legs, she knelt in front of him.

“Don’t even suggest that I go lie down.”

Dora took both of his hands in her own and laid her head down on them in his lap. She took several deep breaths before she could raise her head and look at him.

"You aren't going to die. I will not allow it."

"I might someday, but not today. I want many nights of curling into bed with you. I can't die now."

That made her smile. "I'm going to hold you to that. I will not bury you."

Lee leaned down and kissed her forehead. "You'll never have to bury me. Remnants of the line of Asclepius are burned on a pyre."

Dora swallowed back a sob. She stood and took his face in her hands. She pressed her lips to his burning ones and kissed him all the longing she had for their future. He pulled her to him, wrapping an arm around her waist and one hand in her hair as he drew her down into his lap.

"I shouldn't be kissing you at all," he told her between kisses. "I'm probably going to make you ill."

"It's too late for that worry."

Lee eased back. "We both have work to do."

Dora kissed him once more, grabbing handfuls of his shirt and pulling him close. She prayed to whatever gods would listen to keep this man alive until this was all over. She wanted to breathe him in and imprint this moment on her soul, just in case. She could not finish that line of thought.

Dora ended the embrace but kept her body flush with his, not completely willing to leave. "Marina and I are going to find the pithos today. We will get Petra and stop at houses along the way. We're going to find that pithos if we have to ransack every house and cellar in the valley." Dora's hands curled into fists and her voice took on an edge.

Lee unclenched her hands and took hers in his own. She could feel the fever in his hands and her heart beat painfully. This was her mate. She would not lose him. She would not fail him.

"Come back to me, Dora."

"I will. I promise." Or she would die trying.

CHAPTER 23

"Do you have the ashes?" Marina asked her for what seemed like the fiftieth time.

"I have them. Stop asking."

They were flying over the valley, straight for the Lloyd farm. They had considered searching some houses on their way, but in the end, they had felt a visceral pull to be together. They needed Petra. Dora wanted to touch her and reassure herself that Petra was well. Too many of those who held pieces of her heart were sick or dying.

Dora flew in front, trying to take some of turbulence from Marina, who was struggling more than she wanted Dora to know. Dora's heart constricted, and for a moment it was harder to fly. The deaths she had seen so far were painful, but there were people whose loss would reverberate in her soul for the rest of her life. There was no option of failing today.

The closer they flew to Petra's house, the more dread settled between Dora's wings. She both wanted to know all was well on the Lloyd farm and was filled with fear that it would not be. They landed in the yard, changed, and went into the house without waiting to knock or be greeted.

Petra was at the stove, stirring a pot of soup. She turned to them with a face like a steel mask. Dora knew what that look meant. It was the look you used when you had to keep yourself in one piece or everything would fall apart. She suspected she and Marina both had similar expressions.

"Who is sick?" Dora asked.

Petra continued to stir but turned her face away from the soup. "Most of the ranch hands. Selene developed a fever this morning."

"We are going to find the pithos today. This stops now. We want you to come, if you can." Marina went to stand beside Petra, who had not stopped stirring.

Dora joined them and put an arm around Peter's shoulders. No matter how much they wanted Petra with them, they also knew it might be hard for her to leave.

Petra nodded. "Let me go speak to James and say…goodbye to Selene."

Dora grabbed her arm before she left. "We will find it before any more people die."

Petra gave Dora a smile that held no warmth. "I know we will try, but the gods are not disposed to help us out. Why should they spare us now? Harpies have had to claw our way to everything we've ever wanted."

Petra did not take long and they were up and in the air within minutes.

"Where should we start? Petra asked.

Dora ground her teeth together. Their situation was desperate. "Even though the Mylonis house is closest, I think we should go talk to Magda Renault. Her family knows the most about pottery and urns. Plus, I think she has been hiding something, and I want to know what it is."

Petra was on point and turned around to shout over the wind. "Which of the family are Remnants? Do we know what they are?"

"Magda and one or two of her daughters. They're not anything dangerous as far as I know, but I don't know what they are. Marina?" Dora turned her head to ask and saw the harpy falter. Her heart stopped for a moment as she watched, bunching her muscles to dive left towards Marina.

Before she could move to help her, Marina righted herself. "I'm fine. Styx." Marina took some labored breaths. "I don't know much about the Renaults. Most of the interactions I've had with their family were with the men. They tended to be in town the most, running the ceramics shop."

"Magda is not what you would call the friendliest neighbor I have," Petra said.

"Today, she could be Hades himself and I would go begging if it would help." Dora tried to push all the people burdening her heart aside and concentrate on the task ahead.

The low rasping sound of Marina chuckling in her harpy form sounded over the wind. "I might see Hades before long. I can ask him when I get there if we're still looking for the pithos."

"He'll drag you across the River Styx over my dead body," Petra said.

"Careful what you wish for," Marina replied.

They landed in the yard and changed. Dora watched Marina finger the knife at her waist. "Maybe I should do the talking."

"What, you don't think I can be diplomatic?" Marina took the knife out and twirled it.

Dora elbowed her as she walked towards the door. "We're here to ask some questions. I think your fever is starting to addle your brain."

Petra smiled and said, "I'm certain her brain has been addled since the moment she was born."

Whatever comeback Marina had planned, she never got to say it. The door to the cabin opened and a young girl stepped out. Her hair was in a braid, but half of her hair had come loose. Dora could taste the fear in the air emanating from the girl.

Marina stepped forward, slid her knife back into her belt, and dropped to one knee in one motion, bringing her face a little lower than the girl's pale one. "We're friends. My name is Marina." She pointed behind her shoulder. "This is Petra and Dora. You might remember Dora from a couple days ago when she came by to check on your family. What's your name?"

The girl blinked at Marina and looked back at Dora and Petra. "Leah."

Marina nodded. "That's a nice name. Leah, we want to ask your father some questions. Is he here?"

The girl shook her head. "Momma said he is gone forever. His eyes got red and he went to sleep, but she said he won't wake up again. She put coins on his eyes."

Marina hugged the girl. "I'm so sorry. We need to talk to your mother. Can we come in?"

Leah led them into the house. There was some food on the table, but it had to have been over a day old because it was covered in mold. There were no lamps lit and the fire was cold. Without a word, Petra scooped up the rotting food and threw it outside. Marina started stacking wood for a fire.

"Did you bring anything to eat with you?" asked Marina.

Dora shook her head. "I've barely eaten myself. I was helping out with the sick. There hasn't been any time to hunt."

Marina asked Leah. "Have you eaten today?"

"No. All the berries I picked yesterday are bad and I haven't checked the chickens yet today."

Marina grabbed a basket from against the wall. "Why don't you go look for eggs now while we talk to your mother."

Leah left and Dora went into the back room. Magda sat beside her husband, copper pennies resting on the eyes he would never use again. She did not look up as they entered. Dora could feel Marina at her back and the fever emanating from her. Their time was short, and she could not give Magda the time she wanted to grieve. They needed answers.

"I don't want to talk to you."

Marina started to speak, but Dora held up a hand. "You said you might be able to help us stop this. More people will die until we find the pithos. If you know something, you need to tell us what it is."

Magda sighed and squeezed her husband's cold hand.

Dora looked around the empty room. "Where are the rest of your children?"

Magda stood and faced them for the first time since they entered the room. Her face was set, hard, but Dora sent out some of her own power and could feel the fear and desperation running from Magda like water from a mountain stream.

"Asher is dead. Ruben and Aderes are in the woods looking for berries. Ruben still has a fever, but he insisted on going with his sister. He would've been a strong man. A good man."

"He's not dead yet," Marina said with disgust.

Magda shook her head and led them out into the kitchen.

"But he will be if you don't help us."

Dora nudged Marina to be silent. "Last time I was here, you said you might know some things that could help us. I've seen the ceramics your husband made. I was hoping he or you would be able to tell us some things that might make it easier to find the particular pithos we are looking for."

Magda moved, putting the table between them. "If what you are looking for is as old as the stories say, it will not necessarily be what you expect. You might expect the pithos to be elaborately decorated, but it might also be very simple. It will certainly have more Grecian elements than a household jar, but there is no telling what size it would be. How large does a jar have to be to be filled with the sorrows of the world?"

Dora gripped the back of a chair. "Will there be a maker's mark? Something we can use to identify it?"

"How would I know? I'm not an expert in Greek Mythology," Magda snapped.

Petra ran a hand over her face. "In the myths, the pithos was given to Pandora as a wedding present from Zeus. While he is unlikely to have made it himself, he was a prideful bastard and probably marked it himself. Maybe we are looking for a lightning bolt somewhere on the bottom or in the decoration?"

Dora nodded. "Yes, that sounds like something he would do."

Marina swayed a little, but caught herself on a chair. "We need to get going. This is a big valley with a lot of houses, and I'm not sure I'll last the day."

Dora knew they should leave, but she knew she was missing something. "Is there anything else?"

"What are you going to do once you find the pithos?" Magda asked.

Marina fingered the knife at her belt again. "The myths say we have to sacrifice its protector and replace The Keres' ashes to seal the jar."

Magda's face hardened. "Good luck to you then. You should go. If I can do anything else for you, please let me know."

Dora let out more of her power and sent it snaking towards Magda. The air around her was thick with fear. Marina and Petra sensed it the moment she did, and the three of them straightened.

"There's something making you afraid, making you lie. What is it?" Marina's low voice grated, her harpy showing through.

Magda's hands fisted by her sides. Dora's entire body tensed. Magda was acting like cornered prey.

The door opened and Ruben and his youngest sister, Aderes, came into the room. He was pale and he walked as if every step pained him. He handed his mother a basket then collapsed in a chair.

"That's all we could find."

The basket held a few mouthfuls of berries. Dora's resolve hardened. It did not matter what Magda was hiding. If it would help them, Dora would do anything to get her to tell them. The fingers of her right hand elongated into claws and Dora had to concentrate to make them turn back. She did not, however, stop her power and intention from leaking into the air. Petra and Marina added theirs. The children stilled, looking at the three women.

Aderes, who could not have been more than four, went to stand by her mother. The little girl reached up and blindly grabbed her hand. The sleeve of her dress shifted just enough, exposing her wrist. Circled around the delicate bones was a geometrical pattern, the kind that frequently decorated the tops and bottoms of Grecian urns. The same tattoo that circled her mother's wrist.

Dora swallowed the bile rising in her throat. "The pithos is here. Search the house."

Petra and Marina did not ask how she knew. They went to work. Matthew had once told Dora that his family had been making ceramics for generations, and the contents of the Renault house reflected that. There were jars, plates, cups, and statues everywhere. Marina and Petra piled all the jar or urn shaped items on the table.

Magda shifted, whether to simply move or to escape, Dora did not know. She did not care which. Dora pulled out a chair. "Sit. You and I are going to talk while they look."

Magda sat but kept her arm around the girl. Leah came to stand by her mother. "Ruben, you should go lie down." The boy went to a back room without another word.

Dora did not sit, nor did she conceal any of the threat of violence in her voice. She needed answers. "You and your daughters are Remnants. What line are you from?"

Magda hesitated.

Dora laid her palm flat on the table and elongated her claws. Her voice deepened, on the verge of changing completely. "Now is not the time to hold back what you know. We're trying to save this valley and all its people. I'm trying to save my family. I will do so at any cost."

"And I'm trying to protect mine." She ran a hand over Leah's hair. "We are of Pandora's line."

Petra paused as she placed a small, covered bowl on the table. "Until recently, we didn't know there were any of you left."

"It was what my line wanted. To be forgotten for the follies we unleashed upon the world, to hide what we knew…and what we still possessed."

Marina placed what looked like a sugar bowl on the table. "That's the last of it in the house. She could have hidden it outside in the barn."

"Or buried it. That's what I would do," Petra chimed in.

Dora shook her head. "No, I think it's here."

The three of them looked over the ceramics gathered on the table. Dora separated the most likely ones, the pottery shaped more like urns. There were five, all different sizes, all different designs, but all of Grecian design.

Dora turned back to Magda. "Which one is it?"

Magda's shoulders dropped. "What will you do if I tell you?"

Marina ground her teeth together. "What you should be asking is what we will do if you don't. We don't have the luxury of time."

Dora pulled the pouch of ashes from her pocket. "We add that to the jar and seal it closed again with the blood of the protector."

Magda nodded. She rose and pointed to a jar on the table. The sides were covered in a pastoral landscape, rolling fields and trees. The top, bottom, and handle were wrapped with the same design Magda had tattooed on her wrist. On the bottom of the jar was a lightning bolt encased in a triangle. "It's this one. It's my blood that you need."

Dora lifted the urn. It was smaller than she thought it would be, less assuming.

Marina stepped between Dora and Magda. "How do we know you're not lying and this is the correct one?"

"You don't."

Dora lifted the jar. "Do you know anything more about what we must do? Are there special words we must say?"

"I think you have the knowledge you need to close the jar. The ashes and sacrifice are all that is required. I give you my life freely."

Marina's focus shifted to the two girls. "Petra, they should not be here to see this."

Petra reached her hand out to both girls. Leah was crying, more from the tension in the air than from true understanding, Dora thought. Aderes looked worried, but was trusting in the way only a young, loved child can be. She took Petra's offered hand without hesitation. Her sleeve slipped and Dora saw the tattoo on her wrist again.

"Styx and fire. Stop," Dora put down the urn. "It's not Magda." Dora looked at those small trusting eyes and felt sick. "The protector is Aderes. She's the sacrifice."

"No." Magda threw herself between Petra and the child. Aderes started crying, startled by the quick move and the tone of her mother's voice. "I don't care if the entire world falls apart, you can't have her."

Dora took quick breaths, willing herself not to be sick. "There's no other way. You said so yourself."

Petra looked ill. "It's the girl?"

Dora nodded. "Magda and the girl both have a tattoo on their wrist." Dora pointed to the urn and the geometric ribbon around the top. "It looks just like this. If Aderes has one, that means the power has already passed to her."

"*Aderes* means protector," Petra whispered.

Marina pulled out her knife. "Styx. Styx." She clenched her jaw and her hand holding the knife shook.

"You can't do it," Magda pleaded. "She didn't know. She opened it, but she didn't know. I'll be the sacrifice. I'm of the same line. It might work."

"It won't, though. The gods are cruel. They'd never allow for such an easy end," Marina's voice was heavy and tired.

The four of them looked at each other, all sick at the choice before them, none of them seeing a good way out of this.

Magda sobbed and hugged Aderes. "It's my fault. I wanted to protect her from the truth of what we were for as long as possible. Our marks, they aren't tattoos, they appear when the mantle passes from one generation to the next. Hers darkened four months ago and I had to tell her. She was curious. She's only four."

Marina was still holding her knife in a white knuckled grip. Dora's mind raced. She could barely stomach the thought of what was required of them, but the balance of the entire town rested on this one young girl's life.

"I don't think we have a choice," Petra said.

Marina shook her head. "There's always a choice, but no one wins this one. There's too many lives at stake." She took a step towards Magda and the girls, grim determination in every line of her profile.

"Wait," Dora commanded.

Dora did not want this blood on Marina's hands. Hers had already been defiled by the blood of innocents. She could do this and take the guilt with what she already carried. It was a burden she was willing to bear. It was a sacrifice she had to make to protect her valley and the people in it. A terrible sacrifice, but a required one.

An idea snapped to life in Dora's head.

"Wait," Dora said again. She took two quick breaths to still the swirling sensation in her head. "What did Iris say we had to do? What exact words did Iris use?"

Marina paused. Petra blinked slowly and spoke. "Kill The Keres. Behead them. Burn them and return their ashes to the pithos. The pithos must then be sealed by a blood sacrifice taken from the protector."

"A blood sacrifice taken from the protector," Dora repeated. "Not the life-blood of the protector. A sacrifice."

"But the story in Iris's book said they killed the last protector when the jar was sealed after it was opened," Petra said.

Dora spoke, cutting her off. "But maybe they didn't have to. Maybe death is not required."

Magda's tears ceased, hope effusing her face.

Marina's grip on her knife relaxed a fraction. "Could it be that easy?"

Dora sent a prayer up and said, "It's worth a try."

Dora picked up the pouch on the table. Her hand shook and she hesitated with her palm over the lid. "What will happen when I lift the lid?"

Magda released her daughter and came closer. "Nothing. The evil has already been released. Unlike the myths, only Remnants of Pandora can release the sorrows from the jar. I will lift the lid while you pour the ashes, if you would like."

Dora nodded and Magda lifted the lid. Dora held her breath. Nothing happened. She pulled the strings on the bag and poured the ashes into the jar. Magda set down the lid and turned to her youngest daughter.

She lifted the girl in her arms. "Do you remember the stories I told you of your ancestors and how brave they were when they protected the pithos?" Aderes nodded. "I need you to be brave now. This will hurt, but I won't let anything bad happen to you."

Magda looked at Dora over her daughter's head when she made the last promise, and Dora knew there would be a fight if they did, indeed, need a life to close the pithos. Dora prayed it would not come to that, but she steeled herself for the possibility.

Marina approached the girl with the knife. "I think the top of the arm will be best. It will bleed enough and not do too much damage. Dora here is practically a doctor, and she will be able to bandage you up."

Dora rolled up Aderes's sleeve while Magda held her and spoke nonsense words to her. The girl was calm until Marina brought the knife closer to her.

"Dora, hold her arm over the jar," Marina said.

Dora grabbed Aderes's waving arm and held tight. Dora could feel Marina's power coil beside her, then Marina moved so quickly Dora was barely able to track her. Aderes had a red line on her lower arm and Marina was squeezing the cut to drip blood into the jar. The air around them thickened and time slowed.

"Aderes," Magda said to the child in her arms. "Pick up the lid and place it on the pithos."

Magda leaned Aderes towards the table so the girl could reach the lid with her uninjured arm. The girl picked it up and the weight in the air increased. She lifted the lid and laid it on top of the jar. A shock wave ran out from the jar. Dora's ears popped.

Marina sagged into a chair. "Well, I think that worked."

"Try to open the jar," Magda said to Dora.

"What?" Petra said at the same time that Marina yelled, "Styx. No."

"Did you not listen to me?" Magda snapped. "Only the protector can release the sorrows. If it is sealed and one of you tries to open it, nothing will happen. If we failed, then the lid will lift easily. I think."

Dora stilled herself and closed her eyes briefly before grasping the lip of the jar and pulling.

The lid did not move.

"Thank the gods," Magda said.

Dora ran a shaking hand through her hair. "What now?"

"I know that we will no longer be welcome here. My family, what's left of it, will pack up and be gone by week's end," Magda said. She still held Aderes, whose arm dripped blood onto the floor.

Dora spoke first. "Leah, go find me some clean cloth and a pitcher of clean water." To Magda, she said, "Your family doesn't have to leave."

"But—" she started to protest.

Marina pointed to Petra. "Her husband resurrected Zeus and almost killed us all. He's still here. He makes great cheese."

Petra pointed to Marina. "She causes trouble all the time, but we let her live here too."

Dora added, "We've all made mistakes. Turning Creek is a place for second chances and new beginnings, for everyone. It can be yours too." She took the linen and bowl of water from Leah and started cleaning Aderes's arm. Marina had made the cut sure and not too deep. It would heal cleanly without stitches.

"Besides," Marina said, "since Matthew and Asher are gone, your family is smaller. You might need some help. We can help you."

Dora wrapped up the end of the bandage. "What now? Will the plagues cease? What about the people that are already sick?"

Magda shook her head. "I don't know."

Dora went to the back room to check on Ruben. He lay on top of his quilt. His face was pale, but no longer flushed.

"Is he…" Magda could not finish the question.

Ruben's chest rose and fell in a slow, even rhythm. Dora felt the boy's forehead. It was cool. "He's just sleeping. I don't know if the magic of the jar worked right away. I suppose we won't know until we check on others. Ruben, though, is fine. He will need to rest. You should change the dressing on Aderes's arm for two days. Try to keep it dry and clean it with water."

Petra put a hand on Marina's shoulder. "How do you feel?"

Marina rolled her shoulders and cracked her knuckles. "Better. Tired, though."

Petra stood at the door of the room. "I need to go. I need to go back to the farm."

Marina stood from where she had been sitting. "I need to go home too."

Dora did not know what waited for her sisters. She did not know if they had been quick enough to save the ones they all loved the most.

Dora spoke to Magda once more. "We will try to come check on you soon. If you need help, go to the Mylonis's homestead or north to Petra."

Magda nodded.

Marina paused before leaving. "One more thing. Though you've been given a second chance, know that we protect this town with our lives. You won't be given another. Keep the jar and your daughter safe or things may not end so well the next time."

Tears filled Magda's eyes and rolled in tracks down her face. "Thank you, mistress harpies, for your mercy and justice. I'm sorry that my deception has caused the death of so many. My line will forever be in your debt. May the blessing of the gods be upon you and your daughters."

The three harpies changed and bowed to Magda and Aderes, then turned to each other.

"Fly well," Dora said. "Petra, send word to Iris and let us know if your house is safe."

Petra nodded and left. Dora turned to Marina. "I'll take point. You're still weak from the fever."

Marina used her speed to fly, and Dora pushed wind at their back so they arrived back in town in record time. Marina landed in front of her house and went in. Dora landed in front of the saloon. She changed into her mortal form and stood there, on the boardwalk, her feet encased in lead.

She was afraid of what waited for her inside.

CHAPTER 24

Dora stepped into the saloon, weighed down with dread but propelled by hope. The inside of the saloon was lit only by the light coming in from the front windows. The lamps were out and the fire was banked. Gone were the cries of distress that had been the underlying noise this morning. Now the quiet was punctured only by the sounds of peaceful sleeping.

Dora could check on the patients later. She was looking for one person.

Lee sat on a bench along the back wall. Normally, one of the longer tables sat in front of it, but all the tables had been moved out to make room for the sick and dying. His eyes were closed and his head was resting against the wall. Dora paused halfway across the room to drink in the sight of him, whole and still breathing. Her relief was acute, and she must have made a sound because his eyes, grey and piercing in the dim light, opened and bored straight into her. He gave her a tired smile, and she crossed the room at a fast walk.

Lee opened up his arms to her and she sat in his lap with her legs across his, tucking her head into the crook of his shoulder. Dora took a deep breath and all the events of the summer drifted away. This was her anchor, where she belonged.

"Everyone's fever broke about an hour ago. I suppose that means you succeeded." Lee's chest rumbled against her ear.

Dora sat up and turned to look him in the eye. "We did. The pithos belonged to Magda Renault." Dora told him the rest of the story. He listened without asking questions.

When she was done, he kissed her briefly. "I never doubted you would succeed."

Dora made a rude noise in the back of her throat. "I'm glad one of us was certain. I thought for sure the entire town would die before we found the pithos."

Lee tucked a strand of hair behind her ear, and Dora realized it was still down and probably a tangled mess from flying.

"I probably look frightful."

Lee smiled. "Never."

Dora took his hand in hers. "What do we do now?"

"There's a lot of work to do, but I will not mind the work."

"I'm tired. I think I might mind the work," Dora sighed. A creeping exhaustion was starting to take hold.

Lee kissed both her eyes and her nose, and then gave her a lingering kiss on her mouth. "I will face any mountain before me with a smile because I finally have my partner at my side, for good."

"You're right. I'm not going anywhere." Dora smiled. "I am not that young harpy anymore. I have the family I have made here with Marina, Petra, and Iris, and now I have you. I love you."

Before he could reply, Dora pulled Lee to her and kissed him with all the hope she had been afraid to acknowledge the past few weeks as everything was crashing down around their ears. His arms came around her and there was nothing between them but the love that would carry them through whatever the future held.

***

The rest of the summer was weeks of toil and tears. There were graves to dig and empty larders to fill. In town, on the side of the little church and school house, they buried their dead. Shelly Washburn. L.A. and Johnny, side by side with their wives. Lily and Paul Hughes. Feliks Tumanov. The entire Korman family.

There were also graves to dig outside of town. Matthew and Asher Renault. The youngest Walsh daughter, Nelda. Risto Mylonis. Thomas Neal and his son, Joseph. Dora felt each loss like a weight around her neck. They all did. It seemed unfair that they would have been spared when so many that they loved had been taken.

Families planted large house gardens and gathered what they could. The town pooled their seeds and labor and replanted a number of communal fields. Nina, though young, already wielded the power of Demeter's line in its entirety, and she coaxed the crops, urging them to grow faster. She sat by a different field each day and sang to it, calling to the plants to grow and yield their crops. Before the first snow fell, they gathered what they could and prayed to the gods.

To celebrate, they gathered in the green at the end of Main Street in view of the resting places of those they had lost for a town picnic. It turned into a party that lasted two days, with people who lived outside of town finding beds for the night or putting up temporary shelters.

It was good to be together again in the sunlight and feel thankful to be alive.

Dora cut pies on the second day while Petra and Marina handed out slices. Amy and Agnes Hughes came to the front of the line.

"Aunties…" Agnes started.

"…we want a large piece of apple pie to share," Amy finished.

Dora cut an extra-large slice and handed it over. The girls took it with smiles and went to find a place to sit with Nina. Soon, the older girls were surrounded by two small harpies and a tiny, golden-winged Messenger.

"The twins seem to be happy." Dora handed Marina another piece of pie.

"It took them a few months, but they've settled in. Nina likes having them around." Marina handed George Eisler a piece of pie and smiled at him.

"Good afternoon, ladies," he said.

Dora peered around his shoulder. "Where's Caroline?"

George was holding Melanie's hand, and she looked up to answer Dora. "Momma is too busy visiting and keeping Baby Georgie from crying. She asked us to fetch her a piece."

"One more piece then. Tell her to come over here soon. I want to kiss that baby." Dora handed a second piece to the girl.

Thomas ran through the group of girls, making them screech with laughter as they abandoned their own pie to chase him.

"Poor Reed," Marina said, watching the chaos. "He always wanted a large family, and now he is stuck in one that's chock full of powerful women."

"I think he prefers it that way." Dora cut the last pie and straightened up, stretching the protesting muscles of her back.

Lee walked up behind her and rubbed his strong fingers into her aching muscles.

"That feels wonderful."

"Music to my ears. Will you come and sit with me in the sunshine for a while?"

Dora turned and placed a lingering kiss on his mouth. "I have to go get that thing I have for Iris. Will you carry this blackberry pie to our blanket? I'll meet you there."

"How can I say no to pie?"

"Don't eat it all before I get back."

"I wouldn't do that."

"Yes, you would." Dora handed him the slice of pie. "And one bite does not count as leaving some."

Lee laughed as he walked away and she headed for their office. Lee and Dora still ran his medical practice out of the office on Main Street, spending nights there when they needed to, but they spent most of their nights at her cabin on Silvercliff. They would need to expand it soon, but they still had plenty of time for that.

Dora pulled the cart with its burden around to the green and stopped beside Iris. The green leaves of the tree shook and the two small lemons and the blossoms it bore filled the air with their scent.

Dora knelt beside Iris. "I know your grandmother had a grove in Tuscany where you grew up and I wanted to give you a lemon tree to remind you of her. I grew one of these for you last summer, but it died in the plagues. Nina helped me grow this one over the winter so it would be large enough to bear fruit when I gave it to you."

Iris closed her eyes and took a deep breath filled with the smell of lemons and citrus flowers. When she opened her eyes, they were glassy. She wrapped Dora in a hug, which was made awkward with Iris's growing belly between them.

"My bird, this is one of the most wonderful gifts I have ever been given. I had almost forgotten what the perfume of citrus smelled like in the open air. Of course, now all I really want to eat is lemon cake. This child is going to be born wanting lemons."

Dora's heart constricted with happiness. "Nina said she has woven some protection into the tree so it will not be harmed by our winters."

Dora gave Iris another hug and sat down beside Lee. They had situated their blanket to be nestled in with Iris and Henry, Marina and Reed, and Petra and James.

Lee handed her what was left of the pie. "I saved you some." The pie looked incredibly whole.

Petra piped up. "No, he didn't."

Marina laughed. "He had to go get another piece. He ate the first one."

Lee reclined on one elbow. "I do love pie. I never had pie growing up. The cook my parents employed only made cakes. I never had pie until I left and came west."

Dora rolled her eyes. "At least I know I rank just below pie in your book, then."

She gave him a peck on the cheek. Lee laid down and put his head in her lap. Dora breathed in deep the sense of joy and peace in the air. They were missing many people, but life and love go on, and they still had each other.

Marina and Reed joined them. Marina produced a bottle of wine and they toasted the day. A ways off, Claire sat talking with Daniel Vine. Her face was red from the sun or a blush and she smiled while Daniel told a story. Marina saw the conversation and started to rise. Dora grabbed her arm and pulled her down.

"I don't think you're invited to that conversation."

"I have something I need to tell Claire." Marina crossed her arms.

"Leave it be." Reed shoved the wine bottle back in her hands and she rolled her eyes before drinking. "Besides, I thought you liked him now."

Marina scowled. "I might."

"You just like being obstinate." Dora elbowed her. "The spring air must be getting to everyone. I walked up on Richard and Pearl kissing by the creek this morning."

"Those two have been skirting each other for weeks. I wondered how long it would take them. I'm glad we sent Richard to help Pearl last year. Seems to have worked out for both of them." Petra snatched the wine bottle from Marina. James joined them in time to hear the last comment. Petra leaned against James and sighed.

Dora pointed at Petra. "You *wanted* them to get together. Playing Cupid?"

Petra smirked. "Worked, didn't it?"

The conversation went on about all the trivialities of life that make up family. The air was filled with laughter and life. Dora felt the clean spring air on her skin and the pleasant weight of Lee's head in her lap. She gave her heart over the knowledge that life was violence, love, sorrow, joy, and peace all rolled into one big, beautiful mess. She was in the vortex of life with nothing separating her from the chaos that crashed around her, and she was right where she was supposed to be.

THANK YOU

Thank you for reading the third book in the Turning Creek series.

Would you like to know when the next book is available and win free books? You can sign up for my newsletter at www.wanderingeyre.com. On my blog, you will find all kinds of fun information and general shenanigans. Follow me on Twitter @wanderingeyre, or like me on Facebook at https://www.facebook.com/MichelleBouleAuthor.

I appreciate all reviews. They help readers find books and mean the world to authors.

Turning Creek Reading Order
Lightning in the Dark
Storm in the Mountains
Letters in the Snow
Plagues of the Heart
Journey of the Lost

MYTHOLOGY CODEX

This is a list of mythology characters and mythological locations mentioned in the Turning Creek series and a brief description of each. The information in this codex is for the mythology as it relates to this fictional series. As an author, I have taken some liberty with the original myths.

***

Achilles - The original Achilles was fatally wounded by a shot to his heel because this was the source of his power, speed, and strength. Thomas, the Remnant of Achilles, has the gift of speed and delivers mail in Turning Creek.

Aegis - The aegis is the name for the four warriors who make up the Shield of Zeus which is the title for his bodyguards and henchmen. They are Ioke, Alke, Eris, and Phobos.

Alke - Alke is the personification of strength. He is part of the Shield of Zeus and his main weapon is a sword.

Aphrodite - The Greek goddess of love.

Asclepius - A Greek physician who was granted the power over life and death by the gods. Lee Williams is a Remnant of Asclepius and the doctor in Turning Creek.

Atlanta - Atlanta was a famous huntress who made an oath of virginity to the goddess Artemis, but was later tricked into marriage by Aphrodite. Atlanta, named for the first of her name, travels with her companion and partner, Cyrene, in a quest for the next adventure and hunt. (also known as Atalanta in the Greek myths)

Bellerophon - Bellerophon was one of the hundreds of bastard sons of Zeus who spent his life trying to attain acknowledgement and vindication from the gods.

Cerberus - A three headed dog, the son of Echidna and Typhon, who guarded the door to the underworld for Hades.

Charon - Charon is the ferryman who took souls across the River Styx on their way to the god Hades in the underworld, sometimes also referred to as Tartarus.

Chimera - A monster, sired by Echidna and Typhon, whose front and torso is that of a lion and whose bottom half is that of a snake.

Cyrene - Cyrene was a princess and huntress who once wrestled a lion with her bare hands. The current Remnant of Cyrene travels the world with Atlanta in search of the next greatest hunt.

Demeter - Goddess of the harvest and agriculture. She was one of the few gods who had close ties with humanity because of her purview.

Dionysus - Dionysus, god of the vine, stayed neutral during the battle and Fall of Olympus, making him unpopular with those on both sides. The Remnant of Dionysus, Daniel Vine, owns the saloon in Turning Creek.

Dryad - Similar to a nymph, a dryad is a spirit of the forest, the trees, or other natural phenomenon. This affinity to nature can give them the power to communicate with nature or similar abilities.

Echidna - The original Echidna was called the Mother of All Monsters in the time of the old myths because her children became the nightmares of the Greek era.

Eris - Eris is the personification of strife. He is part of the Shield of Zeus.

Hades - The god and ruler of the underworld.

Harpy - A harpy has the body of a bird of prey and the head of a woman, though their face is more angular in this natural form. They have the ability many Remnants have of taking the form of a mortal when needed. There were four harpies who stood against Zeus in the uprising; Aello, Celaeno, Ocypete, and Podarge. The Remnants of the three surviving harpies lived in isolation from each other, and most of the world, until the current generation.

Hephaestus - Blacksmith to gods, he had the ability to craft weapons of magic and power in his forge, lit by the fires of Olympus. The Remnants of Hephaestus carry some of this original power and are marked with a clubfoot. Henry Foster of Turning Creek is a Remnant of Hephaestus.

Hera - Hera was the wife and queen of Zeus. By the time of the uprising, she had became angry and bitter over Zeus's many affairs and bastard children. She turned a blind eye to the work of the harpies and fled before Olympus fell.

Ioke - Ioke is the personification of onslaught and pursuit. She is part of the Shield of Zeus and her main weapon is the crossbow.

Iris - The original Iris has golden wings, delivered the messages of the gods, and had the gift of prophecy. She shared parentage with the harpies and argued on their behalf often, softening their punishment when Zeus's anger turned against them. The Remnant of Iris, also called The Messenger, is marked with a birthmark of golden wings. The Messenger chronicles the history of the Remnants and the harpies in particular.

Ladon - The Ladon is the serpentine monster child of Typhon and Echidna. Also known as a dragon or a drakon.

Laelaps - A mythical hound, created by Zeus, who never failed to catch its prey

Lernean Hydra - The hydra is another serpentine-like child of Typhon and Echidna. It is a nine headed serpent who occupies bodies of water and spits acidic venom on its victims.

Medea - A powerful and vengeful witch who helped Jason of the Argonauts in many battles and later became his wife, bearing him six children.

Maenads - Maenads are women controlled by Dionysus who turn into raving, mad women. They have been known to tear apart men with their bare hands in their rage.

Manticore - This creature has the head of a woman, the body of a lion, and the tail of a scorpion. It was a meliai, a kind of nymph from the island of Melos.

Medusa - Medusa, in the old myths, was a creature with snakes for hair and eyes who could hypnotise a man. Lily Hughes, the Remnant of Medusa, has the power of persuasion if you look into her eyes.

Minotaur - Child of a queen and a bull, the minotaur guarded a labyrinth, was regularly fed virgins, and was eventually slain by Theseus.

Mount Olympus - The mountain that was the seat of Zeus and the center of his kingdom during the time of the old myths.

Nemean Lion - The Nemean Lion can only be killed by strangulation. It is one of the monster children of Typhon and Echidna.

Nymph - A nymph is a fairy-like creature with an affinity for nature.

Orthus - Orthus is a two-headed hound and the son of Typhon and Echidna.

Pandora - The first mortal woman, named Pandora, was created by Hephaestus as a way to punish men after Zeus became displeased with them. Zeus gave Pandora a storage jar, called a pithos, that contained evil spirits as a wedding present.

Phobos - Phobos is the personification of fear. She is part of the Shield of Zeus.

Satyr - A creature with the lower body of a goat and the upper body of a man. They were creatures of Dionysus and known to harass and sometimes rape women during festivals.

Scylla - Scylla was a sea goddess with a woman's head and torso and the body of a serpent.

Sphinx - The Sphinx had the body of a lion and the head of a woman. It was the offspring of Typhon and Echidna and was known for asking riddles of men and then eating them when they answered incorrectly. The Remnant of the Sphinx is Pearl Nasso.

Styx, River - The River Styx is the body of water that separates the underworld from the living. To swear on the River Styx is to give a binding oath.

Tartarus - Another name for the underworld where souls go to be punished for their bad life choices.

Theoi Meteoroi - The gods and goddesses who controlled the sky and weather. Their abilities and powers varied greatly. They were under the control and power of Zeus and Hera.

Typhon - Typhon was monstrous being. He had one hundred dragon heads sprouting from his neck, a human torso, and a snake body. He is called the Father of Monsters because he sired the worst of the Greek monsters with his wife, Echidna.

Zeus - The Father of the Gods, Zeus was the tyrannical ruler of Olympus. While heralded as an innovator of culture, he ruled with violence and vengeance and held his kingdom together with blood and war. He was notorious for his hundreds of bastard children. Zeus was unseated in the Fall of Olympus which occurred during the uprising led by the harpies.

ABOUT THE AUTHOR

Michelle Boule has been, at various times, a librarian, a bookstore clerk, an administrative assistant, a wife, a mother, a writer, and a dreamer trying to change the world. She is married to a rocket scientist and has two small boys. She brews her own beer, will read almost anything in book form, loves to cook, bake, go camping, and believes Joss Whedon is a genius. She dislikes steamed zucchini, snow skiing, and running. Unless there are zombies. She would run if there were zombies.